Moonlit Nights & Northern Lights

TJ Rose

Contents

Welcome!

Welcome to Moonlit Nights & Northern Lights! This is book two in my Killigrew Street Case Files series, a collection of standalone, inter-connected gay paranormal romances. If you haven't read Bite Marks & Broken Hearts (touch-starved vampire x human he rescues from a demon), you might want to start there.

Content advisories: *mild gore, main character physically and emotionally abused as a child, poor self-esteem, past mentions of racism experienced by one of the main characters, on page anxiety attacks, PTSD (side character and main character)*

I hope you enjoy Rory and Maxwell. They were a riot to write.

— TJ Rose

- Some say the world will end in fire,
Some say in ice.
From what I've tasted of desire,
I hold with those who favour fire.

Robert Frost, Fire and Ice

Prologue

MERIDIAN MEDICAL RESEARCH CENTRE, GREENWICH, LONDON

EIGHTEEN MONTHS AGO

There are three things you should never do on a full moon: drink tequila, break into heavily guarded facilities, or stand this close to the unfairly gorgeous wolf you've been crushing on for weeks. Tonight, I was batting three for three.

"Ready?" Dev whispered, his shoulder pressed against mine as we lurked in the shadow of Meridian Medical Research Centre. The fire-exit door he'd wedged open earlier—during his fake courier delivery—gaped invitingly. Almost too inviting, really. Like those venus fly traps Priya kept on Killigrew Street's kitchen windowsill, that Issac liked to feed toast to.

"Born ready." The full moon burned under my skin like a fever, and I flexed my fingers, trying to ignore the way my wolf scratched at my insides, desperate to break free. Probably not the best night to attempt corporate espionage, but when Dev had texted about a homeless shifter ranting about his missing mate and an unmarked van, waiting wasn't an option. "Though my boss is going to murder me when he finds out I did this without his permission."

"Well, you know what they say." Dev's grin flashed white in the darkness as he eased the door wider. "Sometimes it's better to ask forgiveness."

I threw him a smirk to keep up the pretense that I was super cool, but inside, a spike of icy fear reared its ugly head. What if Seb *didn't* forgive me? What if he kicked me out of Killigrew Street? The thought sent my heart into a panicked spiral, my most painful memories threatening to resurface. Even now, years later, the phantom ache of those severed pack bonds made my wolf whimper. Killigrew Street was the first place that had ever felt like home. Seb, Kit, Priya, and Issac were my family now.

I couldn't lose that.

"You okay?" Dev asked, because I'd frozen mid-stride.

The moonlight caught Dev's profile, highlighting those perfect cheekbones that belonged on a runway rather than skulking around a medical facility. Trust me to fall for a journalist who looked like a supermodel. He smiled at me, and my stomach did that annoying flip-flop thing again. The past few weeks of investigating with him had been torture—the casual touches, the lingering looks, the way his hand would rest on my lower back as we pored over documents.

God, I was pathetic. Here we were, about to break multiple laws, and all I could focus on was how his cologne mixed with his natural scent, creating something that made me want to roll over and present my belly.

"We'll just poke around for a second, then get lost." Dev's voice dropped lower, rougher. That hint of South London in his accent always got stronger when he was excited. "Quick in and out."

"What about the cameras?" I whispered, eyeing the building's exterior.

Dev's smile was smug. "Taken care of. Did a full recon this morning during my 'delivery.' External cameras on this side are down—maintenance issue they haven't fixed. And the internal system…" He checked his watch with practiced nonchalance. "Should be on a loop for exactly twenty minutes starting… now."

"You hacked their security system?!"

"What? No. I know the night supervisor at Sentinel Security. Marcus owes me after I helped someone in his pack." Dev shrugged like having connections to every supernatural in London was perfectly normal. "He's looping the feed from eleven forty to midnight."

"Twenty minutes?" My heart rate kicked up. "That's cutting it close."

"Then we'd better be quick." Dev winked, already moving toward the door.

I nodded, following him through the door like the lovesick puppy I was. But *Christ*, the way his shoulders moved under his fitted black T-shirt should have been illegal.

Focus, Rory. *Focus*. Missing shifter. Possible corporate corruption. Definitely not the way Dev's jeans hug his—

"Watch your step," Dev whispered, catching my elbow as I nearly tripped over a cleaning cart. His touch lingered longer than necessary, sending sparks racing up my arm.

Great. Perfect. I was obviously determined to make a complete tit of myself in front of the hottest wolf in London. At least the darkness hid my blush.

The moment we slipped into the main part of the building, antiseptic hit my nose like a punch. Motion sensors flickered to life, bathing sterile corridors in harsh fluorescent light. Both of us flinched—enhanced senses are a bitch sometimes.

"Seriously, though." I kept my voice low as we crept forward. "Did that guy at the shelter *really* see someone from Meridian bundle someone into a van?"

"He was completely convinced." Dev paused at a corner, scenting the air. "Kept saying nobody would believe him because he was drunk, but he *knew* what he saw. And given the other disappearances..."

I nodded. We'd been tracking missing shifters for weeks—all lone wolves from the streets, all vulnerable. The kind of people nobody would miss.

The moon pulsed again, making my jaw ache, desperate to elongate into its snout. This was a bad idea. We should have run this past Seb.

Should've done anything except break into a facility on a full moon night.

But Dev was already moving deeper into the building, and I'd never been good at making sensible choices.

The research centre's second floor was a maze of identical offices. Dev moved with purpose, like he knew exactly where he was going. I tried to match his confidence, but mostly I was distracted by how the fluorescent lights caught his hair.

"In here." Dev gestured to a door marked *Administration*. "They'll have some sort of paper records."

"How very eco-unfriendly of them."

The office was small, cramped with filing cabinets and a desk that looked like it hadn't been updated since the eighties. Dev immediately started rifling through the nearest cabinet while I bounced on my toes, the moon making me restless.

"We should stay focused," Dev muttered, though I caught the way his eyes lingered on my throat.

"I am focused." I leaned against the desk, deliberately stretching so my T-shirt rode up. "Focused on how good you look in those jeans."

He shot me a look that was half exasperation, half heat. "You're impossible."

"You love it."

The moon surged again, making us both wince. My skin felt too tight, bones aching to shift. Dev must have felt it too, because he paused, rolling his shoulders.

"As soon as we finish here, we'll go for a run together," he promised.

My heart stuttered. Running together meant shifting together. Meant being naked together. But more than that—aside from my brother, I hadn't run with anyone on a full moon since leaving my Highland pack five years ago.

I needed to do something with my hands before they decided to hell with it and grabbed Dev's face. The overflowing bin caught my eye. I upended it onto the carpet, ignoring Dev's tut of disapproval. Most of it was coffee cups and meeting minutes, but underneath—

"Dev." My voice came out sharper than intended. "Look at this."

He crouched beside me, close enough that our thighs pressed together. The paper I'd found was crumpled but legible—a list of names, each with a weird code beside it. P-N. S-V. Some were crossed out entirely.

"I know some of these wolves," I whispered. "That's Old Paul from the shelter near Borough Market. And Janie—she usually sleeps rough near Liverpool Street."

Dev was already pulling out his phone, photographing the document. "What about this?" He passed me another crumpled paper—a delivery note for "specialty restraints" from some company I'd never heard of.

Before I could answer, we both froze.

Footsteps. Heartbeats. Coming closer.

Static crackled through the silence, making my heart leap into my throat. A male voice, tinny through a walkie-talkie: "Second floor clear, moving to admin section."

An answering beep echoed down the corridor.

"Guards. Two of them." Dev's breath tickled my ear.

My hands trembled as I shoved papers back into the bin. *Shit. Shit.* If we got caught here—if Seb found out—my brief career at Killigrew Street would be over before it began.

"Back door. Now." Dev gripped my elbow.

"We can take them." The moon sang in my blood, urging violence.

"Not without risking exposing what we are!"

We crept toward the rear exit, but the moon made my movements jerky, uncoordinated. My hip caught the bin, sending it clattering across the floor. The sound might as well have been a gunshot.

The footsteps pounded toward us. We burst into the corridor, straight into the harsh fluorescent lights—and two uniformed guards.

My heart stopped. The nearest security guard's hand dropped to his hip, and moonlight glinted off something silver. Handcuffs? A weapon?

Dev shifted slightly, positioning himself between me and the guards. The defensive gesture made my wolf howl inside my skull.

A siren pierced the air. Red emergency lights strobed, turning the corridor into a nightmare disco.

Dev checked his watch, confusion flashing across his face. "That's not right—"

"Your mate Marcus screwed us over?" I hissed, adrenaline spiking.

"No! There must be a secondary system or something—"

"Don't move!"

The guard's shout hit something primal—*protect, protect, protect*—and before I could stop myself, I lunged.

Everything happened too fast. One guard tried to grab me, but the moon sang through my blood, turning my muscles to steel. When he seized my arm, I barely felt it—his grip might as well have been tissue paper against the raw strength thundering through my veins. Dev twisted free of the other guard's hold like he was shrugging off a child's grasp. We were too strong, too wild, our beasts too close to the surface.

When the larger man threw an arm around me, instinct took over, and I shoved him with two hands. His head slammed against the wall with a *crack* before he slumped to the floor.

Fuck fuck fuck fuck fuck.

The second guard stumbled backward, fumbling for something on his belt.

"Run!" Dev grabbed my hand.

More footsteps thundered from multiple directions. Police sirens wailed in the distance, getting closer.

We sprinted down the corridor, footsteps echoing off walls. Three more security guards burst around the corner ahead, their uniforms matching the ones we'd left behind. My lungs burned as we skidded to a halt—dead end. A blank wall mocked us, with only a set of double doors to our left.

I slammed my shoulder into them. Pain shot through my arm as the doors refused to budge. The metal reinforcement gleamed under the emergency lights, taunting me.

"Freeze! Hands where we can see them!" One guard raised his radio. "Police are en route."

More heartbeats entered the building downstairs. Among them, a familiar scent hit my nose—crisp cotton, black pepper, lemongrass. This close to the full moon, I could also detect the subtle underlying current of static electricity, marking him as Gifted.

Theodore Maxwell.

Relief flooded through me. Thank fuck. Killigrew Street's police connection would get us out of this mess. For once, I was glad he was telepathic.

Heavy footsteps approached. Maxwell appeared behind the guards, suit slightly rumpled. The bright lights highlighted dark circles under his eyes, even through his glasses.

Theo! Help us! I screamed the thought as loud as I could, imagining neon letters flashing in my brain. *We're here on a case. Dev found evidence of missing shifters.*

Maxwell's dark eyes widened when they landed on me, genuine shock flashing across his face before he schooled his expression. His left hand twitched toward his temple—he was listening.

There's a list. Names. Codes. Something bad's happening here. But you can't take us to the station. It's a full moon. You have to—

"Sir?" One of the uniformed officers turned to Maxwell. "These aren't our suspects."

"No," Maxwell said, jaw tight, eyes never leaving mine. "I don't believe this is connected to our operation, after all."

"But they've still broken in and assaulted security personnel," a different voice interjected.

"Yes," Maxwell said. "They have."

For one breathless moment, Maxwell's expression shifted—something unreadable flashing across his features. He glanced at the window where moonlight spilled through, then back to my face. I could almost see the calculation happening behind those dark eyes: duty versus consequence, law versus supernatural reality. His fingers flexed at his sides. Then his shoulders squared, decision made.

My stomach dropped through the floor as he pulled out his handcuffs. "DI Maxwell, Metropolitan Police. You're both under arrest for breaking and entering, assault on security personnel, and"—his gaze flicked to the unconscious guard—"grievous bodily harm."

No. *No, no, no.* This wasn't happening. This couldn't be happening.

Dev's fingers squeezed mine, his palm sweaty against my skin. The moon pulsed again, making each of my bones tremble.

"Theodore!" The name burst from my lips before I could stop myself. Shit. Probably shouldn't have revealed we knew each other. That was not going to help.

"DI Maxwell, you know this suspect?" asked another officer.

Maxwell's face went carefully blank. "Not that I'm aware of."

"Theo, please," I whispered as he grabbed my wrists. "You can't lock us up—"

"You do not have to say anything. But it may harm your defence—" The cuffs clicked shut. Cold metal bit into my skin.

"Not tonight!" Panic clawed up my throat. "The moon—I won't be able to fight the change!"

"You're going to have to."

"Please! Just call Seb!"

His fingers squeezed my arm. I caught the slight tremor in his jaw, the way his eyes flickered to the window where moonlight streamed through. But he kept moving, steering me toward the stairs, before marching us outside. They guided us to two different cars. Through the window, I watched them push Dev's head down as he ducked into the back seat. The full moon hung above us, impossibly bright, promising violence.

"Please," I begged Maxwell, one last time, but to no avail. The guy barely even looked at me. Didn't give a shit what he was doing to me.

My father's face flashed through my mind—an image of him standing underneath the apple tree near the manor house, regarding me from afar. The very last time I'd seen him alive before the police gunned him down. And here I was, being hauled away by another cop. But this one was supposed to be on my side.

I slumped against the cold leather as Maxwell shut the door. Metal mesh separated me from the front seats. The engine roared to life. I pressed my forehead against the cool glass, watching London blur past. The handcuffs scraped into my wrists, the silver-plated metal making my skin crawl.

Maxwell's eyes met mine in the rearview mirror. For a split second, something like guilt flickered across his face. Good. Let him feel guilty. Let him understand exactly what he was doing to me.

My wolf clawed at my insides, howling for release. The shift wasn't just a *want*—it was a biological imperative. Like trying to hold your breath underwater. Eventually, your body would force you to surface whether you wanted to or not.

And I had hours to go before moonset. Hours, locked in a cell, fighting with all my might against the shift.

The fluorescent streetlights strobed across my face, each flash making my head pound harder. Every cell in my body screamed for transformation. Even my eyesight kept shifting between human and wolf's vision, the world alternating between sharp focus and blurred colours.

I squeezed my eyes shut, trying to concentrate on breathing. In through the nose, out through the mouth. Just like Kit taught me. But my brother wasn't here. Wasn't here to save me this time.

And when he next saw me, he'd probably strangle me to death.

Another wave of moon-fever crashed through me. My spine arched involuntarily, a whimper escaping my throat as the shift rippled under my skin like lightning searching for ground.

Again, Maxwell met my gaze in the mirror, his eyes flicking between me and the officer in the passenger seat. It was only a matter of time before they noticed my increasingly violent spasms. I could only pray they presumed I was in drug withdrawal, or something.

This is torture. Pure torture. Torture, and a betrayal that would leave scars deeper than any physical wound. Fighting the shift for an entire night would be like trying to stop my heart from beating through sheer willpower alone. And he knew it. The bastard *knew* what this would do to me.

Fuck you, traitor, I snarled at him in my mind, channelling every bit of my rage into the words.

This was going to be a long, long night.

1

Present Day

The guide to being a supernatural investigator has exactly one rule about breaking and entering: don't get caught.

Eighteen months ago, I learned the consequences of that the hard way.

But this time was different. This time I was being super careful. Professional.

At least, that had been the plan. Instead, I was failing spectacularly at rule zero—actually getting through the door.

The lock pick slipped for the hundredth time, and I swore under my breath. If only Issac were still alive, he'd be here to help me, and we'd be inside by now. Instead, my knees ached from crouching, and the hallway's motion sensor light had clicked off twice, leaving me fumbling in the dark like the world's worst cat burglar.

"Come on, you stupid thing." I jiggled the pick again, my tongue sticking out in concentration.

Fun fact: most London apartments have standard five-pin locks. Less fun fact: none of my supposedly enhanced abilities were helping me crack this one.

On TV, they always made it look so effortless—just stick the pick in, wiggle it around a bit, and pop! Open sesame. But after twenty minutes of trying, the only thing I'd managed to do was probably void Dev's rental deposit by scratching up his lock.

The irony wasn't lost on me—I'd already be inside if I hadn't lost the spare key he'd given me. The same key I'd sworn I'd return after our breakup, along with his favourite hoodie and the pieces of my broken heart. Instead, I'd shoved it into the pocket of my jeans. The jeans that went through the wash. Twice. My talent for losing things extended far beyond just losing boyfriends. But I needed answers, and they were somewhere behind this stupidly stubborn door.

A therapist would say that breaking into my ex's flat wasn't healthy coping behaviour. But Dev was missing, and I was apparently the only one who noticed something wrong with his absence on any social media feed.

My phone vibrated, and like any self-respecting person with ADHD, I immediately abandoned my task to look at it.

Sebby

Put down the lock pick before you hurt yourself and get back to Killigrew Street. Now.

I jumped, nearly dropping my phone. The screen's glow painted my hands blue in the darkness. My gaze darted up and down the empty corridor, seeking the hidden CCTV that must be tucked into some shadowy corner. Felix had to be watching me—that sneaky little traitor. Why couldn't Felix have lied to Seb and said that the CCTV was broken?

My phone buzzed again.

Now, Rory! Or we'll start the meeting without you.

I stomped down the hallway. Dev's building was exactly what you'd expect for a successful journalist—a converted mansion split into over-priced flats, with high ceilings and crown moulding that almost masked how much you paid for a glorified shoebox.

My footsteps echoed as I descended six flights to the street. London's rush hour roared past. The setting sun cast long shadows across the pavement. I turned left, toward the hidden entrance to the tunnel network leading back to Killigrew Street.

I'd known this was a bad idea, trying to access Dev's flat before Seb returned from Ireland to launch the investigation. But Dev hadn't been online for seven days. Hadn't even *opened* my increasingly desperate messages. And yeah, maybe we'd broken up nine months ago, and I should just let it go, but Dev never went offline. Ever. The man documented his breakfast, for fuck's sake.

His last post had been a perfectly staged photo of avocado toast at some trendy café in Shoreditch. All artful angles and perfect lighting. I'd smiled, imagining him lining up his phone in that way of his. Then I'd swiped to the next photo, to see his stupid new boyfriend shoving said avocado toast into his stupid mouth.

I ducked into an alley between a charity shop and a closed newsagent's, checking for witnesses before pressing a specific brick.

It sank inward with a soft click. The manhole cover beneath me vibrated as machinery whirred below, shifting with a grinding sound.

I heaved up the heavy lid. Cool air wafted from the darkness. I clicked on my phone's torch, stuck it between my teeth, and climbed down the ladder quickly, grimy metal cold under my palm.

The secret tunnel network beneath London had been my saving grace since joining Killigrew Street. No cramming onto the Northern Line with sweaty humans during rush hour for me.

When my brother plucked me off the streets of Glasgow and offered me a job fighting supernatural crime, I thought he was joking when he said our headquarters would be a haunted hotel.

The Killigrew Street Hotel, one of the Victorian era's finest, had been frozen in time since the 1970s when the last paying guest checked out. From the outside, it looked like any other abandoned building awaiting renovation, which was exactly what the neighbours thought we were doing.

"Just contractors," Seb would say with that charming smile of his whenever anyone asked. "Historic preservation work. Very delicate. Very slow." The neighbours nodded, satisfied with the explanation for the occasional strange noises and odd hours. They'd even started a betting pool about when we'd finally finish—the current leader had his money on 2033.

Little did they know our "renovation" involved converting the grand ballroom into a training room, complete with mats and punchbags. The basement was our meeting room and sanctuary. And one day, Seb would surely finally let us transform the honeymoon suite into a cinema room.

Unless he selfishly decided to claim it for himself and Flynn, of course. Now they were sickeningly in love.

At the bottom of the ladder, a rat scurried across a pipe, and I nearly dropped my phone trying not to yelp. The wavering light briefly revealed wall graffiti—a crude dick drawing. Even in secret supernatural passages, humans gonna human.

I jogged through tunnels twisting beneath London like a drunk snake's attempt at civil engineering. Finally reaching Killigrew Street Hotel's basement steps, I took the spiral stairs two at a time, calves burning. Just before the bookcase entrance, my phone buzzed. Signal at last.

Sebby

Oh, and your favourite person is here. Kit says if you refer to him as Detective Dickface even once, you're helping clean the guns again.

"Fuck!" The word bounced off the stone walls. Detective Theodore Maxwell. Because this day couldn't get any better.

My hands clenched into fists, nails digging into my palms. That pompous, rule-obsessed bastard would be there with his stupid suit on, ready to judge everything I did. He'd give me that look—the one that said I was beneath him, just some feral wolf who couldn't control himself.

The memory of cold metal handcuffs flashed through my mind. An entire night locked in a cell during a full moon, fighting every instinct in my body whilst my bones tried to break and reshape themselves. Hours of agony as my wolf clawed at my insides, desperate for release I couldn't give it. The taste of blood in my mouth from biting my tongue to keep from screaming. Fluorescent lights that felt like needles in my skull. The humiliation of resorting to screaming, to begging, only to be ignored.

By dawn, I'd been shaking so violently they'd called a medic, convinced I was having seizures. The wolf had retreated, exhausted and broken, leaving me feeling like a stranger in my own skin for weeks afterwards.

All because Theodore Maxwell didn't step in and save me.

Yes, it was entirely his fault, and nothing to do with your own actions, a snide voice whispered.

My chest felt tight, a toxic mix of anger and self-hatred filling my lungs with lead.

I jammed in the code for the bookcase's release mechanism harder than necessary. Time to face the music. And by music, I meant the world's most irritating telepath.

Every single member of Killigrew Street lounged around on the sofas, their heads swivelling toward me like I'd just tap-danced through the door wearing nothing but a feather boa. Kit's expression was particularly thunderous, but then, that was pretty much my older brother's default.

The weight of their stares pressed against my skin like itchy wool.

"What?" I snapped, shoving my hands into my pockets.

Seb crossed his arms over his chest. His burgundy tailored trousers looked crisp despite having just flown from Dublin. "That's not quite the greeting I expected after cutting our holiday short to return at your rather insistent request."

Flynn hovered next to him, offering me an apologetic grimace. His beach-tousled hair and slight sunburn made it clear exactly what kind of holiday I'd interrupted.

Guilt gnawed at my insides. Flynn had spent months trying to convince Seb to take a break—leaving travel brochures about Ireland on his desk, enlisting Kit's help to clear Seb's schedule. The amount of puppy-dog eyes Flynn had deployed could've filled an animal shelter.

And now here they were, back early all because I rang them screaming about how I was sure my ex-boyfriend had been murdered.

They stood so close their shoulders touched. Flynn's hand rested on the small of Seb's back, and the vampire actually leaned into the touch. It was nauseating, really. I'd never get over how bizarre it was seeing Seb so happy all the time. Well, as happy as someone who'd spent five centuries perfecting his resting bitch face could look.

I'd worked at Killigrew Street for years, and in all that time, Seb had been allergic to sunshine, joy, and my jokes. But now? One look from Flynn and he melted faster than ice cream. Their domesticity was enough to give me cavities. And no, I wasn't jealous. Not one bit.

"Fair point, boss," I said, because it was.

Priya, still bundled up in her favourite purple scarf in May, was the only one who seemed genuinely happy to see me, beaming as she budged up on the sofa, pressing herself into a scowling Felix.

Just as I sat down, something small and grey dropped from the ceiling with a soft thud, landing directly in my lap. Freddy, my zombie ferret, chittered excitedly, his eerie yellow eyes glowing in the dim light of the room. Patches of bone showed through his matted fur as he twisted around, sniffing the air.

"There you are, you little monster," I murmured, scratching behind what remained of his ear. Freddy responded by nipping affectionately at my fingers, his yellowed teeth catching the light.

He'd been dead for a month before Issac had used necromancy to bring him back as a prank. Not everyone appreciated his particular brand of undead charm, but Freddy was the most loyal pet a wolf could ask for—even if he did have a habit of stealing food and occasionally shedding entire clumps of fur.

"Where is he?" I whispered to Priya as I stroked Freddy's tail.

"He stepped into Felix's lair to make a call. Ah—" She elbowed me. "Here he comes. Be nice."

Detective Theodore Maxwell emerged from Felix's cupboard like he owned the place, his expensive shoes clicking against the hardwood floor. The sight of him in that charcoal suit made me grind my teeth together.

Fuck, why did the dickhead have to be so goddamn attractive? Six foot tall, with those broad shoulders stretching the fabric of his jacket, that strong jawline with just the right amount of stubble, and his thighs—they were exactly the kind I'd love to climb if I didn't want to punch him so badly. Even the way his coils were perfectly faded at the sides looked like he'd just stepped from a barber's chair rather than a crime scene.

His steps faltered when he saw me. Just a tiny hesitation, but I caught it. Our eyes met across the room, and his expression darkened into a frown that made his glasses slip down his nose. I frowned back at him... or had I frowned first? Whatever, there was serious frowning involved.

His gaze dropped to Freddy, who was now sprawled across my lap, and his frown deepened into outright disgust. Not that I could blame him entirely—the last time Maxwell had visited, Freddy had pissed on his expensive leather shoes. I considered it one of Freddy's finest moments.

I stroked Freddy's back protectively, drawing comfort from his cold little body.

The tension in the room cranked up several notches. Everyone held their breath, probably waiting for me to call him Detective Dickface to his face... for the hundredth time.

But I was being mature today. Super mature. The most mature wolf who ever matured.

Hey, asshole. Get out of my head, I thought as loudly as possible, just in case he was listening in. He usually was, because he had zero respect for privacy or personal boundaries. *I know you're probably reading my thoughts right now, like the creepy telepathic dickhead you are.*

His left hand twitched toward his temple—his tell—before he caught himself and lowered it. *Ha.* Caught you, you nosy bastard.

I was being ridiculous. I knew that, really. But is there anything worse than having your mind, the most private part of you, invaded without your consent?

Smiling sweetly, I channelled all my rage into screaming obscenities inside my head. *Here's a thought for you: go fuck yourself with that stick up your ass.*

The muscle in his jaw ticced. Good.

Priya elbowed me in the ribs. "Behave," she hissed.

Seb cleared his throat, adjusting his cuffs in that way he did when he was about to be all official. "First, I'd like to thank Detective Maxwell for joining us this evening on such short notice."

Maxwell nodded, his expression carefully blank. "Happy to help."

"So we're all on the same page," Seb said, "Rory is going to begin the meeting by explaining to you all what he relayed to me on the phone."

All eyes locked onto me like laser sights, making my skin prickle. The sofa creaked as I shifted, suddenly hyper-aware of every tiny sound in the room—Kit's heavy breathing, the tick of that ancient grandfather clock Seb refused to get rid of.

My throat went dry. God, I hated that feeling. It yanked me straight back to being fourteen, standing in front of my class while the teacher tapped their foot, waiting for an answer I didn't have. The same hot flush crept up my neck, and my leg started bouncing before I could stop it.

"Um..." I cleared my throat. "So a few days ago, I started getting worried about my ex-boyfriend Dev. He's gone radio silent on social media, which is weird for him."

"Perhaps he's taking a mental health break." Maxwell's deep voice cut through the room like a knife through butter. "Not everyone needs to document their every move online all the time."

The condescension in his tone made my teeth ache, and I swallowed down a retort about Maxwell being too boring to have anything interesting to post online.

"Yeah, you don't know Dev. He's even more addicted to his phone than I am. The man goes live just to document his morning coffee routine. He once did a thirty-minute story about choosing between two nearly identical pairs of shoes."

"So he hasn't posted in over a week now?" Felix asked, fiddling with the cuff of his hoodie.

"Seven days, thirteen hours." The words tumbled out before I could stop them. "Not even a story. Or a like. Nothing."

Maxwell's eyebrows shot up. "Do you check your ex's profile every single day?"

"Umm... yes?" *A completely, totally normal thing to do.* "He posts good recommendations of new places to go around London," I said, but it sounded weak to my own ears. Like explaining why you still had your ex's spare toothbrush under your sink. Just in case.

"That part isn't important, Maxwell," said Priya, and I felt a rush of affection for my best friend.

Yeah, Maxwell.

"I'm just trying to get all the facts." Maxwell's words sliced through the air. "It *is* important if Rory is overreacting."

My muscles coiled tight, ready to spring. The wolf inside me bristled, hackles raised. How dare he? Like I was some hysterical ex who couldn't let go.

"Detective, I'm confident Rory isn't overreacting," said Seb. "Listen to what he has to say."

Priya's hand squeezed my knee, grounding me. The gentle pressure reminded me to breathe, to focus on the warmth of her palm rather than the urge to launch myself across the room and wipe that look off Maxwell's face.

"Actually," I said, my voice steadier than I felt. "I think this might be connected to what happened at Meridian Medical Research Centre."

The temperature in the room plummeted. Maxwell's expression darkened like storm clouds rolling in.

Freddy, sensing my rising anxiety, pressed himself closer against my stomach, his tiny claws digging into my shirt.

"If you remember that," I added, unable to stop myself.

"Do I remember the break-in where you acted without obtaining Sebastián's permission, got caught on CCTV, assaulted two security guards, and compromised any chance of obtaining the evidence you were seeking?"

There was a horrible silence while Maxwell's words stabbed themselves into me. Not tiny pinpricks, but jagged shards of truth I couldn't deny, causing the kind of wound that bleeds internally.

"Yes, Maxwell," I snarled back at him. "The same night when you locked me up in a cell during a full moon!"

I pushed all the painful memories of that horrible event to the forefront of my mind, playing them like a movie in my head while staring directly at Maxwell. His lips pressed together, and his shoulders went rigid. Good. Let him feel my anger. Let him consider how it felt to be trapped, desperate, fighting against the change while concrete walls closed in.

Kit groaned loudly. "Rory, can we please not go over all that—"

"But it's linked!" I practically shouted. "I just know it is! Dev was looking into Meridian. That's how we met in the first place, remember—he was sniffing around for leads about missing shifters. Even after our investigation hit a dead end, after... *that night,* Dev still kept poking around things."

The day after we were caught there, Seb managed to persuade Maxwell to search it properly, but by that point, it was too late. They'd cleared the place out of anything remotely suspicious.

Seb nodded slowly. "We did investigate thoroughly at the time. The reports of missing shifters were concerning—still are."

The trail had gone cold, and Seb had moved me on to other cases. I got it—we couldn't chase dead ends forever when London was bursting with supernatural crime. But Dev... Dev was like a dog with a bone when he caught the scent of a story. There was no way he wasn't keeping tabs on it this whole time.

"Just before we broke up," I said, picking at a loose thread on my jeans. "He had this anonymous letter come through the door, asking to meet him. They said they worked for Meridian. Dev went to the meeting spot at the specified time, but the person never showed. I told you about it, at the time."

Kit's eyebrows drew together, creating that little furrow that meant he was thinking. "I remember. And did that person ever get back in contact?"

My stomach twisted. Dev and I broke up shortly after that, and our communication broke down as well. If Dev had been gathering intelligence this whole time—if he'd uncovered something important—Killigrew Street might have missed out on the information because of our messy breakup. It would be just like Dev to decide he could handle it all on his own.

"I have no idea," I admitted. "He didn't want to talk to me after we broke up."

Maxwell sighed deeply. "So you're saying your ex-boyfriend has been conducting his own investigation into Meridian for nine months, without backup, following anonymous tips?"

My leg bounced faster. We'd been onto something big—I'd felt it in my bones. The thread I'd been picking at snapped, and I wrapped it around my finger until the tip turned purple. My mind raced with all the possibilities, all the things that could have happened to Dev. What if whoever wrote that letter had been watching him this whole time? What if it had been a trap? What if they'd waited until he thought the case was cold before making their move?

The pressure inside me built until I could barely breathe. Dev might be a dick who'd replaced me with a hotter version of myself, but he didn't deserve to disappear. And underneath all my worry about him was this horrible guilt that maybe, if I'd been a better boyfriend, if I hadn't pushed him away, he wouldn't have been doing this alone.

Flynn cleared his throat. "That's not your fault, Rory."

I shot Flynn my most winning smile. Not for the first time, I found myself glad that Seb had found him and his neck rather appealing.

But inside, the memories crashed over me like a tide I couldn't hold back. Dev standing in his favourite coffee shop, the one where we'd had our first proper date, telling me it was over. Just like that. No warning, no discussion, no chance to fix whatever I'd done wrong.

I'd been looking at flat listings on my phone that morning, excited to show him the two-bedroom in Clapham with the tiny balcony. I'd already imagined Freddy sprawling across the sofa, and Dev's journalism awards on the mantelpiece next to my collection of vintage band posters.

The shock had hit me like a punch to the gut, followed immediately by this desperate, clawing need to make him stay. I'd begged, actually begged, right there in front of everyone, asking what I could change, what I could do better. The humiliation still burned.

And when begging didn't work, when he just kept shaking his head with that pitying look in his eyes, I'd lashed out. Said things designed to hurt him as much as he was hurting me. Told him he was pretending to be a serious journalist when all he did was write fluff pieces about fashion trends and call them "cultural commentary on late-stage capitalism." Told him I didn't really see a future with him anyway. Called him shallow and vain and—

God, I'd been such a fucking mess. Such a child. No wonder he'd blocked me on everything afterwards.

"Also, it's not just me who thinks he's missing," I added, desperate to steer the conversation back towards safer territory. "Before I rang you, I called Dev's alpha, and she hasn't heard from him for over a week either. None of them have. They're super worried."

Seb's fingers drummed against his thigh. "There's quite a lot happening at the moment. Marcus Vale's clan is still determined to make my eternal existence a living hell. Only yesterday, they left a drained body in the middle of Brixton park, just to send a message. To be honest, even without your phone call, Rory, we were going to have to cut our Ireland trip short."

My stomach dropped. This was it. He was going to tell me to forget about it.

"However." Seb's eyes fixed on me. "We will investigate. Of course we'll investigate. Detective Maxwell will assist you, as he has the resources we need, and Killigrew Street is spread thin at present."

My mouth fell open. "But—"

"And," Seb continued, his voice taking on that stern edge that meant *shut up and listen*, "I know that as a *professional*, you'll be able to cooperate with him and work effectively as a team."

The word "professional" hung in the air like a threat. Maxwell's lips twitched, and I wanted to throw something at his stupidly handsome face.

"Why can't—"

"Rory!" Seb's voice cracked like a whip.

"Okay! Okay! Perfect!" I snapped. *Oops.* "I mean, thank you. Genuinely."

"I'm sure Maxwell wants to go home for the evening now, but the pair of you can arrange something for tomorrow."

Seb nodded dismissively, and everyone started gathering their things. Kit shoved past me with a grunt that probably meant "we'll talk later," while Priya squeezed my shoulder. Felix disappeared back into his lair.

Freddy scampered down my leg and across the floor, pausing only to hiss at Maxwell's shoes before darting off toward the kitchen. Probably to raid whatever food had been left unattended.

My attention snagged on Seb and Flynn. The way Seb's whole demeanour softened as Flynn stepped closer, like ice melting in spring. Flynn's fingers traced along Seb's jaw, and he nuzzled into his hand, his eyes fluttering closed for just a moment. Flynn murmured something against his cheek and Seb laughed softly, pressing a kiss to his temple.

I could pretend it made me want to retch, but my chest ached watching them. Would anyone ever look at me like that? Like I was their entire world? Dev certainly hadn't. It had been great at first, but somehow, I'd always felt like I wasn't quite enough, wasn't quite what he wanted. And then he found someone who looked exactly like me but... way better.

God, what was wrong with me? Here I was, worried Dev might be dead, and I was still obsessing over how he'd—

A pointed cough cut through my spiral. Maxwell stood there, arms crossed, towering above me. "Tomorrow morning," he said. "Seven a.m. sharp. Text me your address. Don't be late."

I opened my mouth to argue about the ungodly hour, but he was already striding away, leaving nothing but the scent of his stupid lemongrass cologne and the thud of his shoes against the floor.

"Oi."

I turned to find Priya behind me.

"You alright?"

"Am I *alright*? My ex-boyfriend's probably lying dead in a ditch somewhere, and I've been paired with the same dickhead who locked me and him up in cells during a full moon. So I'm absolutely *fantastic*, thanks for asking."

Priya didn't look remotely impressed. She lightly punched my arm. "Don't attack *me* over it, you twat."

My shoulders slumped. "Sorry. I just—" I ran my hands through my hair. "I hate this. All of it."

"Look." She grabbed my wrist, her fingers warm against my skin. "Maxwell is highly competent. He's good at his job. If you want to find Dev quickly, just keep your mouth shut and try not to insult him every five seconds."

I rolled my eyes so hard they nearly got stuck in the back of my head.

"Rory." The tone in her voice made me look at her. "I mean it. This isn't about you and Maxwell's... whatever that is between you two. This is about finding Dev."

The fight drained out of me. She was right. Of course she was right. Priya was always right, which was deeply annoying.

"Fine." I sighed dramatically. "I'll try to play nice with Detective Dickface."

"Rory!"

"That was the last one, I swear." I held up my hands in surrender. "Starting now, I'll be a perfect angel."

She snorted. "I'll believe that when I see it. Text me tomorrow?"

"Course." I pulled her into a quick hug, letting her familiar lavender scent soothe me. "Thanks for always having my back."

She kissed my cheek.

"And if I accidentally shift and pee on his fancy car, it's just marking my territory. That's basically police work, right? Securing the perimeter?"

Priya let out an almighty groan. "Go home!" she snapped, turning on her heel and storming towards the stairs.

Well, then. Seemed like pissing on Maxwell's car was off the table.

For now.

2

Theodore

T he steering wheel creaked under my grip as I checked my watch for the tenth time. Eleven minutes late. My day off wasted, waiting outside Rory's building for him to come down. Brilliant.

My work phone buzzed—a message from the station about another case. I'd normally have checked it, but I resisted. Today belonged to the Devraj Bassi investigation, though every fibre of my being protested spending it with Rory Thorne.

The previous night's text exchange still irritated me. I'd asked for his address three times before a notification popped up, only to vanish seconds later. He'd deleted whatever insulting message he'd sent. Five minutes after that, he'd sent me his address. No other context. No thank you.

Salazar must have lost his mind, pairing us together. The vampire's usually impeccable judgement had clearly slipped. Either that or he enjoyed watching me suffer.

Movement caught my eye. A flash of chaotic blond hair emerged from the building's entrance. Rory's bedhead looked like he'd stuck his finger in an electrical socket—did the man own a brush? Or was this carefully crafted disaster part of his image?

My temples throbbed as his surface thoughts leaked through like water through cracked stone:

...dickface detective actually showed up...could've cancelled...rather eat glass...

I sighed. Spending time with someone from Killigrew Street—the only ones who knew about my telepathy—was always interesting. On one hand, it was a welcome change to be able to freely talk about it. On the other, I felt—all too well—how on edge they were whenever I was in the room.

Rory spotted the car, his scowl clearly visible. Then his features smoothed into careful neutrality as he approached, each step deliberate like he was walking to his execution. The passenger door opened with more force than necessary.

He dropped into the seat without a word, arms crossed. The scent of his shower gel—something citrusy—filled the confined space. The silence felt as dense as London fog, thick enough to choke on.

I waited for the inevitable smart remark, but Rory just stared straight ahead, jaw clenched. The quiet felt wrong coming from him. Usually, I couldn't get him to shut up.

The tension crawled up my spine.

"Good morning to you too." I winced at how sarcastic the words came out.

The paper cup in my cup holder suddenly felt like a terrible mistake. What had possessed me to stop for coffee? The gesture seemed ridiculous now. Yet I picked his up and offered it to him. "It's cold, because you're fifteen minutes late. You take it black, yes?"

Rory's eyes widened, fixed on the distinctive black-and-white striped- cup with its ginger cat logo like he'd spotted a venomous snake in the car. His hands stayed firmly in his lap.

"Okay..." I pulled the cup back toward me, wondering what the fuck I'd done wrong now.

"It's Fat Cat's!" The words exploded from him, making me jump.

I blinked. "Yeah? You love that coffee shop. I've never seen you drink anything else."

His surface thoughts leaked through:

...where the hell does he even live for Fat Cat's to be en route...

Rory's hand hovered over the cup for a long moment, like he was weighing up whether by accepting it he would somehow betray himself.

Finally, he snatched it with more force than necessary. "Thanks," he muttered, the word sounding like it physically hurt to say.

The truth was, I'd gone twenty minutes out of my way to get it, hoping it might ease the tension between us. A peace offering disguised as coffee, because I refused to apologise for doing my job eighteen months ago.

"No problem. Right, Seb suggested we go interview the boyfriend, correct?"

Rory's face twisted into something dark, and an image slammed into my mind with such force I nearly dropped my own coffee. A man with perfectly styled dark hair and warm brown skin was smiling, his arm wrapped around a blond man's chest. The hatred attached to the image burned like acid.

"Yes. Did you manage to get his address?"

"Yes," I replied, then opened my mouth to point out how spectacularly inappropriate it would be for him to interview someone he clearly despised out of twisted jealousy. The words died on my tongue. Not my business. Not my problem if this went sideways.

Rory's thoughts battered against my shields, a hurricane of fragments: *...why him, why him...never good enough...of course he upgraded...*

Christ, the wolf's mind was loud. My temple already throbbed. Maintaining mental barriers around Rory always drained more energy than it should. Most people's thoughts were a gentle stream—his were a tsunami.

I rubbed at my temple, trying to shore up my defences. The motion caught Rory's attention.

"Headache?" The false sweetness in his voice set my teeth on edge.

"I'm fine," I said sharply. "Let's go." I plugged the address into the navigation system. West London, Kensington. Expensive area.

The engine hummed to life, and we merged into traffic. Silence settled over the car, broken only by the wet, deliberate slurping sounds coming from the passenger seat. Each sip lasted longer than humanly necessary, the noise amplified in the confined space.

...bet this is driving him mental...

I kept my expression neutral, eyes fixed on the road. The slurping grew louder, more theatrical, but I refused to give him the satisfaction of a reaction.

Thirty minutes of psychological warfare via coffee later, we pulled up outside a modern apartment complex. Floor-to-ceiling windows gleamed in the morning sun. A doorman stood at attention near the entrance. The building screamed money—worlds away from Rory's slightly dodgy neighbourhood.

...of course he lives somewhere like this...

Rory's thoughts, mixed with a tangle of inadequacy and bitter resignation, hit me like a punch to the gut. I fought back a sigh. Spending time with Rory was going to be difficult unless I could manage to block him better.

My ability had manifested when I was seven—my father's "gift" passed down through three generations of Maxwell men. The first time it happened, I'd collapsed in the school playground, overwhelmed by thirty different voices screaming inside my skull.

Teachers called it a panic attack. My father knew better.

He'd taught me the basics of control, but it wasn't enough. Dad had learnt to manage his telepathy through sheer necessity. First, as a child in Brixton, where his parents had settled after arriving from Kingston, Jamaica. Then later, as one of the few Black officers in the Met during the seventies and eighties, when reading hostile thoughts from colleagues was often more of a burden than blessing.

"You've got to be twice as good to get half the recognition," he'd told me countless times. "And with this gift"—he'd tap his temple—"you've got to be even better than that. People fear what they don't understand."

Through my teenage years, I'd struggled to maintain relationships, friendships crumbling when I accidentally responded to unspoken thoughts. Dating was difficult—enjoying sex with someone when their every insecurity and judgement flooded your mind even more so.

University nearly broke me. Lecture halls became torture chambers of competing thoughts. I'd skip classes, hide in my room, anything to escape the noise. Between that and still processing Dad's death—stabbed whilst responding to a domestic violence call when I was seventeen—my grades plummeted. Ma begged me to drop out, join the force through a different path.

But I was stubborn, determined to prove I could handle it. Determined to make him proud, to carry on what three generations of Maxwell men had started when my grandfather first stepped off that ship at Tilbury Docks.

It took years of discipline to build proper mental barriers. These days, I could usually filter out the background chatter of crowds, limit what leaked through to a sprinkle of surface thoughts only.

...bet he's reading my mind right now...creepy bastard...

I gritted my teeth. Where most people's thoughts were manageable—quiet streams I could dam up or redirect—Rory's mind worked at maximum volume, all the time. His brain fired thoughts in every direction like a machine gun, each one coloured with vivid emotion that made them harder to ignore. Right then, his jealousy and self-loathing swirled together into a maelstrom of hurt.

It wasn't fair. I'd spent decades mastering this curse, learning to function despite it. Then this irritating wolf shows up with his chaos-brain broadcasting on all frequencies—a thunderstorm of thought where others were gentle rain—and suddenly I'm that overwhelmed kid again, fighting for control.

...probably sitting there judging me...

I turned off the engine and caught my reflection in the wing mirror—the same tight curls Dad had worn, cropped close at the sides in a clean fade, though unlike him I was already showing threads of silver despite being only thirty-two years old.

"Before we go in—"

"I know, I know! I'll behave, okay!" Rory yanked the door open, jumped out, then slammed it hard enough to rattle the windows.

"Going well so far, then," I muttered to myself, watching him stalk toward the building entrance.

At least if I ended up murdering him, I'd have the resources to cover it up.

I caught up with Rory at the entrance, my longer strides easily matching his angry stomping. The doorman's eyes tracked our approach, his expression shifting from professional neutrality to mild concern as he took in Rory's aggressive body language.

I pulled out my badge, holding it up. "Detective Inspector Maxwell. We need to speak with one of your residents."

The doorman's gaze flickered between us, lingering on Rory's chaotic hair, multiple ear piercings, and ripped jeans, before returning to my badge.

...odd pair...

"Of course, sir." He stepped aside, swiping his key card to grant us access.

In the pristine hallway, the scent of fresh paint and money surrounded us. I cleared my throat. "So, Ezra Houston. Twenty-five. He's not a shifter, correct?"

Rory shook his head, jaw tight. "No."

I waited for the inevitable snarky comment about wolves dating humans, or some bitter observation about Ezra's wealth. But Rory remained uncharacteristically silent, his shoulders rigid as we walked.

I kept my tone neutral to comment, "And he hasn't filed a missing persons report for his own missing boyfriend."

Rory responded with a grunt that could have meant anything.

"Did you try reaching out to him?"

"Umm..." Rory suddenly found the expensive carpet fascinating. "I think Ezra blocked me on social media."

Something flashed across his face—guilt, maybe shame. What exactly had Rory done to make Dev's new boyfriend block him?

I resisted the urge to find out. That way lay madness, and probably a migraine.

As we approached the door, I had a sudden compulsion to suggest Rory wait outside, but it was too late, because he was already knocking.

It swung open to reveal a man in a pink silk dressing gown that probably cost more than my monthly salary. His honey-blond hair was not dissimilar to Rory's colouring; however, Ezra's swept back from his forehead in artful waves—the kind of style that took an hour to look effortlessly tousled.

...of course he looks like he stepped out of a fucking magazine...

Beside me, Rory's face was a picture, and I almost elbowed him.

"Hello?" A perfect smile flashed, teeth gleaming like a toothpaste commercial.

"DI Maxwell." Displaying my badge, I stepped forward, using my body language to prompt him backward—an old technique that rarely failed. "Can you spare us a second?"

Ezra retreated into his flat, clutching his dressing gown closer. "What's this about?" His accent dripped with private school privilege, each syllable precisely enunciated.

I gestured toward a cream leather sofa that dominated the living space. Through my peripheral vision, I caught Rory's head swivelling like an owl's, taking in every detail of the flat—a crystal decanter caught the morning light, and abstract art pieces dotted the walls.

Ezra did not move. His gaze slid over Rory without a flicker of recognition before returning to me.

"I have a few questions about the whereabouts of Dev Bassi," I said, sliding my notepad out. "You're his boyfriend, correct?"

The transformation was instant. Ezra's carefully cultivated charm vanished, replaced by a scowl that twisted his features into something ugly.

"No," he seethed. "I am not."

I couldn't help but glance at Rory, whose eyes were as wide as saucers.

"I broke up with him just over a week ago. The prick didn't even have the decency to reply to my text."

"You broke up with him over text?" Rory blurted.

Whilst Ezra narrowed his eyes, I tried probing gently at his surface thoughts—always useful to gauge if someone was lying—but only caught fragments. Strong emotions came through clearest. Fear, hatred, desire... those crashed through like alarm bells. But specific facts? Memories? Those required the kind of focus and physical contact that would be completely inappropriate during a police interview.

...oh god, it's the psycho ex...

Now *that* came through sharp and clear, coloured with disgust and a spike of anxiety.

"I... I know you. You're that ex of his. The one who kept leaving laughing face emojis on every single photo we posted of us together."

I swallowed my groan. *Of course.* Ignoring that thread of conversation, I prompted, "Ezra, what happened with you and Dev, precisely?"

"He was cheating on me, the bastard."

"*What?* Dev wouldn't cheat!" Rory snapped.

I rolled my eyes to the back of my head. What sort of voodoo magic had this guy worked to make Rory worship the ground he walked on?

"He was always secretive." Ezra's lips pursed into a moue of distaste. "Disappearing for days at a time with no explanation. Always had these mysterious 'work emergencies' that he couldn't explain."

My detective instincts perked up. Dev hadn't told Ezra what he was. The full moon absences, the sudden emergencies when wolf business called. I tried pressing deeper into Ezra's thoughts, searching for more details, but came up with nothing.

"And then"—Ezra's hand slashed through the air—"the final straw. I had my friend follow him one night. Dev met these two men I'd never seen before. I've got a photo of it. All three of them went into some seedy hotel together." His lips curved into a cruel smile, staring directly at Rory. "You know, if he'd just asked me, I'd have happily had a third join us."

The noise that came from Rory's throat was somewhere between a growl and a choke.

"Not you, though," he said to Rory. "Obviously."

"Alright," I interjected, before Rory could claw his eyes out. "So, what did Dev say?"

"Well, that's the end of it." Ezra's fingers drummed against his thigh. "I sent him the photo with a few choice words about what I thought of his behaviour. Told him we were done. And he didn't even have the decency to respond."

"And you haven't heard from him since?" I pressed.

"Why would I want to?" Ezra's lip curled. "Dev is trash. I should never have lowered myself."

"Can we see the photo?" Rory's voice crackled with tension.

Ezra's glare could have stripped paint.

"The photo, please." My tone brooked no argument. This photo could well be the last time Dev was seen before he disappeared.

With an exaggerated sigh, Ezra snatched his phone from the glass coffee table. His fingers flew across the screen before he thrust it at me.

Rory immediately pressed against my side, leaning in to see. The contact shocked through me—we hadn't been this close since that night when I'd snapped those handcuffs around his wrists. His shoulder dug into my arm, warm even through my suit jacket.

Rory's breath hitched.

The photo showed Dev outside on the street, standing very close to two other men.

Rory's eyes flicked to me meaningfully, then he stared at the photo with theatrical intensity, practically boring holes into it with his gaze.

...WOLVES...I KNOW THEM... he thought so aggressively that I winced, practically feeling the capital letters.

He was so close that his excited exhalation tickled up my neck, and I suppressed a shiver, shuffling away from him.

...SHIT SHIT SHIT, I KNOW THOSE WOLVES...

"Can I send this photo to myself?"

"I don't see why not."

After sending it over, I offered Ezra his phone back. "You've got my number now. Ring me if you hear from him."

"But Dev's not *missing*!" Ezra snapped. "Is... is he?" He looked between the pair of us. "He's not actually missing... right?"

"Keep in touch," I said, heading for the door.

Ezra stared after us, expression glazy, hand frozen halfway through his hair.

I clicked the door shut behind us. Rory's usual vibrant energy had been replaced by something taut and brittle, and he started pacing the hallway like a caged animal.

"Come on, let's go." I set off down the corridor, and to my relief, he followed. "And laughing emojis?" I said. "Come on, really?"

Rory whirled on me, eyes flashing. "I'm sorry, but did you see how Dev replaced me with my fucking *twin*, but taller and hotter?" he spat.

"What?"

"That guy is a model, you know. A literal model. For underwear. A literal *underwear* model. I never had a chance. Guess that's how they met—Dev does modelling on the side."

I blinked, trying to process this information. The idea that Rory thought Ezra was somehow an upgrade was... ridiculous. Sure, the man was polished, but in that artificial way that reminded me of mannequins in shop windows. All surface, no substance. Nothing like Rory's natural energy. Ezra's cheekbones were no match for the way Rory's whole face lit up when he smiled, or that sparkle in his eye that always spelt trouble.

"Calm down. He's not even hotter than you," I said before my brain could catch up with my mouth.

Rory froze mid-stride, staring at me for a long moment. His eyes caught the hallway light, shifting between blue and green like the uncertain edge where shallow waters meet the deep. I could never quite decide what colour they truly were—sometimes as clear as a winter sky, other times harbouring the verdant depths of a Highland forest.

Not that I spent a copious amount of time thinking about Rory Thorne's eye colour, of course.

Those eyes narrowed. "Well, you're hardly qualified to judge, being a straight man."

I snorted. Was this guy for real? "I certainly fucking am. Just because I'm straight doesn't mean I don't have eyes. Let me reassure you, that man is a posh prat. He's got nothing on you." I cleared my throat. "Objectively. So shut up about it, alright?"

Rory's eyes widened slightly, and a hint of pink crept across his cheeks. But then his expression flickered—confusion chasing across his features like clouds across the sun. He opened his mouth as if to say something cutting, then closed it again.

...why is he being nice...what's his angle...don't fall for it...

He stared at me for a long moment, shuffling his weight between feet. Eventually he said, "Thanks, Teddy," using the Killigrew code name he'd assigned me just to wind me up. Yet the ghost of *that* smile played at the corners of his mouth, already transforming his whole face. Something twisted in my chest at the sight—probably indigestion from the coffee. But still, I forced myself to look away from the curve of his jaw, the light catching on his ridiculous number of silver ear piercings.

All of sudden, I couldn't bear our proximity, so I set off at a brisk pace, not talking again until we were back in my car.

"So, who were these wolves you recognised?"

Rory yanked his phone from his pocket, thumbs flying across the screen. "Give me a sec."

His knee bounced up and down, making the whole car vibrate.

"I don't know them well," he said, still scrolling. "Well, I sort of know one of them. But anyway, they're both lone wolves. Packless."

"Huh. Like you?" I knew Rory had left his family pack, who were based up in Scotland, for reasons that had only been hinted at.

A deep crease appeared between his eyebrows. *Ah, fuck.* Clearly this was a sore spot.

"I have Kit," he said finally, voice soft.

...not alone...not like them...

"I'm tethered to him. Sort of. And I have Killigrew Street. They're my pack."

"Right. Sorry. Of course." I shifted uncomfortably in my seat. Foot, meet mouth.

"Found it!" He thrust the phone at me, nearly smacking me in the face. "That was one of the guys, right?"

The photo on Rory's phone showed a pale man, around six feet tall, with close-cropped hair. The background was a blur of neon streaks.

"Looks like it. Where was that picture taken?"

Rory's eyes met mine. "Undertone. You know it, right?"

Ah, Undertone. The "vintage vinyl shop" that fronted one of London's most exclusive supernatural haunts. All sorts of questionable activities went down there, though I made a point of staying clear unless Killigrew work demanded otherwise. The less I knew about what happened behind those hidden doors, the better.

"Yes."

"These two wolves are regulars there." Rory practically vibrated in his seat. "We need to go tonight."

Need? I bit back a groan. It was supposed to be my day off. I'd planned to catch up on sleep this evening, maybe actually cook something instead of living off takeaway.

But Rory's eyes were bright with purpose. Plus, the sooner we tracked down these wolves, the sooner this would all be over.

"I'll pick you up at eight," Rory announced. "It's my turn to drive."

My survival instincts kicked in. I'd seen Rory's car—a rusted death trap held together with hope and duct tape. And his driving... Christ. The one other time I'd been in a car with him, he'd treated London traffic like a Formula One circuit.

"Absolutely not."

He grinned at me. "I absolutely insist."

Resting my head back in the chair, I groaned. "I have to be in bed by eleven."

"Oh my god, you're actually eighty years old, aren't you?" A wicked grin spread across Rory's face. "Do you wear those old man pyjamas with the stripes? And fuzzy slippers?"

"My slippers are perfectly normal."

"Boxers or briefs?"

"What?" My head snapped toward him.

"Just gathering intel. For science."

I started the car, hoping the engine noise would drown him out. No such luck.

"You didn't answer. Boxers or briefs, Detective Inspector Maxwell?"

My head throbbed as unbidden images flashed through my mind—Rory's thoughts hitting me like a sledgehammer. First, me in crisp briefs, so white that they practically glowed against my dark skin, standing on display, quads taut. Then the scene shifted, and suddenly I was lounging in loose navy boxers, casual and relaxed.

...bet he's a briefs man...so uptight...but maybe boxers when he's off duty...wonder if...

Heat creeping up my neck, I jerked the car into the next lane, earning an angry honk from a taxi. "Stop that!"

"Stop what?" Rory's voice dripped innocence, but his thoughts betrayed him:

...definitely briefs...

"You know exactly what." I gripped the wheel tighter, knuckles whitening. "You're doing that deliberately!"

"Oops." He didn't sound sorry at all. "And your temple's doing that twitchy thing again. Dead giveaway, you know."

I forced my hand away from where it had indeed been rubbing my left temple. *Damn it.*

"Besides," he continued, "it's your fault for not answering the question."

"Neither," I snapped. "I sleep naked."

The moment the words left my mouth, I regretted them. Rory's thoughts exploded into technicolor, and I slammed my shields up so fast I nearly gave myself whiplash.

"Really?" His voice squeaked.

"No." I kept my eyes firmly on the road. "And stop imagining it."

I tugged at my collar, suddenly feeling the car's temperature rise several degrees.

"Are you blushing, Detective?" he sang, leaning closer with a wolfish grin. "Did I finally crack your Mr. Professional façade?"

"I'm not—" I cranked up the air conditioning. "I'm dropping you at this bus stop. I need a long break from you before tonight."

Rory chuckled, unbuckling his seatbelt as I pulled in. "Eight o'clock!" he called through the window. "Don't be late!"

"I'm driving!" I shouted back, but he was already weaving through the crowd, that messy blond hair bouncing as he practically skipped away.

I slumped back in my seat. *Fucking hell.* A night at Undertone with Rory Thorne. I'd rather face a pack of feral wolves.

...can't wait to see you in your clubbing clothes, Detective Dickface...

His final thought drifted back to me, clear as a bell despite the distance. I groaned, reaching for the emergency cigarettes in my glove compartment.

Clearly, this was going to be a cigarette kind of day.

3

Rory

The pile of discarded clothes around my feet grew higher as I dug through my wardrobe. A sequined crop top sailed across the room, followed by three pairs of ripped jeans and my favourite mesh shirt.

I'd started this process forty-five minutes ago with a simple goal: find something professional.

Now I had three distinct piles: the "definitely not" mountain by the window that included the glittery monstrosity I'd worn to Pride, the "maybe if I was desperate" heap by my dresser, and the "actually quite promising but missing something crucial" collection on my bed. The black shirts had been circling between piles two and three for the last twenty minutes while I spiralled about whether "professional investigator" meant "boring" or "competent but approachable."

A soft knock preceded Kit's massive frame filling my doorway. "What died in here?"

"My fashion sense, apparently." I held up two nearly identical black T-shirts. The left one was cotton—safe, boring. The right one had just enough texture to suggest I actually gave a shit about how I looked. "Which one says 'I'm a professional investigator who definitely knows what he's doing?'"

"Neither." Kit's eyes narrowed. "Are you sure it's a good idea to go to Undertone with Maxwell?"

"Why wouldn't it be?" I shot daggers at him whilst internally cataloguing whether I could get away with the burgundy shirt if I found my black blazer, except the blazer was somewhere in the laundry pile downstairs and I'd definitely need the specific silver chain that would balance the whole look, but that chain was tangled with three others and— "We're interviewing potential witnesses slash leads. Being professional. Following proper procedure. All that boring stuff he loves so much."

"Uh-huh." Kit leaned against the doorframe, arms crossed. His cardigan stretched tight across his shoulders—the soft grey one he pretended wasn't his favourite. "And the outfit crisis is because...?"

"Because I want to look competent, okay?" I threw both shirts onto the reject pile, immediately regretting it because now I'd have to start over completely and maybe the left one wasn't that boring after all. "And also hot. Because it's a nightclub."

My phone screen caught my eye: 7:15.

Fuck. When had that happened? I'd been debating those two black shirts since quarter to seven, which meant I'd lost thirty minutes to a clothing paralysis spiral while Maxwell was probably already checking his watch and composing mental lectures about punctuality.

"Rory—"

"I know, I know. And I'd feel better if you came with us." I yanked the burgundy button-down from its hanger—sod the blazer, sod the chain, this would have to work. "But Seb's got you in Brixton tonight, right?"

"Yeah. Watching Marcus Vale's clan." Kit's expression softened. "I'd come if I could."

"I'll be fine." I shrugged into the shirt, checking my reflection. Actually, the burgundy worked—made my eyes pop, suggested confidence without trying too hard. "Maxwell might be a dick, but he's a sensible, reliable dick. And I can handle myself."

"That's what worries me."

"Oh, shut up. I promise not to start any bar fights or accidentally set anything on fire."

Kit's deep chuckle echoed down the hallway as his heavy footsteps faded away.

Wait. The burgundy was too formal, wasn't it? Made me look like I was trying to impress him, which I absolutely wasn't, except maybe I was a little bit, but not in that way, just professionally, but—

"Fuck it." I yanked the mesh shirt back off the floor, paired it with my tightest black jeans and threw the burgundy over it as an overshirt. Layers. Versatile. I could ditch the overshirt if the club was too warm, keep it if Maxwell's disapproving stare got too frosty.

My phone blazed again: 7:18. Shit. Maxwell lived thirty minutes away, and I refused to give him another excuse to be a condescending prick about my timekeeping.

I hastily swiped eyeliner across my lids before bolting for the door. My fingers flew across the phone screen as I half jogged to my car.

> Are you sure you and Emma don't want to come to Undertone for your date night tonight?

Priya's response pinged back instantly.

Priya

> No, because I don't want Emma to become vampire food

A laugh burst from my chest as I slid behind the wheel of my not-so-trusty Ford Cortina. Those two had finally got their act together after four months of Priya's not-so-subtle flirting. Flynn had persuaded Emma to get a job at Fat Cat's, and then Priya had repeatedly dropped in, attempting to buy Emma cups of tea so she could read her leaves.

God, it had been painful to watch.

Nowadays, I couldn't help but miss having Priya as my designated single friend. We'd been close since the day we met. She'd made an effort to make me feel welcome at Killigrew Street because Kit had been too on edge about my arrival to do that himself. Priya may not have been all that powerful for a "Gifted practitioner"—her skills basically amounted to teaspoon telekinesis—but she had a heart of gold. For the people she liked, at least.

After Issac died, she'd tried her best to fill the hole the absence of my best friend left in my life. For ages, she'd shown up at my door almost every other evening with food and terrible movies. But post-Emma, I was now often stuck with Kit when I needed company. I loved my brother, but he annoyed the hell out of me.

Though being alone was worse. The silence got too loud, thoughts spiralling into dark places.

I arrived two minutes late, thanks to having to slow down for the three speed cameras en route.

Maxwell emerged from his building, and my brain short-circuited. *Holy shit.*

Detective Dickface was wearing *jeans*. Not just any jeans—dark, well-fitted ones that hugged his thighs in ways his usual suit trousers never did. He'd paired them with a simple black T-shirt under a navy button-up left casually open, the sleeves rolled to his elbows revealing forearms I'd never seen before.

His usual glasses were absent, and oddly, I missed them. They suited his Mr. Serious Detective act.

I clutched the steering wheel, shocked by my own thoughts. What was going on? My earlier interactions with Maxwell had clearly muddled my brain. The way he'd brought me coffee—*Fat Cat's* coffee, of all things—and the compliment about being hotter than Ezra, delivered with such matter-of-fact certainty it had knocked me sideways. For about ten blissful minutes, I'd almost forgotten I was supposed to hate him. I'd caught myself actually *enjoying* his company, teasing him about his underwear choices, like that was an appropriate thing to do.

Get it together, Rory. You can't trust him. Not even a little bit.

Maxwell yanked the passenger door open, wincing at the ear-splitting creak of rusty hinges. He slid in cautiously, as if the seat might collapse beneath him.

"When was this thing manufactured? The Dark Ages?"

"She's a classic." I turned the key, and the engine coughed to life after three attempts.

Maxwell pulled the door shut, only to meet resistance. He tried again, more forcefully, then stared at me, eyebrows raised. Without his glasses, his super thick, long dark lashes were more apparent.

"It doesn't quite shut properly, but it's fine. Honest."

"This thing needs to go to the scrapyard," he muttered, gripping the door handle as I pulled away.

I glanced over, noticing his freshly shaved jaw and catching a whiff of a different cologne than he usually wore. Something woody and spiced that my brain couldn't help but take note of. The scent clung to the collar of his shirt, crisply ironed. Bloody hell, he smelled *good*.

Not that he didn't usually smell good, to be fair to him. Underneath the lemongrass he usually wore, he had this distinctive smell that somehow reminded me of raindrops—the earthy, fresh scent that lingers after a storm breaks the heat. It was... annoyingly nice.

Oops. I'd been silent for too long. Was he reading my thoughts right now, listening to me obsess over how he smelled like a bloody summer rainstorm? God, how embarrassing. My cheeks burned at the thought.

I cleared my throat. "Well, Seb's promised me a new car as soon as I can go a full month without a single parking or speeding fine."

"So... never, then?"

"Fuck off."

My skin prickled as Maxwell's eyes lingered on me, taking in my mesh shirt visible beneath the oversized burgundy overshirt, the eyeliner, my attempt at styled hair.

"What?" I challenged, oddly self-conscious under his scrutiny. "I figured if Undertone is a bust, I'll go out to meet some mates after. You said you had to be home by eleven anyway."

Maxwell grunted in reply.

I pressed on the accelerator, weaving through traffic while my brain ping-ponged between a dozen different thoughts. The case... What if we found nothing? Dev... was he still alive? What would it be like if we found him dead? The missing wolves... were they really connected to this? How Maxwell was going to act at Undertone... would he be his usual grumpy self or actually try to blend in? Should I have worn the other shirt after all? Did he think I looked ridiculous? Why did I even care what he thought?

"Can you stop that?" Maxwell snapped suddenly.

"Stop what?"

He pointed at my hands against the wheel. "That. The tapping."

I hadn't even realised I was doing it. My fingers froze mid-beat, and I scowled at him. "I'm sorry my existence is so fucking annoying to you."

"Do you ever keep still?"

An icy grip seized my heart as every muscle in my body tensed, the words cutting deeper than he could have guessed.

Sit still, Rory! For god's sake, what's wrong with you? My mother's voice echoed from the past, sharp with frustration as I fidgeted through another endless Sunday dinner.

Look at your brothers. Why can't you behave like them? Dad comparing me to my perfectly still, perfectly normal siblings who could sit endlessly without needing to move, to touch, to tap.

You're disrespecting the alpha. Dad's harsh whisper during a pack meeting, his nails digging into my thigh to force me still.

He's doing it for attention. My father's second-in- command, Tariq's dismissive judgement when I couldn't follow the strict formation patterns during pack runs.

Just discipline him properly and he'll learn. Delivered with a sniff while I twisted my napkin into shreds, desperate to quiet the buzzing in my body.

There's something wrong with that boy. Whispered behind hands when they thought I couldn't hear.

The memories washed over me in a sudden, overwhelming wave. My throat tightened. The familiar shame burned hot beneath my skin—that broken feeling that had followed me from childhood. The constant disappointment I caused just by existing as myself.

I glanced over at Maxwell and caught him staring at me with an expression of dawning horror. His left temple twitched under his fingertips.

"Rory, I—"

"I have ADHD, you dickhead," I seethed, gripping the steering wheel with all my strength. "So no, I won't 'keep still' just because it annoys you. And fucking *stop* reading my mind!"

Maxwell flinched as if I'd slapped him. His expression shifted to what might have been genuine remorse.

"Please accept my apology." His voice was softer than I'd ever heard it. "I didn't know. Nobody ever mentioned it," he added, sounding confused.

"You don't know how many times I heard it growing up." Though to be fair, he now had a bit of an idea because he'd read my mind, the creepy bastard. The anger drained from me, leaving a hollow ache in its place. "When I got to sixteen, I finally saw a doctor about it, behind my parents' backs. But they found out anyway, and then forbade me from even trying out ADHD medication. Said it wasn't natural and it would suppress my wolf or some bullshit. They thought I just needed more discipline."

Why was I telling Theodore Maxwell all this? But he was quietly listening, his usual judgement absent from his face, so I continued.

"I ignored them and picked up the prescription. Then, when my mum snooped in my room and found the packets, she threw them away, and I was locked up for three days."

"Christ," Maxwell said, eyes wide. "I don't know much about ADHD," he admitted after a moment. "I'm not sure I've met many people who have it."

How many friends did Theodore Maxwell even have? I pictured him alone in an immaculately tidy flat, his footsteps the only sound as he walked between empty rooms. Then I quickly tried to squash the thought in case he was listening again.

"So the medication helped you?" Maxwell asked.

I glanced at him, searching his face for that familiar judgement—that "god, what must he be like without meds, then" look I'd seen before. But instead, he seemed genuinely curious.

"Helped me? Mate, it changed my fucking life." I drummed my fingers against the wheel, this time deliberately. "There are so many things I didn't realise were ADHD." I laughed, the sound edged with bitterness. "I thought I was just constantly overwhelmed because I wasn't good enough to keep up with everything my parents wanted. But no... turns out I didn't know how to tune anything out."

We stopped at a red light, and I turned to face him properly.

"It was like my brain forced me to pay attention to everything in my surroundings all at once. Sounds are really loud—and that's before you factor in wolf hearing—but on meds, I can actually tune things out. Focus on one conversation instead of drowning in background noise." The light changed, and I pulled away. "And the emotional regulation—I didn't realise so much of the spiralling was ADHD. Now I can have an anxious thought without completely losing my shit."

Stay on topic, Rory, stay on topic.

"Plus, I'm not exhausted all the time anymore. Before..." I faltered for a moment, struggling to articulate something I'd never fully explained to anyone. "I'd be so mentally and physically shattered every day because my brain was working on overdrive just to filter basic stuff. That makes *so* much sense, right?" My voice cracked slightly. "Anyway, I never knew I could be not exhausted."

My words hung in the air. I'd never told anyone how bone-deep tired I'd been my entire life before medication. Not even Kit.

"So, now I can actually cook dinner *and* do laundry at *the same time* without my brain melting," I tried to joke. "If Kit *wants* me to cook. He normally does it, though, because he thinks he's a pro masterchef."

I became acutely aware of Maxwell's silence. The quiet stretched on for so long I wanted to melt into the car seat.

Christ, what was wrong with me? I'd just delivered an unprompted TED talk on ADHD to Detective Dickface of all people. The one person who already thought I was an incompetent disaster. Mortification settled in my stomach like a lead weight.

I sneaked a glance at him. Though instead of the judgement or boredom I expected, his expression was thoughtful, brow slightly furrowed as if processing. I quickly focused back on the road, clamping my lips together. Maybe if I didn't acknowledge my verbal diarrhoea, we could pretend it never happened.

Then Maxwell laughed softly, my head snapping straight back to him. Was he... smiling? Not that sarcastic smirk of his, but something... genuine?

"So that explains why you have the energy of a caffeinated squirrel on speed," he said, his voice light. "And here I thought you were just trying to drive me mad on purpose."

A surprised laugh burst from my chest, and the tension drained from my shoulders. "Annoying you is just a bonus."

"Yes..." Maxwell added, his tone still gentle but with a hint of amusement. "But I have to say, for someone who's supposedly learned how to regulate better... you seem to find it very hard to resist insulting me to my face."

Heat crept up my neck. "Yeah... you bring it out in me, I guess..."

"But seriously, I'll try to do better," Maxwell said, looking out the windscreen rather than at me. "And... try even harder to block out your thoughts. They're just... louder than other people's."

A tiny smile played at the edge of his lips, and I laughed.

"Figures."

He met my gaze. "Figures."

The moment stretched between us, almost comfortable, until Maxwell's phone rang, a loud electronic jingle cutting through the silence. He glanced at the screen, hesitated, then pressed decline.

"Sorry. I forgot to tell my mother we couldn't talk today."

"Aww, Teddy Bear has a standing call with his mummy?" The words slipped out before I could stop them, my default teasing mode reactivated. "Do you tell her about all the big scary criminals you catch?"

The look that crossed his face made me instantly regret my words.

"We do talk most nights. She worries," he said, voice flat. "My father's no longer around. He was also a police officer—not a detective, though he was working up to it. He was almost there, then he was killed in the line of duty when I was seventeen."

"Shit." I grimaced at myself, feeling like the world's biggest asshole. "I'm sorry." There was a long pause before I asked, "Did you always want to be a cop, like him?"

"Yeah," Maxwell said softly. "Even before he died. I used to dress up in his helmet and march around the garden, telling everyone I was going to catch all the bad guys." A ghost of a smile flickered across his face. "He'd come home exhausted—double shifts, overtime, constantly pushing himself. Always studying for the next exam, the next qualification. He'd tell me stories about helping people, making things right. He had this... determination. Like he was trying to prove something to the world every single day." Maxwell's voice grew more distant. "I suppose I've been trying to live up to that ever since. To continue what he started."

My own father's face flashed through my mind—not the warm image I presumed most people had, but the twisted expression of disgust he wore that last time I saw him. The day he told me I wasn't welcome in the pack anymore. Three days before he was shot by an Authorised Firearms Officer during a full moon.

One single well-placed bullet to the heart. A gamekeeper had reported our pack, apparently. Told the authorities the "wolf infestation" was a danger to life.

My pack had been unable to recover his body. No funeral rites for them. All I got was a phone call from my mother three days later, her voice cold as she informed me of his death, like she was telling a stranger. "I thought you should know," she'd said. Not "I miss you," or, "Please come home," or even, "How are you doing?" Just the bare minimum obligation of information before she hung up.

I hadn't spoken to her since.

"My dad's dead too," I said, the words tumbling out of me. "But I don't talk to my mother. Sometimes I think I miss her. Other times she's dead to me." I stared straight ahead at the road. "Sorry, I know it isn't a competition. You must think I'm pathetic, after this morning with Ezra and now all this. I promise I'm not usually like this." Why did I even care what he thought? But I did. Because I always cared what people thought of me.

Maxwell shifted in his seat, turning toward me. "I don't think you're pathetic, Rory."

He sounded so serious that I almost believed him. *Almost.*

"Sure," I muttered, and the awkward silence stretched between us like an elastic band ready to snap.

Maxwell looked morose, his face set in that brooding expression that made him look older than his thirty-something years. Was he always this serious, or was there something in me specifically that brought it out?

The sun was just setting when we arrived. I parked the car down a narrow side street about half a block away, in a legal parking spot so Maxwell wouldn't have to arrest me upon pulling up.

From the outside, Undertone looked like an aging vintage vinyl-record shop. Peeling posters decorated the grimy windows, and a neon sign "By Appointment Only" hung crookedly—a deterrent for humans seeking actual vintage vinyls. Because the real establishment, deep underground, was a nightclub catering to most supernatural persuasions.

"I haven't been here in a while," I said as we walked toward the door. "Seb banned us from hanging here. He's got beef with the vampire who owns the place... Dominic."

Maxwell groaned. "I know."

"But don't worry. Dominic's usually either in his office or the private rooms. He hardly ever mingles with the commoners before midnight."

We pushed through the door, a little brass bell tinkling overhead. Soft jazz music floated through the air—the kind that makes you think of smoky rooms and forbidden pleasures. Inside, the shop was dimly lit, with rows of vinyls arranged in meticulous order.

Even the receptionist, the vampire Marley, seemed to freeze before they smiled, perfect victory rolls framing their face and crimson lipstick accentuating their smile. They sat behind an antique desk, fingers poised over a rotary phone.

"Smaller Thorne," they drawled, voice deep and rich like molasses. "I haven't seen your brother in a while."

Last year, Seb had resorted to sending Kit to buy blood from Undertone, despite its dubious, unethical nature. Needs must when you're a vampire, though.

"Sebastián's got his own personal blood bank these days," I quipped, wiggling my eyebrows suggestively. "His boyfriend comes with all the nutrients a growing vampire needs. Organic *and* free range."

Marley's laugh was surprisingly warm. "Good for him."

I felt Maxwell shift uncomfortably beside me.

"Anyway, we're here for a listening appointment," I said, flashing my most charming smile. "Pleasure tonight, not business."

Marley's perfectly pencilled eyebrow arched. They closed their thick paper ledger with a deliberate thump and stood.

"Follow me."

At the rear wall, three listening booths lined up in a neat row. Marley unlocked booth three with an ornate brass key. The door swung open with a theatrical creak, and they ushered us inside.

The booth's walls were padded with cream leather, and a gleaming turntable sat on a polished wooden shelf. Maxwell dominated the cramped space, and I found myself pressed against his side, acutely aware of how my head barely reached his shoulder.

His body was warm and solid against mine, and I had to tilt my head back to meet his eyes when he glanced down at me. For a moment, his usual scowl softened into something... else? But then Marley reached for a record from a high shelf. As soon as they dropped the needle onto the turntable, hypnotic music filled the tiny space.

The wall behind us silently slid away, revealing a steep spiral staircase descending into darkness. LED strips embedded in the steps pulsed with a soft blue glow, lighting our way down.

"Enjoy your evening," Marley said, their voice already fading as we descended.

The staircase wound down before we finally reached a vast underground space. A curvy female pianist played a bright-yellow grand piano in the middle of the room, her fingers dancing across the keys to a melancholic jazz number. Classic Dominic—always trying to pretend Undertone was a classy establishment before it devolved into a riotous rave by midnight.

Maxwell shifted his weight from foot to foot, adjusting his collar like it was suddenly too tight.

"You look like you're about to be executed," I said, nudging him with my elbow. "Grab that table over there, will you? I'll get us drinks."

I made my way to the bar constructed from stacked vintage speakers, then returned balancing two gin and tonics.

"So, it's just gone half nine. It could be a while still." I pushed a glass toward him. "I went gin and tonic because I thought you'd want something boring."

Maxwell's eyes narrowed as he glanced from my drink to me. "You're driving!"

"I drove *here*," I replied with a smirk. "And I need something to take the edge off if we're going to be interrogating wolves in Dominic Thrift's basement."

Whilst he groaned, I quickly snatched up my glass and took several large sips, the gin burning pleasantly down my throat.

"Fine, I'll drive us back." Resignation etched itself across his face as he pushed his drink toward me. "Your driving made me car sick, anyway. But these better not be doubles."

I paused mid-sip, my eyes widening with mock innocence. "Um... try triple."

"That's not legal!"

I raised an eyebrow, pointing toward the bar where refrigerated glass cases displayed neatly labelled bottles of crimson liquid. "Is it legal to sell pints of blood by the glass?"

Maxwell's expression shifted from outrage to defeat. "There's no way I'm going to be in bed by eleven, is there?"

"Not a chance in hell."

He leaned in closer, his eyes flitting about the room. "And what if they don't come?"

"It's Friday night. They'll show up," I said with more confidence than I felt. "This place is basically the supernatural equivalent of that cantina from *Star Wars*. If you're a shifter in South London who doesn't want to deal with pack politics, this is where you come."

He gave me an off look. "You're a *Star Wars* fan?"

"Don't sound so surprised." I drained half of my second drink in one gulp. The alcohol buzzed through my system, making me feel relaxed for the first time in days. "I contain multitudes."

"That's Whitman, not *Star Wars*," he corrected, then caught himself with a slight flinch. "Sorry. But I like *Star Wars* too. Not only dead American poets."

I stared at him. "Are you... actually semi-interesting, Detective Theodore Maxwell?"

"Probably not," he said, the corner of his mouth quirking up in what might have been the beginning of a smile.

"Do you like *How to Train your Dragon?*"

He frowned. "What's that?"

I gave an exaggerated sigh. "False alarm. Come back to me when you know what Hiccup's middle name is."

The music shifted, replaced by a low electronic beat that vibrated through the floor. The lights dimmed further, and more people began filtering in. A few of them were humans—some likely seeking to earn a fat wad of cash from spending an hour in one of the private rooms with a vampire.

Near the bar, a stunningly gorgeous man with sharp cheekbones leaned against the counter, whispering into the ear of a woman who looked absolutely entranced. The air around him seemed to shimmer slightly.

"Incubus," I muttered, nodding in their direction.

Maxwell's head whipped around. "How can you tell?"

"The slight shimmer," I said. "And the way humans look at them—like they're starving and the incubus is a five-course meal. Plus, they smell different."

"They smell different?"

"Like sugar and sex and something electric. It's hard to describe to someone who doesn't have enhanced senses."

Maxwell stared at the incubus. "I've never crossed paths with one. Well, I don't think so."

"Count yourself lucky. They're a nightmare to deal with—can charm their way out of almost anything." I drained the last of my drink, the gin dulling the sharp edges of my thoughts. "Kit brought one back to Killigrew Street once, for questioning. The incubus nearly talked his way out of it. Even Seb was getting a bit doe-eyed before Priya slapped some sense into him."

The moment I set my empty glass down, a waiter materialised beside our table with two more gin and tonics.

Maxwell let out a small cry.

God, when was the last time I'd eaten? The alcohol was hitting harder than usual, but honestly, I welcomed it. It was quieting the constant worry that had been gnawing at me. A week of Dev being missing, a week of barely sleeping, and now Maxwell was stuck with me when he'd probably rather eat glue.

Just one more drink, then I'll stop.

"Well," I said, taking a generous sip. "Whatever happens next, at least it won't be boring."

4

Theodore

*W*on't *be boring.*

I should be so lucky.

Rory was now four drinks deep, with no sign of the supposed shifters we were here to question. The night was slipping away, and instead of conducting an investigation, I was babysitting an increasingly inebriated wolf with boundary issues.

One drink ago, he'd launched into a sad spiral about Dev Bassi, showing me picture after picture of his face on his phone.

"This was us at Pride," Rory slurred, swiping to yet another image of the missing journalist. "And this one's from his birthday. He hated this photo, but I think he looks perfect."

Honestly, I really didn't get the Dev obsession. Though Rory made his career sound interesting, his curated social media photos screamed pretentious self-absorption. Every image featured the same calculated smile, the same careful angles.

The server approached with another round neither of us had ordered. Rory's eyes lit up as the glasses landed on our table. He reached for one with the enthusiasm of a man who'd forgotten we were here on official business.

I grabbed drink number five, and pushed it out of Rory's reach. My fingers brushed against his as I intercepted the glass, sending a sudden jolt through me.

...warm hands....

Rory pouted, his lower lip jutting out in a way that made him look absurdly young. "That's mine."

"You've had enough," I said firmly. "We're supposed to be *working.*"

...no fun...

"You're no fun," he mumbled, slouching back in his seat. The neon lights caught in his hair, turning the blond strands into something almost celestial. His subtle eyeliner made his eyes larger, more intense somehow. As he tilted his head to stare longingly at the confiscated drink, the club's lights glinted off the collection of silver studs and hoops that lined his ear, dancing in the light with each slight movement. I found myself counting them, wondering absurdly if they'd feel warm or cool to the touch.

Irritated at my own distraction, I forced my gaze away, only for Rory's thoughts to assault my mind.

...I bet he could be fun, though...was Dev fun?...I think Dev was fun...we had fun...didn't we?...until he broke up with me...maybe I wasn't fun enough...

I rubbed my temple, feeling the pressure of too many thoughts threatening to spill into me. Not just Rory's—the nightclub was now full to bursting, and I was suffering from it.

"What was so great about Dev, anyway?" I found myself snapping. "You talk about him like he hung the moon."

Where had *that* bitterness come from? I normally possessed endless patience for listening to people's ramblings. Came with the territory. Yet something about this was pushing my buttons...

Rory's mouth opened, then closed, then opened again like a fish gasping for air. No words came out. For the first time since I'd met the excitable wolf, Rory Thorne was speechless.

I couldn't help it. I laughed. "See!"

The silence stretched between us, unusual and almost unsettling. Rory's constant chatter was as much a part of him as his snark and bounciness. Seeing him without words felt wrong, like witnessing something private.

His face crumpled, every inch of cockiness draining away, leaving something horribly raw and vulnerable behind. "I thought he loved me," he said, voice cracking on the last word. His eyes glistened in the club's pulsing lights, threatening tears.

Fuck. Fuck. *Fuck.*

I wasn't equipped for this. Angry Rory, annoying Rory, even fake-flirtatious Rory—those versions I could handle. But this broken, hurt version? I had no protocol for that.

"It's all my fault that he broke up with me," Rory continued, staring down at his now empty glass. "I was too much. Too needy. Too keen. Desperate, in fact." He laughed, a horrible hollow sound. "Dev was so far out of my league it was ridiculous. Everyone thought so."

I frowned. "Who's 'everyone?'"

Rory waved his hand dismissively. "Doesn't matter. I knew it. He knew it." He traced the rim of an empty glass with his finger. "I just thought maybe... I don't know. That it wouldn't matter. That he could still love me."

His gaze lifted to meet mine, the light catching in his eyes. Blue? Green? Both and neither at once, like sunlight filtering through shallow water. Poetry in colour that shifted with each blink, each change in his mercurial mood. The only constant was their intensity.

"What happened? In the end, I mean, with you and Dev?"

"I suggested we move in together." Rory's shoulders hunched forward. "After that, he started pulling away. Cancelling plans. Working late. Three weeks later, he told me he 'needed space.'" His fingers made air quotes around the words. "Classic, right? Couldn't even come up with an original breakup line."

...never good enough...of course it would end...so stupid...

The melancholy Rory felt leaked into me, seeping through me like poison.

My fingers itched to reach out to comfort him. I clenched my fist into a tight ball, because knowing Rory, he'd bloody well bite me. "Look, Rory, honestly? Dev sounds like a fucking twat. I'm surprised you even want to spend so much time and energy trying to find—"

Rory's eyes suddenly widened, his attention shooting past me toward the bottom of the stairs. "That's them!" he hissed, practically vibrating with excitement.

I turned to look. Two men had entered the club—both muscular, exuding that distinctive predator energy that marked them as shifters. The taller one had a shaved head and a tattoo crawling up his neck, while his companion sported a man bun and a carefully groomed beard. Both wore expensive-looking shirts that strained against their chests.

They matched the photos Rory had shown me earlier.

Thank god. Finally we could get down to actual police work and away from whatever emotional minefield I'd stumbled into.

"Right, you said you know them, yes?" I asked, straightening my posture.

Rory's face contorted into something between a grimace and a smirk. "Um... Did I say that? Well, I sort of do. I met them here once, ages ago, before Seb banned us. But I don't *know* them, know them. Well, you see that one on the right, with the hair? I sort of know his mouth. And... his dick too."

I gasped so hard I choked. "Bloody hell, Rory!"

...wasn't a bad dick either...

Brilliant. Just brilliant. Rory had shagged our primary suspect. This case kept getting better and better. I fought desperately to block out both Rory's wandering thoughts and my own inexplicable irritation at the mental images they conjured.

"And hey, I know his first name, at least! Bradley. I think..." He frowned, swaying slightly in his seat. "Yes, that was it. And his friend, Brody. Or was it Brady...? Anyway, I'll go flirt with Bradley for a bit. Then I'll lead into Dev somehow and hopefully get something."

"Absolutely not," I said firmly. "How would you even do that? Plus, you're not *selling your body* for information. Not to mention that you're now rather drunk, and this is a sensitive investigation. I'll approach them—"

But Rory was already standing, shuffling out of his overshirt, then straightening his black mesh garment that kept drawing various eyes with its glimpses of his bare skin.

I shot to my feet, blocking Rory's path.

"I'm not drunk, Teddy," he said. "Honest. Look, I'll walk one foot in front of the other, all the way."

Before I could physically stop him, he blew me a kiss and staggered away in a ridiculous zigzag, heading straight for the man possibly called Bradley.

I watched, horrified, as Rory intercepted the man, immediately placing a familiar hand on his chest. Bradley's face lit up with recognition, and he leaned down to speak directly into Rory's ear.

The noise of the club seemed to fade around me, leaving only the sound of my own breathing and the distant thump of bass. I just stood there, hovering at our table. My eyes refused to stop following Rory's animated gestures, the way he tilted his head back to laugh at something Bradley said, how his fingers lingered on the man's chest.

Bradley's shaved-headed friend seemed less than impressed. He laughed, shook his head at the pair, and walked past the bar towards the corridor.

I made a decision. We needed information, so splitting up momentarily made tactical sense. Rory was "handling" Bradley—and despite his inebriated state, he was clearly in his element. He might be too drunk for my liking, but he wasn't helpless. We were in the middle of a crowded supernatural club. If Bradley tried anything Rory didn't want, Rory would happily make a scene.

I'd follow the friend—Brody slash Brady—get what information I could, and circle back in five minutes.

I caught Rory's eye across the room and tapped my watch, then pointed toward him. Rory gave me a surprisingly subtle nod before refocusing on Bradley.

Still, as I moved toward the corridor, I couldn't shake the feeling that I didn't want to leave him.

The corridor housed private rooms styled as additional "listening booths." From the sounds emanating through the doors—moans, gasps, and occasional growls—it was clear these spaces served purposes far beyond music appreciation.

The shifter I was following wanted a smoke, not a hookup. I continued to the end of the corridor, where it opened into a brick-walled room, styled as a courtyard, with ventilation that whisked smoke upward. Despite the efficient air circulation, the unmistakable scent of cigarettes hung in the air.

The man stood alone, back against the wall, drawing deeply on his cigarette. *Called it.*

My fingers twitched toward my pocket. I'd been trying to quit for months, but kept an emergency pack for extreme stress. Apparently, clubbing with Rory qualified.

We were alone. I meandered over and pulled out my own cigarette.

"Got a light?" I asked, voice neutral.

He eyed me suspiciously, taking in my appearance with a slow, assessing gaze. After a moment, he produced a silver lighter and flicked it open.

I leaned in, letting the fire catch. "Thanks," I said, taking a deep drag.

"Don't think I've seen you around here before."

"That's because I'm not, usually," I replied on an exhalation of smoke. "I'm a police detective looking into a missing persons case. Journalist named Devraj Bassi. He's a shifter. Ring any bells?"

His expression didn't change, but I caught the slightest hesitation before he took another drag. "Can't say it does."

I pulled out my phone, scrolling to find the photo of Dev with the pair of them.

"Ring any bells *now*?"

He flinched, his eyes widening before he dropped his cigarette and moved toward the door with purposeful strides.

With a regretful toss of my own cigarette, I stepped into his path. "Look, Brody—" He balked at the use of his name. "I'm trying to be reasonable here. But if you don't help me, I'll have to tell Black you were uncooperative."

The shifter laughed, a harsh bark. "Black? You think that's supposed to scare me?"

...shit shit shit...Black?...

Sebastián's reputation did indeed precede him.

"I don't have any information for you, mate," Brody insisted, shouldering past me.

But as he moved, something flashed in his mind—an image so vivid it practically projected itself into my consciousness: Dev Bassi in a dimly lit room, his expression grim, jaw clenched tight. The image was sharp, recent, real.

"Liar," I snapped, the word torn from me before I could stop it.

The wolf's head whipped around, shock written on his face. Then he bolted.

I cursed and gave chase, my shoes slipping on the polished floor. He was fast, but the narrow hallway limited his movement. I lunged forward, catching the back of his shirt.

Brody spun, snarling, eyes flashing amber. His fist connected with my jaw, sending pain exploding across my face. I staggered but didn't let go, using his momentum to shove him sideways.

We crashed into the nearest listening booth, tumbling through it onto the floor, the door slamming shut behind us. The small space amplified our struggle, limbs knocking against walls. He was stronger—shifter strength giving him an edge—but I was determined, fuelled by the knowledge that he'd seen Dev.

Brody's elbow caught my ribs, forcing the air from my lungs. I countered by driving my knee up, creating enough space to flip our positions. We rolled, knocking over a small table. I slammed him against the wall, forearm pressed against his throat.

The wolf's muscles tensed beneath my grip, his skin growing hot. His eyes flickered between human brown and animal amber, pupils elongating unnaturally. A low growl rumbled through his chest, vibrating against my forearm.

...kill him...rip him apart...tear his throat out...

Brody's thoughts crashed into my mind with savage intensity, making me wince. The transformation was beginning—skin rippling, muscles straining as bones prepared to crack and reform. Adrenaline spiked through me. I'd never seen a wolf shift before, and as fascinated as I was by it, pinning a transforming shifter to a wall seemed like a spectacularly poor life choice.

"I wouldn't shift if I were you," I said, voice deadly calm despite my racing heart. "Dominic knows I'm here looking for you." A complete lie, but I delivered it with unwavering confidence.

The mention of Dominic's name cut through Brody's rage. His eyes widened, the amber glow receding slightly.

"That's right." I pressed my advantage. "Dominic doesn't take kindly to wolves shifting in his establishment. Lifetime ban, I believe? And I've heard he has... creative ways of enforcing his rules."

His breathing slowed, the immediate threat of transformation subsiding. I could still feel the wolf just beneath his skin, but he was fighting it back now.

I maintained my grip, ignoring the throbbing pain in my jaw. Blood from my split lip trickled down my chin, dripping onto his expensive shirt.

"Tell me what you did to Dev Bassi," I hissed, tasting copper. "Where is he?"

The wolf's eyes darted to the door, calculating his chances of escape. I pressed harder against his throat.

...can't tell...they'll kill me...

"Who'll kill you?" I demanded, the words slipping out before I could stop myself. *Fuck.* I wasn't usually that sloppy.

Brody's expression changed instantly, fear giving way to something else—realisation, then cold fury.

"You're a fucking telepath," he snarled, disgust dripping from every word.

"You're right. I am," I admitted, easing the pressure on his throat slightly but maintaining my grip. "So don't bother lying to me. Just tell me what I need to know about Dev Bassi, and we can both continue with our evenings."

His eyes narrowed with revulsion. Most supernaturals viewed telepathy as an invasion, a violation worse than physical assault. I didn't entirely blame them.

"Not a chance," he spat. "And don't you dare read my mind. I mean it."

This was the part nobody ever understood about telepathy—it wasn't the convenient superpower they imagined. It wasn't like flipping through a filing cabinet. It was messy, like trying to catch specific words in a hurricane of consciousness. Detailed information required focus, proximity, and sometimes physical contact. The pressure behind my temples was already building as I pushed past his surface thoughts, like forcing my way through thick fog. Each deeper probe sent sharp needles of pain radiating from my skull down my neck.

Even now, with my hands on him, I was only catching fragments. Images of Dev, flashes of fear. The deeper I pressed, the more my vision blurred at the edges, his panicked thoughts mixing with the throbbing in my head until I couldn't tell where his fear ended and my pain began.

I could push harder, dig deeper, but that came with risks beyond just ethics. My father warned me about going too deep into someone's mind. You could get lost, drown in their consciousness.

"Listen," I said, softening my tone. "I don't want to hurt you. Dev is missing, and someone close to him is worried. I just need to know if he's alive, where he might be."

Brody's thoughts flickered briefly to a warehouse, concrete floors, the smell of antiseptic. The image sliced through me, sharp enough to make me blink hard against the sudden spike of pain.

"I can't help you," he said, but his thoughts betrayed him:

...they'll kill me if I talk...they'll kill us both...

I stared at Brody, the truth of his fear pummelling into me. He wasn't just scared—he was terrified.

"I can protect you," I said, loosening my grip slightly. "Official police protection. You'd be safe."

He laughed, a hollow sound that held no humour. "Don't be ridiculous."

"Help me understand." I shuffled back, giving him more space. "Start with Dev. Did you hurt him?"

"No! I swear, we never laid a hand on him. That wasn't our job."

"What was your job, then?"

Brody's thoughts tumbled forward before he could stop them: *Meridian...names...reporting back...*

"You work for Meridian?" I asked.

His eyes widened. "Get out of my head!"

"I'm barely in it," I said. "But you're practically shouting certain thoughts. Meridian Medical Research Centre—what's your connection?"

He slumped against the wall, the fight draining from him. "We never met anyone from Meridian directly. Just some guy who used a fake name. Always met us in different locations, never at the actual facility."

"What did they want from you?"

"Information." Brody rubbed his face. "Bradley and I, we're lone wolves. No pack. They wanted us to identify others like us—packless wolves, especially newcomers to London, ones sleeping rough."

"And do you know what they did with that information?"

I didn't need telepathy to know the answer to that—it was written, plain as day, on his face.

I schooled the distaste from my face. "So, back to Dev. You gave them his name?"

Confusion crossed his face. "No, that was different. Dev isn't packless. They already knew about him. Our job was to pretend to give him information while finding out how much he knew about their operation.

Then we'd report back." Brody looked away. "But we're done with them, now. Promise. Cut ties last week. After Dev. It got... We didn't sign up for..."

"Well, aren't you just a paragon of moral virtue," I said, voice dripping with sarcasm. "Cutting ties after how many wolves disappeared? Your conscience must be so relieved."

"Look, man—"

"So, what did you tell them? What *did* Dev know?" *Enough to get him disappeared.*

Brody's expression shifted. "Dev was pretty sharp, actually. He knew something was off with us from the beginning. We tried to get him talking about what he knew about Meridian, but he kept things vague. Like he was testing us."

"Oh?"

"Yeah, he's good. Had this way of making you want to tell him things without giving anything away himself." Brody's eyes took on a distant quality. "Charming guy, Dev. Gets you talking before you even realise it's happening, you know?"

I clenched my jaw, sudden irritation building. Maybe it was the way everyone seemed bewitched by this journalist I'd never met—Rory still hung up on him nine months after their breakup, this other wolf practically starry-eyed despite being paid to spy on him.

"Well, whatever you fed back to Meridian was obviously enough to—"

The door flew open with enough force to slam against the wall. I spun around, instinctively positioning myself between Brody and the newcomer.

The one and only Dominic Thrift—powerful, ancient vampire and owner of Undertone—stood in the doorway. Resplendent in a deep purple velvet jacket, his platinum hair caught the dim light as he looked us over with cold calculation.

"Well, isn't this cosy?" he drawled, long, sharp nails tapping against the doorframe. "Marley informed me they permitted entry to one De-tective Inspector Maxwell and Rory Thorne this evening." His gaze swept over the dishevelled state of the room, my split lip, Brody's rumpled clothes. "I decided to allow it, as a professional courtesy. But now you're harassing my patrons."

"This isn't—"

"I don't particularly care what it is, darling." Dominic's voice dripped with disdain. "You're upsetting my customers, and that simply won't do." He turned his attention to Brody. "Run along now, sweet thing."

Brody didn't need to be told twice. He scampered past Dominic, disappearing into the corridor without a backward glance.

"You've got five minutes to collect the puppy and leave," Dominic snarled. "Get out of here. And *don't* come back."

Heart hammering against my ribs, I nodded, briskly passing him, heading straight down the corridor. As soon as I reached the dance floor, the migraine that had been threatening all night pulsed behind my eyes, intensified by the strobe lights and pounding bass.

The room had transformed since I'd left. Bodies packed together, writhing in time to music that seemed to physically assault my senses. The air hung heavy—a perfume of midnight desires and abandoned inhibitions.

I scanned the crowd, squinting against the flashing lights. And then I saw them.

Rory, flushed and laughing, swaying to the music with a purple cocktail clutched in one hand. Fury bubbled up inside me. *Another drink. Really?* Wrapped around him like a second skin was Bradley, with that ridiculous man bun that made him look like he'd stepped out of some hipster coffee shop commercial.

Bradley's hands rested on Rory's hips, fingers splayed possessively. As I watched, those hands slid lower, dipping beneath the waistband of Rory's jeans. Rory stumbled, nearly spilling his drink, and Bradley caught him, using the opportunity to pull him closer, whispering something in his ear that made Rory beam up at him.

My head pounded harder, each flash of the strobe lights like hammers against my skull. Fragments of thoughts from the crowd crashed against my already battered mental shields—lust, want, need—a cacophony of desire that mixed with my own churning emotions until I couldn't tell what belonged to me anymore. The careful control I prided myself on was cracking, piece by piece.

Rory's loud laugh drifted over the music, carefree and bright, and something horrible twisted inside me. I'd never heard him laugh quite like *that*.

And the way he was looking at Bradley right now, like he was the centre of his universe...

Something inside me snapped.

Before I realised what was happening, I was cutting through the dance floor, shoving dancers aside with no apologies. Heat surged through my veins—something wild, something primal.

I reached them just as Bradley's hands slipped even lower, cupping Rory's ass beneath his jeans. Rory's eyes were glazed, his movements uncoordinated.

"Get your hands off him! He's drunk out of his mind!" I shouted over the music.

Bradley looked at me, confusion crossing his features. "What?"

My last thread of control shattered. The headache, the crowd's emotions bleeding through my broken shields, the sight of Rory being manhandled—it all crashed together into a mess of fury I couldn't untangle. But watching Bradley's hands roam over him while he was too drunk to properly consent triggered something primitive in me, something that had nothing to do with police protocol and everything to do with an instinct I didn't want to examine.

"I said, he's *mine*!"

The words hung between us, shocking even me. My face flushed hot, but I didn't back down. It was easier this way—easier than explaining duty of care, or that Dominic had kicked the pair of us out.

Bradley's eyes widened as he took in my height, my stance, the fury radiating from me. His gaze flicked between Rory and me, and understanding dawned on his face.

"Oh!" He raised his hands and stepped back, sending Rory stumbling so violently I had to catch him. "Not my fault, dude. He practically threw himself at me!"

I fought the sudden, violent urge to grab that pretentious man bun and yank it right off his head. Luckily for him, after one more grimace in our direction, he twisted, disappearing into the crowd. Hopefully, by the time Brody found him, we'd be gone.

My brain took a moment to register that Rory was now fully leaning against me, his hands fisting the fabric of my shirt. The pain pulsing behind my eyes made everything feel slightly surreal, like I was watching the scene unfold from a distance.

Rory's face lit up with recognition, as if he'd just realised who I was. "Teddy!" he exclaimed, blinking up at me.

I placed my hands around Rory's waist to steady him—and immediately regretted it. My fingers found bare skin through the gaps in that ridiculous mesh shirt he was wearing. The contact sent a shiver up my arms, making me acutely aware of how warm he felt, how solid his smaller frame was.

"We need to go," I said, trying to pry him off me while keeping him upright. "Dominic's kicked us out."

Rory didn't seem to register my words. Instead, he reached up, fingers gently tracing over my cheekbone, sending pleasant tingles dancing across my skin. "Where are your glasses?" he asked, his voice laced with genuine confusion.

"What?" I said, thrown by the question. "I'm wearing contacts. Have been all night."

Rory's brow furrowed as he processed this information, swaying slightly in my grip. His thumb slipped, rasping against my stubble in a gesture that felt almost tender.

"For fuck's sake, Rory," I snapped. "How many more drinks did you manage to consume in the ten minutes I left you?" Clearly his inebriation had reached dire levels, if Rory Thorne was stroking my face.

Instead of answering, Rory's attention shifted to my mouth. "You're hurt!" he exclaimed, his expression morphing into one of genuine concern. His fingers moved to my split lip, touching it with surprising gentleness. "What happened?"

The unexpected care in his voice caught me off guard. In the time I'd known Rory Thorne, I'd seen him angry, defiant, sarcastic, even frightened, but never this openly concerned. Especially not for me. It was... disturbing.

"It's nothing," I said, removing his hand from my face and putting slight distance between us. "Just a disagreement with our friend Brody. While you've been drinking like a fish, I've actually been gathering information."

Rory's face hardened, his concern vanishing. He pulled away from me, swaying slightly.

"I was working as well," he insisted, voice sharp despite the slight slur. "What, you think I was just having fun? Bradley bought me that drink. I had to accept it or blow my cover."

"Your cover," I repeated flatly. "As what? The most enthusiastic dance partner in London?"

...why does he always think I'm so bloody stupid...

"As someone interested in him!" Rory shot back, crossing his arms defensively. "You can't just openly interrogate people. Some of us have to be subtle."

I massaged my forehead, feeling the migraine intensify. "Fine. Did your 'subtle approach' yield any useful information about Dev?"

Rory's defiance crumbled slightly. He looked away, shoulders slumping. "No," he admitted. "We didn't quite get to Dev. He just kept suggesting we head back to his place."

"Fantastic," I muttered, grabbing his arm. "Let's go, before Dominic has our heads on a plate."

I steered him toward the stairs, my hand firmly on his elbow to keep him from stumbling. The throbbing bass seemed to match the pounding in my skull, each beat driving the pain deeper, like a hammer striking the same tender nerve with metronome precision.

A hand clamped down on my arm. A female bartender stared at me with undisguised annoyance.

"Your friend hasn't paid his tab."

I turned to Rory, who blinked owlishly at us both.

"Your tab?" I prompted.

His face lit up. "Oops!" He patted his pockets before producing a battered wallet. "Got it right—"

The wallet slipped from his fingers, contents spilling across the sticky floor. I closed my eyes briefly, summoning patience.

"Sorry," he mumbled, staggering as he bent down.

"Don't." I collected the scattered cards, receipts, and Chinese takeaway fortunes, locating his bank card and tapping it against the machine.

The machine beeped. PAYMENT DECLINED.

Of fucking course.

"One minute, I'll just move some money around," Rory slurred, fumbling for his phone. He jabbed at the black screen repeatedly.

"It's dead," he announced, turning to me with wide, helpless eyes and parted lips.

The look was nothing short of pathetic—part puppy dog, part genuine distress.

"Unbelievable," I muttered, already reaching for my wallet. I'd be damned if I'd admit how quickly I'd capitulated to that look.

I stared at the total, my stomach dropping.

"You're paying me back," I said, pocketing the receipt. "Every. Single. Penny."

Rory grinned up at me with that infuriating smile that made his eyes crinkle. "Do you accept interpretive dance as payment? I've been told my moonlit wolf ballet is quite moving."

I didn't respond, pushing him toward the stairs.

Rory stumbled on the first step. I lunged forward, catching him before he tumbled, wrapping my arm around his waist and half carrying him up.

"I can walk," he protested, leaning heavily against me.

"Evidence suggests otherwise."

We reached the main floor where Marley sat focused on their ledger, not looking up as we left.

When the cool night air hit us, Rory immediately tensed, breaking away to wrap his arms around himself, shoulders hunched as he shivered violently.

It suddenly hit me that he'd lost his shirt. All he had on was that absurd mesh top that left more skin exposed than it covered. The sight of him standing there, hugging himself in the harsh streetlight, looking suddenly cold and sad, stirred something uncomfortable inside me.

Without thinking, I shrugged off my own shirt before holding it out to him.

Rory simply stared at me, then at the shirt, as if he couldn't quite process what was happening. His eyes, still drunk-glazed, widened slightly. It almost looked like he might cry.

"Take it," I snapped, heat rising to my face. Weren't shifters supposed to run hot? "Before I change my mind."

He reached out hesitantly, fingers brushing against mine as he took the shirt. Instead of putting his arms through the sleeves, he wrapped it around himself like a blanket, clutching the fabric at his throat.

My dress shirt swallowed him whole, the crisp blue material draping over his slender frame. Something about the strange sight—Rory Thorne wrapped in my clothing—made my throat go dry. The fabric hung off one shoulder, revealing a pale collarbone and the curve of his neck.

Swallowing hard, I looked away. *What the hell?* My migraines had always had quirky side effects, but this really took the biscuit.

I stormed off toward the car, silently praying Rory could follow without support. Behind me, I heard his uneven footsteps, occasionally punctuated by a muffled curse as he stumbled. I forced myself not to look back.

We reached his sorry excuse for a car. Rory fumbled in his pockets, producing his set of keys with a triumphant, "Aha!"

I snatched them before he could even attempt to unlock the car himself. He laughed, shuffling to the passenger side. We slid in, and he immediately clicked his seatbelt with surprising dexterity.

"Hold that broken door of yours," I instructed as I turned the key in the ignition.

I pulled away from the kerb. With one hand on the wheel, I wiggled a well-deserved cigarette and my lighter out of my pocket.

"Ugh, you smoke? That's disgusting," Rory wrinkled his nose dramatically as I lit up.

"If you don't like it, you're welcome to walk home," I replied, taking a deep drag. The nicotine hit my system, blunting the edge of my headache. I cracked the window, letting the smoke trail out into the night.

"Actually, this is helpful," Rory mumbled, slumping in his seat. "Makes it easier."

"What?"

...every time I find him hot, I can just remember this fucking grim smell...

I stared at Rory, my mind reeling. Had I just heard his thoughts correctly? He actually thought I was... *hot*?

The concept was so absurd I almost laughed out loud. Even before the whole "arresting him on a full moon" thing, Rory Thorne had made it abundantly clear from the moment we met that he despised me. Every interaction was laced with scorn, every look dripping with contempt. And yet...

Well, someone *could* hate another person and still find them attractive. Those weren't mutually exclusive feelings.

Rory started coughing dramatically, waving his hand in front of his face to disperse the smoke.

"Stop being childish," I muttered, taking another drag. "If you're old enough to get blackout drunk at a supernatural nightclub, you're old enough to handle a bit of cigarette smoke."

"It's not—" He coughed again, this time sounding less theatrical and more genuinely distressed. "It's not childish. It's a wolf thing. Wolf senses. Can't—" *Cough.* "Can't stand it."

I glanced over at him. His face had taken on a greenish tinge, and his forehead gleamed with sweat despite the cool night air flowing through the cracked window.

"Stop the car!" he suddenly shouted, doubling over in the passenger seat. "Stop the fucking car!"

I swerved to the kerb, narrowly avoiding a parked motorcycle. "Oh, for fuck's sake," I muttered, throwing my half-smoked cigarette out the window. The second one half wasted tonight.

I'd barely pulled over when Rory fumbled with his door, pushing it open and practically falling onto the pavement. The retching sounds that followed were unmistakable—deep, guttural heaves that ended in splatter against the concrete.

I closed my eyes, leaning my head back against the headrest. The night just kept getting better and better.

...oh god, he's watching me puke my guts out, this is so fucking mortifying...

I grabbed a vaguely clean napkin from the glove compartment and stepped out of the car, walking around to where Rory was still hunched over, retching miserably on the pavement. His slender frame shook with each heave, and something uncomfortably close to guilt twisted in my gut. It probably hadn't been the most polite thing, to light a cigarette in his car without asking.

"Here," I said, holding out the tissue when he finally straightened slightly.

He took it without looking at me, wiping his mouth. "Thanks," he mumbled, voice raspy.

I opened the back door to be greeted by a chaotic junkyard—clothes strewn everywhere, random paperwork, and what appeared to be a half-eaten sandwich growing sentient life. I eventually located a water bottle.

Rory was leaning against the car when I stood up, looking pale and miserable.

"Small sips," I instructed, briefly touching his back as he took the bottle.

He nodded weakly, following my advice with uncharacteristic obedience. While he drank, I glanced at the map on my phone.

"Look, your flat is almost an hour away, and mine is fifteen minutes," I said, the throbbing behind my eyes intensifying. The thought of driving across London with a drunk, possibly still-nauseated werewolf while fighting a migraine was unbearable.

Rory moaned in response, leaning his head against the cool metal of the car.

I hesitated, considering my options. Kit would probably murder me if I brought Rory home in this state. But I could text him something vague—just enough to let him know Rory was safe without inviting his wrath.

"Chips!" Rory suddenly exclaimed, his head snapping up.

"What?"

"I need chips! It's the only thing that will save me. Please?" His eyes were wide, pleading, as if he was a dying man and I had his cure.

Despite my headache begging me not to, I found myself saying, "There's a good shop at the top of my road, which will still be open." Part of me couldn't believe my ears, but it was slightly my fault he'd thrown up.

"Yes. Perfect. Please. Thank you. Sorry for throwing up in your car."

"This is *your* car!" I stared at him incredulously.

Rory blinked several times, looking around as if seeing the vehicle for the first time. "So it is."

The drive to my road had been mercifully short, though Rory's drunken commentary on my "driving like a pensioner" and his demands for curry sauce with his chips—despite having no money to pay for it—still echoed in my ears. I'd caved and bought it for him, then watched in equal parts horror and fascination as he'd tilted his head back and drank the remaining sauce like it was a premium whisky.

...best chips ever...never tasted anything so good...thank god for Maxwell...

His thoughts had been a steady stream of gratitude mixed with genuine euphoria over what was, frankly, mediocre food from the nearest chippy.

Now, as I pulled up outside my building, Rory was slumped against the passenger window, greasy fingers still clutching the empty chip wrapper, looking like he'd just experienced a religious awakening courtesy of Paul's Plaice.

"Right," I said, parking in the guest spot in my building's small car park. The night had been a marathon of madness, and I was more than ready for it to end. "We're here."

To my surprise, Rory walked in a fairly straight line to the front door. Seemed like the chips had indeed saved him from the worst of his drunken state. My shirt still hung off his shoulders, the sleeves dangling past his fingertips.

...I could just pretend to stumble...maybe he'd even princess carry me...

The thought was so clear, so vivid, it might as well have been shouted directly into my ear. I cleared my throat loudly.

Rory's head whipped around, eyes wide with horror.

...fuck, is he listening?...god, it's so infuriating he can just listen to my every thought...

He was right. It was incredibly infuriating—for me. I couldn't simply turn it off. And the worst part? If I admitted I'd heard his thoughts, I'd only confirm his suspicions and increase his paranoia.

So I did what I always did—pretended I hadn't heard a thing and carried on.

The elevator ride to my third-floor flat passed in uncomfortable silence. Rory kept shooting me furtive glances, then quickly looking away when I caught his eye. The close confines of the elevator made his thoughts louder, more intrusive—fragments about the stubble across my jawline, my hands, the way my T-shirt stretched across my chest, my smell.

I kept my expression neutral, pretending I couldn't hear a thing.

Though, as I unlocked my door, a tiny part of me couldn't help but enjoy being wanted. I kept almost everyone at a distance; my last casual relationship was almost a year ago. Between the demands of the job and the complications of being a telepath, dating had always been a minefield. It was nice to feel attractive for a moment, even if it was just drunken appreciation from someone who normally couldn't stand me.

Plus, nothing would ever come of it. Rory's attraction was obviously just harmless fun, fleeting interest that would evaporate with sobriety. Besides, I was straight. Had only ever dated women. The occasional stray thought about a man was just... normal curiosity. Nothing worth examining too closely.

"You can take the sofa," I said, flicking on the lights to reveal my modest living room. Nobody had ever slept on it, but it looked comfy enough. "If you throw up on it, I will kill you."

Rory stood in the doorway, suddenly looking very small as he clutched my shirt.

"Thanks," he mumbled. "For everything. The chips. Not leaving me at Undertone."

Not leaving him? What?!

I nodded stiffly, uncomfortable with his gratitude. It was easier when we were sniping at each other.

"Bathroom's down the hall," I said, to get him out of my sight. Then I raided my ottoman for spare blankets, pulling out the softest ones I owned. Why was I going to such lengths for Rory Thorne of all people? The man who'd been a thorn in my side since the moment we met? The man who had me saved as "Detective Dickface" in his phone?

Blankets all laid out, I grabbed the cushion from the armchair because it was plusher—I wasn't being *nice*, simply professional. I couldn't have him complaining to Seb that I'd left him to suffer.

I headed down the hall to my bedroom. Though as I approached, I found the bathroom door wide open, light spilling into the hallway. And there stood Rory, merrily brushing his teeth.

With my toothbrush.

"Hey!" I barked, stopping dead in my tracks. "That's mine!"

Rory shrugged, foam gathering at the corners of his mouth. "There was only one," he mumbled around the toothbrush.

"I..." Words failed me. The audacity of this man was truly breathtaking.

He turned away from me to spit into the basin, casual as could be, like this was his bathroom and I was the intruder.

Dazed, I retreated to the kitchen. After swallowing down two painkillers, I rested my forehead against the cool metal of the refrigerator, wondering if I was in some sort of fever dream. Rory Thorne was in my house, brushing his teeth with my toothbrush. Had I stumbled into an alternate dimension?

After several cool minutes against the fridge, I regained enough composure to text Kit to let him know Rory wouldn't be home, then poured him a glass of water. He still hadn't returned to the living room, so I went to find him before he helped himself to anything else of mine.

The bathroom was empty.

Strange.

My bedroom door was ajar, the light off. I pushed it open, half expecting to find him rifling through my drawers.

Instead, I found Rory asleep on my queen-sized bed, sprawled atop the duvet with my shirt clutched around him like a security blanket.

God, he looked so different like this. So peaceful. Every sharp edge softened.

But no. No way was Rory stealing my fucking bed, after all he'd put me through tonight.

"Rory," I hissed, stepping closer. "Get up."

Rory responded with a soft snore, burrowing deeper into my shirt.

I stood there, torn between dragging him off the bed and just giving up. My back twinged at the thought of spending the night on my too-small sofa, the day's tension settling between my shoulder blades like concrete.

Maybe I could just stretch out on the other side of the bed for a few minutes, work out the kinks in my spine before resigning myself to my fate...

I clawed out my contacts before I lay down, keeping a careful distance between us. Just five minutes, then I'd relocate to the sofa. Rory stirred but didn't wake, his breathing changing rhythm before settling back into a steady pattern.

I couldn't help but glance at his face again. No smirk, no raised eyebrow, no challenging stare. Just a... softness.

...warm...not alone...safe...

His thoughts drifted to me, unguarded and simple. When was the last time anyone had felt *safe* with me? Usually, I was the harbinger of bad news, the bearer of warrants, the voice telling you your loved one wasn't coming home.

Rory shifted again, mumbling something unintelligible. I found myself attuning to his breathing, the gentle rise and fall of his chest beneath my shirt.

Five minutes stretched to ten. My headache reduced to a dull ache, and my eyelids grew heavy, tension unspooling from my muscles. Rory's rhythmic breathing became a metronome, lulling me toward sleep. *I should move. I really should move.*

But I didn't.

Instead, I let my eyes close, just for a moment. Just until I gathered the energy to get up.

The last thing I registered before drifting off was Rory's breathing syncing with mine, our chests rising and falling in perfect unison, as if we'd somehow found the same wavelength in sleep that constantly eluded us in waking life.

5

Rory

Darkness pressed against my eyelids. The basement again. Cold concrete beneath my bare feet, the musty smell of damp and disappointment filling my nostrils.

"What did I tell you?" Dad's voice boomed from the shadows, each word like hooks tearing through my skin.

I tried to remember what I'd done wrong this time. Was it fidgeting during family dinner? Talking too much when another alpha came over? Or maybe it was the broken vase—an accident, I swear—when I'd been racing through the living room pretending to be a superhero.

"I'm sorry," I whispered, the words automatic, meaningless from repetition.

My father's silhouette loomed larger. "Sorry doesn't fix anything, does it? You never learn."

The familiar knot of dread tightened in my stomach. Would it be the belt today? Or just locked in here until morning? Maybe he'd make me stand in the corner for hours until my legs gave out. Creative punishment was his specialty.

"This is for your own good," he said, stepping closer. "When are you going to learn to control yourself?"

"I'm sorry, Dad," I repeated, because I had no other words.

"Rory, wake up."

I blinked at him, confused. I *was* awake. What did he want from me now? I needed to think, quickly, understand—

"Rory, wake up!"

My eyes flew open, head instantly splitting with pain. A face hovered inches from mine—definitely *not* my father's. Maxwell's dark eyes stared down, annoyed and... uncomfortable?

"Let me go," he said, voice tight.

Horror dawned as I registered my current position—arms and leg tangled around his body, my head resting comfortably on his chest like he was my personal pillow. I was clinging to Detective Dickface like he was my favourite teddy bear.

I recoiled so fast I nearly fell off the bed, scrambling to the opposite edge, dragging the sheet with me. He shot to his feet like I'd electrocuted him, towering over me with that familiar crease between his eyebrows that meant I was in trouble—again.

"What the fuck were you doing in my bed?" I demanded, pulse racing, desperate to cover my mortification with outrage.

Maxwell's expression could have frozen hell. "*My* bed. You stole it, despite me explicitly telling you to sleep on the sofa." He gestured between us. "And then you proceeded to latch onto me like some kind of octopus in the middle of the night. Just now you were squeezing me so tight it woke me up."

Heat crawled up my neck. I'd been having yet another nightmare about my father. It seemed that no matter how many years passed, I'd never truly be able to escape him.

"I always cuddle the duvet when I sleep," I snapped. "Must've gotten confused."

Aside from Priya, I rarely slept in the same bed as anyone—not even hookups. Those guys got a kiss on the cheek and directions to the nearest Tube station before their clothes were fully back on. Yet there I'd been, wrapped around Theodore Maxwell like he was the last lifeboat on the Titanic. *Mortifying.*

"I need coffee," I groaned, pulling away and smacking my dry mouth. My tongue felt like sandpaper glued to the roof of my mouth. Last night was the drunkest I'd been in ages. Memories blurred into fragments of neon lights, bass-heavy music, Bradley all over me, and… "Oh god, I can't believe I threw up on the way home. I haven't done that in years."

Maxwell passed me a glass of water without comment. I gulped it down, spilling some down my chin.

"I need you to leave soon," he said. "I need to shower, get dressed, and go to work. You know, my actual job."

He was still in yesterday's clothes, but so was I, so I could hardly judge.

"The police station can wait," I waved dismissively. "What did we find out last night?"

Maxwell's eyebrow arched. "*We?*"

"Fine, what did *you* find out while I was busy being the diversion?"

He sighed, scratching at his stubble. "Meridian hired Bradley and Brody as informants. They were paid to identify potential shifter targets—specifically lone wolves who wouldn't be missed or who had few pack connections."

My stomach turned. "And Dev?"

"Meridian must have realised he was still investigating the disappearances. The men were tasked with monitoring him, finding out how much he knew, and reporting back." Maxwell crossed his arms. "Though apparently, when the pair of them met Dev, he seemed to suspect them. Dominic interrupted us, so it's unclear what they ultimately told Meridian, but…"

The chips and curry sauce I'd inhaled last night threatened a reappearance. "So Meridian has him?"

"It's looking that way," he admitted.

My shoulders sagged with relief. I'd spent over a week convinced something terrible had happened to Dev while being convinced everyone else would see me as some pathetic ex who couldn't let go. Like I was making mountains out of molehills because I was still hopelessly hung up on him.

"Thank fuck," I breathed, running my hands through my disaster of a bedhead. "Not that he's been kidnapped—obviously that's terrible—but that you believe me. That I'm not just being paranoid."

Maxwell's expression softened almost imperceptibly. "The evidence is pointing that way."

"Okay, so... we're going to storm the place, right?" I perked up, already picturing myself in full action-hero mode, kicking down doors and rescuing Dev. Maybe he'd finally see me as something more than a chaotic mess who couldn't keep his shit together.

"*No.* No, we are not going to 'storm the place,'" Maxwell said, his voice dripping with that special brand of condescension he surely reserved just for me. "I'm going to go to work, and then I'll be in contact this afternoon." He paused, then added pointedly, "Through Seb."

I glowered at him. Clearly, I'd pissed him off somehow. Probably the whole "getting absolutely smashed while on an investigation, throwing up on the way home and needing to crash at his house, leading to stealing his bed and cuddling him to death" thing. Or maybe it was just my general existence.

"So what, I'm just supposed to sit around twiddling my thumbs while Dev could be in danger?" I demanded, ignoring the throbbing in my temples. "Why can't I come with you to the station?"

"Because you're a civilian with no official standing, because you're probably still drunk after the amount you had last night..." He threw me my car key. "And because I said so."

I rolled my eyes so hard they nearly fell out of my skull, and stomped towards the door. My head pounded with each step, a hangover making its presence known.

"Rory, stop."

I whirled around, nearly losing my balance. "What now?!" I snapped, voice sharp.

Maxwell crossed his arms over his chest. His eyes travelled down my torso, lingering on the black mesh top I'd worn to the club last night. The shirt that admittedly now felt sort of ridiculous in the harsh morning light of Maxwell's flat.

"You can't go out like that," he said, one eyebrow raised.

"Are you fucking joking right now?" I gestured wildly. "What, is Detective Dickface suddenly the fashion police too? Worried I'll embarrass you in front of the neighbours?"

He sighed, that familiar sound of exasperation. "It's not that warm out. And it looks like it's going to rain. Just... borrow that shirt again." He nodded toward the blue button-up lying crumpled on the bed—the one I vaguely remembered clinging to last night.

I paused, my next cutting remark dying on my lips. The anger drained from me, leaving only confusion in its wake. Was Maxwell actually... being nice to me? First the chips and now this?

Morning light filtered through the blinds, casting stripes across his face. For a moment, neither of us spoke. Our eyes met, and a jolt shot through me—like static electricity but beneath my skin, radiating outward from my chest. I nearly gasped, fingers twitching involuntarily.

What the fuck?

Maxwell flinched slightly before staring at me, mouth slightly ajar.

I looked away first, rubbing my arms to dispel the lingering sensation. Likely, I was in caffeine withdrawal.

But something unfamiliar still hung in the air between us—not our usual antagonism, no, but something visceral and unspoken that made my wolf pace restlessly inside me.

Maxwell cleared his throat. "Anyway, you'll need to wash that shirt for me," he added, effectively shattering whatever moment we might have been having. "It probably has your vomit on it."

"It does not!" I glared at him, but snatched up the shirt anyway, slipping it over the mesh top, trying to ignore how my fingers still tingled. It still smelt like him—that distinctive smell of raindrops on hot pavement. I inhaled deeper than I meant to, causing him to shoot me an odd look.

God, this guy really hated me.

Without another word, I stormed out of his flat, closing the door with just enough force to make a point.

On Maxwell's street, the borrowed shirt flapped against my thighs in the brisk morning air. He'd been right about the weather—typical

London, grey and threatening rain. The hangover wasn't helping either, each step sending little jolts of pain through my skull.

I found my car next to the building, slipping quickly inside it. Suddenly I was just... alone. That familiar creeping coldness settled over my skin—the one that always ambushed me in moments of solitude. The silence pressed in, amplifying the thoughts I'd been trying to outrun. Dev was in trouble. Real trouble. And here I was, hungover and useless, kicked out of Detective Dickface's flat to await further instructions from the actually important people.

I plugged my phone into the car. When it burst to life, a picture of Freddy eating a cracker filled the screen. My baby's glowing yellow eyes stared back at me, bits of cracker falling from his decomposing mouth.

The notification banner at the top of the screen caught my eye. A missed call, from about an hour ago.

My heart stopped. Then restarted with a painful thud against my rib cage, sending me lightheaded. My fingers froze over the screen, suddenly numb.

Edina Thorne.

Otherwise known as "Mother" if I was feeling polite, which I definitely wasn't.

I blinked, convinced I was hallucinating. Maybe the hangover was worse than I thought. Maybe I was still asleep in Maxwell's bed, drooling on his shoulder. But no—her name remained on the screen, stark and unmistakable.

She hadn't contacted me in years. Not when I was sleeping rough in Glasgow. Not when I moved to London. Not even a text on my birthday.

Why now?

There was no voicemail. Did she... butt dial me? The thought was almost laughable. Edina Thorne, with her calculated movements and rigid self-control, accidentally calling her disappointment of a son? Not bloody likely.

My thumb hovered over her name. I could call her back. Find out what she wanted after all this time.

My stomach twisted into knots. Had someone else died? What if she'd finally decided to apologise? What if—

No. I couldn't think about her and what she may or may not have to say to me. I had an ex-boyfriend to find. Dead or alive, Dev was out there somewhere, and I was sitting in my car staring at my mother's name like a lost puppy.

I tapped Priya's name.

> *be ready in 10, I'm picking you up*

Priya replied almost immediately.

> *it's a saturday and I don't operate before noon*

I tapped my fingers against the steering wheel, considering my options. Flynn would be up for adventure, but he'd tell Seb straight away, the little snake.

A lump formed in my throat as Issac's face flashed through my mind. My partner in crime would have been all over this—already formulating some fabulous plan involving disguises and possibly explosives. But Issac was gone. Dead. No matter how many times I insisted otherwise, the reality was that I'd never again get one of his three a.m. texts with some half-baked scheme.

I swallowed hard and started the car. Kit it was, then.

My brother had just gotten back from his Saturday run when I walked in the door, still in his ridiculous compression leggings and sweat-wicking top. Healthy bastard.

After the turbulent events of last night and this morning, it was a relief to be back with him. Our bond hummed between us, subtle but present. When I'd left my pack, all the bonds with my family members and everyone else had snapped like dry twigs, painful and final. But the thread between Kit and me had somehow survived, stretched thin but never breaking. Not a proper pack bond, but something else—fragile yet surprisingly resilient.

From the way Kit's eyes widened, I must have looked a state. His gaze travelled from my dishevelled hair to Maxwell's oversized shirt hanging off my frame.

"Maxwell texted me last night," Kit said, crossing his arms.

I groaned, slumping against the wall. "What the fuck did he say? That I was a fucking moron, and he hates me?"

"No, that your phone was dead, and he'd brought you back to his flat because you were unwell." Kit raised an eyebrow. "I can see he sugarcoated it. I take it spending an evening together hasn't magically fixed your feelings towards him?"

I thought about waking up wrapped around him, how warm he'd been, the scent of his skin. My stomach did a weird little flip thing that had nothing to do with the hangover.

"He still despises me, yeah," I muttered, looking away.

"Hold on... is that *his* shirt?"

"I lost my one, so I borrowed his. He's making me wash it for him. Because he hates me."

"Rory, you're the one who talks to him like he's a piece of shit."

"But he—"

"Stop. We're not rehashing the night he arrested you for the millionth time. I'll go grey." Kit ran a hand through his hair in frustration.

"You're already turning grey." I pointed to a grey hair nestled in his beard.

"Well, whose fault is that?" Kit shot back, but the corner of his mouth twitched upward. "Anyway, how did it go?"

I filled him in on everything, including the fact that Maxwell said I now had to wait for him to ring Seb, adding in an eye roll for good measure.

"But I want to go to Meridian this morning. Just to check it out."

Kit's expression darkened. "Rory, no. What do you mean 'check it out?' It's not like we're going to be able to see Dev banging on the attic window shouting for help."

"I just want to stand on the road outside it," I said, trying to sound reasonable. "To see what CCTV cameras there are, and stuff."

"We can just ask Felix for that!"

I shook my head, wincing as my hangover protested the movement. "It's Saturday. Seb says we're not allowed to make him do stuff for us on Saturdays."

That was true, but not the whole truth. The reality was more complicated, more gut-level than I could articulate. I needed to see the building with my own eyes, feel its presence. Maybe then I'd know if Dev was in there. Wolves have instincts about these things, after all. Probably.

Kit let out a groan that seemed to come from the depths of his soul. "This is a terrible idea."

"Fine. I'll go alone, then." I straightened up from the wall, summoning what little dignity I could muster in my borrowed shirt and day-old jeans.

"You're still half drunk."

"Am not."

"Your eyes are bloodshot, and you smell like a distillery exploded inside a nightclub."

I gave him my best pleading look. "Kit, please. I need to do this. For Dev. I promise I'll shower first."

He stared at me for a long moment, then his shoulders slumped in defeat. "Fine. We'll take my motorcycle. It'll be quicker."

The thought of the roaring engine made my temples throb preemptively. "God, no. The noise will murder my headache. How about you drive my car?"

"Go shower and change your clothes. You look like you're cosplaying as Theodore Maxwell's one-night stand. It's disturbing."

Twenty minutes later, I found myself a passenger in my own car again. Kit always preferred taking the wheel rather than experiencing what he called my "fairground ride" driving style. The radio hummed with some indie rock station, and I tapped my foot to the beat, partly because I liked the song, partly to channel the anxiety buzzing through me.

Kit wouldn't tell me off for fidgeting. He never did.

My thoughts drifted back to the nightmare I'd had this morning, before I'd woken up in Maxwell's bed. It had been the same one I'd had for years—trapped in our manor house basement in Scotland, Dad looming over me, belt in hand. The air damp and cold, my heart thundering so hard I thought it might burst through my ribs.

Kit hated talking about our childhood. Sometimes I wondered if he was actually even more traumatised than I was, and it was all just repressed under those fluffy cardigans and that perfect posture.

Growing up, Kit had been the golden child. The perfect one. Setting standards that I couldn't hope to meet in my wildest dreams with my chaotic brain and inability to sit still for more than thirty seconds.

I had *hated* him for it. For the entirety of our teenage years, our only interactions consisted of me hurling abuse at him while Kit never replied, never retaliated, never even looked at me—pretending I was invisible. Kit had told me years later that our father had ordered him to act that way, to "not encourage my behaviour."

Now, Kit refused to talk about that time, quickly changing the subject or flat out refusing, saying "let's not dig all that up now" with a tight expression that meant the conversation was over.

I took a deep breath. "I had a nightmare this morning. I was with Dad in the basement. He was about to punish me again."

Kit grunted, sucking in his lips.

"Did he ever punish you down there?" The question had been burning inside me for years.

"Sometimes," Kit said, his voice flat.

He reached forward and turned the radio up, drowning out any possibility of further conversation.

Annoyance prickling through me, I reached over and turned the radio down. *Something* about the morning—maybe the hangover, maybe the worry about Dev, maybe too much time with Maxwell—had cracked something open in me.

"Kit, do you remember the moment you found out Dad was dead? How did you feel?"

His head whipped around, his eyes wide with shock. The car swerved slightly before he corrected it.

"Can you just leave all that stuff?" he snapped, knuckles whitening on the steering wheel. "It's early and I'm trying to drive."

Resisting the urge to tell him I had a missed call from Mum, I turned away, staring out the window at the grey London morning. Buildings blurred past as we drove, my reflection ghostly in the glass.

I remembered so clearly the day Kit left home at twenty-three to join the military as part of a small, highly classified shifter unit. Mum had screamed, Dad had roared. Our father had explicitly forbidden it, but Kit went anyway. Broke his pack bonds by doing so.

He never said goodbye to me. Just... vanished.

For a while, I'd been happy. With perfect Kit out of the way, having disappointed and betrayed them so thoroughly, surely my parents would finally see me? Love me? Accept me as I was?

I was wrong.

Everything got worse. Suddenly I was the future alpha of the pack, the only son left. They needed me to finally buckle down and be the wolf they knew I could be. No more "ADHD rubbish," no more acting out, no more being myself.

It went so badly that eventually I left too, after my father threatened that if I did so, I'd never be welcome back again. Barely twenty and sleeping rough in Glasgow, trying to find a new pack that would take me in. No one wanted the Thorne pack rebel, though. I'd snapped the tethers that bound me to my family, and found nothing to replace them with.

Until Kit found me, and whisked me off to London. Until Killigrew Street. Until Seb. Until Issac, Priya, and now Felix and Flynn.

I glanced at my brother, his jaw still clenched tight, and turned the radio back up. It wasn't his fault he couldn't talk about it with me, as much as I wished he would.

There were many topics filed under "Things Kit Thorne Refuses to Discuss," including his time in the military. My uncle Alex's ex-wife, Moira, had been the one who connected him to a friend of a friend, who got him into a covert programme that exploited shifter abilities under the guise of "enhanced tactical operations." The few times he started telling me a bit about it, he'd often stop mid-sentence, his eyes fixing on something invisible, fingers drumming a rhythm against his glass before he'd change the subject entirely.

I did know that Kit believed the whole programme was so black ops there wasn't even a hint of a paper trail. And whatever happened there had left him with scars that ran deeper than the physical ones.

"I could use some fresh air," said Kit when I started to recognise some of the streets as Greenwich. "Let's park up and walk the rest of the way. When we get to Meridian, we're going to casually walk past it, not gawp up, okay?"

"Sure thing, boss." I gave him a grin and a salute. A rush of gratitude flowed through me that Kit was doing this for me. "It'll obviously be closed anyway, because Saturday."

"Maybe, maybe not." Kit shrugged. "But we are *not* going inside."

Kit found a parking spot on a quiet residential street lined with ter-raced houses.

"We're about ten minutes away," he said, checking his phone. "Re-member, casual stroll, not reconnaissance mission."

"Yeah, yeah."

As we walked, I found myself fidgeting with the zip of my jacket, my mind flashing back to *that* night. Meridian Medical Research Centre sat at the edge of Greenwich Park, named after the famous Meridian Line that ran through the park itself—that invisible thread marking the boundary between east and west. Seemed fitting for a place that might be straddling the line between legitimate research and something much darker.

"The night Dev and I broke in," I said quietly as we turned onto another tree-lined street. "We approached from the back, through that grassy bank behind the building. Dev had wedged open one of the fire doors earlier that day when he'd gone in pretending to be a delivery guy."

Kit shot me a look. "And today we're approaching from the front like normal people," he said pointedly.

"Like normal, law-abiding citizens who definitely aren't planning anything," I agreed with a grin.

We rounded the corner, and there it was—part of the four-storey building visible at the end of the street. Meridian's modern glass façade stood in stark contrast to the surrounding architecture, all sharp angles and tinted windows. My heart started racing, memories flooding back. The harsh blare of the alarms. That awful fight with the security guards. The sickening snap of handcuffs around my wrists.

"Here we are," I hissed to Kit, slowing down as we approached.

Kit gripped my arm, his voice low but firm. "Remember what we—"

Kit's words died in his throat. I followed his gaze. The car park of Meridian Medical Research Centre stretched before us, a flurry of activity where there should have been weekend emptiness. Three large moving vans stood with their rear doors open, and about eight people in dark uniforms scurried between the building and the vehicles, carrying cardboard boxes and office furniture.

"Holy shit!" The words burst from my mouth before I could stop them.

Kit's elbow jabbed sharply into my ribs. "Be quiet, and do *not* stare as we walk past," he hissed through clenched teeth.

We continued our path, trying to look casual while my mind raced. They were clearing out. This couldn't be a coincidence.

As we passed the entrance to the car park, one of the men—a burly bloke with a shaved head—lost his grip on a box. It hit the ground with a crash, spilling what looked like computer cables and wires across the pavement.

"Fuck's sake!" he growled, bending down.

Before Kit could stop me, I darted over, my hands already reaching for the scattered cables.

I heard Kit groan behind me, but ignored him. This was too perfect an opportunity.

"Need a hand, mate?" I asked cheerfully, gathering up a tangle of wires.

The man gave me an awkward look, somewhere between suspicious and grateful. "Thanks," he muttered.

I bundled the cables together, deliberately taking my time. "What's going on here, then? I walk by this centre every day. Has it shut down?"

He stared at me, his expression closing off. "No clue. I'm just paid to move things from A to B." He reached out for a wire still clutched in my hand, clearly wanting me gone.

I handed it back with a friendly smile. "Right, of course. Cheers."

Returning to Kit, I found him glowering at me, arms crossed and jaw tight with barely contained fury.

"What? He needed help!" I protested weakly.

My heart continued to thunder against my ribs as we continued past Meridian.

"They're clearing out. Fuck, Kit, they're *clearing out*!"

"I can see that," Kit muttered, steering us toward a small coffee shop across the street. "Let's sit here for a minute."

Once we'd ordered—both black coffees, though a single spoonful of sugar was pretty tempting—I leaned across the table, unable to contain myself.

"What if Maxwell triggered this? He might have been looking into Meridian yesterday. What if he pulled something up on the police system that set off some kind of alert?"

Kit frowned, sipping his coffee. "I suppose that's possible."

"Or..." I chewed my lip, mind racing. "What if Bradley and Brody haven't actually cut ties with them? Maybe they warned Meridian about Maxwell's questions last night."

"But moving vans on a Saturday morning? That's quick work."

I drummed my fingers on the table. "Not if they were already planning to move. Maybe they've been preparing for this, just waiting for a sign they'd been compromised."

"Or maybe they're just relocating offices and it has nothing to do with us," Kit said, ever the voice of reason.

"On the same weekend Maxwell starts investigating them? After eighteen months of nothing?" I shook my head. "That's one hell of a coincidence."

Kit's eyes narrowed in thought. "If they're moving because of Maxwell's inquiries, it means they have someone inside the police system, or some way of monitoring police searches."

I pulled out my phone, tapping on the contact listed as Detective Dickface.

He answered on the third ring.

"Rory?"

"Don't sound so pleased."

"I told you I'd be in contact this afternoon."

"Kit and I went to Meridian," I blurted out. "They're clearing the place out. Right now."

"Jesus Christ," Maxwell sputtered through the phone. I could practically see his face twisting the way it did when he was trying not to explode. "You did *what?* Please tell me you didn't break in again."

"We just walked past," I said, locking eyes with Kit. "Like normal citizens out for a stroll."

"A stroll that just happened to take you past Meridian."

"Exactly! And they're packing everything up. Moving vans, the whole shebang."

There was a pause, and I could hear the background noise of Maxwell's office—phones ringing, muffled conversations, the clatter of keyboards. Despite his obvious annoyance, his voice lacked the razor edge it usually had when addressing me. Kit's presence clearly made a difference.

"And what has Seb said?" he asked.

"I haven't told him yet."

"You... rang me before him?" The surprise in his voice was unmistakable, almost... touched?

I felt my cheeks warm slightly. "I'm increasingly regretting that fact. Could any of your police searches have tipped them off?"

"It's possible," Maxwell admitted after a moment. "But look, I'm about to go into a meeting. Ring Seb, and I'll check my phone afterwards."

Hanging up, I scrolled through my contacts. "Let's hope he's not *busy.*"

The phone rang for an age before Seb's crisp voice answered, sounding distinctly unimpressed. "Rory, it's Saturday."

I rolled my eyes so hard they practically did a full rotation. Seb never used to care about weekends before he got a tasty boyfriend to snack on. He used to work around the clock, lived and breathed Killigrew Street. Now I could hear Flynn mumbling something in the background, probably something about brunch or farmers' markets or whatever normal couples did on weekends.

After checking that Maxwell had filled him in about last night, I quickly explained about Meridian's sudden evacuation and our theory about police searches possibly triggering their exit, if not Bradley and Brody.

"We'll meet at Killigrew Street at four," Seb said after a moment of consideration. "I'll contact everyone."

I was tempted to argue for an earlier time—every minute wasted might mean Dev's demise, if he was still alive—but I couldn't really push my luck. I was surprised Seb hadn't shouted at me.

After I'd hung up, Kit's eyes suddenly fell to his cup. "Oh, by the way, I messaged Seb this morning while you were in the shower. Got his approval for our little excursion to Meridian."

I nearly choked on my drink. "You what?"

"Protocol." Kit shrugged as if he hadn't betrayed me. "You know how Seb feels about unauthorized missions."

"We were literally just walking past a building!" I protested, feeling a hot flush of betrayal creep up my neck. Kit had gone behind my back, treating me like some rookie who couldn't be trusted. "That's not a mission, that's... that's exercise!"

Kit gave me that infuriating older-brother look—the one that made me feel about five years old. "And yet here we are, watching them pack up evidence that could be crucial to the case."

My phone buzzed before I could argue further. A text from Priya.

Priya

Rory, you're lucky I love you. Emma got us rooftop cinema tickets for Peckham Levels.

A stupid stab of jealousy twisted in my gut. I'd already mentally pencilled in going to see her this afternoon.

Though, what kind of friend gets jealous when their mate finds happiness? A shit one, that's what.

She's got four tickets, so I was about to text you and Flynn.

And now I felt super guilty to go along with my patheticness.

> **Sorry. I love you. Maybe you'll still be able to make it?**

**It's alright. To be honest, it was some black and white art-house thing about the sociopolitical implications of climate change, so you know, maybe
a lucky escape. See you later.**

I looked up at Kit. "So, what are we doing until four p.m.?"

"I'm putting you under house arrest."

The sad thing was, I couldn't even blame him.

6

Theodore

S. Salazar

4 p.m., basement.

I stared at the text message. Just like that, I'd been summoned. No please, no thank you. Classic Sebastián—treating everyone like his personal chess pieces rather than actual human beings with lives of our own.

My relationship with Killigrew Street had begun three years ago, on a day I still couldn't quite forget. When a woman who called herself White had materialised before me on a rain-slicked street, her gloved fingers brushing my wrist, her thoughts crashing into my mind like thunder: *Come with me.*

She'd known my father. She knew what I was. He'd confided in her before death claimed him, left her with the secret I'd spent my life guarding. When she unveiled her proposition—that I become the police link for an underground network fighting supernatural crime—I refused without hesitation.

My father's warnings had echoed like funeral bells: *Stay hidden. Stay safe.* After he died, he'd left my mother clutching photographs and nightmares. How could I willingly take unnecessary risks when his absence had carved such hollow spaces in our lives? When my mother's eyes still searched crowds for a ghost who would never return?

White left me with a blank business card, with only a phone number scrawled in elegant cursive. For weeks it haunted my desk drawer, accusing me with its presence. In quiet moments between cases, I'd trace the numbers with my fingertips, feeling possibility pulse beneath the paper.

My telepathy had always been my private crucible—a gift that isolated me, a power that demanded constant vigilance. Of course, I used it sparingly during investigations. It had to be good for something, after all. But what if I could put my skills to even more use? If I had a choice, surely the moral thing to do would be to help keep London safe from supernatural threats?

And the extra cash White had promised sweetened the deal.

It certainly came in useful. The substantial sums funded cruises for my lonely, single mother who'd always wanted to see the world. Those trips gave her something to look forward to. It was one of the few benefits that balanced out the headaches of dealing with Killigrew Street—especially Sebastián's imperious attitude and Rory's constant provocations. The only one who never grated on my nerves was their quiet tech nerd, Felix. The British-Korean genius had somehow hacked his way into a job there, and I often wondered how he coped with them all day.

At three o'clock, I told my boss I was leaving early to work from home. DCI Harris barely listened, just nodded while on the phone. Being a stellar member of the force came with benefits—like minimal questions about my comings and goings.

Still, I felt guilty about neglecting my actual cases. Two days ago, an ATM had been stolen—ripped from a wall with a digger—and finding "The Midnight Miner" was supposedly my priority, not chasing missing shifters and investigating shadowy medical facilities.

But priorities had a way of shifting when the supernatural was involved. That was the bargain I'd made when I'd finally called White's number. Some days I still wondered if I'd made the right choice.

I rubbed my temple, feeling other people's thoughts pushing against my own. The police station was always an ordeal—too many minds in too small a space.

I couldn't face walking through the tunnels today. The thought of those cramped passageways made me shudder, so I took the Tube instead. Even that was pushing it—the Northern Line was its own special hell for a telepath.

The late afternoon air swept away the cobwebs of my thoughts as I walked toward Killigrew Street. Fat Cat's was closing, Flynn and Priya's friend Emma rhythmically wiping counters whilst nodding along to her headphones, lost in her own private symphony. I'd never quite grasped their near-religious devotion to that café, even if I had made my pilgrimage there yesterday to procure Rory's peace-offering coffee.

Another hundred metres and there it stood—Killigrew Street Hotel, a forgotten monument to Victorian grandeur. Ivy embraced the façade like a possessive lover, climbing stone that had witnessed a century and a half of London's secrets. Windows remained either shattered or shrouded behind wooden boards—eyes closed to the world outside. The once-proud gold lettering above the entrance had surrendered to time. I had to smile at the crooked "FOR SALE" sign—a small fiction, maintained for decades.

I paused, scanning the street for watchful eyes before slipping through the gap in the fence concealed by nature's patient reclamation. My key turned in the side door's lock with quiet precision—at least Salazar honoured what mattered beneath the theatre of abandonment.

The corridors were empty, and I quickly made my way into the lobby. When I reached the desk, I flinched. Dolly, that bloody porcelain monstrosity they all pretended manned the desk, now sported aviator sunglasses with one arm raised in a jaunty wave.

"Christ," I muttered. Probably Rory's doing.

At the basement door, I punched in the code and headed down. Even before reaching the bottom, I sensed them—multiple minds buzzing with activity, and I took a moment to reinforce my mental guards.

A loud, throaty cough cut through the room. Sebastián stood by the sofas, his tailored maroon trousers and cream shirt making him look like he'd stepped from a vintage fashion magazine rather than being the leader of a supernatural crime unit.

The room fell silent, all eyes on me. Had they all been talking about me? Rory actually recoiled, sinking deeper into the sofa as if trying to disappear.

"Afternoon. I believe my presence was requested? Or should I leave?"

"Detective Maxwell." Sebastián's Spanish accent rolled my name with surprising warmth. "Thank you for joining us. Felix is just preparing something, then we'll begin."

I nodded, grateful for the blank void where Sebastián's thoughts should have been. Vampires were the only beings whose minds I couldn't read—a small mercy.

Usually I'd stand, but after last night's adventures with Rory, exhaustion weighed on my bones. I sank into the armchair furthest from him, avoiding eye contact.

Even at that distance, I caught Rory's whisper to Flynn: "Nice scarf."

Flynn was indeed sporting an eye-catching blue silk scarf that seemed excessive indoors.

"No wonder Seb was reluctant to cancel Saturday," Rory added.

I couldn't resist glancing at them, turning in time to see Flynn glaring at Rory. "This is just my outfit today."

A flash of strong emotion leaked from Flynn's mind—a vivid memory fragment of Sebastián's fangs grazing his neck, strong hands gripping bare shoulders. I slammed my barriers up. Some things I *really* didn't need to see.

Thankfully, Felix scurried out of his lair, arms full of laptop and wires. Sebastián moved so Felix could connect to the projector—a feat the five hundred-year-old vampire *still* couldn't manage. The moment Felix finished setting up, the room settled into expectant silence.

"I want to thank everyone for coming in today," Sebastián began, as he straightened his already immaculate cuffs. "Especially Detective Maxwell, who has been working closely with Rory on this matter."

I nodded curtly, trying not to notice Rory fidgeting across the room. I still couldn't fathom how he'd convinced his level-headed brother to participate in that unnecessary excursion to Meridian this morning.

"As of now, we are treating the disappearance of Devraj Bassi as an official missing persons case," Sebastián continued, his tone shifting to something more formal. "The evacuation of Meridian Medical Research Centre, coupled with their apparent connection to missing shifters, gives us sufficient cause for concern. We will be allocating resources accordingly."

Rory's face brightened instantly. "Thank you," he breathed, relief evident in his voice. "I know I've been pushing this, but—"

"We all believe you," Kit interrupted, patting his brother's shoulder. "We always believed you."

"Um, before we continue..." Felix's hesitant voice cut through the moment. He hunched over his laptop, eyes fixed on the screen as if making eye contact might kill him. "I have a slight update for everyone."

Sebastián's posture stiffened almost imperceptibly—clearly this was news to him as well. "Proceed, Felix."

"Well, I just managed to get into Dev's phone," Felix said, fingers flying across his keyboard.

Rory bolted upright. "What do you mean? You told me his phone was off the grid, and that you couldn't do anything?"

Felix pushed his dark fringe from his eyes, swallowing hard. "Well, it pinged back to life about an hour ago..."

Rory's face transformed, twisting into something crudely desperate. "What the actual fuck, Felix?" he snapped, launching forward to the edge of his seat. "You're telling me his phone's been active for an hour and you didn't think to mention it? To anyone?"

Felix shrank back, his face flushing red as he hunched further over his laptop like a turtle retreating into its shell. His fingers froze mid-type, eyes wide with alarm.

"Rory!" Kit's voice cut through the room like a whip crack. "That's enough."

"But he—"

"I said *enough*." Kit's tone left no room for argument—the military edge to it made even me straighten up instinctively. "Do not take your anger out on Felix."

Rory's jaw clenched so tight I could almost hear his teeth grinding. His eyes, bright with anger, darted between his brother and Felix. The flush on his cheeks deepened, and his fingers curled into fists on his thighs, knuckles white.

...why does Kit always have to do this...

Something uneasy fluttered through me as I watched him. For all his irritating qualities, his relentless teasing and boundary-pushing, there was something genuinely painful about seeing him this way—wound tight, being scolded like a child in front of everyone. The urge to say something, to somehow ease that tension in his shoulders, was overwhelming.

Rory was clearly hanging by a thread over this whole situation with Dev. He *should* have been told first, privately, rather than have it sprung on him in front of the entire team.

I cleared my throat and narrowed my eyes at Kit. "Should we let Felix tell us what he's found, then?"

Felix swallowed hard, his fingers nervously tapping the edge of his keyboard. "So, I've had a passive IMSI-catcher simulation running on our network since Rory asked me to monitor Dev's device. I wrote a custom Python script to ping his IMEI number every three minutes through cellular triangulation protocols."

...oh god they're all staring don't panic don't panic should have told Rory first stupid stupid he's going to hate me forever now what have I done...

He turned his laptop slightly, showing a screen full of code and blinking status indicators that meant nothing to most people in the room.

"At fourteen thirty-seven, his phone suddenly authenticated with a cell tower in a remote area. My system immediately initiated a metadata extraction protocol—" Felix paused, noticing the blank stares.

...simple words, Felix, simple words...

"Um, basically I set up a back-door API that hooks into the telecom infrastructure to pull all available device telemetry when it connects."

Flustered, he clicked through to another screen.

"I only managed to scrape partial location data, SMS header information, and app notification logs before the device went dark again. The phone was only active for approximately ten minutes and twenty-three seconds before it either powered down or entered a Faraday environment."

"So where is he?" Rory practically screamed, left leg bouncing so wildly it was tempting to reach over and place my hand there to still it. Thankfully, I had more self-control than that, because I valued my fingers attached to my body.

"The geolocation data is... unusual. The cell tower coverage in that region is extremely sparse, which means the triangulation accuracy is terrible—we're looking at a radius of over ten kilometres rather than the usual few hundred meters. The signal strength was also fluctuating wildly, suggesting either significant terrain interfere—"

"Felix, I think Rory is about to explode," Flynn said softly.

"Right. Yes. Got it." An even deeper pink flush coloured his cheeks as Felix tapped around on his laptop.

The projector flickered, displaying a topographical map with a large red circle encompassing what looked like wilderness—mountains, forests, and not much else.

"Where the hell is that?" Priya leaned forward, squinting at the projection.

Felix zoomed out, revealing more of the surrounding area. The map expanded to show more of the region, including water, and a small cluster of buildings that barely constituted a town.

"So, yeah, it's this random place up in Scotland of all places," Felix said, fiddling with the hem of his hoodie.

"Holy fucking shit."

Rory's voice came out strangled, barely above a whisper. The bouncing leg stopped dead.

A tidal wave of thoughts crashed into me, Rory's mind exploding with such intensity it made my breath catch.

...what the fuck...what the fuck...why is Dev there...anywhere but there...this can't be right...this must be a joke...

I looked back at the map, focusing on the name now visible near the red circle: Glenmoriston.

...home...

"That's... home," Rory said, the words falling like a stone into the sudden silence of the room. "That's our pack. Glenmoriston."

The name Glenmoriston hung in the air like a live grenade.

Rory suddenly jumped up. Without a word, he bolted for the stairs, pounding footsteps echoing through the basement before he disappeared from view.

Kit remained frozen, staring at the projection as if it had personally betrayed him. His mind was completely blank—a static emptiness that spoke volumes about his shock.

I found myself on my feet before I'd even made the conscious decision to stand. I took one step towards the stairs, a strange tightness in my chest.

Everyone's eyes swivelled to me, Priya's gaze particularly sharp and assessing. Her lips curved upwards, questioningly.

What the hell was I doing? This wasn't my circus, not my monkeys.

I had no business chasing after a wolf I barely tolerated on good days. I slowly sat back down, straightening my tie to cover my momentary lapse in judgement. Yet the memory of Rory's unexpected vulnerability about his family during our car journey flashed through my mind. I didn't need to imagine very hard about how he was feeling right now. The phantom sensation of wanting to follow him lingered uncomfortably, like an itch I couldn't scratch.

Kit clearly wasn't moving anytime soon, so Flynn and Priya exchanged glances before both of them trailed after Rory, murmuring in low voices.

"I'm so sorry, I had no idea— I would have told him privately— I just didn't realise—" Felix was practically hyperventilating, his hands fluttering like panicked birds.

Completely having lost control of his meticulously planned meeting, Seb looked dazed, the five-hundred-year-old vampire utterly thrown.

"You didn't have any idea at all?" I asked Felix, trying to keep my tone neutral. The kid looked miserable, hunched in his oversized hoodie, dark circles prominent under his eyes. "About their connection to Glenmoriston?"

Felix's eyes widened at being directly addressed by me. "N-no, Detective Maxwell. I swear. I mean, I know they're Scottish, but I d-didn't. Obviously, I take full respon—"

"Of course Felix didn't know," Kit suddenly snapped, breaking out of his trance-like state to jump to his feet. His voice was razor-sharp as he glared at me. "We don't talk about Scotland. Ever. So how exactly would Felix have known?"

He moved protectively closer to Felix, who looked pathetically grateful for the intervention.

I raised my hands in surrender. "Okay, okay. I was just surprised, that's all."

The irony wasn't lost on me, that Rory had actually shared bits of his past with me during our drive—his struggles with ADHD, his turbulent childhood. Though to be fair, I knew even more from accidentally picking up his thoughts than what he'd willingly revealed.

Kit continued to hover near Felix, carefully maintaining a few inches of space between them. Felix's fingers fidgeted with his keyboard, eyes darting repeatedly toward his lair. The guy looked like he was calculating his chances of escape.

"I should probably... I mean, I could *try* to narrow down the location more precisely if I—"

"That would be helpful," Sebastián said, his voice gentler than usual. "But perhaps take a moment first."

Kit still hadn't moved, his broad frame positioned like a shield between Felix and me, his expression still holding deep concern.

Interesting. This was one of those times where it became extremely tempting to peek inside someone's mind.

Instead, I took my glasses off and pretended to clean them. I'd long ago learned that knowledge wasn't worth the cost. People's inner lives were messy, complicated, and frankly none of my business unless they affected my cases.

Still, I didn't need telepathy to recognise the subtle tension in Kit's jaw, the softness in his eyes when he glanced at Felix, or the way Felix seemed to lean almost imperceptibly toward Kit's presence like a plant seeking sunlight.

The basement door creaked open, drawing all eyes upward. Rory descended the stairs with Priya and Flynn flanking him like prison guards escorting a high-profile detainee. His face was unnervingly blank, eyes slightly puffy.

The room fell into uncomfortable silence as Rory wordlessly reclaimed his spot on the sofa. He sat ramrod straight, hands folded in his lap with uncharacteristic stillness. No fidgeting, no tapping, no bouncing, just an eerie calm that seemed more alarming than his earlier outburst.

"I need to tell you something," Rory finally said, addressing Kit directly.

Kit blinked in surprise.

"Our mother called me this morning when my phone was dead," Rory continued, now addressing the entire room. "I haven't spoken to her since she rang to tell me about Dad's death."

The silence that followed was deafening. Even Felix stopped his nervous typing.

"You don't think that was a coincidence, do you?" I asked.

Kit cleared his throat, expression turned pained. He looked everywhere but at his brother. "I actually know what she wanted. Alexander emailed me yesterday."

...Uncle Alex?...why would he contact Kit?...

Sebastián frowned, his dark eyes narrowing. "Who?"

"Alexander Thorne," Kit explained, his voice carefully controlled. "Our mother's brother. He invited the pair of us to a pack gathering next Friday."

Rory's eyes widened. "Why didn't you tell me? And what did you reply to the email?"

"I deleted it, of course."

Without hesitation, Rory held out his palm. "Well, give me your phone so I can undelete it."

"That's not possible," Kit stated.

"That's... definitely possible," Felix mumbled. "Give it to me."

Kit stared at his brother. The silence stretched between them, taut and uncomfortable. Finally, Kit exhaled heavily through his nose, his shoulders slumping in defeat.

"Fine," he spat, pulling his phone from his pocket. He unlocked it with a series of rapid taps before handing it to Felix, expression pained, like someone submitting to an invasive medical procedure.

Felix's fingers flew across the screen. "Got it," he announced, immediately connecting Kit's phone to his laptop.

The projector screen flickered before displaying an email. The sender line read "Alexander Thorne," with the subject line "Pack Gathering - Attendance Request - Please Read."

The room fell silent as we all read the message that appeared on screen.

Dear Nephew,

I trust this message finds you well, though I suspect my name in your inbox comes as something of a surprise after all this time.

Know that there are still members amongst the pack who miss both you and Rory greatly.

I write to formally invite you both to attend our Spring Equinox Gathering next Friday. Your mother specifically requested your presence, as there are important pack matters that require the attendance of all Thornes by blood. Many other packs will be in attendance—for the Equinox falls on a full moon. It will be the first such gathering in nearly two decades.

I understand there have been "difficulties" in the past, but family obligations transcend personal grievances. Alpha Edina has declared this a mandatory summons for all pack members, regardless of current standing.

You'd be welcome to stay within the estate in the days leading up to the event. Should you decide to attend or not, my door remains open to you both, as it always has been.

Please confirm your attendance by Wednesday.

Your faithful uncle,

Alexander Thorne

"Mandatory summons," seethed Kit. "Like she can wave her wand and have us magically appear. I wish Alex had told her where to stick her invitation."

"I need to go to Scotland," Rory said, his voice unnervingly steady as he stared directly at Kit, chin tilted upward in defiance.

"But... how do we know for sure all this is connected to Dev?" asked Priya.

Rory's arm flew towards the screen. "Really? Dev goes missing, and his phone just happens to ping back to life for a few minutes right by pack land? It's too much of a coincidence, Pri. Come on." He looked to Kit. "We have to go."

Kit's face drained of colour. "I... can't," he whispered, deep remorse etched into every line of his face. His hands were trembling slightly at his sides, a sight so disconcerting I found myself shifting uncomfortably in my chair. "I can't do that. I'm sorry, Rory. But I can't."

"But—"

"You shouldn't go either," Kit interrupted, voice unsteady. "It isn't safe."

Rory's jaw set in his special stubborn way. "I'll go alone, then."

The room erupted into chaos. Priya immediately protested that Rory couldn't possibly go alone, while Flynn suggested that he'd happily accompany him, only to be roared at by Seb. Felix resumed his frantic typing that I suspected was merely pretense. Eventually Sebastián shouted over all of them that he needed everyone else here in London, that they couldn't spare a single person with everything else happening.

I stared at Rory—his blond hair sticking up in defiant tufts, the flush of determination colouring his cheeks. A man who was willing to walk straight into the lion's den for his twat of an ex-boyfriend. The same ex he believed traded him in for a prettier model. Yet here he was...

"Please, Rory," said Kit, his voice cracking slightly. "Don't do this."

The fear in his voice startled me. What could possibly be so terrifying about his childhood home in Scotland that he couldn't even consider returning for his younger brother's sake?

As if answering me, Rory's thoughts crashed into my mind—pure terror, his mind a scattered mess of fragments.

...can't face her alone...won't survive it...she'll destroy me...they'll all see how broken I am...

The raw fear in his thoughts was so visceral it made my stomach clench. Behind all his bravado was someone genuinely terrified of facing whatever awaited him in Scotland.

"I'll do it."

The room fell silent. It took me a moment to realise those words had come from my own mouth.

Everyone stared at me as if I'd grown a second head. Rory's mouth actually hung open, which would have been satisfying under different circumstances.

"I'll accompany Rory to Scotland to support the investigation. With appropriate compensation, of course." I flicked my eyes to Seb, who nodded once. "Double should just about cover it."

Double my typical wage wasn't nearly enough to spend days on end trapped in close quarters with Rory Thorne, but it would have to do.

"You'd do that?" Rory's eyes were wider than saucers, and I glared at him before he started profusely thanking me or something equally horrifying.

I nodded once. After all, my mother could use the extra money to finally renovate her garden like she'd been talking about for years. Plus, I'd never been to the Scottish Highlands—in fact, I'd barely been away in years. Not that this was going to be a *holiday*, of course.

Kit approached me, squeezing my arm with surprising gentleness. "Thank you. I won't forget this."

I swallowed down the urge to promise him that Rory would be safe with me. Because where Rory was concerned, I'd make no such promises.

"When can we leave?" Rory asked, suddenly perking up like a puppy offered a walk. His eyes were alight with purpose, all traces of his earlier distress vanishing.

"I need to call my boss and make up some sort of emergency," I said, already mentally drafting the conversation. In truth, I'd never asked for time off before, and still had most of my holiday days banked up. DCI Harris would probably fall off her chair when I requested leave.

"Monday?" Rory looked so bloody hopeful that I found myself nodding.

Shit. I'd just willingly volunteered to go to the furthest northern location in the UK with the person who hated me most in the world. What the hell was I thinking?

"Brilliant!" Rory clapped his hands together. "That gives us to-morrow to prepare everything. Felix will pull up every map of the area, and I'll have time to find my kilt—"

"Your what?" I choked.

"My kilt," he repeated, as if I was the one being ridiculous. "Can't show up to a formal Highland pack gathering without proper attire. It would be like you turning up to a crime scene in your underwear."

Felix snorted from behind his laptop.

I rubbed my temple, already feeling the familiar pressure of a headache building. This was madness. Complete and utter madness.

And yet, as Rory's face continued to beam over at me as if I were his saviour, I couldn't quite bring myself to dread it.

"So it's settled," Seb announced with finality. "Rory and Maxwell will leave Monday for Scotland to infiltrate the gathering and gather information about Dev Bassi."

A moment of silence settled over the room as the reality of the plan sank in.

"Though..." Rory said, his brow furrowing as he looked between me and Sebastián. "How exactly is Theo going to get into a pack gathering? Human outsiders won't be welcome."

"Right," I said. "I can hardly introduce myself as a police escort."

"But..." Rory's cheeks flushed slightly as he glanced around the room, then back to me. "Well... I mean... you could pose as my boyfriend?"

The words hit my brain like they were travelling through mud, each syllable taking an eternity to register. When they finally connected, I felt as though someone had pulled the floor from beneath me.

"B-boyfriend?" I croaked out, my voice embarrassingly strained.

Priya and Flynn both dissolved into poorly concealed sniggers. Flynn even had to turn away, shoulders shaking with silent laughter.

My mouth went desert-dry. Could I take back my offer? The thought of pretending to be romantically involved with Rory Thorne made my stomach twist into knots I couldn't begin to untangle.

"Would that be a problem, Detective?" Seb asked, one eyebrow arched perfectly. Was this... entertaining him?

I fought against the heat creeping up my neck and into my cheeks. "No," I managed, straightening my tie unnecessarily. "I'm just wondering about our capacity to pull that particular element off."

Priya cleared her throat, looking between us with a mischievous glint in her eyes. "Well, if you're going to play boyfriends, you'll need to work on your chemistry. We can have a trial run, if you like. I'll give you marks out of ten."

I shot her a withering glare, but she continued undeterred.

"Lovers tend not to stand two metres apart at all times," she said, gesturing to the considerable gap between Rory and me. "Perhaps try being at least thirty centimetres close to each other? And maybe stop scowling at him quite so much, Maxwell."

Flynn leaned forward, joining in with enthusiasm. "You'll need pet names too. Maybe not "dickface." Just saying."

"And physical affection," Priya added, her eyes twinkling. "A kiss on the cheek could be quite effective. Perhaps you could have a practise now? Try not to growl at him, Rory."

The room erupted into laughter. Even Sebastián's lips twitched at the corners. I silently begged the hotel's foundations to collapse and end this torment.

Rory remained unusually quiet. No snappy comeback, no mocking grin—nothing. My eyes drifted to him, finding his expression unreadable, his gaze fixed on some invisible point on the wall.

Against my better judgement, I let my barriers slip just slightly, reaching toward his thoughts. I needed to know if he was completely repulsed by the idea, so I could refuse the assignment without causing a scene.

But when I brushed against his consciousness, I found his mind curiously blank, as if he'd retreated deep within himself. What di—

A jolt shot through me, like touching a live wire. The sensation wasn't painful but intense. Rory's head snapped up, his eyes locking with mine as if he'd felt it too.

The room faded away as we stared at each other.

No, that definitely wasn't repulsion radiating from him.

It was something else entirely.

7

Rory

I dragged my suitcase behind me, the wheels clattering against the uneven pavement outside my block of flats. My navy-blue winter coat was stifling in the mild sunshine, and sweat was already prickling at my hairline. Completely inappropriate for London, but Scotland would be colder.

Scotland.

I could hardly believe I was actually going back there. The thought soured my stomach, sent adrenaline flooding through me. My heart hammered against my ribs like it was trying to escape, which, honestly, fair enough.

A tiny squeak emanated from my coat pocket, followed by scratching against the fabric. Freddy always knew when I was distressed. He had an uncanny sense for my moods—probably because he was literally dead and therefore somehow mystically connected to my anxiety. Or something?

"Shh," I whispered, patting my pocket gently. "I know it's hot in there, but it's the only way to smuggle you past Detective Dickface."

The main reason I was wearing this massive coat was so I could sneak Freddy along. No way was I leaving him behind. He'd miss me too much. I'd found him last night in the kitchen cupboards at Killigrew Street Hotel, where he preferred to live rather than our flat. Kit's fault—he claimed Freddy gave him the creeps and was horrible to him.

"Listen, mate," I murmured to the lump in my pocket. "You've got to keep very still and quiet until we're well past London, yeah? I've got snacks in my other pocket that I'll keep feeding you."

Another squeak, which I chose to interpret as agreement.

I looked up and spotted Maxwell sitting in a car—not his, but a sleek red Audi. His mother's car, he'd explained over text messages. An extra security precaution.

As I approached, Maxwell's expression was completely unreadable. The reality of how much time I was about to spend with him suddenly hit me like a bucket of ice water, and my feet froze.

We were about to be stuck together for days on end, if we even survived the endless car journey. Stuck with his judging eyes, his barely concealed contempt. And Scotland... God, Scotland was where my life had fallen apart. What if I had some kind of breakdown and Maxwell witnessed it? He already thought I was a reckless liability. The last thing I needed was to give him more ammunition to prove I didn't belong at Killigrew Street. The familiar feeling of not being wanted sank into my bones, settling like a cold weight.

Maxwell frowned at me so deeply his glasses slid down his nose. *Great.* I was already annoying him, and I hadn't even said good morning. Not that I would have said good morning anyway, but still.

When I find you, you better be fucking grateful for this, Dev.

My new boyfriend wound down the window to glare at me. "Rory, what are you doing?"

My brain scrambled for something to say. "Your mother has a nicer car than you."

"I bought it for her," he said. "She doesn't get to drive it much anymore, though. Are you going to get in anytime today?"

I shook my head, trying to clear the fog of anxiety. With a deep breath, I hauled my suitcase toward the boot of Maxwell's car. He got out and opened it for me, which was unexpectedly considerate.

It was empty, aside from his tiny duffle bag—did he understand we were going for almost a whole week?—and a large metal case packed for us by Kit, which included a Glock and silver bullets, lethal against shifted wolves. Hopefully they'd stay in their case.

"I've never been to Scotland," Maxwell said, helping me lift my very large case inside.

"Well, lucky you, then," I muttered, then felt Freddy squirming in my pocket. I casually patted my coat, hoping Maxwell wouldn't notice the movement.

"You're wearing a winter coat in May?" Maxwell raised an eyebrow.

"Scotland's colder than here," I replied defensively. "I'm sensitive to temperature changes. Wolf thing."

"Right. Another wolf thing."

He was referring to our conversation where I'd explained that we'd have to drive all the way, rather than fly. I'd told him I didn't know any wolves that could bear it. Weirdly, Maxwell hadn't actually argued, apparently resigning himself to his fate of spending countless hours in the car with me. I'd expected at least *some* resistance.

We both got in, and an awkward silence descended as Maxwell pulled away from the kerb. I fiddled with my seatbelt, wondering if I should put some music on or if that would irritate him. The quiet stretched between us, and I held my breath until my lungs felt too big for my chest.

All of a sudden, I couldn't take it anymore, and opened my mouth to finally say "good morning," even though we were a full minute into the journey—

"Look, about the... boyfriend thing the other day. Sorry if I didn't react well."

My head snapped towards him. Had I ever heard him say the word "sorry?"

"I don't want you to get the wrong idea," he continued, eyes fixed firmly on the road.

"Don't worry. I know that you just hate me, rather than being a raging homophobe."

Maxwell sighed, notably not refuting my claim. His fingers tightened on the steering wheel. "I'm just... not the best at acting," he admitted after a moment. "And it's been a fair while since I've had a relationship.

I'm worried I won't be up to the challenge of convincing your family we're... *together*."

I snorted. "Don't worry, Detective. I'll take the lead."

The look of absolute terror that flashed across Maxwell's face was priceless. I couldn't help but laugh, the sound bursting out of me like a dam breaking.

"God, your face!" I wheezed, clutching at my stomach.

Maxwell's lips twitched, not quite a smile, but close. "I'm serious, Rory. I don't want to make things worse for you."

My laughter died. "Trust me, it can't get worse." I stared out the window at the passing buildings. "Though, warning, my mother will hate you by default. When I came out to her, she pretended to accept it. All polite smiles and such. But she was low-key pissed that she wouldn't get a bloodline heir from me." I swallowed hard. "This was after Kit had already left, and we didn't even speak his name anymore."

Maxwell remained silent, but I could feel his rapt attention on me.

"She even suggested I could enter an arranged open marriage to provide children to the pack." I shuddered at the memory. "So, anyway, she's probably not going to react very well to the sight of me hanging off your arm." I grinned at the thought. "I can't wait."

At least I'd be bringing someone like Maxwell home—hot as fuck, successful, intelligent. They'd see I didn't need them, that I was wanted elsewhere. That someone amazing had chosen me.

Maxwell rubbed his left temple, wincing slightly.

Shit. I'd forgotten to guard my thoughts. I needed to be more careful. Compliments were the last thing I wanted him to hear.

Maxwell cleared his throat. "So, your mother is the alpha of that pack now? After your Dad died?"

"Yeah." My fingers drummed against my thigh, a nervous rhythm that matched my quickening pulse.

He looked at me expectantly, that detective stare.

Stifling my sigh, I said, "So I heard, anyway. It all happened three days after I left home."

"How does it all work?" Maxwell asked, sounding genuinely intrigued. "If you don't mind me asking. Kit mentioned to me a while back about how wolves can physically feel others in their pack?"

I found myself rubbing at my chest.

"It's not really physical, not like…" I waved my hand vaguely. "We call them pack bonds. They're like—god, this sounds so cheesy—invisible threads connecting everyone. You feel them here." I tapped my sternum. "Not with your actual nerves or whatever. Deeper."

Maxwell continued to pierce me with his gaze, and my skin prickled as if he was peeling it back, exposing me.

"When you're in a pack, you always sort of know where everyone is. Not like, oh, Sarah's at Tesco's buying milk, but more like… if I closed my eyes, I could point in the direction of any pack member. The closer you are to someone—emotionally, I mean—the stronger you feel it. There's no escape. Family bonds are the worst. I mean, strongest."

I shifted in my seat, suddenly hyper-aware I was anxiously fidgeting. "It's why Kit and I can always find each other, even when we're pissed off at each other. Our tether somehow sort of survived, even after we both left the pack. He's the only one I have left, though it's not the same. We're not exactly a pack."

The car hit a pothole, and I used the jolt to swallow around my tightening throat.

"When a bond breaks—" My voice did that stupid cracking thing. Brilliant. *Shut up, Rory, shut up.* But I couldn't. Kit never allowed me to talk to him about this, and so it was like the words demanded to pour out of me. "It feels like someone's reached inside and snapped something that shouldn't be able to break. It's not just emotional pain. It's…" I shrugged, trying for casual. "It's like your body forgets how to exist properly. When someone dies, you've still got the pack to help you through it. But when you leave—when you cut yourself off from everyone at once—most wolves never experience that level of severance. Waking up gasping because your brain keeps searching for connections that aren't there anymore."

Maxwell was too quiet. I risked a glance at him.

"Did that happen to you?" he asked softly.

I flashed him a smile that felt like baring my teeth. "Turns out ADHD makes pack bonds feel different too. Everything's always too much or not enough. The elders called it 'bond sensitivity'—just another way I was defective. When I left..." I swallowed hard. "Let's just say there's a reason lots of lone wolves don't stay that way for long... one way or another. Your brain's not wired to exist without those connections."

I looked out the window, suddenly fascinated by the passing tower blocks. "Kit helped, once I made it to London. Having one bond still intact, even a... partial one, probably kept me from going completely mental. Those few months in Glasgow..." I trailed off, the name of the city sticking in my throat like a fishbone.

Glasgow. The concrete underpass that reeked of piss. The cardboard that never quite kept the damp out. The hollow ache in my stomach that became so familiar I stopped noticing it. The looks from passers-by—pity from some, disgust from most.

I'd arrived with just enough money for a week in a hostel. After that ran out, I'd tried other packs. Three of them. As soon as I'd dropped the Thorne surname, their expressions had changed. Turns out my family were known as righteous, posh snobs who thought they were better than the rest, especially city wolves.

Then there were the two blokes with knives who'd cornered me behind a supermarket, demanding my backpack. I'd had nothing worth taking except my ID and a photo of my mum from before everything went wrong. The wolf inside me had howled to be released, claws itching beneath my skin. But I'd swallowed it down, handed over my backpack with shaking hands, and walked away with nothing but the clothes I wore.

The weight of Maxwell's stare prickled across my skin. He'd definitely listened in. I couldn't bring myself to care.

"Why didn't you just come to London straight away, if Kit was there?" Maxwell asked softly.

"We weren't actually talking at that point." I squirmed in my seat. "It's a long story. But eventually a wolf from another Highland pack spotted me, managed to get Kit's number, and told him what was going on." I remembered the black eye I'd been sporting, courtesy of a much larger homeless man who wanted my sleeping spot. "The next day, he just appeared on the street, right in the underpass where I was camping."

The emotions tied to the memory came flooding back. Shock, horror, *relief*.

"I told him to fuck off, then I burst into tears like a baby."

"And he took you back to London?"

"Yeah. Three days later, I was Killigrew Street's newest employee." I attempted a laugh that came out more like a strangled cough. "Biggest regret of Seb's five-hundred-year life, I'm sure, hiring me."

A sharp squeak pierced the air, followed by frantic scratching against my coat. *Shit*. I'd been so caught up in our conversation that I'd completely forgotten about Freddy.

"What was that?" Maxwell frowned, glancing over at me.

"Nothing! Just my stomach—"

Before I could finish, Freddy erupted from my pocket like a furry grey missile, launching himself onto the dashboard. His matted fur stood on end, yellow eyes glowing with hunger as he bared his yellowed teeth at Maxwell.

Maxwell screamed—not a manly shout or dignified yelp—but a full-on, spectacular high-pitched banshee wail that probably shattered several nearby windows. The car veered sharply left, tyres screeching as we hurtled toward a lamppost.

My body moved before my brain caught up. I lunged across the center console, one hand grabbing the wheel, the other shoving Maxwell's frozen arm. The car straightened with inches to spare, tyres bumping against the kerb before settling back onto the road.

Maxwell's chest heaved with rapid breaths, eyes wide behind his glasses as he stared at Freddy, who was now innocently sniffing the air vents.

"What. The. ACTUAL. FUCK." Each word exploded from Maxwell with increasing volume. "You've brought that... *thing* on our trip? Without telling me?" His voice dropped dangerously quiet to add, "Are you completely mad?"

"He's not a *thing*, he's a ferret," I corrected, reaching for Freddy who skittered away, clearly enjoying his newfound freedom.

"*Rory!* Why have you brought a dead animal into my car?!"

I winced. "Technically, he's *un*dead."

Maxwell's face went through an impressive range of expressions—shock, disgust, horror, finally settling on pure, unadulterated rage.

"I couldn't leave him behind!" I protested, finally managing to scoop Freddy up. "And look, he's perfectly harmless."

As if to prove me wrong, Freddy chose that exact moment to launch himself into the air, landing on the steering wheel and snapping his sharp teeth at Maxwell's fingers.

"He's going to get us killed!"

I scrambled to open my coat pocket, fumbling for the crackers. Freddy's little nose twitched frantically.

"Come on, you monster," I coaxed.

Freddy's yellow eyes locked onto the treat. He abandoned his assault on Maxwell's hand and scurried across. I stroked his fur as he gnawed on the cracker.

"See, I have him perfectly under control," I said, giving Maxwell my most winning smile.

"You still haven't explained why he's coming with us. And to be frank, I don't get your obsession with that rat."

"I was never allowed pets as a kid," I said, scratching behind Freddy's partially exposed skull. "Animals get nervous around wolves, apparently. So when I moved to London, getting Freddy was one of the first things I did for myself. Straight away, I loved him so much."

My throat tightened unexpectedly. "When he randomly died one day, I was devastated. Like, proper crying-for-days devastated. That's when Issac... he brought him back. Mainly as a joke, I think."

Maxwell snorted. "That sounds like how I remember him. Though, obviously, I didn't know him well," he added with a quick glance.

"Then Issac died. And now Freddy's all I have left of him." I scratched behind his ear. "Issac was my best friend. The first proper friend I had in London, aside from Kit. Maybe the first real friend I ever had."

Maxwell was quiet for a moment. "I'm sorry for your loss."

"The thing is," I continued, words tumbling out before I could stop them. "Freddy shouldn't still be... you know, moving around. When a necromancer dies, everything they've reanimated is supposed to die again. Properly, this time."

I stroked Freddy's fur, feeling the familiar ridges of bone beneath. "For a long time, I thought that meant Issac was still alive somewhere. But every time I brought it up, everyone at Killigrew Street would get this look, like I was some pathetic kid who couldn't accept reality. So I just... stopped talking about it. Easier that way, right? Just another thing to bottle up and pretend doesn't exist."

The words tingled bitter on my tongue. I forced myself not to think of my brother who refused to talk about Scotland before this car conversation fully descended into impromptu therapy.

My cheeks burned as the realisation hit that I'd now burbled on about myself for the entire duration of the journey. Was this trauma dumping? Was I trauma dumping on my archnemesis?

"Sorry," I sighed. "You probably didn't want to hear about all that. If you put on some music, I promise I'll do my best to shut up."

His cheek twitched. "What music does Freddy like?"

I wound his tail around my finger. "He's quite partial to a bit of drum and bass, now that you mention it..."

"Not a chance in hell."

"But—"

"No," Maxwell said firmly, though his voice had lost its edge. "Driver picks the music. Shotgun—and their undead rodent—shut their cake holes."

I gasped dramatically. "First *Star Wars*, and now *Supernatural*? Detective Maxwell, you absolute nerd."

He shifted in his seat. "I don't know what you're talking about."

"You know, I thought you'd only watch history documentaries or sit there with a notebook during *University Challenge*. Wait till everyone hears about this." I pulled out my phone, grinning wickedly. "Did you know that Seb and Flynn spend half their time watching *Buffy*? You know, when they're not gazing lovingly into each other's eyes, or Seb's not munching on Flynn's neck? But maybe the three of you can start a cinema club together."

"Put that phone away. Now."

"Make me." I waggled my eyebrows, already typing.

Maxwell took his eyes off the road just long enough to make a grab for my phone. I twisted away, pressing myself against the passenger door.

"Seriously, Thorne?" He kept one hand on the wheel but reached over with the other.

I batted his hand away. "Eyes on the road, Detective! You're meant to uphold the law, not break it."

"Give me the bloody phone." He made another swipe.

I curled protectively around my mobile. "Not a chance."

Maxwell's fingers brushed against my side as he reached, and I flinched, letting out an embarrassing yelp.

His eyes flicked to me, a dangerous realisation dawning. "Are you... ticklish?"

"No," I lied, clutching the phone tighter.

A wicked, rare smile spread across his face. "Interesting."

The next time he reached over, his fingers deliberately dug into my ribs. I squirmed, an involuntary laugh bursting out as I tried to protect both my dignity and my phone.

"Stop it!" I gasped between laughs, my coordination failing as he found exactly the right spot between my ribs.

In my moment of weakness, Maxwell snatched the phone from my hand and slid it into his jacket pocket, looking infuriatingly pleased with himself.

"That's cheating," I wheezed, trying to catch my breath.

"That's strategy," he corrected, a hint of smugness playing at the corner of his mouth. "You'll get it back when we stop for food."

I slumped back in my seat, but couldn't maintain my outrage for long. "Fine. But at least tell me what music the great Detective Inspector deems acceptable for this journey."

Maxwell's answer was to press a button on the car stereo. The car filled with soaring voices—dozens of them—singing in what sounded like Latin, backed by a full orchestra.

"Oh my god," I groaned, sinking lower in my seat. "Is this... like, church music? You're such an old man."

"I'm thirty-two."

"In your soul, you're at least seventy."

"It's Mozart," he said, as if that explained everything. "It's classical."

Freddy chose that moment to scamper from my lap onto the dashboard, where he began doing what could only be described as a zombie ferret conducting session, his tiny paws waving in time with the dramatic crescendos.

Maxwell's eyes widened. "Get that thing off my—"

"Look! He loves it!" I crowed triumphantly. "Freddy's got sophisticated taste! He thinks he's conducting the London Symphony Orchestra!"

"Thorne, I swear to god—"

But I could see it—the smile he was violently fighting, the way his shoulders had loosened from their perpetual tension. For a moment, with the late afternoon sun streaming through the windows, the ridiculously dramatic choral music playing, and Freddy's bizarre little dance, it almost felt... normal. Like we were just two blokes on a road trip, not a wolf and a telepath who hated each other, heading toward my personal nightmare.

Instead, I leaned back, closed my eyes, and let myself enjoy the moment while it lasted.

8

Theodore

The journey was taking ages. What should have been a straightforward drive had devolved into a nightmare of congestion and road closures. I'd spent most of the afternoon gripping the steering wheel, inching forward at a snail's pace.

Though the endless crawl of traffic became almost bearable as surprisingly pleasant conversation flowed between us. At one point, Rory launched into a passionate defence of Priya's tea leaf readings, leaning forward in his seat with those expressive hands of his punctuating every point.

"She predicted Kit would break his arm last winter, three weeks before it happened," he insisted.

"Coincidence," I countered, though I found myself fighting a smile at his indignation.

"You're just like Kit," Rory groaned, slumping back. "I heard you comparing your ridiculous morning runs the other day. Who actually enjoys getting up at dawn on weekends?"

"People who appreciate quiet," I said, which earned me an eye roll.

As miles of tarmac disappeared beneath us, I discovered Rory had an encyclopedic knowledge of pastries served in London cafés, a surprising passion for true crime podcasts, and absolutely no filter between his brain and mouth. Somehow, I minded less than I should have.

Eventually, we circled back around to Dev.

"Do you think he's alive?"

The intense way Rory asked the question—as if I truly knew the answer—startled me. I almost found myself promising that Dev would be fine before catching myself. Promises were dangerous things. I'd certainly learned that after a decade on the job.

"The fact that his phone came back on is a good sign," I offered instead, keeping my eyes fixed on the road ahead. "Most missing persons cases where technology reactivates—"

"That doesn't mean anything," Rory cut in, shaking his head. "Remember that episode of *Vanished Without a Trace* I was telling you about? The killer kept his victim's phone charged for weeks, posting on their social media, texting family members. What if someone's just using his phone as bait? Or what if they've got him locked up somewhere near the signal tower? Or maybe they've got his finger to use for the fingerprint ID and—"

"Rory," I interrupted, "we don't know anything yet. That's why we're going."

He nodded, fiddling with his sleeve. "It's just... mad, isn't it? That it's somehow linked back to my old pack land? Of all the places..."

"You said Dev's alpha has no idea what he'd be doing up here?"

"Yeah. Christina says she'd send up shifters herself to look for him, but doesn't want them torn to pieces. She's super grateful that we're doing this."

I glanced at him, noting the tightness around his eyes. The loyalty this man showed toward the ex who broke his heart was remarkable—Dev was a lucky bastard to have someone like Rory still in his corner, even after walking away from such unwavering devotion.

"Dev must be quite something," I said carefully, "to inspire this kind of dedication."

"He is," Rory said, then fell silent. "You think it's strange, don't you?"

"Just a little," I admitted.

Rory sighed. "Dev was... he was one of the first people who chose me, you know? After I left Scotland. I mean, I could have tried joining one of the London packs, but..." He shrugged, looking uncomfortable. "When you've been rejected once, it's hard to believe it could work out the next time. Plus, most wolves, they hear about someone cutting themselves off from their birth pack and they assume there's a good reason for it. That you're defective somehow."

He shook his head as if clearing it. "Anyway, I dated loads of people after moving down. One-night stands, casual things that lasted a short while. But with Dev, it was different. It was the first time I thought, 'Oh, this could actually be something.' You know? Like maybe I could have what other people had—someone who'd stick around, who'd want to build something proper with me."

Oh, Rory. My throat felt oddly tight.

"Don't get me wrong, Dev was a dick to me. But you don't just… abandon someone who was there when you had nothing, you know? Even if they broke your heart. Even if they're now fucking someone who looks like a better version of you."

The bitterness in that last sentence was sharp enough to cut, but underneath everything he said, I heard something else entirely—a fierce, protective loyalty that had little to do with romantic love and everything to do with refusing to let go of the people who'd chosen him when he'd been convinced no one would.

We stopped for food at a roadside service station, where we lost an extra twenty minutes for Rory's second burger to arrive after the first one apparently hadn't filled him up. Another "wolf thing." Then Priya sent five messages in a row demanding to see Rory's tea leaves. Rory rolled his eyes, but dutifully photographed his mug from multiple angles.

Finally settling back in the car, I glanced at the clock and suppressed a groan. It had hit rush hour, and we still hadn't reached the Scottish border, let alone begun the long drive to the Highlands.

A dull throb started behind my left eye. I touched my temple, feeling the migraine threatening to take hold. Reaching into my jacket pocket, I fished out a small bottle and tapped two tablets into my palm.

"Are you okay?"

I swallowed the pills dry. "I'm getting a headache."

"From me? Are my thoughts too loud again?" His brow furrowed with what looked like genuine concern—a trick of the light?

"No, it's not you. It's just from driving all day." And the amount of people in the restaurant with their noisy thoughts hadn't helped. I rubbed my eyes. We were supposed to do the entire journey today—what was a ten-hour drive without any stops or traffic. But we still somehow had over half of it yet to go.

Rory squirmed in his seat. He was finding it difficult being trapped in the car all day, even if he hadn't moaned—aloud—once.

"I wonder..." I said.

"What?"

"I wonder if it'll be too late now by the time we get there? To your family's estate, I mean. Maybe we should break up the drive by staying somewhere, then arriving tomorrow morning?"

Rory sighed with palpable relief. "Oh, thank god. I'm desperate to go for a run."

A flash of imagery crossed my mind—Rory racing through woodland, fur gleaming gold in moonlight. I wasn't sure if I'd picked it up from his thoughts or if it was my own imagination.

Though beneath the immediate relief, I sensed something else—gratitude for the extra preparation time before facing his family. The tension that had been building in him all day seemed to ease slightly.

I shifted the car back into drive. "We're not stupidly far from the border. Should be loads of options there."

"Yeah," Rory agreed, leaning back into his seat.

As I pulled back onto the motorway, Rory promptly leaned against the window, his eyes drifting shut. Within minutes, Freddy had climbed onto his head, making a nest in his messy blond hair before curling into a small, grey ball. The ferret's matted fur blended with Rory's chaotic hairstyle in a way that would have been comical if it weren't so... oddly endearing.

A few minutes later, Rory was fast asleep, his breathing deep and even. The constant energy that typically radiated from him had settled into something peaceful.

I found my eyes drifting towards him every few minutes as I drove, still processing everything he'd told me earlier. The pain in his voice when he'd spoken about leaving his pack, the stark vulnerability when mentioning Issac. The levels of emotion that had radiated from him had been intense—waves of grief, loneliness, and a desperate need for acceptance that I hadn't expected.

Strangely, I hadn't minded dealing with it. There was something about seeing beneath Rory's chaotic exterior that made me want to...

I shook my head. *Understand him.* Yes, that was it.

As we approached the border, the traffic worsened. Rory started to stir, stretching in the confined space like a cat waking from a nap. Freddy tumbled from his perch, landing in Rory's lap with an indignant squeak.

"Where are we?" he mumbled, voice thick with sleep.

"Not far now."

His leg immediately started bouncing, a nervous, restless energy returning to his body.

"Let's find somewhere, then," I suggested, noting his discomfort. "You've been trapped in this car long enough."

"I'll ring Felix to book somewhere," Rory offered, reaching for his phone.

"He's not your bloody PA, Rory. Look it up on your phone."

Rory tapped at his screen, then frowned. "It's dead."

"Why is your phone *always* dead?"

"I'll use yours," he said, reaching to yank my phone down from its navigation holder.

"No!" I snapped.

Rory's hand froze mid-air. "Why don't you want me on your phone?"

"Because I don't."

I didn't trust him not to snoop. My phone was like a crime scene—revealing far too much about me. Not because there was much to find, but because of what wasn't there: no group chats, or social media. A couple of messages from my work buddy George planning our occasional hiking trips. The camera reel housed photos of landscapes only.

And then there were the notes. Dozens of them, fragments of poetry I'd written late at night when sleep wouldn't come. Words I'd never show anyone, certainly not Rory Thorne, who'd have a field day if he discovered "Detective Dickface" wrote sonnets about moonlight and longing. Christ, I'd never hear the end of it.

"If you've got porn in a locked folder, Felix can totally hack into that, by the way. Trust me, I have experience. I think I scarred him for life."

I threw my charging wire at his face.

Then, as if a miracle had decided to bless me, I spotted a sign by the roadside. "Oh look, a B&B."

"Especially when he saw the one of—"

"Please don't."

I knew he was only winding me up—that goddamn twinkle was back in his eyes again, the corners of them doing the crinkly thing.

I turned off the motorway, navigating down increasingly narrow country lanes. Each twist in the road seemed to heighten Rory's restlessness. His fingers drummed against the dashboard, tapping out an irregular rhythm.

He'd somehow managed to resist asking the "are we nearly there yet" that looped around his mind.

Finally, we pulled into a tiny village—barely more than a cluster of stone buildings huddled around a single main street. The sign for "Heather's Haven B&B" swung gently in the evening breeze, its paint faded but welcoming.

I parked in the small gravel lot beside the building. Rory was out of the car before I'd even switched off the engine. He remained outside as I entered the B&B's tiny reception room to find it empty.

After ringing the small brass bell, I cast my eyes over the numerous tourism leaflets scattered all over the place. Through the window, Rory stretched his arms above his head like he was trying to touch the sky. The fading sunlight caught in his hair, turning it to gold as he tilted his face upward, eyes closed.

"Can I help you?"

I almost jumped out of my skin. Turning, I found a cheery-looking woman behind the desk.

"We need rooms for the night," I said, glancing back through the window where Rory had wandered over to examine a weathered stone wall, running his fingers along the moss-covered surface.

"Beautiful view, isn't it?" the receptionist said, and I snapped my attention back to her.

"Yes..."

"How many rooms?" she asked, tapping at her computer. "We have two left."

I hesitated, then felt confused at myself for hesitating. "Umm... yes, two..."

What the hell was that pause for? I needed two rooms. Of course I needed two rooms. One for me, one for Rory. Separate. As they should be.

The receptionist looked at me curiously, her gaze drifting to the window where Rory was visible. Her eyes flicked between us, a small smile forming on her lips.

"You sure about that?" She winked. "You don't look sure."

"Yes, I'm—"

She suddenly started bashing her keyboard with theatrical force. "Oh, silly me! Honestly, I think I need my eyesight checked. I'm afraid we actually have just the one room available, sir. With one bed." At this, she sighed dramatically. "Though it *is* queen-sized." Another wink, more obvious this time.

I stood there, stunned into silence, as she slid a key across the counter. My brain offered precisely zero helpful responses. I should have corrected her. I should have insisted on checking elsewhere. I should have done anything except stand there like an idiot while she assumed Rory and I were—

Christ. How was Rory going to react?

"Breakfast is served between seven and nine," she continued cheerfully, then proceeded to witter on about this and that, including countryside walks and the dinner menu that evening.

I nodded mechanically, my fingers closing around the key as my brain struggled to catch up with what had just happened. *Tell her you need the other room.* But my mouth refused to form the words, and my tired brain started replaying the entire scenario, wondering if maybe I'd imagined the winking, that she did only have one room after all.

I stepped outside, the key heavy in my hand. Rory had wandered over to a small patch of grass where Freddy was now scampering around his feet, the ferret's matted fur almost blending with the ground.

"We've got a slight problem," I called out.

Rory looked up. "What's wrong?"

"There's only one room available." I held up the key, dangling it between us like evidence at a crime scene. "With, um, one bed."

His eyes widened. "Oh."

"Yeah."

Rory shrugged. "It's fine. I'll sleep in the car."

"Don't be ridiculous," I said, the words tumbling out sharply. The image of him curled uncomfortably in the back seat made my chest prickle. When had I started caring about Rory Thorne's comfort? "You're not sleeping in the bloody car."

"I've slept in worse places." Something dark flashed across his features.

"We'll manage with the one room. It'll be fine."

Rory studied my face for a moment, then whistled for Freddy, who scurried up his leg and into his pocket with surprising agility for something half decomposed.

"Fine," he conceded. "But you're not sleeping on the floor or whatever. I'm not letting you play the martyr and then sulk about it."

For fuck's sake, what have I done?

If I hadn't been tired from driving all day, I would have managed that situation like a normal human being.

Or perhaps I *was* losing my mind. Because for a split second, when she'd winked at me, there'd been a flash of... something. Not revulsion. Not horror. Just a brief, treacherous thought of what it might be like to—

No. Absolutely not. I was overtired. That was all.

Yet the receptionist's knowing smile continued to haunt me as we trudged upstairs to room seven, grabbing two vile-looking coffees from a vending machine en route.

The room was small but cosy—floral wallpaper, wooden beams crossing the ceiling, and a queen-sized bed dominating the space. A tiny bathroom was visible through a door to the right.

One bed. One very clearly not-quite-large-enough bed for two grown men to share without some level of proximity. I swallowed hard, the room shrinking around me. Or maybe it was just that Rory, already peering at the view out of the window, seemed to fill whatever space he occupied with his energy, his movement, his very presence.

The door clicked shut, and Freddy jumped out of Rory's pocket and started weaving around in mad circles. Rory headed to the bed and began stripping it of its excess pillows. I watched, confused, as he arranged them in a neat line down the middle of the mattress, creating a barrier.

"There," he said, stepping back to admire his handiwork. "Now we can both sleep in the bed without a repeat of the octopus situation."

"Yes," I said dryly. *I'm sure this was exactly what the receptionist had in mind.*

I should have felt relieved. This was practical. Sensible. Problem solved with minimal fuss. So why did I feel a strange disappointment at the sight of that pillow barrier? It was ridiculous. I should be grateful for Rory's unexpectedly mature handling of the situation.

I set my bag down with more force than necessary. Tomorrow we'd reach his family's estate, and this strange, confusing day would be behind us. One night. I could survive one night sharing a bed with Rory Thorne.

Couldn't I?

"We'll have to share a bed when we get there anyway," said Rory.

I stared at him, my brain struggling to process his words. "What?"

"You know, because of the whole couple thing? I'm not sure we're going to be particularly convincing if we insist on sleeping in two rooms." His tone was casual, almost flippant, but I caught the flash of fear in his eyes.

"Oh, right. Yes."

My stomach dropped as the reality of our situation crashed over me, my pulse quickening. We'd be sharing a bed not just tonight, but potentially for days. Nights upon nights of lying beside him, separated by nothing but a flimsy barrier of pillows—if that. The thought sent a confusing jolt of what felt like nerves through me.

But who wouldn't be nervous spending that much time with someone who hated you?

"There will be a sofa or something, though," Rory added. "We can take turns. Or you can just have the bed because you are doing me a favour after all."

Is that how he saw me accompanying him? As if I were some reluctant participant, dragged along against my will?

"I'm being paid to come with you," I pointed out, slightly clipped.

Rory pulled a very strange expression before looking away. "Yeah, I know."

Silence fell awkwardly between us. For some reason, it felt like I'd said the wrong thing entirely.

I cleared my throat. "It'll be dark soon, and you can go for a run."

Rory's face brightened instantly, the tension draining from his shoulders. It was remarkable how quickly his mood could shift.

I hesitated, then added, "Can I... come with you?"

Rory's eyes widened, and he blinked rapidly. "Okay," he said after a moment, the single word carrying a weight of surprise. Then his eyes bulged, and he shouted, "Fuck!"

I twisted to see Freddy nose deep in the small paper coffee cup, which I'd taken one sip of and rejected. The ferret's matted grey tail twitched with alarming enthusiasm.

"Quick!" Rory scrambled to his feet. "You know what he's like on caffeine!"

I lunged, but Freddy, sensing the approaching threat to his beverage consumption, leapt straight up into the air with supernatural agility. Coffee droplets scattered across the floral wallpaper as he sailed past my outstretched hands.

"Gotcha!" I made another grab for him, but the little bastard twisted mid-air and sank his yellowed teeth deep into the flesh between my thumb and forefinger.

"ARGH!" The scream tore from my throat as white-hot pain shot up my arm. Freddy dangled from my hand like some demented Christmas ornament, his glowing yellow eyes rolling back in what looked suspiciously like bliss.

I shook my hand frantically, trying to dislodge him, but his jaw had locked with rigor mortis determination. "Get him off!" I shouted, dancing around the small room like I was being electrocuted.

Rory rushed over, but instead of helping me, he immediately started cooing at the ferret. "Oh, Freddy, sweetheart. You naughty boy. Let go of the nice man."

I stared at him incredulously, still trying to shake Freddy loose. "I'm bleeding!"

He only gently stroked Freddy's fur whilst the creature remained firmly attached to my hand.

"RORY!" I bellowed.

"What?" He looked up at me with genuine confusion, as if it were perfectly normal to prioritise a zombie ferret's emotional wellbeing over a human bite wound.

"Here, hold still," Rory said, having the audacity to *giggle* as he gently pried Freddy's jaw open.

I stared down at the bleeding puncture wounds. "Brilliant."

"Oh, stop being such a baby." Rory was practically vibrating as he headed for the tiny en suite. "I'll get you some tissues. But honestly, you just need to be nicer to him if you want him to like you."

"I don't want him to like me," I called after him, glaring at the ridiculous creature who was now whizzing around at lightning speed, chasing his own tail like a dog. "Why would I want him to *like me?!*"

A couple of hours later—in which I'd caught up on some of my actual police work—darkness had properly fallen. Rory began squirming restlessly, repeatedly looking out of the window at the night sky.

"Okay, it's probably fine now," he said, stretching his arms above his head. "Which is good, because I'm getting hungry again. Hopefully, I can catch a rabbit or something."

I stared at him. "The wrap was huge!" I'd fetched us two falafel wraps from the kitchen, and even given him the last bite of mine after he gave me puppy-dog eyes.

"Wolf thing," he said with a shrug. Reaching to his left ear with two hands, he started systematically removing his earrings. When he caught me staring, he said, "I can leave a few of the larger hoops in, but most of them just ping off and spray everywhere if I don't take them out before I shift. And I can't afford to keep losing them, because some of them are white gold, because you know, silver."

It took a considerable effort for me not to make a comment about how impractical it seemed to bother wearing them at all.

Rory whispered sweet nothings into Freddy's ear, then grabbed a small drawstring bag from his luggage. I followed as he darted down the stairs, taking them two at a time. Typical Rory—always moving like he was being chased.

We crossed the car park, where the gravel gave way to woodland. The trees loomed dark and mysterious in the moonlight, their shadows stretching across the ground like reaching fingers.

The light caught the pale planes of Rory's face as he surveyed the woodland ahead of us, making his features appear sharper, more defined. "By the way," he said, "if you lose me once I shift, just listen for whatever's making the most noise and follow that. It'll probably be me."

I stared at him. "Why can I *still* never tell when you're joking?"

"Maybe you're just not very good at reading people," he said with a grin. "Bit concerning for a telepathic detective, that."

"I'm excellent at reading people. You're just..." I searched for the right word. "Chaotic."

"Chaotic?" Rory's eyes lit up. "That's definitely a compliment." He laughed, a genuine sound that filled me with something light and buoyant, like helium. "But you'll get used to me, eventually." He was quiet for a moment, then added, "Well, if you decide to hang out with me—with Killigrew Street—more, after this. I'm surprised that you never really do."

I stared at him. The words stuck in my throat as I remembered the Christmas gathering—lingering in the basement doorway of the hotel, hearing Rory's voice drift from below: *"Urg, but why is Detective Dickface coming? He'll probably arrest us all for having too much fun."*

"You've never made me particularly welcome," I said finally.

Rory's expression shifted, guilt flickering across his features. "That's true. That's just *me*, though. The others have always been lovely to you. You could have come to stuff, and just ignored me."

I couldn't argue with that. Seb had extended invitations. Kit had offered drinks, and weekend runs. Priya often tried to include me in their banter. Felix attempted eye contact that lasted a whole second.

"Rory," I said, quite seriously. "You're impossible to ignore."

He gave me a lopsided smile that made my heart skip a beat. I could still detect guilt radiating from him. I *almost* felt bad for making him feel that way, even though he'd been an absolute wanker towards me. Was that all behind us now? Possibly, as long as I never needed to arrest him again.

"God, it's beautiful out here," Rory said suddenly, tilting his head back to look at the stars. "So peaceful. Makes me realise how much I need to get out of London more."

I gazed upward at the vast expanse above us. Away from London's light pollution, the night sky swam above us, delirious with stars—a velvet canvas punctuated by countless pinpricks of light, some merely whispers, others shouting their brilliance across the void.

"You can see the stars so much clearer here," I murmured, almost to myself. "I've heard that sometimes in Scotland you can even see the Northern Lights?"

"Yeah, you can. Not in May, though. You need winter, with the long nights. I saw them just a few times when I was growing up." His voice softened with something like nostalgia. "It's a rare occasion—you need a combination of clear skies, strong solar activity, blah blah blah. Once, when I was about twelve, there was this incredible display—green and purple waves dancing across the sky." He gestured with his hands, mimicking the movement. "Kit and I were asleep, but my dad woke us up to watch. It was... magical."

The word hung between us, a rare moment of Rory speaking about his past without bitterness.

"I've never seen them," I said. "Always wanted to."

Thirty-two years old, and I'd never seen the Northern Lights. Or the pyramids. Or the Great Wall of China. I'd sent my mother off on holiday to see all those places, while I buried myself in case files and midnight coffees. Days blurring into weeks into years—time slipping through my fingers like water I never thought to cup my hands and save. Until suddenly I was here, standing in a beautiful moonlit forest with Rory Thorne of all people, wondering when my life had become a collection of postponed dreams.

My father would have understood the dedication, at least. He'd worked himself into the ground chasing his own dream—desperate to make detective, to prove himself worthy of more than the beat. Eighteen years on the force, and they never gave him the chance. He knew why—knew it had nothing to do with his record or his skills, and everything to do with the colour of his skin. When he died in the line of duty at forty-three, I was seventeen and drowning in grief. But I made myself a promise at his funeral: I'd achieve what he never could. I'd make detective. I'd do it for the both of us.

Of course, duty and purpose were more important than tourist traps. But standing under this vast sky, I couldn't help but wonder if I'd traded too much of living for the job—if I'd become so focused on honouring his memory and taking care of Ma that I'd forgotten to actually live.

We walked in silence for several more minutes, venturing deeper into the trees until Rory finally stopped in a small clearing. The moonlight filtered through the canopy above, dappling the forest floor with silver light.

"So," Rory said, placing his bag on the ground.

My pulse quickened. While I'd seen both Kit and Rory as wolves a few times before, I'd never actually watched the shift. And there was something about Rory right now, his blond hair almost silver in the dappled moonlight, that made me desperate to see it. There was a new energy about him—something wild and barely contained.

This was a side of him I hadn't seen properly. Not Rory the pain in my ass, but Rory in his element. Rory as he was meant to be.

I realised I was staring and cleared my throat. "I've never actually seen a shifter turn before," I admitted. "Can I... watch you do it?"

I instantly regretted the words as they left my mouth. Too intimate. Too revealing of my fascination.

Heat crept up my neck as Rory turned to face me, eyebrows raised.

"A, I'm pretty sure you don't want to see me naked," he said, counting on his fingers. "B, it's not exactly a spectator sport..."

...oh my god there's no way I want him to see me like that...

His anxiety hit me like a slap.

"And C," Rory continued with forced lightness, "it's messy and gross and you'd probably throw up."

I shifted my weight, suddenly acutely aware of how the leaves crunched beneath my feet. "Sorry, I shouldn't have asked. It was inappropriate."

"It's fine," Rory said, his voice oddly soft. "I get why you'd be curious. But trust me, it's not pretty."

I winced. "I didn't quite realise."

"Yeah, well." He shrugged, then gestured vaguely toward a dense cluster of trees. "I'll just go over there, do my thing, and come back considerably furrier."

I nodded, still feeling like an idiot, suddenly realising that Rory probably hadn't wanted me to even come out with him this evening. Why had I weirdly declared I'd come? It wasn't like I could actually run with him—I'd just end up crashing into trees in the dark while he bounded ahead.

I was still frozen in place when I heard it—a series of sharp cracks followed by a muffled groan that made my skin prickle. The sounds emanated from the thicket where Rory had disappeared.

Another crack, louder this time, like breaking branches. Then a sound that wasn't quite human—a strangled cry that cut through the night air.

What was happening to him? I'd known intellectually that shifting involved physical transformation, but I hadn't expected this—hadn't expected it to sound like torture.

A muffled whimper reached me, sad and helpless. Before I could stop myself, I took a step forward, every instinct screaming at me to help him.

"Rory?" The word escaped before I could catch it, barely above a whisper.

More sounds—wet, wrong sounds that made my stomach lurch. Was this normal? Was he hurt? How would I even know the difference?

A rustling in the undergrowth stopped me mid-step. Then suddenly, he burst from the thicket.

Where Rory had vanished, a wolf now stood, moonlight alchemizing his golden fur to silver. He was smaller than Kit's wolf form, but what he lacked in size, he made up for in presence. His fur seemed to capture the moonlight itself, glowing around the edges like a halo.

Wild thing wreathed in silver light,
Beauty carved from moon and night.

I laughed softly at the two hoops still adorning his left ear, glittering with each movement of his head. The wolf's movements were fluid, graceful in a way human-Rory's never quite managed to be. Those eyes, though—unmistakably Rory's, bright with intelligence and that familiar mischievous glint.

I couldn't look away. In that moment, I understood why humans had both feared and worshipped wolves throughout history. He was magnificent. His facial markings were striking—darker fur outlined his eyes like natural kohl, making them appear even more vibrant, whilst his muzzle bore subtle streaks of cream.

Rory trotted toward me, his bag dangling from his jaws. He dropped it at my feet, then looked up at me with what could only be described as a wolfish grin, tongue lolling slightly to one side.

I bent down to pick up the bag, slinging it over my shoulder. "Great. I've been demoted from Detective Inspector to coat check attendant."

Rory barked once—a sharp, happy sound—then began bouncing around my legs, transformed into pure energy. He circled me, playfully nipping at my shoelaces, then darted away only to rush back again. I couldn't suppress my laughter.

It made perfect sense for Rory's wolf to be all unfiltered joy, without the constant need to maintain his human façade. I couldn't help but feel an odd surge of jealousy—when did I ever get to drop the weight of everything and be free like this?

Rory nudged my leg with his head, looking up at me expectantly. My hand hovered uncertainly above him. Was I allowed to touch? God, I wanted to. His fur looked impossibly soft, catching the light in ways that made my fingers itch to discover if it felt as magical as it looked.

"Aren't you something," I said, admiration shining through my voice.

His tail wagged furiously at the praise, and he pressed closer against my leg, clearly fishing for more attention. The universal language of "pet me, I'm magnificent."

But what if he bit my hand off? This *was* Rory we were talking about, after all.

Rory nudged me again, more insistently this time, then pressed his head directly into my palm.

Permission granted.

I knelt down, hesitantly at first, then with growing confidence buried both hands in his fur. It was even softer than it looked, like the velvet of my mother's prized evening jacket I'd secretly touch as a child, thick and warm beneath my fingers. Rory leaned into my touch, eyes half closing in pleasure.

Silk spun from starlight, warm as breath.

I stood there, my hands still tingling from the warmth of his fur, watching as Rory bounded around me. There was something different about the telepathic connection with a shifted wolf. Kit had explained it to me once. In wolf form, shifters followed base senses and didn't necessarily stick to human-like thoughts. Hearing wolves wasn't the structured sentences or clear images I sometimes caught from humans, but rather impressions, emotions, instincts.

From Rory, I felt waves of something like pure contentment radiating outward. Not thoughts exactly, but a buzzing energy—relaxed happiness streaming from him in pulses. It was strangely infectious. I found myself smiling as he continued circling me, occasionally pressing against my legs or looking up with those bright eyes.

After a few minutes of this, I realised he was still lingering around me rather than taking advantage of the freedom the forest offered.

"You should go run," I told him, gesturing toward the trees. "That was the point of coming out here, so..."

His ears immediately flattened against his skull, and I felt a ripple of something like disappointment. It was almost funny, that Rory's wolf counterpart actually seemed to *like* me. Rory would surely be fuming about it when he changed back.

"Go on. I'll wait here for you."

Rory hesitated, then nudged my hand one last time. With a final glance over his shoulder, he took off into the night, a golden streak disappearing between the trees.

And just like that, I was alone.

The silence felt sudden and absolute. The forest sounds rushed in to fill the void—rustling leaves composing whispered verses, distant owls punctuating the night with mournful refrains, the occasional crack of a branch—but they only carved Rory's absence deeper. It was strange how quickly I'd grown accustomed to his constant presence, his chatter. Now the quiet felt oddly hollow, a poem missing its most vital line.

I leaned against a tree and looked up at the fragments of night sky visible through the canopy. How odd to miss the company of someone who, just days ago, I would have paid good money to avoid.

I'd been standing there for about twenty minutes, alone with my thoughts, when a twig snapped nearby. My head jerked up, scanning the darkness. A flash of golden fur appeared between the trees, and relief washed over me. He was back.

Rory trotted into the clearing, and I opened my mouth to greet him. Then I noticed what was dangling from his jaws.

A rabbit. A very dead rabbit.

And not just that—Rory was absolutely covered in blood. It matted the fur around his muzzle, stained his chest, and had somehow even splattered across his back. He looked like he'd just walked off the set of a horror film.

Before I could process this grisly sight, Rory padded directly to me and dropped the mangled corpse at my feet with what could only be described as a proud flourish. He sat back on his haunches, tail sweeping enthusiastically across the forest floor, looking up at me with bright, expectant eyes.

I stumbled backward, nearly tripping over a root. "Jesus Christ! Get that thing away from me!"

Rory didn't move. The rabbit remained where it was, a bloody offering on the forest floor, while Rory's tail continued its happy rhythm.

"I'm serious! What the hell am I supposed to do with that?" I gestured wildly at the dead animal. "Take it to a taxidermist? Mount it on my wall?"

As I glared at him, I felt something that could only be described as laughter—a bubbling, effervescent amusement that radiated from him in waves. He was enjoying this. The little shit was enjoying my discomfort.

And here I'd been, minutes earlier, actually missing his company. Thinking profound thoughts about his absence. What had I been thinking? This was Rory Thorne—the same irritating man who'd been driving me mad for years, just in a different form. One that apparently thought bringing me bloody carcasses was appropriate.

Rory nudged the rabbit closer to my feet with his nose, his mental laughter growing stronger.

"No," I said firmly, backing up another step. "Absolutely not. And this is the last time I ever come with you to shift."

But even as I said it, I knew it was a lie. Because despite the blood, despite the dead rabbit, despite everything—there was something captivating about him like this. Wild and free and utterly himself. No pretense, no walls, just pure Rory.

He bounded around me in circles, still radiating that mental laughter, and I found myself fighting a smile. It was hard to stay properly annoyed when faced with such obvious joy. Even if that joy came at my expense.

"Fine," I sighed, running a hand through my hair. "You've had your fun. Can we go back now? Before you decide to bring me an entire deer?"

Rory made a sound that was somewhere between a snort and a huff. As I watched him, resplendent in the moonlight, I couldn't help but wonder what it would be like sleeping beside him tonight. To lie next to the man who, just moments ago, had been this wild, magnificent creature. The man whose fur had been impossibly soft beneath my fingers. The man who'd looked at me with those bright, knowing eyes.

Imagining his human form lying next to me in the dark later, blond hair splayed out across the pillow as he inevitably hogged the blankets, something shifted inside me—a tectonic plate moving just enough to change the landscape. This wasn't just professional curiosity or reluctant tolerance. This was... *attraction*. To another man. To Rory Thorne, of all people.

The realisation stole my breath away, sent my head spinning. Somehow, I *was* attracted to Rory—to his wild spirit, to his annoying laugh, to the way he moved with such freedom whether on two legs or four.

And now I was about to share a bed with him, not to mention pretend to be in love with him in front of dozens of strangers, once we arrived in Scotland.

Bloody hell.

Fucking hell.

I was so completely, utterly screwed.

9

Theodore

Warmth. That was my first conscious sensation. Warmth and the soft rhythm of another person's breathing against my chest. My nose was buried in something soft that smelled like citrus and pine—Rory's hair. One of my arms was wrapped around his waist, my hand splayed across his bare thigh, thumb grazing his hipbone. His back was pressed firmly against my chest, his body fitting perfectly into the curve of mine.

I froze, suddenly wide awake.

What the bloody hell had happened to the Great Pillow Wall of China we'd constructed last night? The defensive barricade had been standing tall and proud when we'd gone to sleep, with me pointedly facing away from Rory, clinging to the furthest edge of the mattress like a man afraid of drowning.

Now the pillows lay scattered and defeated around us, as if they'd never stood a chance against whatever gravitational pull had drawn me across the bed and directly into Rory's personal space.

Thank fuck I'd worn an old T-shirt and tracksuit bottoms, so there was some semblance of barrier between us—Rory had declared he was sleeping in just his underwear last night, saying he was hot from the run. Wolf thing.

This was all absolute madness. Yesterday's realisation in the woodlands—that I was *attracted* to Rory fucking Thorne—had thrown my entire self-concept into disarray.

I wasn't sure what was more shocking: that I was attracted to another man, or that I was attracted to Rory Thorne, who openly referred to me as his "archnemesis."

Besides, I was *straight*. Always had been. Right?

Yet a tiny voice reminded me of moments I'd carefully filed away over the years: the lingering glance at my university roommate as he changed after rugby practice; the inexplicable tension whenever my sergeant at the academy stood too close during firearms training; the way I'd often avoided the locker room at the gym...

Perhaps "straight" had been a convenient simplification, a path of least resistance. My father had been the epitome of traditional masculinity—a dedicated cop who'd married young, raised a son, and died in the line of duty. Following his footsteps had been easier without added complications.

With so much of my life being an uphill battle—hiding my telepathy, facing racial prejudice in the force, caring for Ma after Dad died—perhaps I'd subconsciously decided not to overcomplicate things further. One less battle to fight. One less difference to explain.

Not that I'd even managed to date many women. My romantic history was embarrassingly sparse for a man in his thirties—a handful of short-lived relationships that fizzled out before they truly began, leaving nothing but awkward memories and unanswered text messages.

My telepathy made dating a minefield of unintentional intrusions—catching stray thoughts during intimate moments, hearing unspoken disappointments, sensing when someone was losing interest before they'd even admitted it to themselves. I'd never even gotten as far as considering telling a partner about my "gift." The mere thought of that conversation was enough to make me break out in a cold sweat. Far easier to keep relationships brief and superficial.

Loneliness had become so familiar I hardly noticed it anymore—just another constant, like the weight of my job, or the persistent hum of London traffic outside my window.

And yet here I was, wrapped around another person like my life depended on it, my body betraying years of careful distance in a single night of unconscious movement. Not just any person, either. Rory Thorne—infuriating, chaotic, wildly beautiful Rory—who'd somehow burrowed his way past defences I'd barely understood I'd built.

I needed to extract myself from this compromising position before he woke up and realised what I'd done.

I held my breath, listening to the steady rhythm of Rory's breathing. If I moved carefully—very, very carefully—I *might* be able to free myself before he woke up. Before he realised. Because I'd never live this down.

...look who's the octopus now, Teddy...I can't believe he's done this after being disgusted the other morning...I wish I could reach my phone...take a picture for evidence...

Due to the fact we were squished like sardines, Rory's thoughts easily filtered through my mental barriers. Not asleep, then. Not asleep at all.

The little shit was awake and fully aware of our current situation. And enjoying my discomfort. Again.

I kept my breathing deliberately slow and even, feigning sleep while my mind raced. Being this close to Rory made it impossible to maintain any level of barrier—his thoughts flowed into my consciousness like water through a sieve.

...he's still asleep. Perfect. Let him wake up and realise he's the one who can't keep his hands to himself...

Rory's smug satisfaction radiated through his thoughts...

Which then took an unexpected turn.

...god, he's so warm, though. Like a bloody furnace...

I felt him shift slightly, settling more comfortably against me, and his thoughts drifted in a new direction.

...his arm is so heavy. All muscle. How did I not know he was this fit? Wonder what the rest of him looks like. Always hides under those suits...

Christ. This was veering into dangerous territory. I should move, should break this connection, but that would mean admitting I'd been awake, listening to his private thoughts. And we still had days of this trip ahead of us.

...wonder how big his cock is. Surely as big as the rest of him. Feels pretty damn generous pressed against my back. Bet he'd fill my mouth perfectly. Thick and heavy on my tongue...

I fought to keep my breathing steady as Rory's thoughts became increasingly explicit.

...bet he tastes so good. God, I'd love a taste. Would he be gentle or would he grab my hair and take control?...

The vivid imagery flooding from Rory's mind made it increasingly difficult to maintain my charade of sleep. My body flushed from head to toe, and I focused on counting backward from one hundred, desperately trying to ignore both Rory's fantasies and my dick's traitorous response to them.

Because one wrong move now would make the rest of this trip unbearably awkward.

...wonder what he'd look like on his knees for me. Those intense eyes staring up through those sexy glasses, all that authority completely surrendered...

Rory's imagination spiralled, painting vivid flashes of mental pictures that flooded into my consciousness. Me on my knees, mouth stretched around his cock, him thrusting into my throat. Rory's waves of imagined pleasure shot straight to my own groin, and I clamped my lips shut to suppress a groan.

...his mouth would be so hot and wet around me. I'd grab his head with both hands, make him take all of me...

The vision continued to unfold in graphic detail, each image more explicit than the last. Rory had a fantastic imagination, I'd give him that.

...I'd finish all over his face, get my cum all over him, watch him with those glasses splattered...

It was no use. I couldn't control my body's reaction anymore. My cock hardened painfully against the thin fabric of my tracksuit bottoms, pressing unmistakably against Rory's lower back. Panic surged through me as I realised there was no hiding it—the evidence of my arousal was firmly wedged against him.

...bloody hell, is that his dick?! Jesus Christ, it IS massive...

To my horror, instead of pulling away, Rory deliberately pushed back against me, shuffling so that the crevice of his ass nestled my straining cock, the movement sending shockwaves through my entire body.

...shame he's straight. And that he hates me. I think he actually might be quite nice, as well. Maybe I should stop terrorising him...

His thoughts paused briefly before concluding:

...nah. That's boring...

Each tiny shift of Rory's body against mine sent fresh waves of agonizing pleasure through my groin. When he arched his back slightly—perhaps stretching in his pretend sleep—my cock throbbed painfully.

Christ, how long had it been? Eight months? A year? The dry spell had clearly affected my self-control because the pressure building at the base of my spine was unmistakable. I was genuinely at risk of coming in my briefs like a bloody teenager, just from this contact.

Rory wiggled his hips back against me. Even biting into the side of my cheek didn't stop my dick from pulsing, desperate to rut against him. My heart pounded a frantic rhythm as I realised I was dangerously close to the edge. If I didn't move now, there would be no hiding the evidence. The mortification would be complete.

Then Rory made a sound—a soft, breathy little noise in the back of his throat—half sigh, half moan.

That tiny sound broke me.

Without any plan, I quite violently shoved him away from me, leapt to my feet, and practically ran towards the bathroom.

"Morning, Detective Teddy Bear." Rory's voice was thick with sleep and smug satisfaction. "Didn't know you had it in you."

I slammed the bathroom door behind me, turning the lock with trembling fingers. Spinning the shower dial to its coldest setting, I yanked the water on full blast. The pipes groaned in protest, but water soon cascaded down in what I hoped would be an icy deluge.

I stripped off my clothes with desperate haste, then stepped under the spray, bracing for the shock of cold.

But even as icy water pelted my skin, raising goosebumps across my chest and shoulders, my cock remained stubbornly, painfully erect. It jutted out from my body, proudly swollen, twitching with each pulse of my heartbeat, completely unmoved by the freezing temperature. If anything, the contrast of cold water against my burning skin only heightened every sensation.

Ice cannot quench what fire has lit,
Cannot calm what chaos has been writ.

"Fuck it," I muttered, taking myself in hand.

Do not think of Rory, lying in that bed, I commanded myself. *Do not think of his warm, firm body under your hands, the shape of his mouth, or those porn-worthy images he projected, or—*

Oh, who was I kidding?

My hand moved faster, grip tightening as my imagination took over, fuelled by Rory's earlier fantasies still seared into my brain. The cold spray faded from my awareness as heat built inside me, a gathering storm beneath my skin.

For some inexplicable reason, my mind fixated on Rory's fantasy where I was on my knees before him, looking up as he loomed over me. His fingers pawing roughly at my hair, controlling me as he used my mouth at a punishing pace. I'd never before fantasised about a dick in my mouth, but now I wondered desperately about the feel of it on my tongue. What it would be like to surrender completely, all control abandoned as Rory took what he wanted from me.

He'd be so loud about it—of course he would be loud, it was Rory—making those obscene noises in the back of his throat. The same breathy sound he'd made against me in bed that had nearly undone me completely.

I stroked myself with bruising intensity, the pleasure building to an almost unbearable peak. My breath came in harsh pants that echoed off the tile walls.

Then I heard something—a faint, rhythmic sound from beyond the bathroom door. Was it possible? Was Rory touching himself right now, lying on that bed where I'd left him?

I could find out. I could lower my barriers, reach out with my mind, try to hear his thoughts from here…

It was an invasion of privacy. Unethical. Wrong.

I did it anyway.

His thoughts crashed into mine like a tidal wave—fragmented, chaotic, and burning with desire.

…so fucking hot…want him so much…Christ, his cock…want to suck it so bad…need to…

Rory's euphoria flooded through our connection, his climax building in tandem with mine. The double sensation—my own physical pleasure layered with the echo of his—was overwhelming.

When his orgasm hit, the force of it reverberated through our mental link, pushing me over the edge. I came with shocking intensity, streams of release pulsing from me as waves of pleasure crashed through my body. I had to shove my knuckles into my mouth to muffle my cry of ecstasy.

I rested my forehead against the cold tiles, my chest heaving. What the actual fuck had just happened?

My blood pounded in my ears as the connection faded, leaving me alone with the aftermath of the most powerful orgasm I'd ever experienced—and the damning knowledge that I'd just crossed a line that could never be uncrossed.

I staggered to the sink and gripped the porcelain, forcing myself to look in the mirror. The man staring back at me looked wrecked—eyes wide and pupils still dilated, a flush burning across my cheekbones. The water from the shower had made the hint of silver at my temples more pronounced against the tight coils. I ran a shaking hand over the fade at the sides, a futile attempt to restore some semblance of control.

"Get a grip, Theo," I muttered to my reflection. "This is Rory fucking Thorne we're talking about." The thorn in my side. The same infuriating shifter who challenged every decision I made. The same person whose mind I'd just invaded in the most intimate way possible.

I dragged both hands down my face. Then I marched back outside dressed only in a towel, determined to pretend nothing had happened. The cool morning air hit my damp skin immediately—the window was wide open, curtains billowing in the breeze.

Rory had stripped the bed completely. The sheets and pillowcases were bundled in his arms as he turned to face me.

"Thought I'd help the cleaners," he said, gesturing to the bare mattress with his chin. His hair was tousled, cheeks flushed.

"Right." My voice came out embarrassingly hoarse. I cleared my throat, adjusting my towel.

Rory looked at me, his eyes tracking a water droplet as it slid down my chest. With every ounce of my energy, I maintained my mental barrier. Something flickered across his face before his usual mask of irreverence slipped back into place.

"I still can't believe you manhandled me like that this morning," he said, tossing the bundle of bedding onto the floor. "I think I've got bruises from your death grip. Do you always cuddle your prisoners that aggressively, Detective?"

I didn't respond. My pulse hammered a desperate rhythm—*be normal, be normal, be normal*—while my tongue lay frozen. Each heartbeat only stretched the crackling tension tighter.

"I mean, if you wanted to cuddle, you only had to ask," Rory continued, his voice taking on a nervous, rapid-fire quality. "Though I should warn you, I charge extra for spooning. Consider last night a free trial. Method acting for later, I suppose? Getting into character for our star-crossed lovers routine?"

Stomach churning, I gathered my clothes and retreated back toward the bathroom without meeting his gaze. There was no way I could have Rory's eyes on me right now—not when the memory of what I'd done was still so fresh, the awkward confusion still churning in my gut.

"I'll just get changed in here," I managed, already closing the door between us.

Back in the bathroom, I eyed the tiny window above the toilet, measuring it against my shoulders. It was barely wider than a shoebox. Still, I found myself genuinely calculating whether I could squeeze through the narrow opening. If I exhaled completely, dislocated both shoulders, and possibly broke several ribs in the process... maybe?

The three-storey drop on the other side would be the cherry on top of this disaster sundae. I'd either break both legs or land in those thorny bushes I'd spotted yesterday.

At least it would solve my current predicament. Death by rosebush seemed marginally less painful than facing Rory after what had just happened.

I pressed my forehead against the cool glass, peering down at the concrete below. The drop looked even more lethal from this angle. Perfect. I could picture the report now: "Cause of death: acute embarrassment followed by gravity."

I turned away from the window with a silent curse. I had a possible homicide to solve, a case to close, and a professional reputation to salvage—if only I could remember how to look Rory in the eye without feeling the echo of his pleasure still reverberating through my mind.

10

Rory

The Scottish countryside was showing off, and I couldn't even properly enjoy it. The sunlight broke through the clouds in dramatic rays that would've made Kit grab his camera. Mountains rose majestically against the horizon, their peaks disappearing into wisps of cloud, and heather painted the hillsides in patches of purple. The occasional cluster of sheep dotted the landscape like tiny cotton balls scattered by a careless child.

My wolf senses were already heightening as we neared pack territory. The window, cracked open just an inch, brought a symphony of scents—the sharp tang of pine sap from the forests to our left, the sweet musk of heather warmed by sunlight, the earthy richness of peat bogs, and beneath it all, the faint mineral smell of granite that formed the bones of these mountains. Home smells that bypassed my human brain and spoke directly to my wolf, stirring memories I'd tried to bury.

Luckily, I was rather distracted—busy suffocating in the awkward silence that had settled between Maxwell and me since we'd left the B&B this morning.

My phone buzzed against my thigh.

Priya

Guess what?

Just caught Flynn trying to break into room 303 FOR THE THIRD TIME. Honestly, that man. He won't let it go.

Anyway, can you keep texting Kit to reassure him you're still alive? He's so stressed he's snapping at everyone. Even Felix.

Can do. And really???

Yes, really. Now poor Felix is traumatised and Kit is feeling awful even though he won't admit it. But anyway, how's it going?

This was followed by a stream of shifty eye emojis that made me instantly suspicious.

what?

What do you mean, what?

I stared at my phone. Priya was never this cryptic unless she was fishing for something specific.

how long until you arrive?

only a couple of hours now.

and you and Maxwell have survived this long in the car together without killing each other?

I glanced sideways at Maxwell, who was gripping the steering wheel like it might try to escape. His jaw was clenched tight enough to crack walnuts. I'd obviously really upset him with my teasing about the cuddling this morning.

The way he'd bolted from the bed made it clear how disturbed—disgusted, even—he was to have woken up wrapped around a practically naked me. And if he had any idea what I'd done in that bed while he was showering, he'd probably die. My cheeks burned at the memory of how hard I'd come. God, what kind of person wanks thinking about someone who can't stand them?

What made it even more annoying was how different things had been last night in the forest. When I'd shifted, Maxwell had suddenly smelled like ambrosia to my wolf—the intoxicating blend of cedar, rain-on-pavement, and that sharp black pepper and lemongrass scent altered my brain, and suddenly something inside me demanded to press against his legs. Maxwell hadn't seemed to mind at all. In fact, he'd stroked my fur with those long fingers of his, scratched behind my ears in ways that had made me melt. He'd even *smiled*. Smiled at *me*. And I'd loved it, leaning into his touch shamelessly like some overgrown puppy, even bringing him that rabbit as a gift. Which, in retrospect, might not have been my brightest idea. But still.

Then, earlier, I had to go and ruin it with my stupid mouth, making jokes about the cuddling. Now we were back to square one—worse than square one—with him acting like I was radioactive. Typical Rory behaviour, always bollocksing things up just when they finally started going well.

In a futile attempt to fix things, on the journey today, I'd been fighting to be my best, least-irritating self, which mainly involved completely shutting my mouth, to be honest. It didn't help that ever since last night, I was hyper-aware of his scent—the black pepper and lemongrass radiating seemingly from his pores made it impossible to focus on anything else. Every time he shifted in his seat, a fresh wave would hit me, and my wolf would stir restlessly beneath my skin. Distracting didn't even begin to cover it.

> we're sat in silence right now because i've pissed him off. think he hates me more than ever tbh

The three dots appeared and pulsed for an eternity.

> I wouldn't be so sure

> what?

Maxwell cleared his throat, making me jump, and for some reason, I frantically jabbed at my phone screen, turning it off.

"So. It's not long now," Maxwell said, his voice cutting through the silence. "You want to run me through some of who is likely to be there when we arrive? Things I should know, et cetera?"

"Yeah, of course," I replied, shoving my phone into my pocket.

It made sense that he'd want to know all about them, considering he was about to literally walk into the den of vipers with me in order to find Dev. The only issue was, I hated talking about my family. Like, properly hated it. The kind of hate that sits in your stomach like a rock and makes your throat close up.

Now I was an hour away from seeing them all again after all these years. The reality of it hit me like a punch to the chest, winding me. Suddenly, the car felt too small, the air too thin. My lungs couldn't seem to get enough oxygen, and my vision started to blur at the edges as nausea seeped through me.

My hands began to shake as I leaned forward to grip the dashboard, the mountains outside the window spinning sickeningly.

"Rory? What's wrong?" Maxwell's voice seemed to come from very far away.

"I—" My throat closed over, the words trapped like prisoners behind bars. My chest felt like it was being crushed by an invisible weight, heart hammering so hard I thought it might crack my ribs.

The car lurched suddenly, tyres crunching on gravel as Maxwell yanked the wheel to the left. We bumped and jolted down into a shallow ditch at the side of the road before the engine cut off.

"Take a deep breath," Maxwell said, his voice firm but gentle.

I hadn't even realised I wasn't breathing. The edges of my vision had started to darken. I dragged in a shaky inhale, the air burning my lungs like I'd swallowed fire.

I wanted to apologise, to make some joke about how pathetic I was being, but I didn't trust my voice. My mouth opened and closed uselessly, like a fish tossed onto dry land.

Maxwell's hand reached out, hovering uncertainly around my thigh without touching it. The awkward hesitation was like a knife to my gut. Christ, now he couldn't even bear to fucking touch—

His warm palm landed on my thigh, fingers curling around the muscle with surprising strength. The heat of his hand seeped through my jeans, anchoring me back to reality. His grip tightened, thumb pressing into the side of my leg in small, circular motions. It wasn't tentative or disgusted—it was solid, present, real.

And bloody hell, that hand was so close to where I'd imagined it this morning. My body flushed hot with the memory once again—how I'd stroked myself thinking of those long fingers wrapped around me instead, how I'd bitten my lip to keep from moaning his name when I came. The ghost of that bliss rippled through me before I quickly squashed it down.

"Are you okay?" Maxwell asked softly.

My chest loosened slightly. I focused on his warm, steady hand, and with each breath, the roaring in my ears quieted a little more.

"Just... give me a minute," I managed, leaning back against the head-rest and closing my eyes.

The car fell silent except for the sound of our breathing, which somehow had synchronized without either of us noticing. *In, out. In, out.* The weight of his palm against my leg remained constant, his thumb occasionally making small, reassuring circles.

"We don't have to do this, you know. We can still turn back."

I shook my head, forcing myself to take another deep breath. "No. We're not turning back now. Not after you've driven us all the way up here. Besides, I already told my uncle we'd be there. He's... actually the one I'm looking forward to seeing. Out of all of them. But I'm sorry. I know you didn't sign up for me to be having constant panic attacks the whole week," I tried to joke, peeling my eyes open.

Maxwell's expression softened, the early afternoon light catching in his eyes, turning them the warm amber of whisky in a crystal glass. "Considering what you're about to face, I'd be more concerned if you weren't anxious. Though it'll all be okay, Rory. We can leave at any time if it gets too much. But I'll be there to help you through it."

I shot Maxwell a look at the words. Suspiciously nice words. Oh god, had I managed to make him feel *sorry* for me? *Great work, Rory. He already thought you were a loser after you got drunk and cried about Dev, and now he thinks you're pathetic.*

At my expression, he quickly removed his hand from my thigh, sitting up straighter in his seat. The loss of his touch was immediate, like stepping from warm sunshine into shadow.

"As your colleague, of course," he added stiffly.

I couldn't help but laugh. "Look, you only have an hour to perfect your doting boyfriend act, Maxwell," I said, the familiar rhythm of our banter further helping to ground me.

"Don't remind me," he muttered.

"Keep driving," I said. "And I'll tell you about my family."

Maxwell looked like he was going to argue, but then turned on the ignition.

"My family isn't exactly what you'd call... functional," I said, staring out the passenger window as he pulled back onto the winding Highland road. "The Thorne Pack is old money, old traditions. Very old traditions."

Maxwell nodded, eyes fixed on the road. "Your father was the alpha?"

"Malcolm Thorne," I said, the name tasting bitter. "Shot by an armed officer three days after I left home. Mum rang to tell me. That was the last time we spoke. I didn't go to the funeral. If there was one—she said they couldn't even retrieve the body."

"I'm sorry," Maxwell said quietly.

I shrugged, feigning indifference. The thing about abusive fathers dying is that you're supposed to feel something definitive—grief or relief or closure. I felt none of those things. Just... hollow. "He wasn't exactly father of the year."

"And your mother?"

I laughed, the sound bitter and twisted. "Edina Thorne. She's the alpha now, which is actually progressive by their standards. Most Highland packs would've passed leadership to another male relative." Out of the window, the mountains grew more familiar with each passing mile. "She's... cold. Proper. All about appearances. The kind who'd rather die than have anyone think there was something wrong with her children."

Maxwell glanced at me briefly. "Like with your ADHD?"

"Like anything that didn't fit her perfect pack image." I fiddled with the seatbelt strap. "When the teachers suggested I needed assessment, she told them I just needed more discipline."

"And your mother knows I'm coming?" he asked, shifting slightly.

"Oh, definitely. Alex would have relayed everything I said, including that I was bringing my boyfriend." I shot Maxwell a sidelong glance. "She'll hate that you're human. She'll hate that you're a cop even more. The Thorne Pack doesn't exactly have warm feelings toward law enforcement."

"I figured we wouldn't be telling them I'm a Met detective anyway. Doesn't really go with the whole undercover thing."

"Good plan. Wolves and cops don't mix well."

"Yet we're such a convincing couple," Maxwell said dryly.

I snorted. "Just remember to look besotted. And try not to flinch when I touch you."

"I don't flinch when you touch me," he protested.

"Oh, really?"

I lifted my hand toward his face. Maxwell's eyes widened, tracking my approaching fingers like they were venomous snakes. He jerked away sharply.

"Ha! See?" I crowed, laughing at his reaction. "You almost dislocated your neck."

Maxwell scowled, eyes fixed firmly on the road ahead. "I'm driving."

Before he could protest further, I reached out again—quicker this time—and ruffled his perfectly styled hair. The short, tight coils sprang back immediately after my touch, as if defying my attempt to mess them up.

As my fingers brushed against his scalp, that same weird electric current I'd felt twice before sparked between us—warm, alive. A zing that travelled from my fingertips straight down my spine, settling somewhere deep inside me.

Maxwell sucked in a sharp breath, his whole body tensing.

I yanked my hand back, glaring at him to mask whatever my face or thoughts might have been revealing. "Why does that keep happening? You feel it too, right? Is it when you're trying to read my mind or something?"

"No," Maxwell said, his voice tight as he fixed his gaze on the road. "I've never experienced anything like that before." He reached up to touch his head where my fingers had been, his movements stiff and controlled. "It must be a wolf thing."

I barked out a laugh. "Oi, only I'm allowed to say something's a 'wolf thing,'" I said, making air quotes with my fingers. "That's like me saying your constant brooding is a 'telepathy thing.'"

Maxwell's lips twitched, almost forming a smile before he caught himself. "I don't brood."

"You're brooding right now!" I pointed at his furrowed brow. "Look at that face. That's the face of a man composing sad poetry in his head while it rains outside."

"I'm concentrating," he muttered, though his lips curved upward.

I leaned back in my seat, watching him from the corner of my eye. The static between us still lingered in my fingertips, like an echo of something I couldn't quite understand. Whatever it was, it definitely wasn't a "wolf thing" I'd ever experienced before.

But if Maxwell wanted to write it off as supernatural weirdness, that was fine by me.

All too soon, we crested a hill, and my stomach dropped.

"There it is," I said, pointing ahead to where the vast estate was finally coming into view in the valley below. Thorne Manor stood imposing against the landscape, grey stone walls rising from the mist.

"Jesus," Maxwell muttered.

"Welcome to my childhood home," I said, my voice hollow. "A beautiful prison with a spectacular view."

Maxwell fidgeted with his shirt collar, and I could practically feel the anxiety radiating off him. "So, if we're concealing my identity, what profession should I say I am? I could say I'm a... teacher? Accountant?"

I glanced over, surprised by his nervousness. Detective Inspector Theodore Maxwell, actually worried about something? I considered his question for a moment, watching the familiar landscape roll by.

"You could easily pass as an accountant," I teased, earning me a glare through those nerdy glasses I was growing rather fond of.

"Gee, thanks." He sighed, adjusting his grip on the wheel. "And what about... us? How did we meet?"

I stared at him blankly before realising what he meant. Right. The boyfriend cover story.

"Don't worry," I said, a slow grin spreading across my face. "I'll think up something fun on the spot."

The look of absolute horror that crossed Maxwell's face brightened my day.

"That's exactly what I'm afraid of."

As we descended toward the iron gates, I added, "I'm sorry in advance for any bullshit you have to put up with as my fake boyfriend. These guys are nothing like the city shifters. They're the sort that still believe humans are beneath them."

"Wonderful," Maxwell muttered. "Anything else?"

"Just try not to be alone with any of them," I said. "They can smell fear."

Maxwell shot me a look. "Are you trying to make me nervous?"

"Is it working?"

He didn't answer, just drove forward, toward the ghosts I'd been running from for five years.

The gates remained still, and for one delicious moment, I indulged in fantasy. They'd stay shut. We'd shrug, turn the car around, and head back to London. *Sorry, Dev, we tried!* Back to my normal life, away from this place and all its painful memories.

Then the gates began to creak open.

"Here we go," Maxwell murmured, putting the car into gear.

We drove through, the gates closing behind us with an ominous clang. The manor house wasn't immediately visible through the trees—we still had about half a mile of winding private road ahead.

"The whole estate is surrounded by this bloody wall," I explained, gesturing to the high stone barrier that ran alongside the road. "Nearly ten feet tall in places. The locals hate it."

"How big is the property?"

"About two thousand acres. The manor and gardens are at the center, then it's just miles of forest, hills, streams… perfect territory for wolves." I sighed. "Perfect place to hide."

Was Dev right here, within these very walls? The thought sent a chill through me. I'd asked Felix repeatedly to check over all of the location data we'd gathered from his phone pinging back to life for those few minutes, but apparently we couldn't obtain a more accurate estimate. It could have been here, or miles and miles away.

I stared out at the misty landscape, trying to make sense of it all for the millionth time. Why would Dev be up here, so close to my family's territory? Not on holiday, certainly. Dev was a city boy through and through. He'd complained incessantly about the lack of decent coffee when we'd visited Brighton for a weekend. The idea of him willingly venturing into the Scottish wilderness was absurd.

He didn't come willingly.

I knew it in my very core.

The road curved, and suddenly Thorne Manor appeared before us in all its gothic glory. Three storeys of weathered grey stone, mullioned windows, and a slate roof that seemed to touch the clouds. Gargoyles perched at the corners, their faces worn smooth by centuries of Highland rain.

Could Dev be locked within the depths of the manor's halls? Maybe even the basement, where I'd spent many a night myself?

Maxwell pulled into a small gravel parking area to the side of the house, the tyres crunching as we came to a stop. "Bloody hell," he whispered. "I can't quite process that you grew up here. Neither you nor Kit act like you came from this sort of money."

Before I could make a joke about stealing some crockery to fund buying a new car, movement caught my eye. The massive oak front door swung open, and several figures emerged onto the steps.

Shit. I'd hoped we might slip in unnoticed, maybe have a moment to prepare myself. No such luck.

Please not her, please not her, I silently begged, scanning the faces.

Relief washed through me. No sign of my mother. Instead, my uncle Alexander stood at the front, his short grey hair and beard neatly trimmed as always. Beside him was my cousin Isla, her bright ginger hair unmistakable even from this distance. There was also a man I didn't recognize—tall, dark-haired, probably in his forties.

As we watched, Alex turned to the stranger, exchanged a few words, and the man nodded before heading back inside.

"That's my uncle," I said, unbuckling my seatbelt with suddenly clumsy fingers. "And my cousin."

"Stay here," I hissed at Freddy, napping by my feet.

My hand was shaking so badly I had to stuff it into my pocket as I climbed out of the car. The distance between us and the manor steps seemed impossibly vast—each step forward was torture, the crunch of stones beneath our feet the only sound breaking the Highland silence. I couldn't remember how to walk normally. My shoulders hunched forward of their own accord, my free hand swinging awkwardly at my side. What did people usually even do with their arms?

Suddenly, Maxwell's warm fingers wrapped around mine, pulling my hand from my pocket. I let out a rush of air in surprise, turning to look at him in shock.

Right. The boyfriend act.

But this... this felt different. He was squeezing my hand tightly, his thumb rubbing soft, reassuring circles against the back of my hand. That wasn't pretend. That wasn't for show. That was... comfort.

I couldn't bring myself to look at him as my heart rate skyrocketed, the steady *thump thump* in my chest drowning out even the sound of our footsteps. With Maxwell's hand in mine any nerves about approaching my uncle faded away.

"Rory," Alex greeted calmly when we reached the steps, his familiar Scottish burr washing over me. His eyes flicked between us, clearly trying to take in Maxwell while maintaining his composure. All I'd mentioned in my email was that I'd be bringing my boyfriend.

I opened my mouth to respond, but nothing came out. Five years of silence, and now I couldn't even manage a simple hello.

Maxwell didn't let go of my hand as he extended his other toward my uncle. "Theodore," he said, leaving off his surname. "Thank you for having me."

"Aye, of course," said Alex smoothly. "You're most welcome." His eyes flicked to me as an amused smile crossed his face—because Maxwell wasn't going to be welcome here at all, and we both knew it.

"Rory," Isla stepped forward, her voice gentle. "It's nice to see you."

I stared at her, momentarily stunned. Gone was the gangly teenager I remembered. Now she stood tall and confident, her bright ginger hair framing a face that had lost all its childish roundness. No longer were we pups chasing each other around the estate, playing hide-and-seek in the forest. I'd heard through our very limited grapevine that she was studying medicine in Edinburgh—it was possible she was also here against her will this week.

"You too," I managed, my throat tight, then blurted out, "Where's everyone else?" desperate to fill any silence that threatened.

Alex cleared his throat. "I said it would be best for just us to greet you. We thought we'd show you to your room, help Bernard with your things."

Bernard? I was surprised he was still here. The head of household staff had been nearing retirement when I left five years ago, always grumbling about his aching knees while sneaking me extra biscuits when my mother wasn't looking.

Then the rest of Alex's words registered, and panic shot through me.

Your room.

Our room, in the house I'd lived in for so many painful years.

My feet felt rooted to the gravel as memories crashed over me like ice water. The grand entrance hall with its sweeping staircase where Father had once dragged me down by my ear. The formal dining room where I'd endured countless silent meals, every scrape of cutlery amplified in the strained quiet. The library where both Ma and Dad had lectured me for hours about my responsibilities to the pack while I fidgeted, unable to focus, earning his disappointment again and again.

And my old bedroom—the one place that should have been a sanctuary. Instead, it had been where I'd spent countless nights staring at the ceiling, listening to arguments about what to do with the broken wolf cub who couldn't sit still, couldn't follow instructions, couldn't be normal.

"Rory?" Maxwell's voice cut through the fog, his hand squeezing mine. "You alright?"

I blinked, realizing everyone was staring at me.

"We're staying in the house?" I blurted out.

Alex's expression softened slightly. "I've put you in the east wing. Away from..." He trailed off, but I knew what he meant. Away from my parents' rooms. Away from my old bedroom. Small mercies.

I nodded, unable to form words as I stared at the manor's façade. The stone seemed to loom larger with each passing second, the windows watching me like judging eyes.

"We don't have to stay here," Maxwell murmured, so quietly only I could hear. "We can find somewhere else. In the town, perhaps."

Yes, the town—some blessed distance.

A deep crevice split across Alex's forehead. "I dinnae think your mother—"

"What about Primrose Cottage, Dad?" Isla interrupted. "I overheard Samuel saying the roof was fixed now." She turned to us. "I'm not sure how clean it is, but if you're desperate..."

"Yes," I said immediately. "Perfect."

Alex sighed, then nodded. "Wait here."

He disappeared inside, leaving us lingering awkwardly on the doorstep. Was he talking to my mother, getting her approval? My skin prickled with unease. Was anyone watching us, from one of the numerous windows? If I still had my pack bonds, I'd be able to sense how many wolves were in the manor house. But I didn't. Only phantom pain where they'd once existed.

"Your home is beautiful," said Maxwell politely to Isla, and I had to suppress laughter at his efforts.

Isla shrugged, her eyes drifting to the manor's stone façade. "Not really my home anymore. And to be honest, I'm surprised you came back." Her gaze returned to me, curious and probing. "Everyone is."

I shifted my weight, and Maxwell's iron-clad grip increased its fervor.

"The email sounded like a summons," I said, trying to keep my voice light despite the heaviness inside me.

Isla nodded, though suspicion clouded her face. "And Kit?"

"He's rather sensibly staying home," I replied, unable to keep the bitterness from my voice. Lucky bastard, safe in London while I faced the wolves' den.

"And is it true you guys live together in London now?" The question held genuine curiosity—wondering how Kit and I had gone from despising each other to being roommates.

"Yeah," I said, forcing a grin. "City rental prices, right? Kit threatens to throw me out over my messiness every other month, but he loves me dearly."

Isla smiled, but it didn't quite reach her eyes. "I was sorry to hear he couldn't make it. I always liked Kit." She glanced toward the house, lowering her voice. "Mum did too."

The mention of Moira, her dead mother, caught me off guard. No one in the pack ever mentioned her casually. "Yeah, she was... she was kind to him."

"To both of you," Isla said, something unreadable flickering across her face. "She understood what it was like to feel different in the pack."

I shifted, unsure how to respond. The Moira I vaguely remembered had been distant. And in the years leading up to her death, she spent more and more time away from the pack. When Kit had told me, once I'd reached London, that it had been Moira who put him into contact with someone who helped him enter the black ops shifter unit, I'd been surprised. I'd wondered if my parents had found out, and that was the final nail in Moira's coffin.

Before I could formulate a response to Isla, Alex reappeared, wiggling a set of keys. I exhaled with relief, grateful for the interruption. One awkward conversation successfully dodged, approximately fifty more to go.

"Voila. All sorted." Alex tossed the keys in the air and caught them with a flourish.

Dragging me with him, Maxwell headed down the steps towards the car, clearly already eager to escape the joyous family reunion.

"Hold on," Alex called after him. "You'll need to leave the car here."

Maxwell turned, frowning. "Why?"

"We like to keep all vehicles by the manor house. The estate is essentially a wilderness reserve. No cars beyond this point."

Maxwell didn't look impressed. "Then how exactly are we supposed to get to this cottage?"

"Golf buggy," Alex said, gesturing toward a small green vehicle parked nearby. "We can load your bags on that."

Five minutes later, I had Freddy hidden in my pocket, then we all crammed into the tiny buggy with the luggage precariously balanced around us. Alex drove, with Isla squished beside him in the front, while Maxwell and I were wedged together in the back. Maxwell's hand was wrenched away from mine in the process, and now my palm felt cold, still tingling from the memory of his soft skin against mine.

The buggy bumped along a narrow path through the woods, jostling us with every rock and root. Maxwell's thigh pressed against mine with each turn, something he made no effort to stop.

"There's a dinner this evening," Alex shouted back over his shoulder, the wind carrying his words. "Eight o'clock. Your attendance is... suggested."

I barked a laugh. "Is it now? Who will be there?"

"Close family only."

Great. Still over a dozen wolves. Judging eyes. Bonds I used to have, now shattered.

Isla twisted in her seat. "Look, I don't want to be here either. We'll suffer through together, promise."

"We'll come," I said, because the whole point of this mission was to infiltrate and interrogate, not to hide away and cry about my childhood being a shitshow.

The buggy rounded a final bend, and Primrose Cottage appeared before us—a small stone building with a thatched roof and pink rosebuds climbing up its walls. It looked like something from a fairy tale, quaint and utterly disconnected from the imposing manor house.

As we climbed out and started unloading our bags, Isla smiled. "This will be nice for you. You can pretend you're just on a normal romantic getaway!"

I let out the loudest snort.

Then promptly remembered that was maybe *not* an appropriate reaction.

Quickly, I turned to Maxwell, capturing his arm and beaming up at him like he was my personal sun.

"Teddy here doesn't need a picturesque cottage to be romantic, do you, baby?"

Maxwell's eyes bulged for a second before he pulled his face into a grimace-smile that looked physically painful. Then his hand found the small of my back, and before I could process what was happening, he leaned in close. His lips brushed my ear as he murmured, "Careful there, Terrier."

Trust him to make my ridiculous code name sound like the hottest thing he'd ever whispered. And when he pulled back, the transformation on his face sent a jolt through my entire body. Gone was Theodore Maxwell, perpetually stern detective. In his place stood a man with eyes that sparkled with joy, a devastating smile that revealed perfect teeth—and bloody hell, were those *dimples*?

"Darling," he purred, his voice a warm caress I'd never heard before. "Why don't we get settled in? After all that time in the car, I'm rather looking forward to stretching my... legs."

My brain short-circuited. The suggestive tone, the raised eyebrow, the hand now tracing small circles on my lower back, the staring at me like I was a particularly delicious dessert...

Alex cleared his throat loudly, shifting his weight from foot to foot. "Right, well, we'll leave you two to... settle in."

"It was lovely meeting you both," Maxwell continued, his thumb now pressing into the sensitive spot just above my hip. I bit back a squeak as he pulled me against him. "Rory's told me so much about his family."

I pinched his side where my relatives couldn't see. His smile didn't falter, but I felt his fingers dig into my back in retaliation.

Isla's wide eyes darted between us, a small smile playing on her lips. "We'll see you at dinner, then. It'll be the usual over-the-top affair," she warned me.

"We'll be there," Maxwell assured them, his free hand coming up to brush an imaginary strand of hair from my face.

I leaned into Maxwell's touch before reaching up to straighten his collar, letting my fingers linger. For the act, of course.

As Alex and Isla climbed back into the buggy, Maxwell waved enthusiastically with one arm while the other remained firmly around my waist. He maintained his besotted expression until they disappeared around the bend in the path.

The moment they were out of sight, I expected him to drop his arm and jump away. Instead, he kept his grip firm, leaned down, and said low against my ear, "Your uncle was watching us like a hawk. Some of his thoughts... I had to make it convincing."

His breath was warm against my skin, and I fought back a shiver. When he finally released me and stepped back, I forced myself to take a deep breath to refocus myself.

"Didn't know you had it in you, Detective," I said, trying to sound casual while my heart stumbled over itself.

Maxwell's face settled back into its familiar stern lines, dimples vanishing like they'd never existed. "There's a lot you don't know about me, Thorne." He picked up his bag and headed toward the cottage door.

"Let's get inside and make a game plan for this dinner. You can start filling me in on the pack."

As I watched Maxwell unlock the cottage door, the reality of where we were—who we'd be facing in just a few hours—should have sent me spiralling into panic. But instead, a strange calm had settled over me.

It took me a moment to recognize it. Maxwell wasn't just tolerating this mission or doing his job. He was committing fully, putting himself between me and my family.

He was on my side.

Suitcase in hand, I followed him inside, my fingers absently tracing the spot on my forehead where his hand had brushed. The warmth of his touch lingered there like a shield.

The apprehension was still present—a low hum beneath my skin at the thought of facing my mother, the pack that had beaten me down and ultimately rejected me. But it was different now. Manageable. I wasn't walking into the lion's den alone.

"You were really good at that," I said suddenly.

Maxwell paused his inspection of the cottage's spacious reception. "Good at what?"

"The boyfriend act. You really sold it." I aimed for casual, but my voice came out oddly sincere.

He shrugged, not quite meeting my eyes. "Just doing my job."

"Well, you're good at your job, then. And... thanks. For being here."

Maxwell stilled, then gave a short nod. "We're partners on this. I've got your back, Thorne."

Partners. The word settled something inside me, unexpected and warm. Like finding solid ground after an eternity of treading water in the dark.

He shot me a piercing look through his glasses. "Just stop calling me Detective Dickface and we can call it even."

My face split into a grin. I looked directly at him, broadcasting loudly... *What about in my own head?*

"No."

Aww, but you love it, though.

"I really, really don't."

"Alright then, Teddy Bear," I said, blowing him a kiss before dashing past him to the stairs, not looking behind to see his reaction. Because I wanted to imagine a smile dancing across his lips.

11

Theodore

Have you arrived? Rory isn't answering his messages.

His phone is perpetually dead, so that could be why. Yes, we arrived an hour ago. We haven't seen the bulk of your family yet - that pleasure is tonight.

Three dots swirl, then stop. Swirl, then stop.

Finally:

I'm eternally in your debt for going with him. I can't tell you how much of a coward I feel.

No sweat. I'm enjoying the fresh country air.

Keep a close eye on him for me. I'm worried about how he's going to react, being back up there.

I stared at Kit's message, thumb hovering over the keyboard. *Keep a close eye on him.* The weight of that responsibility settled on my shoulders like a physical thing. A week ago, I would have laughed, but now, here I was, pretending to be Rory Thorne's boyfriend in the Scottish Highlands, my fingers itching to reassure his brother that it wasn't just him in Rory's corner.

The cottage was quaint—exposed beams and stone hearth. The living room had that unlived-in quality of a holiday rental, with generic landscapes on the walls.

I checked my watch, and my stomach knotted. Earlier, we'd sat down and Rory had started going through some of what he still knew about the key players of the Thorne Pack. Now, in forty-five minutes, I'd meet them at dinner. I'd faced murderers and monsters, but meeting Rory's estranged family made me uneasy. Perhaps because I knew how much it mattered to him, despite his cavalier attitude.

My phone buzzed. Mum's name flashed on the screen. I glanced at the ceiling—Rory was still showering upstairs. I was safe to take the call.

"Hey, Ma."

"Theodore! How are you, darling?" Her tone suggested she hadn't heard from me in months, not days.

"I'm all good, Ma. I know I said I'd call you when we arrived yesterday, but we actually had to stop over somewhere. We only got to Scotland today."

"Did my car get you there alright?"

"Yeah, smooth sailing. Thank you again."

A pause. "And how's George?"

My stomach lurched. I hadn't *explicitly* mentioned George's name when I'd asked to borrow her car, but she'd assumed, as he'd joined me on a few hiking trips before.

"Actually..." I started, not entirely sure what I was going to say. "I'm not up here with George."

A long silence, then... "Theodore James Maxwell! Are you telling me you're on some romantic getaway and you didn't tell your own mother?"

The accusation in her voice made me wince. But perhaps it was easier if I went along with this, then tell her it had fizzled out.

"Something like that."

She squeaked—an actual squeak of delight. "Tell me about her! What's she like?"

I found myself thinking of golden hair catching sunlight, of quick wit and infectious laughter. "They're... brilliant. Funny. Brave to the point of recklessness sometimes. Always says exactly what they're thinking."

"Oh, Theodore, I'm so pleased! You know I've been hoping you'd find someone special. Maybe I'll finally get those grandchildren I've been pestering you about."

The image slammed into me—Rory surrounded by two small children, running circles around him in some sun-drenched garden. The sound that escaped my throat was somewhere between a choke and a laugh.

The shower shut off upstairs.

"Listen, Ma, I've got to go—"

"Of course, of course! I won't bother you again. Just... call me when you're back in London, yeah? I'm so happy for you, love."

I fought to calm my racing heart as floorboards creaked above me.

"Hey, Teddy Bear," Rory called down. "I forgot my towel. It's in my luggage."

I sighed, but found myself rifling through his chaotically packed suitcase anyway, still sprawled across the living room. Freddy snapped his razor-sharp teeth at me, as if guarding Rory's toothbrush and underwear.

Upstairs, the bathroom door was closed, steam escaping through the gaps.

I knocked twice. "Delivery service."

The door cracked open just enough for Rory's damp face to appear, blonde hair darkened and plastered to his forehead. Cheeks flushed, a scattering of droplets shimmered in his eyelashes.

"My hero," he said, extending one bare arm.

I handed him the towel, but the door shifted slightly wider. My eyes betrayed me, dropping downward before I could stop them. I caught a glimpse of wet thigh, the sharp curve of his hip, before Rory deftly adjusted his position behind the door.

Our eyes met, and my face burned hotter than the steam billowing from the bathroom.

"Can I help you with something else, Detective?" His voice was teasing, but with an underlying tension.

I froze, standing there for an awkward moment, pulse hammering in my neck. Then I wordlessly pivoted and headed downstairs, my thoughts in disarray, wondering how I was going to make it through this entire evening without having a breakdown or my body betraying me.

When I heard him coming down, I turned to the window, feigning interest in the misty moor. The countryside stretched in watercolour washes of purple and green, but I wasn't seeing any of it. My peripheral vision was consumed by Rory's reflection—hair dripping, nothing but the towel knotted precariously at his waist.

I swallowed hard and pressed my forehead against the cool glass.

"Which jumper should I wear?" Rory's voice broke through my determined study of a rock formation.

Despite my better judgement, I turned. Beads of water traced paths down his shoulders, catching the light. "What? Why are you asking me?"

"Because... you're the only one here?"

Rory held up two jumpers—one a safe beige, the other a chunky cable knit in a rich, vibrant hue that caught my attention. It was the exact same impossible shade as his eyes—that mercurial blue-green that shifted like water, never settling on a single hue, defying description even to a man who collected words like treasures.

"That one," I said, nodding towards it before I could stop myself.

He tossed the beige one aside and reached for the chosen jumper. My gaze betrayed me, dropping to the lean expanse of his torso—the defined ridges of his abdomen tensing as he stretched, the contours of a landscape I had no right to map. A narrow trail of dark-gold hair descended from his navel, disappearing beneath the fluffy cotton that hung dangerously low on his hips.

I turned back to the window. Nature had never seemed so fascinating.

"Good choice," Rory said behind me. "Kit says it brings out my eyes."

I made a noncommittal sound, not trusting myself to speak. To tell him how much it intensified that changeable colour that reminded me of deep forest pools in summer, of stormy seas in winter, of everything wild and untamed that I shouldn't want but couldn't stop thinking about.

Thank fuck I was the telepath, and not him.

Though Rory wasn't blind. Or stupid.

"Though, isn't it a fancy dinner or something?" I smoothed down the front of my crisp white button-down, suddenly self-conscious. At least I was wearing dark jeans.

"I don't give a shit." Rory glanced up from wrestling with his phone charger, his eyes widening slightly. "You look nice, though."

I blinked, momentarily stunned into silence. Had I just received an actual, genuine compliment from Rory Thorne? The same man who'd spent the better part of eighteen months referring to me exclusively as "Detective Dickface"?

"But maybe..." Rory abandoned his charging cable and approached me slowly, as if I were a wild animal he was trying not to startle.

He reached for my arm, his fingers hovering near my wrist. I made no move to stop him. With surprising delicacy, Rory took hold of my cuff and began rolling the sleeve up my forearm, his movements deliberate and precise. Every brush of his fingertips against my skin sent ripples of awareness through me. He folded the fabric neatly, three turns that ended just below my elbow.

I extended my other arm without a word, watching as he repeated the process. Where his fingers grazed my skin, the static heat between us intensified, every tiny hair on my arm standing to attention.

"Much better," he murmured, stepping back to assess his handiwork.

Zap.

There it was again—that electrifying shock, jumping between us like a living thing. Our eyes snapped together, and I froze, waiting for him to laugh it off as a "wolf thing" again. But instead, his teeth sought his lip, worrying at the skin there, his gaze dropping momentarily to my rolled sleeves before darting away.

Well, if he didn't want to talk about it, I sure as hell wasn't going to mention it.

Twenty minutes later—after waiting for Rory's phone to charge to thirty percent, and then for him to say a rather extended goodbye to Freddy involving multiple kisses on his creepy little head—we finally left.

The evening air carried a bite as we walked towards the manor, the misty landscape swallowing the sun's fading light. Rory walked beside me, his steps slowing as we approached the main path. His earlier bravado seemed to have evaporated, replaced by a tightly wound tension.

"He hid it well," I said, breaking the silence. "But your uncle was very suspicious of me earlier."

Rory glanced sideways at me, his lips quirking up slightly. "Of course he was suspicious. They all will be. You're not pack." He shrugged. "But don't worry so much about Alex. He's not that close with my mother. He's the only nice one."

We followed the winding path through a copse of silver birch trees, their pale trunks ghostly in the fading light.

"Is he?"

"Honestly, Uncle Alex is... different. He's my mum's brother, Oxford-educated doctor. One of the few who ever left Scotland—most pack members are born, live, and die within a hundred miles of the estate. He was always the progressive voice in family arguments. Actually listened when I talked about wanting medication. Couldn't override my parents, but he tried. His dead wife, Moira, she was actually the same. Bit of a rebel by pack standards. She and Alex were the reasonable ones. When I came out, Alex was the only one who didn't look at me like I'd grown a second head. Mum and Dad went mental—not about the gay thing specifically, but about how it would 'complicate pack dynamics.' Alex told them that the pack needed to modernize with the rest of the world."

He kicked at a stone, sending it skittering ahead of us.

"Gatherings were the worst. Every time I let my impulses win, or I said something inappropriate, my parents would get this look—like I was deliberately trying to embarrass them. But Alex would always step in, make some joke to defuse the tension. He'd defend me when no one else would."

"So Isla's mum is dead?"

Rory scoffed. "Pack says she died in an accident about seven years ago, but there were always whispers that my father had something to do with it. She and my dad clashed constantly. She'd openly challenge him in front of everyone. It was horrible. When she died, we were told a young wolf from another pack had wandered onto our territory during a wolf moon, and they'd fought, and she'd lost. But then the rumours started. I'm not sure what Alex thinks. Maybe he was happier pretending. Being packless is the worst fate imaginable for most wolves. You lose your anchor, your support system. Without a pack, you feel... adrift. Purposeless."

"That's not how you feel though, right?" I asked him, eyeing him carefully.

He bit into his lip. "I have Kit. That's enough. Anyway, Isla was only thirteen when her mother died. She's studying at medical school now, in Edinburgh, I think. I wonder how much she even comes back here."

"How many wolves are in this pack?" I asked, suddenly apprehensive of how many teeth might snap at me tonight.

"Around thirty."

"*Thirty*?!" I couldn't stop the pounding of my heart. Perhaps I should have brought the silver bullets Kit had packed...

"Yeah, it's one of the biggest around here for sure. Everyone lives pretty spread out across the land, so it's not like you see everyone all the time. There's the main manor house—massive old stone thing that's been around for generations—and then cottages and smaller houses dotted around the estate."

"And... what do the humans in the area think about it all?"

"That we're—" He caught himself. "*They're* some new age cult thing. We used to joke about it ourselves, sometimes. But all us kids in the pack would sometimes get teased about it at school. Until they realised we were all stronger than them, with short tempers."

Abruptly, Rory stopped walking as a memory surfaced, so emotionally charged I saw it as if it were my own.

Rory, pinned against the brick wall of the primary school by a boy twice his size. Others circling, calling him "cult boy" and "freak." The panic rising in his chest, the wolf inside him desperate to break free, to fight back. Then Kit appearing like a guardian angel, yanking the bigger boy off him with strength no teenager should possess.

...*"Touch my brother again, and you'll regret it."*...

"Rory?"

...*that was before everything changed between us...before Kit left me...*

"Rory?" I repeated, I touched his arm, trying to pull him back to the present. "You okay?"

He blinked, shaking his head slightly. "Yeah. Sorry. Anyway..." He shuffled forwards, kicking the ground. "Out of everyone, we can count on Uncle Alex. Trust me on this."

"I'll form my own opinions, if you don't mind. You shouldn't trust anyone here completely."

"Oh, here we go with the detective routine." Rory rolled his eyes, though a smile played across his lips.

"I... am literally here as a detective, investigating a missing persons case."

Eventually, Thorne House loomed ahead, its windows already illuminated though the sun had only begun to set. The golden light spilled across the manicured lawn, creating long shadows that stretched toward us like grasping fingers.

Rory stopped abruptly, his gaze fixed on the house, shoulders drawing up tight. "It'll be the first time I've seen her since I snapped all my bonds," he said.

I almost asked who, before realising he was talking about his mother. The current alpha. The woman who'd mistreated—fuck that, *abused*—her son to the point he chose to leave everything he'd ever known behind to sleep rough in Glasgow.

Looking at his face—openly worried in a way I'd never seen before—a fierce protectiveness rose within me that had nothing to do with our pretense.

But I could *pretend* it did.

For the second time that day, I grabbed his hand, firmly interlacing our fingers, squeezing until Rory's forehead smoothed back out.

"I hope you're ready for this, Maxwell," Rory muttered as we approached the manor's entrance, his hand tightening around mine.

"Don't call me Maxwell," I found myself saying. "I'm not using my real last name. Plus, that would be a weird thing to do... call your boyfriend by his surname."

Why did I care quite so much? Everyone at the station called me Maxwell—even George, who I'd known since academy days, still called me Maxwell when we met for pints or hikes outside of work. The formality had become so normal I barely noticed it anymore.

The only person who ever called me Theo was my mother.

Rory blinked at me, his eyebrows rising slightly. "Okay, Teddy."

I groaned. "I was thinking more along the lines of Theo. You know, my name?"

"Teddy is such a cute pet name, though, don't you think?" He grinned at me, horizon-wide, and for a moment, I forgot to tell him no.

Because he was already dragging me through the large oak double doors, through to a marble-floored lobby within a grand entrance hall, its vaulted ceiling adorned with elaborate plasterwork. From somewhere to our right, the buzz of conversation flowed—multiple voices overlapping in animated discussion, punctuated by occasional laughter.

An older man with silver hair and impeccable posture appeared from a side door. His eyes widened fractionally as they landed on Rory.

"Master Rory," he said. "It's been quite some time."

"Bernard." Rory grinned at him. "This is my boyfriend, Theodore."

Bernard's gaze shifted to me, assessing. "Yes, we were told that you were bringing a... boyfriend." He blinked at me as if he couldn't believe his eyes. "Welcome to Thorne Manor, sir. May I take your coats?"

The moment Bernard turned away with them, Rory's hand shot out to grab mine again, the movement so swift and desperate I nearly laughed. His palm was clammy against mine, his fingers trembling slightly.

As we approached the source of the noise, waves of anxiety radiated from Rory. Surface thoughts leaked through my mental barriers despite my best efforts.

...they'll all be staring...

...should never have come...

...what if she...

Yet Rory marched determinedly, practically dragging me along.

I stopped abruptly, yanking on his arm. "Hold on a second." I caught his other hand, drawing him close. His wide eyes searched my face, panic swimming just beneath the surface. "Hey," I murmured. "Breathe."

Rory's gaze darted towards the noise, then back to me. "I am breathing!"

I squeezed his hands, where he wasn't quite able to hide his trembling. "You don't have to prove anything to them. You're here because you chose to be, not because you owe them anything."

His jaw tightened, but he nodded, some of that old stubborn fire flickering back into his expression. "Right. Fuck them if they don't like it."

"That's my Terrier," I said quietly, and was rewarded with the ghost of his usual grin.

We stepped into a spacious parlour dominated by antique furniture—leather armchairs, mahogany tables, and floor-to-ceiling bookshelves. Around a dozen people were scattered throughout the space, dressed smartly in brown overcheck woollen waistcoats or pantsuits. The moment we entered, a hush fell over the room. Every face turned in our direction, the pin-drop silence absolute.

I held very still, waiting for Rory's reaction, waiting for him to make some sort of sarcastic comment about the dramatic welcome, or break the tension with his usual easy laughter.

But nothing came, and the moment stretched painfully, Rory's hand gripping mine so tightly my fingers began to tingle.

Eventually, Alex cleared his throat. "Rory! Good to see you," he called out too loudly, moving towards us. His voice seemed to break the spell, and conversations gradually resumed around the room.

Rory's face was the very picture of misery, his usual animation completely gone.

Alex took a few steps towards us, but froze as another man materialised, nodding curtly at Rory before turning to me with an extended hand.

Yanking my own hand free from Rory's death grip was quite a feat.

"Tariq Fraser," he introduced, handshake firm and measured. "Second to Alpha Thorne."

Tariq was as tall as me, his salt-and-pepper beard meticulously trimmed against brown skin. I attempted to read his surface thoughts, but encountered nothing—a smooth, blank wall where the usual static of consciousness should have been.

"Theodore," I returned eventually, as Tariq pierced me with his gaze.

"What a pleasure," he replied with a snarlish smile that spoke volumes. "We so rarely have humans join us. Aside from our staff, of course."

I swallowed down a bubble of laughter that threatened to burst out of me. What a twat.

Beside me, Rory had gone rigid. His breathing had shifted—shallow, controlled, like someone trying very hard not to bolt.

"Rory," Tariq said, his tone carrying the weight of authority and disapproval. "You look... well."

"Fraser," Rory replied, his voice tight in a way I'd never heard before. His hands clenched at his sides.

A flash of memory burst through my telepathy, from Rory's panicked thoughts. Suddenly there was cold stone pressing against my back as I looked up at a younger Tariq towering above me, his voice booming: *"Discipline, boy. Your father expects better."* The sharp sting across my cheek, the burn of tears I refused to let fall.

The memory vanished as quickly as it had come, but judging by the way Rory seemed to shrink slightly under Tariq's gaze, those old wounds had left their mark.

It was already no wonder Rory had hightailed it out of this place and never looked back.

"Where is she?" Rory asked.

"She's coming. She'd have heard you arrive."

As if summoned by magic, the room once again quietened as a woman entered. I'd have recognised her as Edina Thorne by her nose and chin, so similar to Rory's, but I didn't need to make the connection myself—the entire room reacted to her presence.

One by one, the pack members sank to their knees, faces bowed to the floor. Only Rory and I remained standing. I looked around in bafflement, feeling indeed like I'd stumbled into a cult, like Rory had said earlier. My gaze shot to him—he remained stoic, though he didn't seem surprised by this bizarre display of subservience.

"Rise," Edina commanded, her voice carrying effortlessly across the room without being raised.

The pack members stood in unison, the synchronicity of their movement unsettling. I couldn't help but be surprised by the diversity of the pack. People of various ethnicities mingled throughout the space—not the homogeneous group of white Highlanders I'd perhaps subconsciously expected. Hopefully, that meant I wouldn't face racism on top of displeasure that Rory had brought home a human male as his boyfriend.

Dressed all in black, Edina moved towards us with predatory grace. I stared into her eyes, momentarily afraid I'd see Rory's mercurial blue-green gaze reflected back at me. Relief washed through me when I found them to be a pale, icy blue instead—beautiful but cold, lacking the warmth and mischief that animated her son's.

"Detective Inspector Theodore Maxwell," she said, extending her hand.

My blood froze. Beside me, Rory inhaled sharply. How did she know my full name and title? When Rory had emailed Alex to confirm our attendance, he'd only mentioned bringing his new boyfriend.

I accepted her handshake, her skin cool and dry against mine. As our palms connected, I reached out with my telepathy, trying to catch even a whisper of her surface thoughts.

Nothing. Only a blank wall where consciousness should have been.

My mind reeled, a sudden wave of dizziness washing over me. How the hell did she know who I was? Acid churned in my stomach as possibilities raced through my mind. Five minutes into the mission, and my identity was already completely compromised. Was Killigrew Street exposed? Was Rory in danger?

I forced my expression to remain neutral, tamping down the rising panic with practiced control.

"You must be Edina. Thank you for having me here."

Her smile was all teeth. "My pleasure. I do hope you'll find our little gathering... educational," Edina continued, scrutinising my face. "It's so rare we have someone of your... professional standing join us."

All of a sudden, my lungs constricted as the room pressed in around me. The collective gaze of the pack members felt heavier with each passing second.

I needed a moment to think, to process what the hell was happening and how badly compromised we were.

I just needed a minute. Just one bloody minute to get my head together.

Across the room, I spotted a crystal decanter and glasses on a side table. An escape route.

"Let me grab us some water," I said, squeezing Rory's hand once before releasing it.

I didn't wait for his response, moving deliberately through the crowd, fighting the urge to run. My hands trembled slightly as I reached for the decanter, pouring water into two crystal tumblers.

Cold sweat prickled across my forehead. Did Edina already know we were here looking for Dev? Had she warned her entire pack about my telepathy?

I reached out tentatively with my mind, probing the thoughts of nearby wolves. Just like with Edina and Tariq, I encountered nothing but blank nothingness.

Taking a steadying breath, I turned back toward the room, glasses in hand. This time, I deliberately made eye contact with each pack member I passed. Their smiles were polite, even welcoming, but their eyes told a different story—cold assessment, thinly veiled disgust. They knew. They all knew what I was.

My skin prickled uncomfortably, every instinct screaming danger. The sensation of being an unwelcome intruder intensified with each step, the weight of their collective disdain pressing against me. I'd barely told a soul in my life about my gift, and this was why.

I handed Rory his water, noting how his face fell as he glanced down at the clear liquid.

...thanks for abandoning me and leaving me alone with her...plus I need something ten times stronger than this...

The familiar irritation in his mental voice was almost comforting amidst the sea of blank minds surrounding us.

"Will ye be running with us this evening, Rory?" Edina asked, addressing him only, her voice carrying the weight of command.

I expected Rory to immediately decline. Instead, confliction crossed his face, his eyebrows drawing together. Did he think it might somehow help our investigation? Or was he simply afraid to refuse his mother directly?

Before he could answer, someone tapped Edina on the shoulder, drawing her attention away. I seized the opportunity, grabbing Rory's elbow and steering him toward a quieter corner of the room, hoping the ambient noise of conversation would mask our words.

I felt dozens of eyes following us—the spectacle of the runaway wolf and his telepathic detective boyfriend providing the evening's entertainment. We were the main attraction in this twisted circus, and I hated every second of it.

I leaned in close to Rory's ear, as if we were sharing an intimate moment. His hair tickled my nose.

"Your mother somehow knows I'm a telepath," I whispered, my lips nearly brushing his earlobe. "They all do. They're guarding their thoughts when they're near me, or when I look their way."

Rory pulled back slightly, his eyes widening with interest rather than alarm. "You can do that?" he asked, sounding excited, like I'd just revealed some fascinating new superpower rather than a critical security breach.

"With a conscious, constant effort, yes," I replied, struggling to keep the exasperation from my voice. "It requires focus and mental discipline."

Rory's face broke into a grin. "Nah then. Pass. Sounds hard."

I rolled my eyes to the heavens above. "But this is a serious security breach. How the hell do they know who I am?"

"I don't know," he said. "She has a deep well of resources. But Kit has always suspected she's had tabs on us this whole time. It makes sense to have had us watched even closer after she sent the invite."

"Tabs? This is more than *tabs*, Rory. This makes no sense. It's impossible for her to know."

My thoughts raced, searching for any explanation. Before this evening, I'd only met Alex and Isla. Was it possible one of them possessed some kind of telepathic detection ability? Apparently shifters could tell when a human was Gifted, but not usually anything more specific than that, as far as I was aware.

Unless...

A cold feeling settled in my stomach. What if there was a file on me somewhere? Something that documented my telepathy. Some list, unknown even to Killigrew Street, and White? White had found me because she knew my father. Who knew how many others knew about him? If he had been documented somewhere, then it was entirely possible I'd inherited more than just his telepathy. I'd inherited his place on someone's watchlist.

The thought that someone might have been tracking me my entire life, even before I knew what I was, chilled me to the bone.

"Ah, fuck," Rory hissed, distracting me. "There he is."

I shifted slightly so I could see who he meant out of the corner of my eye. A dark-haired man in his late twenties stood by the fireplace, meticulously dressed in what looked like a bespoke suit, nursing a tumbler of amber liquid. A pale scar bisected his left eyebrow, giving his already severe features an even more intimidating edge.

The man's gaze found Rory's across the room, and his lip curled into what could generously be called a smirk.

"Well, he looks like a good time," I muttered.

"That's Callum Reid," Rory said through gritted teeth. "Complete tosser. We've hated each other since we were kids. He was an orphan the pack took in. Immediately jealous of me and Kit for being the alpha's sons."

Callum raised his glass in a mock toast towards us, the gesture dripping with condescension.

"Right," Rory said, jaw set with determination. "Fuck this."

Before I could stop him, he grabbed my hand and marched us directly towards the fireplace. I had no choice but to follow, wondering what fresh hell I was about to witness.

"Rory," Callum said, taking a deliberate sip of his drink. "Back from the dead, are we? And with... *company*." His eyes raked over me with obvious disdain. "And there I was thinking we'd never see you again, after your grand exit. After you told us so vehemently that you don't belong here."

To Rory's credit, he didn't flinch. "Oh, I don't," he said merrily. "We just fancied a holiday, didn't we, Teddy?"

He squeezed my hand so tightly I could have sworn my bones crunched.

"Yes. It's so interesting to see where Rory grew up," I said, causing Callum's eyes to narrow at me.

"Ah, but has he told you what he was like as a child?" Callum asked me with a horrible smile. "Our little Rory here was quite the handful, weren't you?"

Rory's grip on my hand tightened impossibly further, but his smile never wavered. "Something like that."

Callum swirled his drink. "The tantrums, the defiance, the complete inability to follow simple instructions. It was quite entertaining for the rest of us." He turned to me with false sympathy. "I hope for your sake he's finally grown up."

Every muscle in my body coiled tight. It took every inch of my self-restraint not to punch him in his smug face. "Rory's told me all about his time here," I said, my voice carefully level. "Including the people who made it difficult."

Callum's eyebrows shot up in mock surprise. "Difficult? We were the ones who had to deal with him." He grinned wickedly, addressing me directly to ask, "Tell me, does he still struggle with authority? Or have you managed to house-train him?"

The blood roared in my ears. I'd arrested actual criminals who showed more respect for basic human dignity than this bastard.

"Callum," Rory said, his voice dangerously quiet.

"What? I'm just sharing fond memories with your... boyfriend."

I opened my mouth, ready to tear strips off this sanctimonious prick, but Alex's voice boomed across the room before I could speak.

"Callum! Come here a moment, would you?"

Alex's gaze flicked between us and Callum, who for a moment seemed like he may not move. Then, with visible reluctance, he straightened his jacket and walked away.

"Well, he was a piece of work," I muttered.

"Told you," Rory said, but his usual spark was dimmed, shoulders curved inward.

"Did I see you just deliberately enter a conversation with Callum?" a low voice said behind us.

I turned to find Alexander's daughter, Isla, with her bright ginger hair.

"Isla!" Rory exclaimed with genuine warmth.

They embraced briefly, and I caught a flash of her thoughts—

...still can't believe he actually came back...

Had Isla not been instructed to control her mind? Or perhaps, she didn't care to?

"He was glaring at us from across the room," Rory said.

"Maybe he was wondering how you managed to bag someone so hot." She glanced at me with a half smirk. "Or was plotting your death," she said cheerily. "Probably a mix of both. He's been boasting for years about how you'd never dare show your face here again."

"What do you mean, bag someone so hot?" Rory said, with a pretend scowl on his face. "If anyone, Teddy is the one punching up."

"Dream on," I said, earning me an elbow to the stomach.

"Anyway, how is our dear Callum these days?" Rory asked, voice dripping with sarcasm. "Still licking Mother's boots?"

"From what I hear, worse than ever," Isla rolled her eyes. "He's practically her shadow now. Reports everything back to her. Every conversation, every slight, every perceived challenge to her authority. It's pathetic."

I sneaked a glance at Callum. He was pretending to listen to Alex, but his gaze was now fixed on Isla with an intensity that bordered on uncomfortable.

"Also..." Isla said, her voice dropping to a disgusted whisper. "Three times since I moved to Edinburgh Callum has 'accidentally' run into me. It's ridiculous."

"What do you mean?" Rory asked. "Has he got a thing for you or something?"

"Thing?" Isla scoffed. "More like an obsession. Last Christmas he got drunk and cornered me in the library with mistletoe."

Rory sniggered. "Sorry. Poor you. God, I'm glad to have one friend here."

Isla's expression shifted. "You know," she said very quietly. "I've really missed you these past five years."

Rory's face softened immediately. "Isla—"

"No, I mean it," she continued, her voice barely above a whisper. "I barely come back here anymore. Maybe twice a year, if that. Christmas and Midsummer, and even then only because Dad guilts me into it. I hate it here. The constant politics, the way everyone watches everyone else, waiting for someone to step out of line. The way they all bow to Edina like she's some sort of goddess. The way people *still* like to gossip about Mum's death even though it was seven years ago."

Rory reached out and squeezed her hand. "I'm sorry. I should have stayed in touch better. I just... I couldn't bear any connection to this place."

"Don't apologise," Isla said firmly. "You were brave to leave. Braver than I've ever been. You were the smart one," she said, looking directly at Rory. "Getting out when you did. Making your own life."

"Sorry to interrupt," I said gently. "But Isla, Edina knew my full name, and title. Even though we never told a soul. Do you know how?"

Green eyes widened. "Well, she wouldn't have let you through the gate if she didn't know who you were." She cocked her head. "Who are you?"

Before I could respond, the sharp sound of glasses clinking cut through the room. A hush fell immediately.

"Dinner is served," a voice announced from the doorway.

We followed the procession through to another grand room, dominated by a long table that must have seated more than twenty, though not every place was set. Relief washed through me when Alexander and Isla took seats vaguely opposite us.

An elderly woman with elegant grey braids wrapped in colourful fabric settled beside Alexander, introducing herself as Nessa Okonkwo. Her eyes lingered on me with unmistakable curiosity.

"Theodore Maxwell," I replied, offering my hand.

"We so rarely entertain humans at our table. Especially Detective Inspectors."

She said my title like it was a joke that amused her. I gritted my teeth. These people were determined to make me feel as uncomfortable as possible, and it was working.

Throughout the first course—a blood-rare venison carpaccio that turned my stomach—my telepathy reached out tentatively. Wisps of *something* floated from the nearest wolves before their minds snapped shut, sensing the intrusion. Their sustained mental defence impressed me.

Alexander's thoughts remained open, whether by choice or ignorance of my abilities. Nothing juicy filtered through—just concerns about rearranged work meetings and hopes of escaping the pack run later.

I still couldn't believe Rory hadn't flat-out refused his mother's request. Hopefully he understood that he wouldn't be leaving my sight at any point, especially not to run off into the wilderness with the family that broke him.

The second course arrived—more meat, this time a barely seared rack of lamb. I eyed my fork on the way to my mouth. Was this even safe for me to eat? Or even, could the food be poisoned?

I pushed the lamb around my plate, trying to locate anything green. "Do all wolves have something against vegetables?" I joked, attempting to lighten the atmosphere. "Or is this just Scottish cuisine?"

Nessa's laughter cut through the tension. "Our diet does tend toward protein, Detective. Especially before a run." Her dark eyes twinkled with amusement. "Some of the game tonight is fresh meat that we caught on a recent hunt."

"In the estate?"

"And the general Highlands." Her smile tightened almost impercep-tibly. "We do leave our prison. For short periods."

The word "prison" hung in the air between us. Was she trying to test me? I kept my expression neutral, maintaining eye contact with her as I took another tiny bite of the bloody lamb.

My gaze flicked to Rory beside me, radiating misery. His leg tapped an anxious beat until his palm slammed against it, stilling it abruptly.

How would I survive a whole week up here? The only way to end this torment was to get the information we'd come for—namely, the whereabouts of Devraj Bassi.

I'd never felt so out of my depth. My ordered world I navigated daily—the one where my badge carried weight and my telepathy gave me an edge—had evaporated the moment we crossed the threshold of Thorne Manor. Here, I was just prey among predators, the lone human in a sea of wolves with gleaming teeth and ancient grudges.

The familiar confidence that carried me through homicide scenes and interrogation rooms had abandoned me completely. My training meant nothing here. What good was police procedure against pack law? What use would I be fighting creatures who could tear me apart in seconds?

Every instinct screamed that we should leave immediately. This wasn't just uncomfortable—this felt dangerous. I could call Kit, force him to talk some sense into his brother. We could be back in London by morning.

"Teddy?" Rory's elbow dug into my ribs, jarring me from my spiralling thoughts. "Alex is trying to talk to you."

I blinked, forcing my attention back to the table. Alex was watching me expectantly.

"Sorry," I managed, plastering what I hoped was a convincing smile across my face while my heart tried to escape my rib cage. "Miles away."

"I hear you're a detective in London," Alex said, his Scottish accent pronounced on the city name.

Everyone has heard that, I almost spat at him. They probably knew my shoe size and blood type too.

"That's correct."

"And how did you two meet?" Alex pressed, glancing between us with undisguised curiosity.

Before I could formulate a response, Rory piped up beside me, that trademark mischievous glint in his eye. "Let's just say it involved handcuffs."

I laughed too loudly, the sound brittle and forced. "Oh, I do love his sense of humour," I said, squeezing Rory's forearm with barely disguised warning. "I'm afraid we actually met in a coffee shop."

...boring...

Rory's dismissive thought floated into my mind, clear as a bell, with an edge of challenge to it.

"The nicest little independent coffee shop," I said, letting my eyes linger on Rory's face. Something in me decided to throw caution to the wind—perhaps it was the absurdity of our situation, or maybe I just wanted to see Rory squirm.

"This little place with black and white striped cups," I continued, watching recognition dawn in Rory's eyes. "I used to go almost an hour out of my way each day just for the chance to bump into him."

Beside me, Rory completely stilled. Even his thoughts, normally a constant barrage against my mind, had fallen silent.

"I saw him there every day for months before I worked up the courage to talk to him," I continued, warming to my fabrication. "He'd always order these ridiculous concoctions—caramel this, extra whip that—while I stuck to plain black coffee."

Rory's mouth twitched as he clearly had to fight his instinct to correct me— in Killigrew Street meetings he always took his coffee black, like me, and mocked Felix for his cavity-inducing drink orders.

Alexander and Isla watched us with undisguised interest, clearly enjoying these romantic revelations.

"And even then, when I finally spoke to him, I pretended my phone had died and I needed to borrow his charger, rather than ask him out directly." I shook my head, letting out a self-deprecating laugh. "Can you believe that? Me, a detective who interrogates hardened criminals for a living, completely tongue-tied by Rory."

"I made him wait three more visits before I gave him my number," Rory interjected. "He looked so sad, I eventually took pity on him, and asked him if he enjoyed activities other than staring at me in coffee shops."

I reached for Rory's hand, which lay motionless on the table. "I couldn't bring myself to ask. I thought for sure he'd say no. That someone like him—funny, vibrant, full of life—wouldn't look twice at someone like me."

Rory remained frozen, his eyes fixed on me with an odd expression. For once in our acquaintance, I'd managed to render him completely speechless. No quip, no deflection, no rapid-fire commentary.

Isla made an "awww" noise, clasping her hands together. "That's adorable."

Rory's gaze burned into the side of my face. The room seemed to shrink around us, the other dinner guests fading into background noise.

"What do you mean?" Rory finally asked.

I turned to meet his eyes, finding myself suddenly trapped in their unfathomable blue-green depths. The lie had started as a performance, but something in his expression made the words feel weighted with unexpected truth.

"Exactly what I said," I replied, silky soft. "I couldn't process the idea of someone like you finding me attractive."

"Right." Rory snorted, but the sound lacked his usual confidence. His fingers twitched ever so slightly against mine, a subtle tremor that betrayed the storm beneath his carefully composed expression.

"It's true," I continued, squeezing his hand, lifting it off the table for effect. "I thank my lucky stars every night that I met you."

The words hung between us, fragile and dangerous. Something shifted in Rory's expression—a flicker of confusion, of vulnerability. His usual armor of sarcasm and bravado cracked just enough for me to glimpse what lay beneath.

And then I felt it—waves of sadness suddenly radiating from him, so potent they nearly took my breath away.

...nice fantasy...

The thought slipped through, crystal clear and achingly melancholic. It wasn't embarrassment or discomfort at our charade—it was genuine sorrow. I couldn't stand the desolation seeping out of him. Before I could think better of it, I found myself leaning closer, pressing a kiss to his temple.

His hair, soft against my lips, carried the clean scent of his shampoo. I lingered there a heartbeat too long, my own chest tightening with an emotion that felt eerily similar to what I was experiencing second-hand from him.

I wanted to tell him that someday, he would be loved just as fiercely as he deserved to be. That the right person would see him—truly see him—beyond the chaos and bravado. That someone would cherish every part of him, from his mischievous smile to his boundless energy to the vulnerability he tried so desperately to hide.

But then, the thought of another man's lips pressed to his messy hair sent a vicious snap of jealousy through me, and I interlaced our fingers more forcefully. The possessiveness startled me—this sudden, primal urge to stake a claim on this person who drove me mad on a daily basis.

Irrational.

Ridiculous.

Yet, undeniable.

Rory drew his brows together, bewilderment seeping through our connection. His confusion brushed against my consciousness like fingertips against skin, only heightening my own disorientation at whatever was happening between us. His eyes searched mine, seeking answers I didn't possess.

You and me both.

"That's so lovely," Isla said, breaking the moment with genuine warmth. "I'm so glad you're happy in London, Rory."

Her sincere comment earned her several sidelong glances from the other wolves, including her father, followed by some low rumblings.

A sharp, ringing sound cut through the dining room. Every head turned toward the head of the table, where Edina Thorne sat like a queen on her throne, Callum and Tariq on either side of her.

Edina rose slowly, her movement deliberate and graceful. The room fell into immediate silence.

"This evening is special," she began, her voice carrying effortlessly across the table. "Tonight marks the beginning of our run-up to the spring equinox, when our pack will welcome many others from across Scotland to our ancestral lands."

Her gaze swept the table before landing, with pointed deliberation, on Rory.

"And what a pleasure it is to have old friends join us for the occasion, eh?"

The word "friends" hung in the air. My hand squeezed Rory's thigh beneath the table, anticipating an outburst that never came. Instead, he remained perfectly still, his face a careful mask.

"The equinox represents balance," Edina continued. "A time when light and dark exist in perfect harmony. Perhaps it is also time for us to find such balance—to heal old wounds and forge new paths forward together."

A murmured ripple of assent shot through the wolves, and Edina smiled at them all, before returning to her seat.

The rest of the meal passed with excruciating slowness. I finally managed to secure a few potatoes with the next meat course, a small victory in this carnivorous battlefield. Beside me, Rory maintained pleasant conversation with Alex and Isla, his voice carrying none of the tension I could feel vibrating through him.

I tried to focus on the conversations happening around me, catching fragments of dialogue from the wolves seated nearby. Interestingly, not all seemed enthusiastic about the impending pack gatherings. Whispered concerns about "territory disputes" and "the old ways" filtered through, suggesting discord beneath the unified front.

Finally, mercifully, after a serving of coffee, the meal drew to a close, and Edina once again stood. "I will see you all in an hour for the run," she announced, her eyes falling once again on Rory with unmistakable expectation.

The remaining wolves began to disperse as staff appeared silently to clear the table. I exhaled slowly, tension draining from my shoulders. *Thank god.* That was more than enough for one night. I needed space, silence, a moment to process everything. To recharge before whatever fresh hell awaited us next.

"Shall we head back to the cottage?" I murmured to Rory.

"I'll use the bathroom, then we can say goodnight to Uncle Alex and Isla." He jerked his head to where they stood by a bookcase, finishing their drinks.

As I watched Rory walk away, a peculiar sensation washed over me—something akin to abandonment, as ridiculous as that sounded.

For goodness sake, Theodore. He's going to the bathroom, not emigrating.

Yet the absurd impulse to follow him persisted. What was I planning to do? Stand guard outside the door? Hold his hand while he pissed? Laughable, but the humour felt hollow against the mounting unease crawling up my spine.

Why was I suddenly pathetically dependent on Rory Thorne's presence? The man who'd been nothing but an irritation since the day I'd slapped handcuffs on him. The man whose chaotic energy and blatant disregard for procedure had driven me to the brink of professional madness more times than I could count.

And yet here I stood, fighting the irrational urge to trail after him like a lost puppy, terrified of being left alone in a room full of predators wearing human skin. I clutched my tiny china cup of coffee close to my chest, taking minuscule sips so that I'd be busy in Rory's absence.

Pull yourself together, for fuck's sake.

"Detective Maxwell." Tariq Fraser materialised at my elbow, his voice low and measured. "A moment of your time?"

"Of course," I said, heart sinking.

"I understand your... protective instincts toward Rory," Fraser said, his tone measured in that particularly Scottish way that suggested he understood nothing of the sort. "But you should know that pack business is pack business. Tonight's run is a sacred tradition. Humans aren't welcome."

I bit back several retorts that would have done nothing for diplomatic relations. "That's perfectly fine," I said instead, keeping my voice even. "Rory won't be attending either."

Fraser's eyebrows lifted slightly. "Oh?" He paused, dark eyes cold and assessing. "I have to say, I'm surprised you're here."

"Oh?" I mimicked. "And why is that? I'm simply here at my partner's request."

"Right. You're here as Rory's... *partner.*"

The way he emphasised the word made my teeth grind together. How much did he know? Was it possible he knew about Killigrew Street? About the true nature of our relationship—or rather, our lack of one?

"Yes," I said firmly. "As his partner."

Fraser nodded, that infuriating half smile still in place. "Of course. Well, enjoy your evening, Detective. I'm sure we'll speak again soon."

He turned and walked away, leaving me standing alone in the dining room. I scanned the space for Rory, but there was no sign of him. Alex and Isla had disappeared as well.

The remaining wolves cast occasional glances in my direction, their expressions ranging from curiosity to open hostility. Standing here alone was like being a wounded gazelle surrounded by lions.

I pulled my phone from my pocket when it vibrated in my hand.

Going on the run. It could be helpful. Will meet you back at the cottage in two hours, max. x

PS: Could you feed Freddy for me? I'll try and bring him back a squirrel or something, but he'll want some crackers.

PPS: Phone about to die. Soz.

My fingers tightened around the phone, fury rising like a tide. The utter fool was deliberately putting himself in danger, without so much as a discussion. For a moment, I considered tearing the manor apart room by room until I found him. But what then? Drag him out by his ear like a misbehaving child? Create a scene that would only further complicate our already precarious position? No. He'd made his choice.

The night air bit at my face as I stepped onto the manor's stone terrace. Stars pricked the inky darkness above, seeming unnaturally bright this far from London's light pollution.

"I'm going to fucking kill him," I whisper-shouted at the stars, who twinkled back at me in sympathy.

Trees loomed on the path ahead of me, darker and more menacing without Rory's presence beside me. Just perfect—abandoned to walk through the Scottish wilderness alone, surrounded by who-knows-what supernatural threats.

When he finally returned to the cottage, we were going to have words. Many of them. None particularly pleasant.

12

Rory

I leaned against the ancient rowan tree, its gnarled bark rough against my skin. The "Kissing Tree," we'd called it as teenagers—not for any romantic reason, but because its twisted trunk had split and rejoined, creating what looked like two trunks embracing. It stood a good fifteen-minute walk from the manor, our unofficial meeting spot for night runs.

The dinner still clung to me like smoke—every sideways glance, every pointed comment, every moment where I'd felt like a specimen under glass. But worse than all of that was the memory of Maxwell's voice, soft and certain, spinning that beautiful lie about falling for me in a coffee shop.

For one ridiculous moment, I'd let myself believe his words. I'd sat there, frozen, as he painted this picture of someone—him—going an hour out of their way just for the chance to see me. Someone tongue-tied and nervous, grateful for my attention rather than exasperated by my existence.

Nice fantasy.

That's what I'd thought, and fuck, the sadness that had washed over me in that moment had been mortifying. Here was Maxwell, playing his part perfectly, and I'd nearly let myself get swept away by the pretence. Nearly let myself imagine what it would feel like to be loved like that—completely, desperately, without reservation.

But it wasn't real. None of it was real. After this, we'd go back to London, back to him thinking I was an idiot, back to the careful distance we maintained between us.

The decision to join the run had crystallised in that moment of bitter clarity. If I was going to be here, if I was going to face all this pain, then I needed to do something useful. Something that justified putting myself—and Maxwell—through this torture. We needed to do everything possible to find information about Dev.

The thought of returning to the cottage later had icy dread shooting through me. That cold hatred would return to Maxwell's eyes after days of... whatever this was between us.

But maybe, if I could learn something tonight—anything that might help us find Dev—then the cost would be worth it.

The moon called to me, its pull irresistible despite being three nights away from full. I quickly removed most of the piercings from my ears, stuffing them into my jeans pocket, then stripped off my remaining clothes. I left it all in a haphazard pile near the trunk, burying my dead phone within the nest.

Finally time.

A mix of relief and excitement coursed through me. My wolf form felt right in ways my human form never did. No more constant buzz of thoughts, no more feeling too loud, too much, too inadequate.

The night air prickled against my naked skin as I closed my eyes and let the change take me.

First came the burning—fire racing through my veins like I'd downed six espresso shots at once. My bones cracked and reshaped with excruciating precision, each snap a familiar agony that still made me want to scream. My jaw elongated, teeth sharpening to points as my spine curved and shortened. I fell forward onto hands that were no longer hands but paws, claws digging into soft earth. The world fractured into kaleidoscopic colours as my senses heightened—too bright, too loud—the way my mind felt on my worst days, but purposeful now, directed.

Then, as the last of my muscles shifted into place, my scattered human thoughts shattered.

Pain fades. Power floods.

Scents assault first—damp earth, rotting leaves, rabbit trail three hours old. Mouse heart patters beneath fallen log. Moon pulls. Not thought. Command.

Muscles bunch. Claws dig. Earth gives way.

Run, run, run.

Howl builds in chest. Old instinct. Pack call.

No answer comes. Lone wolf now.

Scent hits first. Male-wolf-threat. Familiar-rival. Approaching from downwind.

Eyes catch movement. Human shape emerges between trees. Scar on face. Callum. Male-wolf-rival.

Hackles rise. Teeth itch to bare.

Stand ground. Don't retreat. Don't challenge. Watch.

Male-wolf-rival smirks. "We don't meet over by that tree anymore."

Circle once. Keep distance. Show not afraid, not submissive. Not challenging either.

"Everyone else is over on the other side of the stream. Miles away."

Pack location. Invitation? Trap? Hard to know. Trust not easy. Wolf mind wants simple answers. Human thoughts try to surface.

Male-wolf-rival approaches. Too close. Circles me. Assessing. Judging.

"You know, I forgot how wee you are, even as your wolf." Laughing. "As if you could ever have been an alpha anyway. It's funny, really, thinking about it now."

Words sting worse than teeth. Size-shame. Pack-position-shame.

Instinct surges. Lunge? Bite?

No. Bad choice. Outnumbered. His territory. His pack now.

"Why did you come back here, Rory? Nobody wants you here. Not even Edina. Not really."

Pack-bonds memory stings in chest. Broken things.

Circling closer now. Showing dominance. Testing boundaries. Testing patience.

"And your 'detective inspector boyfriend' is fooling nobody. How much did you pay that idiot to come up here with you? Or does he accept payment in the form of blow jobs?"

Rage-fire explodes through blood. Not-pack insults *mine*. Unforgivable.

"I'm glad that big gob of yours has some use—"

Muscles bunch. Spring forward. Teeth aim for throat.

Male-rival drops. Body already twisting. Bone-crack sounds fill air. Fur erupts from skin. Challenge accepted.

Bodies collide. Teeth snap at air. Black-fur-rival larger. Heavier. Teeth find shoulder. Pain flares. Blood-scent sharp.

Roll away. Speed advantage. Circle-strike-retreat.

Bodies tumble down slope. Black-wolf slams weight down. Pins chest. Air pushed from lungs.

Twist hard. Teeth find leg. Bite down. Bone crunches. Pain-howl fills forest. Grip loosens.

Break free. Blood drips from muzzle. Mine and his.

Rival-wolf limps forward. Eyes promise pain.

Rage burns. Want to fight. Want to prove stronger-faster-worthier.

But no help coming. No Kit-brother to stand beside. Alone.

New thought cuts through fog. Raindrops-lemongrass-safety waits. Detective-mine waits.

Want him. Need safe-den.

Twist body. Launch away from rival-wolf. Paws find earth. Sprint between trees.

Behind, rival-wolf howls. Chase begins. Heavy paws thunder after. Bigger but slower. Injured leg slows pursuit.

Forest thins. Cottage lights appear through trees. Safe-den ahead.

Circle around. Find back of den. Blood loss makes head swim. Legs wobble.

Collapse beneath window. Curl tight. Lick shoulder wound. Taste copper-blood.

Door crashes open. Raindrops-lemongrass-mine rushes out.

"Rory? Oh, thank god. Fuck, are you hurt?" Worried. Heart beats fast-fast in chest. Can hear blood rushing beneath skin.

Answer with throat-sound. Whine-admit pain. Too tired to pretend strength.

Arms slide beneath body. Careful-touch around wounds. Lift up against warm chest.

"Christ, you're so heavy."

Carry into den. Place on soft-nest.

Want closeness. Need safety-comfort. Drag body forward. Rest head in lap. Warm-thigh beneath cheek. Breathe in raindrops-lemongrass-mine scent. Home-scent now.

Gentle fingers stroke behind ears. "You're going to be okay." Voice steadier now. Less fear-scent. "I can't actually see anywhere that's hurt. Just a lot of blood. Is it all yours? I'm going to call Kit."

No! Kit-brother will make leave. Growl builds in chest. Warning-sound.

"Okay, okay. Got it. But you're calling him yourself, later."

Fingers resume stroking. Pain eases slightly under gentle touch.

"What am I supposed to do with you like this?"

Strokes bring joy. Not want strokes stop. But need to show not badly hurt. Need human-words to explain.

Must change back. Must become two-legs again. Need human-words to explain.

Concentrate. Pull at the human beneath fur. Call it back.

First shudder ripples through muscles. Body rebels. Wants to stay wolf. Safer as wolf. Easier as wolf.

Bones begin to crack. Pain sharper now. Fur receding into skin that feels raw, exposed. The world's edges starting to blur, colours fading.

My perception shifts as human senses return. The vibrant tapestry of scents fades last—raindrops-lemongrass-Maxwell becoming just... Maxwell again.

The final twist of transformation leaves me naked and shivering on the cottage floor, human once more. Every muscle screams in protest. My shoulder throbs where Callum's teeth tore through.

The room spun. *Focus, focus!*

The cold clarity of human thought slammed back into me. I'd abandoned Maxwell via text message. I'd gotten into a fight to the almost-death with Callum.

Oh shit. Maxwell was going to absolutely murder me.

The concern in his eyes would soon harden into that familiar cold fury. The little bubble we'd been building over the past few days was about to pop. Spectacularly.

And that hurt far worse than any wolf's bite could.

Just say sorry, Rory. That will be a good start.

"Bloody hell," I said instead, through chattering teeth. "Well, that went well, wouldn't you say?"

"No, I would not say," Maxwell snapped, throwing a blanket on top of me. Possibly because I was shivering, but probably so he didn't need to see my dick. "Are you okay?"

I lay still, cataloguing the damage. Shoulder definitely bitten. Ribs ached with each breath. Various scrapes and bruises, but nothing catastrophic. The shift had already healed the worst of it, though not as completely as I'd hoped.

"I'm okay," I croaked.

"Are you sure?" Maxwell's voice was tight.

I ran my hands over my torso, wincing as I pressed against my left side. "Possibly a slightly fractured rib?"

Maxwell pointed toward my shoulder. "What happened there? Did you get *bitten?!* What the fuck happened, Rory?"

I touched the wound gingerly, the puncture marks where Callum's teeth had sunk in. The bleeding had stopped, but it was still raw and angry. If I'd stayed shifted longer, it would have closed it better.

"As soon as I shifted, Callum found me. Alone. I wasn't in the right meeting spot. So nobody else was around."

"And he just full-on attacked you? Jesus Christ!"

"Well. Sort of. Yes, he attacked me." I swallowed, looking away. "Though *technically* I jumped on him first. But he provoked me. Verbally!" Another burst of rage at Callum's words about Maxwell flooded through me.

Maxwell sighed deeply, tilting his head back to stare at the ceiling beams, pressing both hands either side of his glasses.

Can we go back to the part where you were stroking behind my ears?

I pushed myself up to sitting, clutching the blanket around my waist, ignoring the protests from my battered body. My suitcase was still at the bottom of the stairs. *My clothes! My phone!* They were still by the tree. I opened my mouth to tell Maxwell we needed to go get them immediately, before wisely snapping it shut. If anyone caught the scent of my stuff, hopefully Felix's security system would keep them out of my messages and emails.

I had bigger concerns, because Maxwell paced the small cottage living room like a caged animal, his footsteps heavy on the wooden floorboards. With each turn, his scowl deepened, and I could practically hear his teeth grinding.

"This is exactly what I was worried about," he muttered, more to himself than to me. "I knew something like this would happen."

I struggled to my feet, wobbling slightly as my head spun. The blanket slipped, and I grabbed it quickly, securing it around my waist. My shoulder throbbed with each heartbeat, but I'd had worse. Much worse.

"Have you seen Freddy since you came home?"

He gave me a death stare. "Seriously?"

"Yes, Maxwell, seriously. It's all fine now. Calm down."

He stopped dead in his tracks. The sudden stillness was more unnerving than the pacing had been. When he turned to face me, his eyes were dangerously calm, like the surface of water just before it freezes.

"Calm down?" His voice was quiet, controlled. Terrifying. "You're actually telling me to calm down right now?"

Cold dread shot through me and I wished more than anything that I could turn back into my wolf. The human part of me knew I'd stepped into dangerous territory. I'd seen Maxwell's explosive anger on a few occasions when I'd pushed him too far. But this was something else.

"Umm... you know what? I take it back. Don't calm down. Keep um... keep uncalming."

Maxwell's eyes narrowed to dangerous slits. "Don't you dare make jokes right now."

I tried to shift my weight, wincing as pain shot through my ribs. "Look, it's not as bad as—"

"As what?" Maxwell cut me off, his voice rising. "As bad as abandoning your partner in the middle of hostile territory? As bad as running off with the people we're actively investigating? As bad as getting yourself torn apart by another wolf?"

"I didn't completely abandon you," I protested. "I texted!"

"Oh, brilliant. You *texted*." Maxwell's laugh was hollow, bitter. "A dead battery and 'going for a run, laters' is your idea of proper communication? While I'm left trudging through pitch-black countryside where I could've been attacked at any moment?"

Fuck. That was true. And I hadn't even considered it. Guilt flooded through me, and I clutched the blanket tighter around my waist. "Maxwell... I'm so sorry. I didn't think of that. The cottage isn't that far from—"

"I don't actually care about that!" Maxwell slammed his hand against the wall, making me jump. "I promised your brother I'd keep you safe. I made a *promise*, Rory."

"I don't need a babysitter," I snapped, my own anger flaring. "I'm not some helpless moron who needs constant supervision. I can protect myself."

"Really? Because evidence suggests otherwise." He gestured wildly at my wounded shoulder.

I straightened despite the pain, pride stinging worse than my injuries. "I was trying to further our investigation! You saw what they were like today—closed ranks, suspicious. You couldn't read their minds, and they're so guarded, they're hardly going to let the slightest thing slip, are they? I need to earn their trust!"

"By getting yourself killed?"

"By trying to be one of them!" I shouted. "Running with the pack was a chance to get closer, to learn *something*, maybe!"

The anger seemed to drain from Maxwell suddenly as he studied my face. "Did you want to run with them to feel close to a pack again?"

The question caught me so off guard, I inhaled sharply. I looked away, unable to meet his gaze as something tender and painful stirred inside me. "No. It... it would have been horrible, anyway."

"How so?"

"Running beside them but not being able to feel them. Being physically there but still... disconnected. It's worse somehow, being right next to what you can't have." I risked a glance up at him. There was a glimmer of understanding in his eyes. "Look, I just want this whole thing over as quickly as possible. I barely held it together today with Edina pretending to be mother of the year. I want to find Dev and go home. That's all."

"So your brilliant plan was to run off without talking to me and get into a fight?" Maxwell stepped closer. "Did you consider for one second what would happen if you didn't come back? If they'd all suddenly decided to finish what Callum started?"

"I knew what I was doing!"

"Did you?" He was close enough now that I could smell mint on his breath. "Because from where I'm standing, you never think things through. You never consider anyone else. Never stop to consider the consequences."

His words stabbed into me, in the same spots where my parents' voices had carved permanent wounds. *"You never think things through. You never consider anyone else."* How many times had I heard those exact words? How many times had teachers, my parents, pack elders thrown them at me like stones?

"That's not fair," I managed, but my voice came out small as the familiar shame crept up my throat, hot and choking. I was eight years old again, being told I was selfish for forgetting to do my chores. Twelve, being called reckless for climbing too high in a tree. Fifteen, hearing that I was too impulsive, too chaotic, too *much* for anyone to handle properly.

Maybe they were all right. Maybe I really am just broken.

Maxwell's expression shifted, his anger dissolving into something that looked almost like horror. "I didn't mean—" He stopped himself, jaw working as he struggled with something. "You're not broken, Rory. It's just... Do you even care about your own wellbeing? Or are you so desperate to prove yourself that you'll risk everything?"

"I care about solving this case," I said through gritted teeth. "I care about finding Dev. I care about not spending one more day in this nightmare than necessary."

"And what about the people who care about you?" Maxwell asked quietly. "What about them?"

The question crackled in the air like a live wire, something in his tone sending my heart into an erratic beat against my possibly fractured ribs.

"Don't pretend you care about me," I said. "I'm just an assignment. A problem you're stuck with."

Something sparked in Maxwell's eyes—hurt, maybe, or anger. "Is that what you think?"

"Isn't it true?" I challenged. "You've made it perfectly clear how you feel about me from day one, Maxwell. Even before you arrested me that night."

"You have no idea how I feel," he growled, and suddenly the air between us seemed to thrum with something beyond anger.

"Then enlighten me," I whispered, my heart still hammering. "How do you feel?"

Maxwell's hands clenched at his sides, like he was fighting some internal battle. He took a half step closer, the space between us shrinking. "You're impossible," he murmured, shaking his head slightly.

"I'm not sure that's a feeling, Detective Maxwell." I retreated a step, but couldn't resist adding, "Perhaps you should be more specific." My heart skipped a beat as he followed, advancing like a predator.

"It is when it comes to you," he said. "Impossible. Infuriating. Reckless."

With each word, he moved forward, and I backed away until the cool plaster of the cottage wall pressed against my bare shoulders. The blanket slipped slightly, and I clutched it tighter, suddenly aware of my near-nakedness.

"Still not feelings," I challenged, tilting my chin up. "Those are just adjectives."

Maxwell's breath hitched. He moved forward suddenly, one hand landing on the wall beside my head, effectively caging me in. The manoeuvre left me breathless, with his soft exhalation ghosting across my forehead. His size should have made me feel trapped, claustrophobic—I usually despised being cornered—but right then, there was something almost thrilling about being caught in Maxwell's orbit.

"You want feelings?" His voice dropped to a near whisper. "I feel terrified every time you're out of my sight. I feel like I'm losing my mind when you pull stunts like tonight."

I could feel the heat radiating from his body, smell the faint scent of his black pepper and lemongrass cologne mingling with sweat and forest air. *Raindrops-lemongrass-Maxwell.*

The wall behind me was solid and cool, a stark contrast to the warmth emanating from Maxwell as he leaned in closer.

"That sounds suspiciously like caring," I said, my voice a whisper.

His eyes met mine, defiant and vulnerable all at once. "Maybe it is."

Maxwell's eyes flickered down to my lips, then back up so quickly I might have imagined it—except for the way my entire body responded, a violent shiver coursing through me like a shockwave. For one wild, irrational moment, I imagined what it would be like to kiss him. Detective Dickface. The man who'd arrested me, when he was supposed to help me. The man who drove me absolutely mental. What a stupid, impossible thought.

My whole body began to quiver as a strange combination of fear and longing shot through me. And perhaps that was why I found myself saying, "So what? You care enough to lecture me but not enough to trust me to handle myself?"

"Trust has to be earned, Rory."

"And what have I been doing all this time?" Fucking hell, what more did he want from me? With both hands, I shoved against his chest, but he barely moved. "I've been trying my hardest since day one to impress you."

"*Impress me*?! By taking unnecessary risks?" he growled, his other hand slamming against the wall on the opposite side of my head, fully caging me in now.

The heat of his body enveloped me, and with it came that scent—raindrops on sun-baked pavement, elemental and consuming. It filled my lungs, clouding my thoughts, making my wolf stir beneath my skin.

"By making my job of keeping you safe impossible?" he continued, leaning closer until his anger seemed to radiate between us like summer heat.

"Your job," I repeated, the words bitter on my tongue. "Right. That's all you ever really care about."

"That's not what I meant—"

"No, I get it. I'm just a task to be managed. Another problem for Detective Dickface to solve."

His eyes flashed dangerously. "I've told you to stop calling me that."

"Make me," I taunted, tilting my chin up defiantly.

Maxwell's tongue darted out to wet his bottom lip, leaving it glistening in the lamplight.

What would those plush lips feel like against mine? Would he taste of the mint I could smell on his breath, or the red wine he'd had with dinner? Or would he taste like he smelled—like the promise of rain, like relief after unbearable heat? Would he hold me so softly, or clutch me tightly, while he—

With a growl that sounded almost feral, he grabbed the back of my neck and crushed his mouth against mine.

It wasn't gentle. It wasn't sweet. It was pure frustration and pent-up anger—all teeth and desperation.

I gasped against his mouth, shocked to my core, my body frozen between fight and surrender.

For one long, suspended moment, I couldn't move, couldn't think.

Then something primal took over. I fisted the collar of his shirt, rising to my tiptoes to return his kiss with equal ferocity. My tongue slid against the seam of his lips, demanding entry, and when he opened to me, he made a pleased sound deep in his throat that vibrated through my entire body.

Was I unconscious? Was this some outlandish fever dream brought on by my injuries?

The cool metal of Maxwell's wire-framed glasses grazed my cheek as I tilted my head. His other hand found my waist, fingers digging into bare skin so tightly it was as though he were afraid I might disappear—or perhaps fighting the urge to pull me even closer.

The blanket slipped dangerously low, barely clinging to my hips. His hand on my neck slid up to tangle in my hair, and I fit our mouths together more firmly. The stubble along his jaw rasped against my palm, my fingers delighting in collecting this new sensory detail about a man I'd only ever observed from a safe distance.

No, this wasn't a fever dream. Dreams faded at the edges—this only grew sharper, more intense with each passing second. Dreams couldn't make your pulse race like this, couldn't make your skin burn where his fingers pressed into flesh.

He removed any space between us to press me against the wall. I slipped a hand under his button-down shirt to trace the contours of his abdomen and his breathing hitched. I quickly swallowed the sound, savouring it like a secret I'd stolen from him.

Everything grew hazy except for the feel of his solid chest beneath my hand, the way our lips moved together, and the heat of his breath mingling with mine. A hunger began to build, spreading through my veins like wildfire. I pushed my tongue deeper, groaning at the silky heat of his mouth, at the way he tasted of that minty toothpaste, but also so much more.

Beneath the artificial spearmint lay something intoxicating—something that matched his scent perfectly. Like the first rainfall after a drought, like thunder breaking silence, like salvation.

When we finally broke apart, both gasping for air, his eyes were dark and wild, his lips swollen. I stared at him, my brain struggling to catch up with what had just happened.

"This is completely unprofessional," he murmured, voice ragged.

"What, has the great Detective Maxwell finally lost control?" I said, inches from his lips. I pulled back slightly to reach up to pluck his glasses from his face. "Let's see if removing these helps you to relax."

Whilst snatching his glasses out of my hand, he silenced me the only effective way he'd discovered so far: by pressing his mouth to mine.

He claimed me again, deeper, hungrier this time. The hand in my hair tightened, sending delicious tingles across my scalp, a pleasure that bordered on pain. But I needed more, needed to taste him again.

I nipped at his bottom lip, drawing a startled gasp from him before diving back in, invading his mouth with desperate strokes, chasing away the last remnants of toothpaste to find what I truly wanted—that taste of summer rain, of something wild that called to me on a level I couldn't explain. My whimper of approval vibrated between us as I pressed closer, craving more and more. All that mattered was getting closer, tasting deeper, drowning in him.

The idea that Maxwell was kissing me, actually *kissing me*, was so absurd, so impossible that it spun me even dizzier. Maxwell hating me made sense. Maxwell kissing me? That was madness.

But his hands on my skin felt real. The heat of his mouth against mine felt real. The racing of my heart felt real.

Raindrops-lemongrass-Maxwell.

The scent that had guided me through the dark forest. The scent I'd followed back to safety. The scent that had become a beacon, a north star in my wolf form.

Raindrops-lemongrass-Maxwell.

Wait. No. Not quite that.

Raindrops-lemongrass-*mine.*

That's what I'd called him. *Mine.*

Panic shot through me like ice water. I broke the kiss, shoving against him. Though his hand remained on my hip, he shuffled back, his eyes opening, confusion swirling in their depths.

Mine. My wolf had claimed him. Without my permission, without my conscious thought.

"Wait, wait, wait, but... what are we doing?" I gasped, my hand flat against his chest, his heartbeat thundering beneath my palm, echoing in my ears like a drum. My head spun, a dizzy cocktail of desire and confusion.

Maxwell's eyes blazed as he stared down at me, his breath coming in short bursts. "Getting this out of our system," he rasped.

This? What was "this?" The tension that had been building between us since that night at Meridian? The undeniable pull I felt toward him despite the fact he hated me?

"But... you're straight. You're totally straight. So straight."

Maxwell's gaze dropped deliberately to where my rather erect cock had tented the blanket. "If you say so," he murmured, one eyebrow arched in challenge.

A mad urge to cover myself with my hands surged through me, but before I could move, Maxwell's hands slid down my back and grabbed my ass through the blanket, kneading firmly with both hands. I gasped at the possessive touch, my knees nearly buckling.

In one smooth movement, he twisted me around so that he was against the wall, then settled his thigh between my legs—his very large, very muscular thigh—and pulled me toward him. The pressure against my aching erection sent sparks shooting through me, drawing an embarrassing whimper from my throat.

"Go on," he whispered against my ear, his hands still gripping my ass, guiding my body in a deliciously slow grind against his thigh. "Show me how straight I am."

Stunned wordless, my mouth did the only thing it could—latched onto Maxwell's once again.

Our kiss was all-consuming. Each brush of Maxwell's tongue against mine had heat flushing through my veins like liquid fire, turning my blood to molten lava.

Desperate, needy whimpers slipped out of me, and he responded with a groan that vibrated through his chest and into mine, his hands tightening their grip on my ass as he pulled me harder against his thigh.

"Fuck," I gasped against his lips, the hands tangled in his shirt gripping tightly.

Maxwell growled and yanked my head back by my hair, exposing my throat. The sharp sting against my scalp sent a jolt of pleasure straight to my dick. His other hand slid up my back, carefully avoiding my injured shoulder—a fleeting moment of tenderness in the midst of our frenzy that somehow made everything hotter.

"You like that?" he murmured against my neck, tangling his fingers deep in my riot of curls.

Fuck, yes, pull harder. I love it when—

He tugged again, harder this time, and I couldn't stop the raspy moan that escaped me. His lips curved into a smile against my skin. My hips bucked against his thigh, seeking more friction, more pressure, more of everything. *This damned blanket—*

And a second later it was gone, Maxwell having whipped it off the second I'd had the thought. The cool air hit my overheated skin, but I barely noticed, too consumed by the blissful friction of Maxwell's jeans against my bare cock.

His mouth found mine again, hungry and demanding, as his hands guided my hips in a rhythm that had me seeing stars. I rocked against him, chasing the building pressure at the base of my spine, my fingers moving to dig into his shoulders.

"I'm going to come on you," I panted, half plea, half warning, wholly mortified. Because when Maxwell snapped out of this, he was never going to be able to look at me the same again.

"Hey," he said, capturing my chin to lift my face, staring intently into my eyes. "I'll be able to look at you just fine." He brought his mouth to my ear, as if whispering a secret. "In fact, I'll remember how fucking hot you looked, rubbing yourself against me like this."

His words sent me hurtling over the edge. My body tensed, every muscle locking as pleasure exploded through me. I cried out, throwing my arms around his neck, burying my face into it as I came in hot pulses across his thigh, my entire body shuddering with the force of my release. Raindrops and lemongrass and white-hot heat enveloped me at the peak, like a storm breaking inside me. Wave after wave crashed over me, leaving me gasping and clinging to Maxwell like he was the only solid thing in a world that had suddenly turned to quicksand.

For a moment, I hung suspended in bliss, my body a collection of nerve endings humming with satisfaction. The room spun back into sharp edges and solid shapes, revealing my feet swaying inches above the floorboards—Maxwell was supporting my entire weight, his arms wrapped around me like steel bands, his breath coming in hot, ragged puffs against my ear.

"Fuck," I mumbled, face still buried in his neck, inhaling his intoxicating scent, the strength of it almost overpowering. My legs felt like jelly, utterly useless.

Between us, a sticky mess covered his jeans. But he had asked for it, hadn't he? Practically demanded it with that commanding voice and those strong hands guiding my hips.

I became acutely aware of something hard pressing against my hip—Maxwell's own considerable erection straining painfully against his jeans. That couldn't be comfortable.

Slowly—giving him plenty of time to stop me if he wanted—I slid my hand down his chest, past his stomach, until my fingers brushed against the outline of his cock. He drew in a sharp breath.

"Can I suck you off?"

The question hung between us for one breathless moment. Then Maxwell's arms loosened their grip, and I slipped to the ground, hitting the floorboards with a soft thud. Looking up, I found his expression had shifted, his brows drawn together.

"What, too gay?" I tried to joke, but it came out sounding strained and panicked.

"No," he snapped, his voice sharp enough to make me flinch.

"Then what's the problem?" I asked, fingers still hovering near his belt buckle.

"You're injured, Rory." His fingers traced a path from my wrist to the edge of my shoulder wound, which was barely bothering me with all the pleasant distraction. "You need to rest."

I rolled my eyes dramatically. "Seriously? That just now wasn't particularly restful. What's the real problem? Scared you won't be able to look me in the eye after you've seen me on my knees for you?"

Something flashed in his eyes—that spark I'd seen before when I pushed his buttons just right.

"No," he practically seethed. "I'm more concerned you won't be able to handle what you're asking for."

"Your lack of evidence is disappointing for a detective. Let's collect some more data points, shall we? Exhibit A, my mouth." I flicked open his belt buckle with slightly shaking fingers, the metallic clink sounding like a dare in the quiet room. "Unless you've suddenly developed performance anxiety?"

A low, guttural sound—half growl, half groan—escaped Maxwell's throat. In one swift movement, his hand shot out to grip the back of my neck, fingers threading through my hair with surprising strength. He guided me downward with firm pressure, not rough but undeniably commanding, until my knees hit the floorboards with a satisfying thud.

I grinned up at him, then with a wink, my fingers wiggled underneath the elastic band of his briefs as I remembered how much I'd wound him up that time in the car, when I'd taunted him with questions about his underwear. I yanked down both garments, my fingers brushing against the coarse curls at his groin. And then, jutting up with proud glory, his cock sprang free.

His rather massive cock.

Fuck that, *his extremely massive, oh-my-god-it's-humongous cock.*

A cock I'd promised was going in my mouth.

My jaw actually dropped as my eyes blinked in disbelief at its thick, swollen head and the sheer bloody length of it. Smooth, formidable, throbbing, it completely filled my vision, dominating the space between us. I licked my lips, my eyes tracing its slight curve.

Maxwell was unable to hide the nervous edge in his laugh. "You thought I was exaggerating, didn't you, Thorne?"

I ignored him, already moving my mouth towards it, overwhelmed by the urge to worship this magnificent creature. My lips parted, eager to trace every glorious vein, to map the contours of its impressive length with my tongue.

One hand went straight to his base. His cock pulsed beneath my hand, seeking, demanding. My mouth began with reverence, a slow drag of my tongue along the underside of his shaft, tracing the prominent vein that pulsed beneath my touch. Maxwell's breath caught, a soft hiss filling the cottage as his head fell back against the wall. His cock twitched against my tongue, responding beautifully to each delicate exploration.

"Jesus fucking Christ," he breathed.

I painted wet circles around the base, taking my time, learning the geography of him—the slight ridge where shaft met pelvis, the velveteen softness of skin stretched taut over hardness. My hands steadied his hips, but they strained against my grip, seeking more than this teasing worship.

Maxwell's fingers threaded through my hair, not pulling, just resting there with a trembling restraint that told me how close he was to losing control. I glanced up through my lashes to find his eyes locked on me, dark with hunger, his chest rising and falling in shallow bursts.

I dragged my tongue upward in a languid spiral, savouring the salt of his skin, the heat radiating against my lips. When I reached the crown, a glistening bead of precum had formed at the tip.

One taste. That's all it took.

The flavor exploded across my tongue. Salt. Musk. Maxwell. Lemongrass. Raindrops.

Something in me snapped.

I took him in.

Hard.

With a hunger that made time fracture around us, my lips stretched around his considerable girth as I welcomed him into the wet heat of my mouth. And *oh.* The taste of him—the *weight* of him—rewrote every fantasy I'd ever entertained.

A strangled sound tore from his throat as I began to move, my tongue mapping every ridge and vein with devoted attention. His hips jerked involuntarily, seeking more, and I gave it to him, drawing him deeper until I could feel the blunt head of his cock nudging the back of my throat.

"Christ," he gasped, his voice wrecked and desperate.

I set a rhythm that had him trembling against the wall, my mouth working him with increasing fervor. His fingers tightened in my hair—not pulling, but anchoring himself as I lavished attention on every inch of him. The cottage filled with the sounds of our shared desperation: his ragged breathing, my soft moans of appreciation, the wet slide of lips and tongue.

I hollowed my cheeks and drew him in even deeper.

Not all the way—not as far into my throat as I'd like—but enough.

Enough to hear that broken sound tear from his chest.

Enough to know I was ruining him.

I was making him make those noises. *Me.*

"*Rory!*" he cried, my only warning as he pulsed hot and thick across my tongue. He tried desperately to pull away, but I held him fast, drinking him down greedily, gorging myself on the taste of him. My wolf howled with satisfaction, a primal pleasure at having him on my tongue, down my throat. When I finally pulled back, my chest heaved as I caught my breath.

Maxwell's dick still glistened with traces of saliva and cum. I leaned forward again, dragging my tongue slowly along his length, cleaning him thoroughly as he groaned above me, his fingers still tangled loosely in my hair.

I sat back on my heels, finally taking in the full picture of us—Maxwell, breathless against the wall, cum-covered jeans pooled around his ankles, shirt rucked up.

Maxwell seemed to have the same thought. He kicked off his jeans and pants, then reached down to snatch the blanket from the floor. He wrapped it around his waist, while I remained kneeling there, utterly naked.

"There's no need for this to be awkward," I said quickly, the words tumbling out. "It's just sex."

Though something about those words didn't feel right on my tongue. Something about those words sent a flutter of panic through me.

"I'm not feeling awkward," Maxwell said, his voice stiff, his posture even stiffer as he clutched the blanket around his waist like a shield.

It was such a blatant lie that I laughed, loudly.

Sighing deeply, Maxwell crossed the room and threw himself on the sofa, wiping his face with his hand. Just as I was about to remind him whose idea that whole thing was, he spoke.

"I'm sorry. I am feeling awkward. I'm not going to sit here and say, 'we shouldn't have done that,' like a twat, but I'm not completely blind to the consequences either."

I joined him on the sofa, wincing slightly as the movement tugged at my shoulder. I'd definitely overdone it. Placing a cushion over my dick for some semblance of modesty, I said, "What consequences? Seriously,

I'll be totally normal tomorrow. My usual, irritating self." I paused. "Actually, slightly less irritating, because of the super hot sex, but that's a positive consequence, so there."

A genuine laugh escaped him then, his shoulders relaxing slightly. He looked at me when he said, "You know, I don't usually enjoy sex."

I blinked at him. "What? Why?" How could someone who kissed like that, who touched like that, who made those sounds, not enjoy sex?

Maxwell sighed, running a hand through his short coils, the tight curls springing straight back into place. "It's... complicated. Being a telepath during sex is..." He searched for words. "I can make it good for the other person, obviously. I know exactly what they want. But I also hear their insecurities, their comparisons to previous partners." His voice dropped low. "You know, when they're thinking they've had better. When they're imagining someone else."

"Oh." I hadn't considered that. "That's... not ideal."

"And before you shout at me, it's literally impossible to block thoughts when I'm having sex. There's too much direct skin contact. And it's... too intimate a moment."

"Normally I hate you reading my mind," I said. "But it was actually so great that you knew what I wanted. Knew I didn't want gentle treatment." I grinned wickedly. "Knew I like dirty talk."

"That was actually just a guess." A slight smile played at his lips.

"But... did you enjoy that then, or not?" I asked, an anxious knot coiling in my gut.

Maxwell's face softened. "I enjoyed it very much. Sorry if that wasn't clear. Actually, I've never had sex with anyone who knew about my gift before."

"Never?"

"Not many people know about me." He shrugged. "My mother. Killigrew Street. That's it."

"You never told any of your ex-girlfriends?"

Maxwell fixed me with a pointed look. "You've spent eighteen months abusing me for 'reading your thoughts' even when I'm doing my damnedest not to."

"Fair point," I winced. "Sorry about that."

He sighed, his gaze drifting to the window. "Plus, I've always been scared they won't believe me. That the next day, a team of psychiatrists will turn up, ready to cart me off to the psych ward."

I watched the shadows play across his face, seeing him—really seeing him—perhaps for the first time. *How lonely it must be, carrying a secret like that.*

"Well," I started tentatively, "maybe sex with someone who knows about it will be better for you. Great, even." I cleared my throat. "You know, in case we need to, um... 'get it out of our system' again, or something."

Maxwell laughed, the sound warm and rich. "I have a feeling you'd just merrily voice your desires aloud anyway."

"True." I grinned. "I usually have no problem being very vocal during sex. My ex before Dev, Jamie, used to say I was so loud the neighbours were sending him death—"

I cut off as Maxwell visibly flinched. He looked away sharply, but not before I caught the unmistakable flare of anger in his eyes.

Zap.

That sensation again—like a bolt of electricity arcing between us, connecting us. But this time it wasn't just a tingle or a flash. This time it felt like someone had hooked jumper cables to my ribs and cranked the power to maximum.

The force of it knocked the air from my lungs. My entire body jolted, muscles spasming as the current ripped through me. My vision blurred at the edges, and for a moment, I swore I could see the air between Maxwell and me crackling with blue-white energy.

My hand flew to my chest, pressing against my sternum where the sensation had centred.

"Fuck," I gasped when I could finally breathe again, still dizzy from that overwhelming scent that seemed to have seared itself into my senses. "Did you—"

But one look at Maxwell's face told me everything. His hand mirrored mine, pressed flat against his chest. "What is this... this *thing* that keeps happening to you?" he demanded. "I've never come across anything like it before. And don't just say 'wolf thing' again. What is it?"

Panic flared through me. Because I *did* know what it was. Or I thought I did, anyway. And there was no way that Maxwell could know.

I forced my mind blank, imagining a pristine white wall.

Like that's not suspicious, Rory.

Gah, stop thinking about how that's suspicious!

"I'm going to go wash quickly," I blurted, scrambling off the sofa and nearly tripping over my own feet in my haste to escape.

I bolted for the bathroom, shoulder pain flaring, not looking back. I slammed the door behind me, leaning against it as I tried to catch my breath.

"No, no, no," I murmured to myself, pacing the tiny bathroom floor. "Why is my life always so complicated?"

I washed my body, then splashed cold water on my face, staring at my reflection in the mirror. My hair looked like I'd been dragged through a bush backwards, but that was no different. It was the deranged, terrified look in my eyes that made me seem like a stranger.

The first times the zap had happened, I'd brushed it off. A weird static electricity thing. Maybe Maxwell's telepathy interacting strangely with my quirky brain. But there was no denying it anymore, not after that.

I'd never felt anything like it with anyone else. Not with Dev, not with any of my previous relationships or hookups.

It wasn't something that was heavily discussed in my pack. Or if it was, it wasn't something that teenage me paid attention to—too busy hating my life and being hormonal to learn about mate bonds.

But I was fairly sure that this was what it was. It felt different from the bonds I'd had with my pack. Pack bonds were comfortable, familiar, like a well-worn jumper that fit perfectly. They felt like belonging, like home. Even the weird not-quite-pack-bond thing I had with Kit—that tenuous thread that somehow survived despite everything—was nothing like this. This thing with Maxwell was demanding, almost painful in its intensity. It pulled at something deep inside me, something I couldn't control or ignore.

I had asked Kit about it once. In a very rare moment of candour, he'd told me extremely briefly that he'd fallen in love with one of his comrades during his time in the covert military unit. I'd asked him if he'd felt that magical mate bond thing I'd heard a bit about. Turns out no, he hadn't. I'd asked him if he'd ever felt it. And then he looked so sad, I stopped asking him about it.

I wish I'd asked him more questions, like, "If it happens to me, how do I make it stop?" Because I needed it to. Immediately. Before Maxwell found out and thought I was an even bigger freak than he already did.

In some sort of bizarre twist of fate, Maxwell wasn't actually straight after all, and even more bizarrely, he wanted to fuck me.

Wanted to *fuck* me.

Not be my bloody mate, tethered to me for all of eternity, in all of our soulmate reincarnations, if our species's stories were to be trusted.

This was so typical of me. My stupid brain must be glitching out. Muddling up my attraction to a hot man, who I'd had mind-blowing sex with and was *sometimes* a bit nice to me, with something more. No cosmic connection, no mate bond, no destiny. Just sex.

I'd done this before. With Jamie, I'd planned our future wedding after three dates. With Dev, I'd pushed him away when I asked him to move in with me. I always came on too strong, too fast, too much. It was why everyone left me in the end—tired of my intensity, my neediness, my everything-all-at-once approach to relationships.

"It's just sexual attraction," I muttered to myself. "Nothing else. Maxwell will never want you like that."

I needed to sort out my priorities. We were here to find Dev, solve a case, and *maybe* have some more casual sex along the way. Nothing more.

With a deep breath, I straightened my shoulders. There would be no more zaps. The next time I felt it, I'd fight against it with all my might. And I wouldn't now look for extra meaning in every glance or touch. I would be cool, casual Rory. The kind of bloke who could have sex with someone without planning a future together.

Even if every cell in my body was screaming otherwise.

A knock at the door, then it creaked open slowly. Maxwell's head poked through. His glasses were back on his face but sitting slightly askew, giving him an endearingly dishevelled look.

"So, I've had a good look for Freddy, but there's no sign of him."

My heart did this pathetic little somersault that I absolutely refused to acknowledge. Because only I could turn "bloke remembers conversation about missing zombie ferret" into "clearly destined to be together forever." Still, the fact he'd actually looked... I bit my lip hard, forcing down the soppy smile trying to escape.

"That's okay. He's probably just out feasting on the Scottish sheep. I'm sure he'll be back tomorrow morning."

"Riiiiight." He suddenly looked hesitant. "So, I'm about to drop dead from exhaustion, but I wanted to check before I went to sleep that you're okay with sharing the bed..."

"Yeah, no worries," I said, trying to sound casual despite the way my heart skittered about. "I'll just quickly build the pillow barrier for us."

His face fell so dramatically that I couldn't help but burst out laughing. A warm, tingly sensation flooded through me when his lips quirked upward, my joke finally landing.

"Bold of you to assume I'd let you near me after you snored directly into my ear last night," he shot back, adjusting his glasses with mock indignation.

"I do not snore!" I clutched my chest in mock offence.

"You sound like a chainsaw attempting to cut through concrete."

"Slander and lies!"

As we moved toward the bedroom, a creeping anxiety wormed its way into me. What if Maxwell woke up tomorrow morning filled with regret? What if the harsh light of day made him realise he'd made a terrible mistake letting another man suck him off? It was a tale as old as time—blokes who were curious, experiment, then panic afterward and disappear.

But Maxwell was stuck with me. Not just up here, but while we still both worked for Killigrew Street.

Fuck, if he quits because of this, Seb will kill me.

"So," I said, trying to sound casual as I flopped onto the bed. "Not that straight after all, huh?" I waggled my eyebrows suggestively. "I'm rather pleased I was the one to turn the great Detective Inspector Theodore Maxwell to the dark side."

Maxwell shrugged, a touch too stiffly. "Sexuality is fluid. I actually think maybe I've always been attracted to men, just never acted on it." His words came out almost rehearsed—had he been waiting to announce this to me?

"So... you're not like, freaking out at all?" I asked, watching his fingers drum a pattern against his thigh.

Very slowly, he sat on the edge of the bed, folding his arms tightly across his chest. "Are *you* freaking out? What happened to 'it's just sex?'" His voice was steady, but his eyes wouldn't quite meet mine.

I propped myself up on my elbow, ignoring the twinge in my injured shoulder. I didn't believe Maxwell's attempt to appear completely unfazed. I needed to throw him a lifeline. Give him a chance to shut this down before it went any further.

"Well, in that case, I was thinking..." I paused, gathering my courage. "Tomorrow morning, it would be best to um... properly get it out of our system, don't you think?" I shot him a wicked grin to cover up my bubbling anxiety—that he'd reject me, say that once was enough for him. Say that we needed to forget it ever happened, for professional reasons.

"Hmm." Maxwell tilted his head to one side, making a show of pondering the question, and my stomach knotted. "I suppose it's important that it's *completely* out of our system, yes."

Butterflies exploded across my nervous system, but I forced myself not to react.

"Before we get straight back to finding Dev, of course," he added quickly, as if reminding himself as much as me.

"Of course," I said.

The realisation sent a wave of guilt flooding through me. Here I was, flirting and joking while my ex-boyfriend was still missing, and we hadn't made any headway on the case. But the way Maxwell looked at me—like he was seeing something worth wanting, even as fear flickered behind his eyes—made it hard to focus on anything else.

When we both crawled under the covers, we left a generous amount of space between us, an unspoken reinforcement of our "it's just sex" agreement. My leg started bouncing beneath the duvet almost immediately—a restless rhythm that matched the spiralling thoughts in my head. What if Maxwell changed his mind? What if Dev *was* in real danger while I was here selfishly focusing on whether Maxwell wanted to keep kissing me or not? The mattress shook slightly with each bounce of my foot.

Maxwell spent several minutes lying stone still, staring at the ceiling, his breathing carefully measured. Then, almost hesitantly, his hand crept across the mattress—pausing twice as if he might change his mind—before finally making contact with my elbow. His touch was feather-light at first, uncertain, before settling into softly caressing up and down my arm. The restless energy in my leg began to ebb, the bouncing slowing to a gentle tremor before stopping altogether.

And when I finally fell asleep, it was to his fingertips brushing tenderly around the angry marks Callum left on my shoulder, as if he could stroke my pain away.

13

Theodore

Knock, knock. Knock, knock.

The sound yanked me from sleep, my consciousness resurfacing like a drowning man breaking through dark water. My eyes snapped open to unfamiliar shadows dancing across an unfamiliar ceiling. For several disorienting seconds, I couldn't remember where I was.

Knock, knock. Knock, knock.

Insistent now, demanding.

I tried to move but found myself anchored in place by a warm weight. Rory. He was draped across my chest like a living blanket, one leg thrown rather possessively over mine, his face buried against my neck. His breath tickled my collarbone in slow, even puffs.

Dead to the world.

The knocking came again, more urgent this time.

"Rory," I whispered, gently attempting to disentangle myself. He responded by clutching me tighter, mumbling something incomprehensible against my skin. I carefully extracted my arm from beneath him, then lifted his leg off mine, earning nothing but a soft snore for my efforts.

I slid out of bed, my bare feet hitting the cold wooden floor as my hand fumbled for my glasses on the side table. The cottage was still cloaked in near-darkness, though the window showed the faintest hint of dawn's light. Who the hell would be knocking at this ungodly hour?

Padding down the narrow staircase, it wasn't until I reached the bottom that I realised I was wearing nothing but my briefs.

Well, if they were going to knock at this ungodly hour, they could hardly complain.

The knocking resumed, three sharp raps that seemed to echo through the silent cottage. My mind flashed to Callum, the wolf who'd attacked Rory. Had he come to finish what he started?

My sleep-addled brain vaguely registered I should grab something—a kitchen knife, a poker from the fireplace—but as I approached the door, I let my telepathy reach out instead. Two minds waited on the other side. Two minds that felt... familiar.

Taking a deep breath, I unlatched the lock and pulled the door open.

The astonishment struck me so forcefully my heart fully seized.

"Umm... surprise!" Felix whispered, his face illuminated by the soft glow of his phone screen. Behind him stood Priya, her arms crossed against the Highland chill.

"What the—" I stared at them, convinced I must still be dreaming. "How did you— Why are you—"

"We've been trying to call you both for hours," Priya said, pushing past me into the cottage. "Let me tell you, we've had such a time of it, getting up here."

I stepped back wordlessly, slack-jawed as our unexpected visitors entered the cottage.

Felix shuffled in behind Priya, looking distinctly uncomfortable, his shoulders hunched as if trying to make himself smaller in the unfamiliar space.

Priya immediately took charge, flicking on lights and illuminating the small living area. I quickly scanned the floor for any compromising evidence, a brief fear that I'd imagined throwing my jeans in the washing machine yesterday taking root.

Abruptly, a blur of matted grey fur shot out from Priya's coat pocket, accompanied by an unearthly squeak. Freddy scampered across the floor and bolted up the stairs.

"But..." I managed, my brain still struggling to process their sudden appearance.

"The little mite met us at the gate. Marched us two miles or so to a hole in the wall." Priya extended her elbow, which was scraped raw, the skin angry and red. "Wasn't fun, but we managed. Then we walked another twenty minutes, because Freddy was clearly concerned about Rory's phone."

She reached into her bag and pulled out a bundle of clothes—the ones Rory had been wearing yesterday—and his phone, tossing them unceremoniously on top of the suitcase still open on the floor.

"Almost gave poor Felix a breakdown, following Freddy, because he kept leading us away from your phone's location."

Priya's stream of words were making little sense in my sleep-deprived state.

"But... why are you here?" I asked, running a hand through my hair.

She blinked owlishly at me. "Is that really how to greet someone who's been travelling for nine hours straight, including an overnight flight, to get here as soon as possible?"

"You flew here?" I asked, though it should have been obvious.

"After you rang Seb, we booked the earliest flights to Inverness."

As soon as I returned to the cottage alone yesterday, I'd rung Seb to tell him my identity was somehow completely compromised. I'd managed to avoid explicitly telling him Rory had run off alone.

"You didn't tell me you rang Seb."

A voice from the top of the stairs made my heart immediately kick into overdrive. Rory stood there, his hair tousled from sleep, wearing nothing but a tatty oversized T-shirt that hung off one shoulder, revealing the mess Callum had made of his shoulder.

"We were... busy..." I managed, as my eyes drank in the sight of him.

Rory took the steps two at a time, flinging his arm around Priya as if he hadn't seen her in months.

"Um... hi. I'm here too," said Felix from the shadows.

"Did you want a hug?" Rory offered brightly.

"No, thank you," Felix replied.

"I have to say, I'm surprised to see you here, Felix," I said. Killigrew Street's tech expert rarely left his lair of screens and equipment.

"Well, Flynn volunteered but wasn't allowed to come, and I wanted to help, you know, after..." Felix fidgeted with the sleeve of his hoodie.

I fought the impulse to roll my eyes. "So Flynn wasn't allowed, but you were? Your life is just as important as Flynn's," I said firmly. "It's dangerous here. Rory was attacked yesterday." I gestured to the many patches of blood still visible across the floor and furniture.

"You were attacked?" said Priya, gently inspecting Rory's shoulder. "You didn't tell Seb that!"

"We were... busy..." Rory said, meeting my eyes, his lips twitching into a secret smile that sent a shiver right through me.

I forced myself to look away, suddenly very aware of my near-nakedness in the middle of the living room.

Rory turned back to Felix and Priya, his expression growing serious. "Maxwell's right, though, it's dangerous for you here. The cameras at the gate would have picked you up. Plus, the shifters will catch your scents. You can't just secretly hang out here. This isn't a holiday park. Random visitors aren't exactly welcome. And to be honest, your appearance is going to compromise our efforts," Rory continued, running a hand through his chaotic bed-hair. "Maxwell and I are supposed to be a couple visiting family, not hosting a reunion."

As he said my name, he caught my eye again, and I couldn't help but think that he was thinking the same thing as me—that these two had picked one hell of a time to show up. Because as much as we needed all the help we could get finding Dev, we needed to talk properly about what the hell happened yesterday.

"I'm just going to pull some clothes on," I mumbled, dashing for the stairs. I did want clothes, but more than that, I wanted a moment to myself.

Last night, I'd told Rory I wasn't freaking out.

I lied. I was completely freaking out.

I'd grown used to our antagonistic relationship over the last two years. The constant bickering, the pointed jabs, the repeated insults, the way he deliberately pushed my buttons—all of it had become familiar territory.

I knew how to navigate those waters. But this? This was uncharted territory. Dangerous territory.

What made it worse was the looming dread of what would happen when this inevitably came out. Would Seb fire me? The thought of facing him, of him finding out about my ludicrously unprofessional behaviour, filled me with mortification.

Before we slept, I'd been close to asking Rory not to tell anyone at Killigrew Street about it. But the words had died in my throat. I didn't want him to think I considered it a mistake or some kind of experiment. Because despite my panic, despite everything logical in my brain screaming that this was a terrible idea, I didn't regret what we did.

Now his best friend had waltzed through the door before I even had a chance to talk to him.

And sorely interrupted the plan you two had to further "get it out of your systems" this morning.

Not the time, not the time!

After hastily locating a light jumper and jeans, I trudged back downstairs to catch Priya saying, "So you really want us to leave?"

"I don't *want* you to leave," Rory said, "but it's not safe—"

A series of urgent electronic beeps cut through the tension. Felix's eyes widened as he fumbled for his rucksack, dropping it to the floor with a thud. He yanked out his laptop and threw himself into an armchair, fingers flying over the keyboard before the screen had fully illuminated.

"What is it?" Priya leaned over his shoulder.

Felix's face lit up. "Dev's phone is back online again!"

The change in Rory was instantaneous. His entire body seemed to vibrate with renewed energy, his eyes wide and hopeful. "What? Where? Can you track it? Is he using it right now? Is he near us? Fuck, Dev might actually be okay!"

...Dev might be okay, he might be okay...

As I watched Rory crowd around Felix, continuing to bombard him with excited questions, I felt a sharp, unexpected twinge in my chest. Jealousy. This was exactly why you didn't get involved with colleagues.

Especially if it involved having sex with the person you were helping to find the missing ex-boyfriend of.

Another series of electronic beeps punctuated the tense silence. Felix's expression fell, his fingers dancing frantically across the keyboard.

"Annnnd it's gone again," he announced, not looking up from his screen.

Rory shuffled closer, practically hanging over Felix's shoulder. "But do we have the precise location this time?"

Felix didn't respond, his face bathed in the blue glow of his laptop, eyes narrowed in concentration as he tapped away with almost manic intensity.

I watched Rory's anxiety building—his shoulders tensing, the slight bounce in his stance. Before he could annoy the hell out of Felix, I gently took his arm.

"Let Felix focus," I said softly.

Rory's head snapped toward me, eyes wide with surprise. I tensed, preparing for him to pull away or snap at me for presuming to tell him what to do. But instead, he nodded, the fight draining from him as he allowed me to guide him away.

Priya's eyes keenly followed us as I led Rory to the tiny kitchen tucked into the corner of the cottage. There never was getting much past her.

I filled a glass with water from the tap and handed it to him. He leaned against the counter, taking small sips, his eyes fixed on some invisible point beyond the window. His ears looked bizarrely bare without his array of hoops and studs in. I missed them.

For several horribly long moments, neither of us spoke.

"How's your shoulder?" I finally asked, desperate to break the silence.

"Honestly, it's fine."

The awkward silence resumed, stretching thin between us. I searched for something else to say, anything to dispel the strange tension, but my mind remained stubbornly blank.

Rory shifted his weight from one foot to the other, his thoughts leaking into my mind, clear as a bell:

...oh my god, why is this so awkward, I'm dying...

I took a deep breath and made the executive decision to do the most British thing possible in a crisis—make tea.

I opened cupboards until I found mugs, and filled the kettle, grateful for the mundane task to occupy my hands while my mind raced. The cottage kitchen was barely large enough for one person, let alone two, but Rory lingered, leaning against the counter beside me.

I needed to say something—anything—to dispel the awkwardness, but the right words wouldn't come to me.

The kettle clicked off. I busied myself with teabags, buying time as I arranged my thoughts. I reached for the sugar, spooning out a generous amount for Felix's mug.

Suddenly, Rory's hand shot out, wrapping around my wrist and stopping me mid-motion. "That's the salt, you numpty," he said, his fingers warm against my skin.

I blinked down at the white granules. "So it is." I raised an eyebrow at him. "But... numpty? Really?"

A tiny chuckle escaped me, and then Rory snorted, and somehow that broke the dam. We both dissolved into laughter—the kind of uncontrollable, slightly hysterical laughter that only comes after unbearable tension.

"You clearly didn't get enough sleep last night," Rory managed between gasps.

"And whose fault is that?" I countered.

Rory leaned in close, his face inches from mine. "Yours, if I remember rightly, Detective," he said, voice low and teasing. My pulse quickened as his gaze dropped briefly to my lips. "I'm glad to see Priya and Felix," he murmured, "but I really wish they'd arrived just a few hours later."

"Me too," I whispered back, surprising myself with my honesty.

"What the fuck are you two conspiring about?" Priya shouted from the living room. "Get back in here!"

After locating the actual sugar, we carried the four mugs into the living room. As I handed Priya her tea, she gave me an annoying smirk.

"Who knew a couple's retreat in Scotland would be the thing to make you two bury the hatchet?"

Rory scoffed. "Are you joking? We hate each other more than ever. Maxwell won't stop lying about me snoring."

Priya's eyes widened. "You're sleeping in the same bed?!"

"There's only one bed, Priya! Only *one* bed!"

"Umm, guys?" Felix's uncertain voice cut through. "Dev's phone location? You know, the thing you were so excited about two minutes ago?"

Rory's head snapped around. "Right! Yes! Sorry, Felix." He practically bounded back to Felix's armchair. I followed, grateful for the timely interruption.

"So," Felix began, fingers still tapping away. "This time I managed to triangulate the signal much more precisely using a modified cell tower spoofing technique." He glanced up briefly, catching our blank expressions. "Um, basically I tricked the phone into connecting to my virtual network instead of the actual towers."

Priya leaned over his shoulder. "And?"

"And..." Felix turned his laptop around, displaying a topographical map with a small red dot pulsing in what appeared to be wilderness. "I've got it narrowed down to within fifty meters!"

"That's... in the middle of nowhere," I observed, squinting at the screen.

Felix nodded. "It's about seven miles northeast of here, deep in the Glenmoriston forest. There's no road access—at least none that shows up on any maps."

Rory leaned over. "That's not pack land. And you're correct. No roads around there. I know the area, though."

"How long would it take to get there?" Priya asked.

"By foot?" Rory said. "Three, maybe four hours. The terrain is pretty rough—lots of elevation changes, dense forest. And we'll need to cross one of the tributaries of the Moriston—not the main river itself, but a smaller stream that feeds into it. Luckily we won't have to climb any mountains, per se."

"There's no way we can drive?" I asked, already knowing the answer.

"No," Felix confirmed, fiddling with the map. "Besides, even if we tried off-roading with quad bikes or something, the vehicle signatures would definitely be picked up by anyone monitoring the area. Walking is the best option."

"Then we walk," Rory said. "The challenge will be smuggling you two out of here. We'll have to creep the long way back to the manor house, off the main path. Then Maxwell and I will bring our car to the edge of the gravel. You guys can jump in, hopefully undetected by the cameras, and then we'll drive through the gate, and find somewhere to park the car." He marched with confident strides toward the stairs, as if lit with renewed purpose.

"Wait," said Felix. "Just to be clear, Dev's phone only connected for a few minutes this time. And..." He hesitated. "It didn't make any calls or send any messages. It just... connected."

"What are you saying?" asked Rory, blinking at him.

"You know what he's saying, Rory," said Priya. "He's trying to manage your expectations."

A sudden, visceral image slammed into my mind with such force that I nearly dropped my mug.

Dev's body sprawled in a forest clearing, limbs at unnatural angles. Blood matting his dark hair. Eyes open, vacant, staring at nothing. The rich smell of decomposition mingling with pine.

The image wasn't mine. It had burst from Rory's mind with such intensity that my defenses crumbled. I staggered slightly, gripping the back of the armchair to steady myself.

"Maxwell?" Priya's voice sounded distant. "Are you alright?"

I blinked, forcing the horrific image away. Rory stood frozen, his face drained of colour, hands trembling slightly.

Our eyes met. He knew I'd seen it.

"I'll... go get dressed," he said, voice unnaturally calm. "Everyone, be ready to leave in fifteen minutes."

Without waiting for a response, he disappeared up the stairs, footsteps quick and deliberate.

Felix and Priya exchanged glances.

"Well," Priya said, breaking the uncomfortable silence. "Look at Mr. Organised, ordering us around. Has Maxwell been rubbing off on him?"

I half choked on the last sip of my tea, the words twisting themselves into an innuendo.

"You okay there, Detective?" Priya asked, eyebrow raised.

"Fine," I managed, setting down my mug. "Just... went down the wrong way."

She pinned me with her gaze.

God help me if she ever found out exactly how Rory had been rubbing off on me.

Killigrew Street meetings would never be the same again.

The Highland wilderness stretched before us in all its rugged glory—a panorama of heather-covered slopes, ancient pines, and rocky outcrops. In the distance, a mountain peak loomed against the slate-grey sky, its summit lost in wisps of cloud. If I'd been here on a hiking trip, I'd have appreciated its beauty more.

My shirt clung to my back, sweat trickling down my spine despite the cool air. Rory, in a ridiculously bright tie-dye T-shirt that rather distractingly clung to his frame like a second skin, had set a brutal pace from the moment we'd left the cottage. The short sleeves left his arms bare as he moved with determined strides, as if he could outrun his own dark thoughts by sheer physical exertion.

I'd fallen back with Felix, who held a tablet connected to a satellite transceiver to help keep us on track.

"You could put that away, you know," I suggested, wincing as he nearly tripped over an exposed root.

"Can't," he muttered, not looking up. "Just in case Dev's phone pings again. You never know."

Ahead, Rory gesticulated wildly as he spoke to Priya. My stomach tightened. What was he telling her? Just how *busy* we were last night? I couldn't imagine Rory keeping anything from her.

My phone buzzed in my pocket. Seb, perhaps, responding to my earlier updates?

I pulled it out, surprised to see Kit's name instead.

Kit

Just got to Killigrew Street to find out that Priya and Felix have gone to Scotland. I don't know how on earth Priya convinced Seb it was a good idea, because I wasn't there last night when it got decided. But it isn't safe, especially for Felix. They need to come home.

Rory's already on their case. In the meantime, we'll look after them. Don't worry about Felix. He's in his element.

I quickly snapped a picture of Felix, who was now squinting at his tablet in the sunlight, lower lip caught between his teeth in concentration.

Felix looked up. "What was that for?"

I hit send.

"For someone who's missing you."

Confusion clouded his expression. "What?"

I pretended to concentrate on avoiding thorny brambles, and my phone soon buzzed again.

> **Thank you. Can you tell Rory to call me back?
> I've left him about twelve voicemails. Priya
> said Callum attacked him?**

> **He hasn't had much time to call you since
> that happened, to be fair. We've been busy. I
> promise that he's okay.**

The vague path we were following narrowed, then disappeared entirely. What had been challenging terrain became an obstacle course of fallen trees, dense undergrowth, and sudden dips where water had carved gullies into the earth. The forest closed in around us, branches reaching like grasping fingers, dimming the drizzly daylight.

"Still on track?" Rory called back, after some time marching through this, his voice tight with strain.

Felix nodded, though his earlier enthusiasm had faded. "About half a mile to go. We're heading straight for the signal location."

I watched Rory's shoulders rise and fall with a deep breath. Priya moved closer to him, her hand finding his elbow.

"Try not to imagine the worst, Rory."

Rory gave a hollow laugh. "He's hardly going to be sitting around having a picnic by himself, is he?"

As we continued walking, my brain couldn't help but imagine what would happen if we did find Dev's body. Rory would be absolutely devastated. Someone would need to make sure he didn't touch the body, contaminating evidence. Someone would probably need to comfort him.

A sudden image of him sobbing, throwing himself at my chest blared to life in technicolour clarity. That would be typical behaviour for mortal enemies, right? I would be allowed to wrap my arms around him and hold him tight while he grieved?

Though comforting Rory would be Priya's job, wouldn't it? She was the one with her arm linked through his now, murmuring reassurances

I couldn't quite hear. The one he truly trusted. The one who hadn't arrested him and thrown him in a cell during a full moon.

The forest grew thicker still. Branches snagged my jacket, thorns catching on my trousers. The air felt heavy, laden with moisture and the rich scent of decomposing vegetation. Twice, I had to save Felix from slipping, both times imagining Kit's face if he returned to London with a single scratch on him.

"We're getting very close," Felix said, voice barely above a whisper, as if speaking too loudly might disturb whatever—or whoever—waited for us ahead.

I nearly collided with Felix when he stopped abruptly, tablet held out in front of him like a divining rod.

"This is it," he announced, his voice carrying an unnatural cadence in the dense forest. "We're right at the centre of the ping radius."

The location itself was unremarkable—just another patch of undergrowth surrounded by towering pines. No buildings, no clearings, nothing to suggest why Dev's phone would be here of all places.

I scanned the area, slipping into detective mode. "Spread out," I instructed, keeping my voice calm and authoritative. "Look for anything unusual—disturbed ground, personal items, footprints. Stay within earshot."

Rory immediately pushed forward, trampling through ferns with desperate energy. Priya took the opposite direction, methodically examining the forest floor. Felix hovered near the centre, still staring at his tablet as if it might reveal more secrets.

I moved in a wide arc, eyes sweeping back and forth across the ground. The forest felt oppressively silent, as if holding its breath.

Then a shriek tore through the stillness—Rory.

My heart lurched violently against my ribs. My stomach twisted into a knot of dread as I sprinted toward the sound, branches whipping at my face. The forest blurred around me, my mind conjuring images of bloodied earth and sightless eyes, of Rory crumpled beside a body gone cold.

I burst through a thicket to find Rory on his knees, shoulders hunched, head bowed. I dropped to the ground beside him, my hand instantly finding his back.

"Rory," I said through breathless pants, scanning for the body.

But there was no Dev. Instead, Rory was staring down at a phone—a sleek, latest model iPhone, screen cracked and dark. The device was half buried in decomposing leaves.

"Look," I said, pointing to a thin wire trailing from the phone into the undergrowth. I gently lifted it with a stick to reveal a small external battery pack, slightly weathered. Where the wire connected to the pack, the insulation had frayed, exposing copper strands.

Priya and Felix crashed through the foliage behind us, both breathing hard.

Felix immediately crouched down, examining the setup. "Huh. Maybe this explains the extremely intermittent signal," he said. "The connection is damaged. When moisture conditions are just right, it might create enough of a circuit to power the phone for a few seconds or minutes—long enough to ping a tower before dying again."

"Right," said Rory, flatly.

I studied him. He'd clung onto that minuscule shard of hope, that we'd find Dev alive out here, sitting around waiting for rescue. Now that was shattered.

The hand that was still on Rory brushed up and down his back in soothing strokes before I forced myself to stop—suddenly thinking that there was a chance Rory would rather Priya and Felix didn't know about... *us*. Perhaps he would be embarrassed to have them discover he'd lowered himself to someone like me, who couldn't be further from the vibrant, colourful types he probably surrounded himself with. Someone he openly despised.

I lowered the stick and pulled out my phone, snapping several photos of the device and its surroundings from different angles. This was evidence now. Proper evidence.

"We need to do a thorough search of the area," I said, reaching into my jacket pocket for a plastic evidence bag I habitually carried. "See if we can find anything else. Anything at all."

As I carefully sealed the phone and battery pack, I couldn't help but feel a prickle of guilt. Normally, this would be the moment I'd call in a full forensics team, have them comb the entire area with meticulous precision. We'd set up a perimeter, bring in cadaver dogs, establish a command post. The works.

Now that we had concrete evidence suggesting Dev might have met with foul play, was it time to involve the authorities? The Scottish police would certainly have grounds to investigate. We could construct a plausible story—Dev was Rory's friend who'd mentioned hiking in the Highlands before disappearing. We'd tracked his phone here out of concern. That narrative would be enough to mobilize significant resources.

But the supernatural element complicated everything, as usual. If Dev's disappearance was connected to Meridian's interest in shifters, bringing in regular police could create more problems than it solved.

"I'm going to hold off on calling this in officially," I said, tucking the evidence bag into my inner pocket. "We'll see what Seb says later."

Rory nodded, his face grim but determined. "So what now?"

"We search," I said. "Properly, systematically."

I quickly organized us into a grid pattern, marking out sections of forest with Felix's help. He used his tablet to divide the surrounding area into search quadrants, each roughly twenty meters square.

"Stay within sight of at least one other person," I instructed. "Look for anything unusual—clothing, blood, disturbed earth, anything that doesn't belong in a forest."

The next three hours passed in painstaking, muddy work. We combed through underbrush, examined the bases of trees, peered into hollow logs. The rain started again, a persistent drizzle that soaked through my jacket and made the search even more challenging.

Rory shifted into his wolf to better pick up Dev's scent, if there was any trace of it left to detect. While I methodically examined my quadrant, I kept one eye on the golden wolf darting through the forest.

Every fifteen minutes or so, Rory would bound back to me, pressing his warm body against my legs. The first time, I froze, unsure how to respond. But his expectant look broke through my hesitation, and I found myself reaching down to scratch behind his ears.

The wolf leaned into my touch, eyes half closing in what could only be described as bliss. I chuckled despite myself, fingers sinking into his thick fur.

"You're like a puppy," I murmured. "Just with far sharper teeth."

Rory made a huffing sound before darting away again.

This pattern repeated—Rory following scent trails, then returning to check in with me. Each time he approached, he'd press harder against my legs, sometimes nearly knocking me off balance. And each time, I'd obligingly stroke his head or scratch that spot behind his right ear that made his back leg twitch.

It really was funny how much he seemed to like me as a wolf.

By mid-afternoon, we'd covered nearly half a square kilometer around the original site. Felix, who'd been examining the forest floor with surprising enthusiasm, considering I'd never seen the man outside, finally straightened up with a wince.

"I think we're done for now," I declared.

"That would be good," Felix said. "I want to see what I can recover from Dev's phone."

14

Theodore

Hours later, we collapsed into the cottage living room, a tableau of muddy exhaustion. I sank into the armchair, my muscles protesting every movement. Rory sprawled across the sofa, one arm flung dramatically over his eyes. Felix hunched over his laptop at the dining table while Priya perched on the floor, her back against the wall.

"I could murder a cup of tea," Felix mumbled, not looking up from his screen where Dev's phone sat connected by a tangle of wires.

"On it," Priya announced with surprising vigor, pushing herself up. "I have loose camomile in my bag. Perfect for stress and exhaustion."

"I'll just have one of the normal teabags," I requested.

"No, let me make everyone this. You'll love it."

I lacked the energy to argue further. She clearly wanted to read everyone's leaves—I'd have to wash my mug out before she could.

The cottage fell into weary silence, broken only by the gentle clicking of Felix's keyboard and the distant whistle of the kettle. My eyes drifted closed. I was going to need to take an actual holiday when I returned to London, to recover from all this.

"Oh!" Felix's exclamation jolted me awake. "It's working!"

We all gathered around his laptop where Dev's phone screen, still in an evidence bag, had flickered to life, displaying a lock screen with a photo of a sunset over London.

"Do you know his password?" Felix looked to Rory.

For the first time since finding the phone, Rory's face brightened. "Yeah, I still remember it!"

I passed him a plastic glove, and he carefully slid the phone out, placing it on the table.

Rory's fingers hovered over the screen. "It's his mum's birthday and the last two digits of his postcode." He tapped in the sequence, then frowned as the phone vibrated and flashed red.

"Incorrect password," Felix said, rather unnecessarily.

Rory sighed. "He's probably changed it to his new boyfriend's birthday or something," he said moodily.

"Don't worry about it," Felix said quickly, already connecting another cable. "I don't actually *need* the password. Give me twenty minutes, and we'll be in."

I accepted the steaming mug of tea that I didn't actually want from Priya. "You're not reading my leaves."

She pouted, eyes wide with mock innocence. "What about if I get to see, but I keep it to myself?"

"No."

"But what if it's helpful for the investigation, Maxwell?" Rory chimed in.

I glared at him. "Keep out of it. And you should use these twenty minutes to call Kit. He keeps texting me. He's going mental."

Rory groaned. "He'll just beg me to come home. He's so tightly wound about this whole thing."

"I was surprised when he refused to come with you," I admitted, blowing on my tea.

"It's okay. I understand it would be too much for him. Kit's..." Rory paused. "He's sensible to stay away."

"Kit had an equally tough time growing up here?"

"Oh yeah, for sure. He refuses to talk about it, and as a kid, I didn't see it that way at all. I thought he was loving life—golden child, favourite of the entire pack, future alpha—had it all. Even popular at our local high school. Played football, made girls drool, you know, the lot." Rory's voice softened. "I used to think it was so unfair. Me, hating everything about my life, thinking I was a broken thing until I finally got my ADHD diagnosis, whereas he just sunnily breezed through everything." He stared into his mug. "But looking back at it through an adult lens, and from the brief things he's said... he had a tough time of it, for sure. I mean, obviously there's a reason why he 'randomly' upped and left one day."

"Hmm. Well, you need to go call him," I said firmly. "Go on. Go."

Rory's eyebrows shot up, his lips curving into a smirk. "God, you're so bossy," he said with an exaggerated eye roll, his tone carrying more than a hint of flirtation that made my pulse quicken. Something must have shown on my face because he immediately straightened, clearing his throat. "Right, then. I'll go upstairs. Be right back."

As his footsteps retreated, I drained my tea in three long gulps.

The second I set the empty mug down, Priya's eyes lit up.

"No, Priya."

"What if I massage your temple for you?"

"No."

"What if I promise not to tell Rory about that adorable little smile you give him when he's not looking?"

Every molecule in me froze, ice cold.

"*What*?!" I managed, heart seized into a tight ball.

"What if—"

"Oh, for fuck's sake!" I shoved the mug toward her, desperate for any distraction from what she'd just said. "Fine. I don't care. It's all rubbish anyway."

I glanced at Felix, wondering if he was listening. As he was shaking with suppressed laughter, I'd say he was.

Priya turned the mug three times counterclockwise before peering inside. Her face remained completely blank. After a few more seconds, she silently placed the mug on the table.

"Well?" I snapped.

"What?"

"What did you see?"

"I thought you said it was all rubbish? Why would you want to know what I saw?"

I glared at Priya, trying to push past her innocent expression to the thoughts beneath. But all I encountered was an absurd mental image of yellow rubber ducks floating in a bathtub, complete with little sailor hats. One of them was smoking a tiny pipe.

"I didn't know you were such a fan of rubber ducks," I said, rubbing at my temple as the beginnings of a headache formed.

"Sure you don't want that head massage?" she asked sweetly, wiggling her fingers.

"No thanks," I muttered, reaching for my phone. The last thing I needed was Priya's hands anywhere near my head while she was broadcasting rubber ducks doing the backstroke.

"Five minutes or so," Felix announced, not looking up from his work. "The encryption's tougher than I expected, but I'm getting there."

I nodded and stepped away, scrolling through my missed calls. Several from Seb. Brilliant.

I called him back, moving toward the kitchen.

"Teddy!" Seb answered immediately. Hearing my code name coming from him felt odd, after all Rory's teasing. "I've been trying to reach you since yesterday!"

"Sorry, Noctule," I said, keeping my voice low. "We were busy searching the woods. We've found Dev's phone."

"I gathered as much from Magpie's messages. I tried to call last night to tell you they were on their way, but you didn't answer."

"Sorry about that. Reception's spotty out here. Anyway, Magpie thinks he can crack the phone in the next few minutes. After that, they'll probably need to leave. To be honest, I was surprised to see them on our doorstep after you said you couldn't spare anyone for this mission."

"Well, that was before you sounded the alarm about Terrier's pack knowing your identity, but most importantly, *knowing that you're a telepath*. My mind is still reeling from that news."

"I know," I said. "I suppose they could have immediately run the plates on my mother's car, and then linked her to me, if they have access to that level of resources, which they probably do. But as for the telepathy…"

"If I thought Terrier would actually follow the instruction, I'd order you both home. I don't like this, Teddy. I don't like this at all."

"Me neither."

"Keep me informed, and your phone off silent."

"Yes, boss," I said jokingly, as I never called him that, even though the others did.

He made a sound that might have been a laugh. "And Terrier hasn't sent you grey yet?"

"Oh, he's sent me completely grey. I've aged about fifty years."

After a chuckle, Seb hung up.

"We're in!" yelled Felix, and the sound of Rory's footsteps bounding down the stairs quickly followed.

We gathered around Felix's laptop like pigeons fighting over a chip, jostling for space in the small cottage living room. Rory ended up smushed into me, his breath hot across my collarbone as he leaned forward to see better. The bright fabric of his shirt pressed against my arm, causing gooseflesh and making it nearly impossible to focus. My mind quickly wandered to last night—his mouth on me, the softness of his hair between my fingers—and heat rose to my cheeks. *Not now, for god's sake.*

A fragment of anxious thought drifted into my consciousness:

...too close, everyone's too close, I can't think properly when they do this...

I glanced at Felix, noting the tension in his shoulders and the way his hands had stilled over the keyboard.

"We should give Felix some breathing room whilst he works his magic." I stepped back and gave Rory and Priya a meaningful look.

The other two budged back by approximately five centimeters. I continued to glare at them until they finally gave him space. Felix's shoulders immediately relaxed, and I caught the grateful look he threw my way.

"Right, then." I cleared my throat. "What have we got, Felix?"

"He's got a million missed calls. From Rory, but also someone named Sakshi."

"That's his alpha," said Rory.

"I'll open his texts." Felix tapped the screen, bringing up a cascade of Dev's message threads.

"Jesus," I muttered, scanning the names. "He's been busy."

Dozens of different contacts populated the list—all names I didn't recognize, but the breadth of Dev's communications was staggering.

"Oh! Click on Ezra," Rory instructed. "His new boyfriend. Look, he hasn't opened the last message."

Felix obliged, and the screen filled with their conversation. At the top sat the same photo we'd seen at Ezra's flat—Dev standing with Bradley and Brody outside a building. Beneath it, Ezra's final message glowed accusingly:

Ezra

> **Really, Dev? You chose these two to mess around with, out of all people? And to think, I almost believed that lie about your sick mother. Don't bother coming to my flat. If you want your stuff back, I suggest you look in the bins outside my building. It's where you belong.**

Beside me, Rory let out a snigger, his shoulder shaking against mine.

I turned to him. "Is that appropriate right now?"

"What?" Rory's eyes widened innocently. "Come on, this is exactly what I'd expect from Ezra. He's so dramatic." Rory shrugged. "Besides, I'm sure Ezra and Dev will merrily get back together after we deliver Dev safely back to London." The bitterness I expected from that statement was glaringly missing. *Interesting.* Was he finally getting over Dev?

Felix scrolled further up through the conversation, revealing a nauseating parade of selfies—Dev and Ezra sending kissy faces, heart emojis, and... *intimate* photos back and forth.

Rory made an exaggerated retching sound. "Oh my god, make it stop."

"I take it you weren't this sickening with him?" Priya asked, eyebrow raised.

"Absolutely not," Rory declared, though the slight flush on his cheeks suggested otherwise.

That little bubble of jealousy grew inside me again. Jesus, what was I, a pathetic, lovesick teenager? "Let's look at his other conversations," I found myself snapping. "You guys are so easily distracted. I don't know how you get anything done."

"Who put you in charge?" said Rory, with a smile.

...but I like it...

I deliberately sighed loudly and moved my gaze to the screen.

"Look, this one is about a missing persons case," said Priya.

And as Felix methodically scrolled through conversation after conversation, a disturbing pattern emerged. We read in silence as the full scope of Dev's investigation materialised before us. Dev had reached out to shifter connections across major cities, using subtle, coded language. Manchester, Liverpool, Cardiff, Glasgow. He never directly mentioned "shifters" or "wolves," instead referring to "one of us" or "people like your brother."

"Bloody hell." Priya pointed to a message from a contact named Morgan in Cardiff. "Three gone without a trace since February."

"And here." Rory jabbed at another exchange. "Two more in Manchester just last month."

My stomach tightened as the evidence mounted. By my count, at least fifteen shifters had vanished across the UK in the past six months—and these were just the ones Dev had managed to document.

"I can't believe he didn't bring this to Killigrew Street," Rory said suddenly, his voice tight with frustration. "All this time, he was building this case, and he never once thought to..."

...probably didn't want any more interaction with me...my fault, as usual...

The thought was so loud and raw that my hand instantly flew to his shoulder, squeezing it gently. "I'm sure he was just about to come to you. He was gathering evidence before presenting his findings."

Privately, I harboured less charitable thoughts about Dev. The journalist struck me as an arrogant asshole who likely believed he didn't need professional support for his little "investigation." It wasn't like he could even publish all this as a story. The fool should have brought this to Seb months ago.

"Wait—stop scrolling!" Rory lunged forward, nearly knocking Felix's laptop sideways. "I know her! Carrie MacGregor—shifter woman, slightly older. She helped me out when I was sleeping rough in Glasgow. Lives there in one of the city packs."

Felix clicked on the thread, and immediately I could see this conversation was substantially longer than the others. The timestamps stretched back over four months, leading right up to Dev's disappearance.

The story unfolded piece by piece: Carrie's second cousin Ewan, who'd struggled with alcohol dependency, had vanished without a trace. She'd filed an official missing persons report, but when the police investigation stalled—unsurprisingly, given the chronic underfunding of Scottish police forces—she'd taken matters into her own hands.

Carrie MacGregor

> **The more people I talk to, the more I realise how much bigger this is than Ewan. How is it possible our kind have been disappearing for years, and nobody has ever noticed?**

> **Just few enough, I suppose. And it's the same picture across the country - they know exactly who to target to remain undetected.**

This systematic targeting suggested organisation, resources, planning—a level of sophistication far beyond random opportunistic abductions.

Just what exactly was going on here?

Felix continued scrolling until we reached messages from just days before Dev's phone went dark. Carrie had sent an audio file with a brief message: *"From the friend I told you about on the phone. Listen immediately."*

"Play it!" Rory demanded, practically vibrating with tension beside me.

Felix clicked on the file.

The audio began with a jumble of muffled sounds—paper rustling, fabric brushing against what must have been a hidden recording device, indistinct voices weaving in and out of audible range:

"...don't understand why we need to..."

"...facility nearly ready..."

Static swallowed several seconds before the audio suddenly cleared.

"Look, we have acquisition quotas to meet here." The voice was male, authoritative, with a clipped London accent. *"As per our agreement."*

"But this isn't like the earlier batches! Those were lowlifes we could pick up from street corners." This voice was deeper, rougher, defensive. *"This is a completely different ballgame."*

"We're only asking for five. And we're paying Meridian handsomely. With due respect—"

"With due respect, have you seen your specification list? Finding shifters that meet your criteria is hard enough, let alone—" The audio deteriorated into crackling static as footsteps approached. A third voice joined the conversation, the words barely audible through the interference, something about "timelines" before the recording abruptly ended.

The cottage fell into stark silence. I could hear my own heartbeat, the weight of what we'd just heard settling over us like a dark shroud.

Priya was the first to break the silence. "It seems like Meridian might be acting as some sort of middleman."

Felix nodded, fingers still poised over the keyboard. "And whoever is 'ordering' these wolves, has recently changed the rules of their game."

He scrolled down, revealing more of the conversation between Dev and Carrie.

> did your friend manage to get anything else to you?

> just those maps I emailed you. I'll ring you later to catch up properly.

"Maps? What maps? Let's see them!" Rory pressed forward, pushing against Felix.

"Give him a chance to click, Rory," I said, placing a restraining hand on his arm.

Rory made a frustrated noise in his throat, somewhere between a growl and a whine. "Sorry, Felix."

Felix's frantic fingers froze, and he turned to Rory with shock written all over his face, blinking owlishly. "That's okay. I'm used to it now anyway."

"That doesn't mean you should put up with it," I told him.

He stared at me as if I was speaking in alien.

"Okay, great talk, now let's get on with it," snapped Priya.

The tense silence hung in the cottage as Felix continued his work. After a few moments more, Dev's emails appeared on the screen. It took Felix nanoseconds to bring up the right attachments. Aerial maps filled the screen, vast swathes of green space broken by scattered settlements.

"There," Priya said, pointing at a red rectangle that encircled a cluster of buildings.

"That's definitely the Highlands." Rory leaned forward, his shoulder pressing against mine.

"Your family's land?"

Rory shook his head, studying the map intently as Felix zoomed in. "No. And it's not near where Dev's phone was either. It's northwest of here."

The next map zoomed in on the red rectangle, a detailed view of a building complex made up of four separate structures.

"The email doesn't have an elaboration of what exactly these maps are," Felix said. "I guess they spoke about a lot of this over the phone? But I'll be able to locate the buildings online. It'll be listed as something."

Priya tapped her nails against the wooden table. "The question is, did Dev come up here of his own accord to investigate all this in person, or was he taken and brought up here?"

"I'm going to ring Carrie," Rory announced, already pulling out his phone as Felix pulled up the number for him.

We watched as he dialled, waited... *frowned*. "No answer—her phone is off."

An uneasy feeling crept across my shoulders. "Hmm."

"I wonder if I can get the number of her alpha," said Rory before chewing on his lip. I barely resisted the urge to reach over and tug it free. "I think Kit might know the name. He might know someone who can help. I'll message."

While Rory typed furiously on his phone, Felix made a small noise of discovery. "I've found a text message Dev drafted to Rory but didn't send."

My eyes darted to Rory, who looked up sharply, shuffling back towards the screen.

> **Hey, I need to talk to you. Hopefully in person? I know we haven't seen each other in a while. But it's about everything at Meridian. This is wild, but I've found evidence that your family might be somehow connected? Can we meet? I know I hurt you, and you probably don't want to see me ever again, but this is really important.**

Rory's face paled, and his throat worked as he swallowed hard. "Well, I'm sure Carrie will have all the answers," he said, his voice brittle with forced confidence.

His phone vibrated—Kit had already come through with a number. Rory immediately dialled, putting the phone on speaker.

"Hello? This is Rory Thorne. I'm looking for Carrie MacGregor? Sorry to bother you, but her phone is off, and it's urgent."

A gruff male voice responded. "Who's asking?"

"I'm a friend. I've been trying to reach her."

"Well, you're out of luck. She hasn't been seen for two weeks. Since the end of April."

Rory's eyes snapped to mine, wide with alarm. The date matched up almost perfectly with Dev's disappearance.

"Two weeks? Is that normal for her?"

"No," the voice said.

"Did you know that she was investigating missing shifters?" asked Rory.

A long pause stretched across the line. When the voice returned, it was sharper, more guarded. "Who exactly are you? And how do you know about that? Did you say you're a Thorne?" There was an edge to the man's tone now.

Rory paused before answering. "I'm not in the Glenmoriston pack. I left them years ago."

Another stretched silence.

"Let me know if you find out where she is," he said at last. Then hung up before I could interject and demand more information.

"Well, that was helpful."

Knock, knock, knock.

Three sharp taps on the front door had all four of us jumping out of our skin.

A dark look crossed Rory's face as he inhaled sharply through his nose. "Time's up. They're here."

Rory

*K*nock, knock, knock.

The sound came again, and I groaned, moving towards the door.

I'd already caught their scent. Tariq stood on the other side of our cottage door. And with him, that unmistakable stench of undiluted arrogance that could only be Callum Reid.

"Stay there," I muttered, my stomach clenching as I opened the door just a crack to prevent them from seeing our unexpected guests.

"Hello?" I kept my voice casual, like I wasn't panicking about the evidence of our investigation spread across the cottage.

Tariq stood ramrod straight in his usual formal posture, Callum slightly behind him, glowering. The scar through his left eyebrow was tugged downwards as he scowled at me. He had no signs of injury from our scuffle—either they'd healed or were hidden under the thick hoodie he wore. Had he even told anyone we'd fought? I wondered what my mother would think of her precious protégé ambushing me in the woods.

"We've got a message for you from Edina," Tariq announced, his tone clipped and efficient as always.

"Did she not fancy the walk herself?" I asked, leaning against the doorframe.

Tariq ignored my jab. "There's a taxi waiting for your *guests* at the gate."

"What guests?" I asked with mock innocence.

Before I could stop him, Tariq shoved the door wide open, pushing past me with Callum hot on his heels.

For a long, uncomfortable second, Tariq raked his eyes over the cottage—the blood still on the floorboards, Maxwell's hostile stance, arms folded, Priya and Felix sitting very still at the table.

"I'm not entirely sure what you were thinking, but the pair of them need to leave, *now*. We graciously decided to allow one outsider"—he slid his eyes to Maxwell, voice laden with disgust—"as a peace offering. But this? This is too far." He glared at Priya and Felix, and Felix visibly flinched, looking terrified as he slammed his laptop shut.

The sudden movement drew Tariq's attention to the computer. Panicking that he might declare he was seizing it, I jumped in with, "They were just here for a flying visit. I forgot my toothbrush, and they offered to bring it to me."

Tariq did *not* find that amusing. "The taxi's waiting."

"It's okay, Rory," Priya said, standing to gather her bags. "We'll go stay in the town."

Callum growled, low and threatening, and I wanted to punch him in the face. Or tear his throat out.

"You're not welcome here," Tariq stated coldly. "Not on pack lands, or in our town."

Our town. As if they actually owned every piece of it. The hatred bubbled up inside me—my family always thinking they could possess and control everything around them.

"It's okay, Priya. You're needed back in London anyway. I'll be home soon," I said, trying to sound reassuring.

Tariq moved towards the front door, holding it open expectantly.

"Jesus, give them a moment," I snapped. "Look, I'll walk them to the gate, okay? You can go back to the manor and watch from the cameras."

"We've strict instructions to personally ensure they get in that taxi," Tariq replied, "and then escort you to Edina."

The mention of my mother set off a riot in my chest, each heartbeat a panicked tap dance. A wave of nausea crashed over me, and suddenly

I was twelve again, standing outside my father's door, waiting for punishment, his disappointment in me already seeping into my soul.

Maxwell materialised at my side, his hand finding my arm, and squeezing tight. "We'll all walk to the gate together to make sure our friends get in the taxi safe and sound," he told Tariq with a horribly fake smile.

A sudden squeak had me swivelling towards Felix. His eyes were wide with terror—Callum's hand was on his shoulder, his fingers coiled with unmistakable threat.

"Get off him," I snarled.

Before I could move, Priya swung around and drove her elbow straight into Callum's stomach. He doubled over with a grunt of surprise, then straightened up, face contorted with rage as he hissed at her.

My vision clouded red. I lunged forward, ready to tear Callum's throat out, when Maxwell's arms locked around me from behind.

"Let's go," Maxwell said firmly in my ear, his grip tightening as I struggled against him. "Let's. Go."

I could feel my wolf raging inside me, clawing to get out and defend. Defend my family. Defend the pack I'd built for myself. But Maxwell's arms around me grounded me, even as I trembled with fury.

"It'll only make things worse," he murmured into my ear.

Tariq's face remained impassive. "After you," he said coldly, gesturing towards the open door.

Within moments, Priya and Felix were packed and out of the door. We marched in silence towards the gate, Tariq and Callum bringing up our rear like vicious guard dogs.

When we reached the gate, it was already open, the taxi waiting a short distance outside. Tariq and Callum hung back within the perimeter of the wall, while Maxwell said brief goodbyes at the entrance, leaving me to walk them to the car.

Felix looked relieved at the sight of it, quickly jumping into the back seat, hugging his bag to himself like a blanket. His first Killigrew Street experience outside of his lair had certainly been an action-packed one.

Priya lingered with her hand on the taxi door, glancing back at the manor house with obvious concern. "Well, that was... intense. Sorry we have to go."

"Believe me, you don't want to spend any more time here than you have to."

"I can see why." She studied my face carefully. "Are you going to be okay? Because I saw how Callum was looking at you in there, and I don't like leaving you here."

"I'll be fine. Maxwell's here."

"Speaking of Maxwell..." She lowered her voice. "So, tell me quickly. What's going on?"

"The taxi driver looks pretty ready to leave."

"So don't keep him waiting."

I sighed, glancing back at where Callum and Tariq were watching us like hawks. "It was just one time. Last night. Just a casual hookup. Burning off pent-up anger towards each other. Nothing more to it."

Priya's expression softened with concern. "Don't give me that rubbish. I saw the way you were running over to him earlier. Your wolf was practically licking his face. What if this is more than just sex?"

I scoffed, though my pulse skyrocketed. "I'm not being his baby-bi experiment. We're colleagues. Professionals. And stuff." I swallowed hard. The truth was, I wasn't sure my heart would take it—seeing him at meetings, working with him, if we actually dated and it went south. Which it inevitably would. "I'd usually happily be any hot man's guinea pig. But not with him. Not after everything."

There was a long pause as Priya studied my face. "Rory."

"What?"

"You're taking the safe option here. Closing yourself off to new possibilities. Don't overthink this. Trust your instincts."

I whacked her on the head. "Sorry that I'm trying to be a mature, sensible adult for once."

"If you were a mature, sensible adult, you wouldn't be planning on fucking his brains out the moment you get back to that cottage."

"Get in the taxi," I told her.

"This is great, though," she continued cheerily. "Everyone now owes me twenty each. Even Flynn didn't believe me. The fool."

"*Get in that taxi.*"

She laughed and finally got in, waving at me sadly as the taxi pulled away.

I raced back towards Maxwell, who stood waiting for me. Callum and Tariq lingered nearby, staring over—clearly waiting for me to join them to see my dear mother.

My stomach twisted into knots. I'd rather face a pack of rabid wolves than have another conversation with her.

Maxwell stepped in front of me.

"I'll see you back at the cottage, I guess," I said, trying to sound casual despite the anxiety crawling up my throat.

"Not a chance. I'm coming with you." He folded his arms across his chest, stance wide and immovable. "The last time you were out of my sight, you came back bleeding. You're not leaving my side ever again."

Oh. Why did that sentence cause my stomach to explode into a thousand fluttering butterflies?

"I mean, until we get back to London," he added, spoiling the moment with his signature scowl. "Then you're Seb's problem."

"Gee, you really know how to make a guy feel special," I said. "But seriously, I'll be fine."

Maxwell shook his head. "I'm not budging on this. Besides, it fits with our cover story." He reached out to grab my arm, his fingers warm against my bare skin. "Your fierce, overly protective boyfriend isn't going to let you go alone," he said, while squeezing my arm, his thumb gliding over my skin.

I almost told him he was giving me very mixed signals, but it probably wasn't the time for that conversation.

Tariq and Callum marched us to the house. Maxwell surprised me by sliding his hand down my arm, his fingers intertwining with mine. The simple gesture sent a rush of pleasant tingles through me, and the knot of terror at facing my mum loosened slightly.

As we climbed the steps, Tariq said, "Theodore, you can wait in the lobby. Edina wishes to speak with her son alone."

Maxwell's grip on my hand tightened. "Rory isn't going anywhere without me," he stated, shooting a scathing look to Callum.

Before Tariq could respond, the manor's heavy oak door swung open with a sharp creak. Isla emerged, ginger hair pulled up in a harsh ponytail, freckled face flushed. "Rory, are you okay? I've just heard what happened."

"It's all fine," I said quickly, not wanting to cause more drama. "My friends shouldn't have popped up uninvited. That's on them."

Isla turned to glare at Tariq and Callum. "They were hardly staging an invasion. Christ, you'd think they were carrying pitchforks the way you all reacted."

I caught the way Callum's entire posture shifted when Isla spoke. His shoulders straightened, his eyes raking over her like he wanted to devour her whole.

"Edina has requested to see Rory," Tariq told her pointedly.

Isla's expression softened with sympathy as she looked at me. She reached out to touch my arm gently. "Good luck. You know, I'd love it if we could spend some time together before the gathering on Friday. If you're not too busy, of course." She shot a knowing look at Maxwell, complete with a cheeky wink.

Standing there, watching my cousin's genuine concern and warmth, I felt a stab of guilt. Maybe I'd been too quick to write off my entire family in my head. It made me think that perhaps I could make an effort to reconnect with the nicer ones who weren't actively trying to kill me.

"I'd like that," I found myself saying, surprised by how much I meant it.

"Edina is waiting," snapped Callum.

I laughed. "We haven't spoken properly in years. I think she can wait five more minutes."

We entered the house, and I caught sight of Bernard scurrying across the corridor. Isla and Callum peeled off at the entrance hall, leaving us to follow Tariq up the spiral staircase to the first floor. The path was achingly familiar from my childhood—too many times I'd been marched up these same steps.

Despite the anxiety gnawing at my insides, I reminded myself that I was returning here as my own person. Not part of the pack, not a manipulated child anymore, but a confident, accomplished—*semi*-accomplished—adult, with my wonderful, sexy-as-fuck, extremely intelligent boyfriend beside me. Well, pretend boyfriend.

We reached the door of my father's old office—clearly now Edina's. Tariq knocked, two sharp raps.

My mother was sitting at her desk when we entered. Her gaze swept over me, lingering with obvious distaste on my tight-fitting tie-dye shirt—the bright pinks and purples seeming to offend her personally. Tariq bowed to her before silently retreating, shutting the door behind him.

The office was exactly as I remembered it, complete with the Scottish flag hung on one wall and landscapes of the Highlands on the others. The desk's feet had been carved to look like wolves' heads, their snarling faces frozen in eternal aggression.

She addressed Maxwell. "I expected Rory alone."

"You might need to readjust your expectations, then," Maxwell replied coolly. "Rory has asked me to be here with him."

Edina made a clicking noise with her tongue, a habit that had always set my nerves on edge.

Maxwell moved to take a seat in front of her, dragging me along with him. I sank into the chair, trying to appear more confident than I felt.

Edina eyed me for a long moment. "The intruders made it to their transport successfully?" Her tone made it clear she already knew the answer.

"Yes. I didn't realise they were coming. They... just wanted to see where I grew up."

"They know what you are? What we are?" she asked carefully.

I panicked, not quite knowing the right answer. "Um... no..."

Edina laughed, the sound brittle. "You were never any good at lying, Rory. But you can drop the pretence. I know that you all work together in London, under a vampire called Sebastián Salazar."

I gasped, my mind reeling. "How—"

"You thought we'd let Kit go without keeping tabs on him?" she asked. "As soon as he left the military to head to London, we had people on it."

My mind was reeling—Kit and I had no idea. We hadn't heard from our pack in so many years, it was like they existed in a different universe. To learn we'd been watched all this time... was unsettling, to say the least.

"How much do you know?" I asked.

Edina shrugged. "To be clear, I dinnae really care what the pair of you get up to. You've left my pack, made your choice. My point is, you don't need to play games with me."

"So why did you invite us back here, then?" I demanded. "You tried to ring me for the first time since Dad died, and then Alex made it sound like you were desperate for us to come in his email to Kit."

"Desperate is a strong word," she replied, leaning back in her chair. "But you and Kit are still my sons, and I'd like a distant, cordial relationship with you both. Other packs have been asking about you."

I scoffed. "Of course. It's all about appearances."

"Not just that. And I've wanted to reach out for a while," she continued. "When Callum suggested—though slightly last minute, I confess—that the Spring Equinox Gathering could be a suitable time to reconnect, I agreed."

"Callum?" I couldn't believe my ears. "Did you know he attacked me last night?"

"He told me everything, aye. Including who made the first strike."

"Rory came back bleeding," Maxwell interjected, scowling so deeply his glasses slid down his nose.

"I trust Callum's assessment of the situation." She waved a dismissive hand. "Those two have always had their issues."

Maxwell leaned forward, his voice dangerously calm. "So you're not going to discipline Callum for almost killing your son?"

Edina's gaze slid from Maxwell to me, her eyes cold. "Let's stay on topic, shall we? Rory, I'm glad you decided to come up early, because I would like to move forward."

"Well, I'm not interested in any sort of relationship, especially one just for appearances. You've got Callum now anyway, your perfect little lapdog. I only came up this week to see Uncle Alex and Isla, and to get closure."

Edina frowned. "Closure?"

I laughed, the sound hollow. "You really have no idea, do you? What you put me through when I lived here?"

Her face froze. It took a while for her to say, "Your father was... harsh, that is true. But he was just trying to teach you discipline. You needed structure. Your mind was always... everywhere. Your... condition... made you unpredictable. Dangerous, even. The pack couldnae afford that kind of liability. How else could you learn? And he was harder on you because he saw potential. Don't you see that was a compliment? That's how we learn—through challenge and hardship."

Beside me, I felt Maxwell shift in his seat. I looked over to find his face thunderous. I reached across to grab his knee.

Yet my own vision blurred with rage. I wanted to scream at her, throw the objects on her desk at her, to shout that all I ever wanted as a child was a mother who loved me, a father who didn't beat me with a belt and lock me in the basement.

But I took a deep breath and said, "Well, I hope you're happy with the result of your methods. Because neither Kit nor I became your perfect successor. We'd both rather have died. We moved countries to get away from you."

My mother visibly recoiled, and I rejoiced in my small victory. "How is... Kit?" she asked, tensing—clearly desperate for information about her favourite son after all these years.

I *could* have told her how equally traumatised Kit was, how my parents' behaviour pushed him to join the military unit that further fucked him up in ways that I didn't even understand yet, on top of everything he experienced here. That he couldn't even bear to talk about our childhood.

Instead I said, "He's doing great. Brilliant, in fact. He laughed at Alex's email. The idea of bothering to come up here to see you was hilarious to him."

Edina's fingers drummed against the polished oak of her desk. "Is there any way Kit would consider coming up?" A flicker of something—vulnerability, maybe—passed across her face.

I paused, genuinely surprised by the question. Was there a slight maternal instinct beneath Edina's many icy layers—a mother aching for her firstborn? For a brief, unsettling moment, I felt a twinge of sympathy for her.

Then I remembered Kit's face whenever our childhood was mentioned. The nightmares he still had. The way he'd lock himself in his room on the anniversary of the day he left.

"Nope. No way," I said flatly. "You're never going to see him again."

The softness in her eyes hardened instantly. Her lips pressed into a thin line, jaw tightening as she rose from her seat with deliberate slowness.

"You may leave now," she seethed, her voice a controlled blade. "I shall see you at the gathering on Friday."

I stood, teetering on the balls of my feet. A part of me was unsure if I should ask her about Dev—maybe I secretly wanted to see a look of genuine confusion across her face. Because although Dev was convinced my family was involved with his investigation, I didn't want to believe it, despite hating them.

The question hung in my throat, but I swallowed it down. Not yet. Not until I knew more.

"Goodbye," I said, marching to the door without looking back.

When we were outside the manor, at the bottom of the steps, Maxwell stopped me with a gentle hand on my arm.

"You did a great job just then," he said, his voice uncharacteristically soft. "You were right. You didn't actually need me there at all."

I turned to him, studying the afternoon light on his face, the genuine respect in his eyes. Something bloomed inside me, warm and fragile.

"You're wrong," I whispered, reaching up to stroke his cheek, enjoying the slight roughness of stubble beneath my fingertips. I leaned in and pressed my lips gently against his cheekbone, lingering for a heartbeat.

It happened the moment my lips touched his skin—a surge of electricity that shot through me like lightning finding earth. My entire body seized with it, a current flowing from my lips through my chest and down to my toes. I gasped against his skin, fingers involuntarily clutching at his shirt.

With the shock came that scent—raindrops on hot pavement—but amplified, as though the sky had opened above us and drenched everything in a summer downpour. It filled my lungs, my head, making me dizzy with its intensity. For a moment, I could have sworn I felt the phantom sensation of rain on my skin, despite the clear afternoon sky.

Maxwell jerked back, his eyes wide with shock, pupils blown. His hand flew to the spot where my lips had touched, and he stared at me with a look of bewildered wonder.

He opened his mouth—likely to ask for the hundredth time what the fuck was going on—and panic flashed through me. I couldn't risk telling him. Not while I was enjoying this fragile thing between us so much. Not when it would send him running a thousand miles from me.

So I did the only thing I could think of—I lunged forward, grabbed his face between my hands, and crushed my mouth against his. Not a gentle peck, but a desperate clash of lips and teeth. I swept my tongue against his, swallowing his question, replacing it with a groan that vibrated through both our bodies.

For a heartbeat, he stood frozen, clearly caught off-guard by my sudden attack. Then his hands found my waist, pulling me against him with a force that made me gasp into his mouth. Whatever he'd been about to say was forgotten, lost in the heat building between us.

When we finally broke apart, Maxwell cleared his throat, his glasses askew. "Let's go back to the cottage," he said breathlessly. He quickly added, "To um... see if Felix has sent us anything else yet."

"That," I said, unable to keep the grin from spreading across my face, "sounds like an excellent idea."

16

Rory

We practically ran back to the cottage through the golden evening light, turning the walk into some sort of playful race—completing the journey in record time before bursting through the door, tumbling over each other as we jostled to be first inside.

The door slammed shut, and in a blink, Maxwell caught me—strong arms circling my waist like he was apprehending his most wanted fugitive—and in one decisive motion, hoisted me upwards as though I weighed nothing. I shrieked in surprise, then laughed, instinctively locking my legs around his waist, my arms finding anchor around his neck as he carried me into the kitchen. The sudden height gave me a new vantage point, looking down into those dark eyes now dancing with intention rather than their usual scrutiny. His lips found mine, seeking and demanding, as he placed me on the counter.

Maxwell's hands slid under my shirt, fingers working against the tight fabric that clung stubbornly to my skin.

"Did you wear this stupidly tight shirt today just to torment me?" he murmured against my lips.

"Obviously," I replied, grinning. "Did it work?"

He traced the curve of my spine with blunted nails, making my back arch, his fingers oh-so warm against the cottage's chill.

"Too well."

One of my hands tangled in his hair, scratching with just the same amount of pressure as he was giving me. I kissed a path along his stubbled jaw, mouthing my lips against the coarse hair. I finally reached his waiting tongue. A hint of camomile tea still lingered, and my ears caught the rapid thrum of his heartbeat, matching the frantic pace of mine.

I tightened my legs around him, drawing him closer to the counter's edge. The position had my hardening cock pressing against the firm plane of his stomach while his own growing erection nudged against the counter beneath me. Rolling my hips forward, I sought more contact, more friction, dragging myself against him with a low moan that he swallowed with another kiss.

Maxwell's hands traced fire along my skin, and all I could think about was how much I wanted him—all of him. My mind raced with possibilities as his mouth moved against mine. I wanted to drop to my knees right here in this cottage kitchen, take him into my mouth again like I had last night. The thought of his taste, his weight on my tongue, made me harder. Or maybe this time he'd be the one to sink down, those lovely lips wrapped around me...

Oh, the things I wanted to do with him. I rarely found anyone I felt comfortable bottoming for—usually seeking partners that wanted me to top. But with Maxwell, I ached for him to twist me around, to bend me over this very counter. Or maybe he'd prefer the bed, where he could watch my face as he pushed inside me. The images flooded my mind, each more explicit than the last.

Then Priya's voice echoed in my head: *"What if this is more than just sex?"*

The thought hit me like a bucket of ice water, even as Maxwell's hands continued their exploration of my body. Because she was right.

I didn't just want to fuck Maxwell. I wanted to fall asleep with his arms around me, wake up to his octopus hugs and sleepy morning face. I wanted to surprise him with breakfast in bed—maybe French toast, which I was actually half decent at making. I wanted to go for walks with him that didn't involve searching for my ex-boyfriend's dead body. I wanted to see his rare smile when I said something unexpectedly funny. I wanted to keep winding him up, to have him glower at me until he cracked, bursting into laughter. I wanted to peel back each of his layers, to discover all the soft parts of him he kept so carefully hidden. To map every corner of his guarded heart.

I didn't want this to end when we got back to London.

The realisation terrified me. This was Theodore Maxwell—Detective Dickface—the man who'd arrested me during a full moon. The man I'd spent the last year and a half insulting. The man who was only up here with me in Scotland because it was his job. The man who'd never even kissed another man before this.

Maxwell's hand crept up my thigh to land on my cock, squeezing lightly through the denim of my jeans, and I gasped at the contact, pushing up into him—but the spiral of thoughts wouldn't stop.

"Wait," I said, against my better judgement, heart sinking like a stone. "Hold on a moment."

Maxwell jumped back as if I'd slapped him, his hands flying up in surrender.

"I'm so sorry," he blurted, eyes wide. "I didn't mean to—I thought you wanted—"

"No, no," I said quickly, hopping off the counter and reaching for him. "That was all great. So great. You didn't do anything wrong. It's just..." I tore a hand through my hair, struggling to find the right words. "Is this just sex?"

He blinked at me. "What?"

"Is this just sex?" I repeated, my heart fluttering wildly, sending me dizzy.

Maxwell frowned, adjusting his glasses. "That's what you told me it was yesterday."

"I know, but I say a lot of things." I sighed. "You might have noticed by now."

He studied me for a long moment, his expression unreadable. "What are you saying?"

I fidgeted with the hem of my shirt, suddenly unable to meet his eyes. "I'm not sure."

Maxwell retreated further, exhaling loudly.

My eyes darted around the cottage kitchen, desperate for something to focus on that wasn't Maxwell's increasingly concerned expression. That's when I spotted a bottle rack mounted on the wall near the window. I reached it in three quick strides, scanning the collection until I found a bottle of single malt whisky, about half empty, its amber contents glowing like liquid gold.

I brought out two heavy crystal tumblers that looked like they'd seen their fair share of Highland evenings, poured just myself a glass, leaving the bottle on the counter.

I turned to find Maxwell staring at me like I'd completely lost my mind, which, to be fair, wasn't entirely inaccurate. "Well," Maxwell said, "what *are* you sure of?"

"Why do *I* have to be the one to put my cards on the table first?"

Maxwell rolled his eyes so far back I thought they might disappear into his skull.

"Let's play truth or drink," I suggested, swirling my whisky. "Three questions each."

"Are we twelve?" Maxwell asked, voice dripping with disdain.

"Please?" I said, then stared at him until he sighed, reached for the whisky and poured himself the tiniest amount.

"I'll go first." I leaned forward, studying his face. "Do you still hate me?"

Maxwell frowned, a genuinely almost convincing display of puzzlement. "I've never *hated* you, Rory. You've infuriated me. Made me want to bang my head against the wall. Made me want to shake you on more than one occasion. But I've never hated you. Not in the same way you hate me. I mean, *hated* me." He raised an eyebrow. "Do you still hate me?"

"No." I took a tiny sip of whisky. "So... do you like me?"

A long pause. He stared at me through his glasses, his eyebrows a squiggle. "Do I... like you?"

"Yes. You have to answer, or throw back that whole drink."

He sighed, long and deep, a sound of resignation. "Yes, Rory. Yes, I like you."

My heart did a weird little flip. It was a simple admission, but hearing those words in his serious, slightly exasperated voice made my skin tingle.

Though it wasn't enough.

"But do you *like*, like me?"

Maxwell looked to the ceiling and mumbled what might have been a prayer.

I moved closer, one hand on my hip. "Well?"

He met my gaze, his wide hazelnut eyes studying me carefully. The lusciously thick eyelashes I was so jealous of fluttered as he blinked slowly. "Listen, I'm going to be honest here. This is all quite... confusing for me. And very... sudden. Possibly I hit my head a week ago and I'm in a coma right now, and this is all one crazy dream. But... yes... I think— no, I *know*. I do like you. *Like*, like you. Which, considering you drive me absolutely mad, is quite frankly terrifying and completely impractical, but here we are. I think I might *like*, like you very much. What about you?"

I briefly considered pretending to contemplate the question for a moment, but I could tell the honesty he'd just given me had cost him. So he deserved my own.

I brought two hands to each side of Maxwell's head, cradling his face between my palms. I focused intently, channelling every ounce of sincerity I possessed into a single thought:

...I think I might like, like you very much as well...

I pushed the thought forward with all my might, willing it to cross the barrier between our minds, infusing it with the tangled mess of emotions churning inside me—the warmth, the fear, the longing.

Maxwell's breath audibly caught. His eyes widened behind his glasses, lips parting in surprise. He leaned down, trying to capture my mouth with his, but I ducked away, sliding my hands down to rest on his shoulders.

"You still have one more question left," I said softly. "It has to be fair."

I still had a dozen more questions I desperately wanted to ask him, like "but do you want to see me when we get back to London," and "what fruit is your favourite on French toast," and "why do you make me feel so warm and tingly inside?"

But I kept silent, awaiting Maxwell's final question.

He considered me, his gaze searching my face. "What's that weird electric thing that keeps happening to you? I know you know what it is."

Fuck. Not that.

Visualising a white brick wall in case he decided to cheat, I reached over to pick up my glass and downed the drink in three large gulps, the amber liquid burning a fiery trail down my throat. I gasped for air afterwards, my eyes watering.

Then I threw my body at him before he could demand the truth. Because I almost wanted to give it to him. But I didn't want to spoil this fragile thing between us with delusional suggestions of forever.

Not when he actually *liked*, liked me.

He caught me with a soft sound, wrapping his arms around me as I stretched upward on my tiptoes to kiss him deeply. I wanted Maxwell's hand on my dick so badly I could scream with it—and then suddenly his hand was there, cupping me through my jeans, squeezing with just the right pressure.

Maxwell's breath ghosted against my ear, making me practically melt into a puddle as he whispered, "Can I taste you?"

My brain short-circuited. Four simple words that nearly sent me over the edge right there. *Yes, yes, yes,* my mind screamed, every cell in my body vibrating with want.

Maxwell pulled back slightly, dark eyes searching mine. "I want to hear you say it."

"God, yes," I managed to gasp out, my voice embarrassingly breathy. "Please. Before I combust."

The corner of his mouth twitched upward in satisfaction. "You know, I think I like you desperate."

And suddenly he was moving at lightning speed. His fingers found the button of my jeans, making quick work of it and my zip. I hopped awkwardly, helping him as he tugged them down my legs with an urgency that made my heart race.

The sound of Maxwell's knees hitting the kitchen tiles had me quivering in anticipation. He reached for my underwear... then froze. His eyes widened comically behind his glasses as he stared at the bright pink fabric adorned with cheerful yellow rubber ducks.

"Fun, right?" I said, wiggling my hips slightly.

Maxwell still looked semi-shocked, blinking rapidly as though trying to process what he was seeing. But then something shifted in his expression—a softening around his eyes, a quirk of his lips—and he leaned forward, pressing his open mouth against my hipbone. The hot slide of his tongue made me shudder, my hands finding purchase in his tight coils.

With a boldness that surprised me, he grabbed the waistband of my ridiculous underwear with his teeth and began dragging them down, his hands coming up to knead my ass cheeks firmly.

And then suddenly, there I was—completely exposed, my cock proudly jutting between us. A wave of anxiety washed over me as Maxwell stared. What if he didn't really want this? What if he felt obligated to reciprocate after last night? What if—

"Rory," Maxwell said, voice firm but gentle. "What is it going to take to convince you that I'm attracted to every part of you, including your dick?"

"Umm..." I laughed weakly. "A fucking killer hot blow job?"

"No pressure, then," he muttered, swallowing visibly. For a moment, something flashed across his face, and I caught the nervousness he was trying to hide. "You know, I obviously haven't done this before, so... 'killer hot blow job' might be a bit of a stretch. Will marginally adequate do?"

My heart gave a tiny squeeze. "Maxwell, you could probably read me the phone book right now and I'd come. I don't actually need killer hot. I just need you."

His expression softened as he reached up, stroking over the dark blond thatch of hair above my dick, his fingers surprisingly gentle as they traced patterns through the coarse curls. I fought hard not to purr like a kitten.

The first touch of his tongue—right where I wanted it, right over my tip, where precum trickled out—had my eyes closing, as I let myself sink into the sensation. I quickly forced them open again, because I wanted to savour every bit of this with every single one of my senses.

I was just in time to catch Maxwell's mouth widening, his lips stretching around me as he took me in. The most exquisite silky heat enveloped me, making my breath hitch and my fingers clutch desperately at his shoulders.

He didn't hesitate. His enthusiasm left no space for doubt as he worked me with surprising skill, taking me deeper with each bob of his head. The way he moved—like he was savouring the finest delicacy and wouldn't allow anyone to interrupt his feast—had me making noises I'd definitely deny later.

All my previous concerns evaporated like smoke. Because there was no way Maxwell wasn't into this. Not when his eyes kept flicking up to meet mine, dark and intent. Not when he was gripping my thighs with those gloriously large hands, fingers pressing insistently into my skin as though he'd arrest me if I dared move away.

My fingers once again found purchase in his coils, their texture familiar now. I thrust forward slightly, unable to help myself. Maxwell chuckled, the vibration rippling through me and dragging a broken moan from my throat. He settled into a rhythm, his cheeks hollowing as he sucked, the pressure making my toes curl against the kitchen tiles.

My knees started to shake, threatening to buckle entirely. Thank god for Maxwell's firm grip on my hips, his strong hands holding me steady while he continued his glorious assault.

One of his hands began to wander, sliding from my hip around to the curve of my ass. He hesitated there, his touch questioning.

Yes, please. Please, please, please, please.

Maxwell's eyes flicked up to meet mine, confirmation sparking in their depths. His fingers traced the cleft of my ass, and then—*oh, fuck*—he pressed just slightly against my hole, the barest hint of pressure.

I gasped, my back arching involuntarily. It was too much, too good—I was going to come embarrassingly fast if he kept this up.

"Wait," I panted, tugging lightly at his hair and pushing against his shoulder.

Maxwell pulled off with an obscenely wet sound, his lips swollen and glistening. He wiped the drool from his mouth with the back of his hand, looking up at me with questioning eyes.

"Rory, if you're about to ask me if I *like*, like you again, that really will be the death of me."

"Do you want to fuck me?" tumbled ungraciously out of my mouth.

Maxwell's mouth made an O of surprise, his eyes widening behind his glasses. After a moment, he cleared his throat. "Is that what you like?"

I shifted my weight, fighting the urge to cover my glistening dick with my hands. "I mean, normally I prefer to top, but yeah… sometimes."

With Maxwell, the idea felt right in a way it rarely did with others. There was something in the careful way he touched me that made me want to surrender completely. The thought of being completely vulnerable with him—of letting go of control for once and trusting someone else to hold all the spinning pieces of me together—was intoxicating. My mind whirred for more words to say, but I couldn't quite bring myself to articulate how safe he made me feel despite our turbulent history.

Maxwell said nothing, his expression unreadable. Tension hung heavy between us, growing more awkward with each passing second. *For fuck's sake, Rory, why did you have to go and fuck it up again? We were having a perfectly nice time—*

"You fuck me, then."

I blinked, certain I'd misheard him. "What?"

"You heard me." Maxwell stood, adjusting his glasses with that precise little movement I'd come to recognize. And adore. "You prefer to top, so do that."

Typical. The one time I really need him to read my mind, and he doesn't.

Something in his tone made me narrow my eyes. "Are you trying to prove a point? That you're so one hundred percent definitely bisexual, that you absolutely want a cock up your ass?"

"No," he said, too quickly. "It's just... logical."

"Logical?" I snorted. "Have you ever even touched yourself there before?"

Maxwell pursed his lips in a way that was almost comical. "That's irrelevant."

"It's extremely relevant! You can't just decide to bottom like you're picking what to have for lunch." He'd said it himself—this was all very sudden for him.

"I'm trying to do what I thought you'd prefer," he said, his voice measured and careful. "I want this to be good for you."

"Good for me?" I threw my hands up. "This isn't about checking boxes on some satisfaction survey. This is about what feels right for both of us."

"And that means I can't be... accommodating?" His eyebrow arched perfectly.

"No, it means—" I growled in frustration. "Look, Maxwell, I need your cock inside me right now, or I swear to god I'm going to die. Like, actually die. Is that what you want? My death on your conscience?"

"Fine, then!" Maxwell's voice was edged with frustration.

"Fine!" I echoed.

My cock hadn't deflated throughout this exchange. Not even a little bit.

Then a horrible realisation struck me. "Fuck!" I exclaimed, smacking my palm against my forehead. "We don't have condoms!"

Maxwell blinked at me, his expression shifting to disbelief. "You didn't bring any?"

"Why the fuck would I have brought condoms?" I gesticulated wildly. "This isn't actually a couple's retreat, as much as we're pretending it is."

"I thought you'd have some in your wallet or something."

"Do I seem the type to be that prepared?" I asked, throwing my hands up. *Not that any of mine would even fit you anyway,* I resisted adding.

Maxwell's lips quirked. "Point taken."

"But I got tested like a month ago," I offered, shifting my weight. "All clear."

"A month? And you... haven't had sex since then?" Maxwell asked, his tone carefully neutral.

I scowled, crossing my arms over my chest. "Obviously not, else I'd have said. I'm not at it with different blokes every night, you know."

"Sorry," Maxwell said, looking genuinely contrite. "The way you and Priya talk sometimes made me think that you... erm... enjoy a very healthy sex life."

"Are you calling me a man-whore because I occasionally have casual sex?" I demanded, my voice rising an octave.

Maxwell's eyes widened in horror. "Fuck, no! Look, I'm really sorry." He ran a hand across his face, clearly mortified.

Oops. I'd probably slightly overreacted.

"I guess..." he continued. "I'm very aware that you're much more sexually active than I am. In fact, I haven't had sex in ages—coming up to a year now." He glanced away for a moment. "But anyway, to the best of my knowledge, I'm completely safe. I had a bunch of annual checkups earlier this year, STDs included."

By now my cock had finally gotten the message and deflated considerably. Maxwell noticed—his eyes dropped to my groin before he reached out and took me in hand, gliding his fingers very slowly up and down.

"I'm trying very hard not to read your mind right now," he said quietly, his thumb tracing a delicate circle over my sensitive head. "But I'd very much like to know what you're thinking."

"I'm thinking that we should go upstairs before we fight again, because I really do need you to fuck me senseless."

Maxwell immediately dropped my dick, took my hand in his, and guided me toward the stairs. His fingers laced through mine, warm and certain, as he led me up each step.

My heart fluttered wildly as we ascended the stairs, Maxwell's hand still firmly grasping mine, his grip deliciously tight.

"I have lube, by the way, in case you were wondering," I said. "It's in the zipped pocket of my suitcase from ages ago."

He paused at the top of the stairs, turning to look at me with his signature arched eyebrow. "The suitcase whose contents are still scattered across the floor like a clothes bomb detonated at the bottom of the stairs?"

I glanced down at the explosion of my belongings—T-shirts, trousers, and socks flung in every direction like shrapnel.

"I guess I should probably bring that up now," I said, reluctantly letting go of his hand and bounding back down the stairs. I rummaged through the disaster zone, finally locating the small bottle. Victoriously, I held it up.

Then, I left my suitcase exactly where it was, taking the steps two at a time to rejoin him on the landing.

Maxwell's eyes darkened, a low growl rumbling from his chest. "You're bloody infuriating, do you know that?"

I waggled the bottle between us, my grin widening. "You secretly love it, apparently."

He stared at the lube. "Piña colada flavour? Really?"

"What's wrong, too fun for you?"

Without warning, Maxwell's hands were on my shoulders, propelling me down the corridor with surprising force. My back hit the bedroom door, which swung open under our combined weight. He marched me backward until my legs hit the mattress, pushing me down onto the bed.

I barely had time to bounce on the springy surface before Maxwell was looming over me, his fingers gripping the hem of my tie-dye shirt. In one violent motion, he yanked it up and over my head, tossing it somewhere.

Cool air kissed my bare chest, though the tremor that ran through me had more to do with the hunger prowling behind Maxwell's dark eyes, his breathing sharp and uneven.

"Take your clothes off, then," I said.

Maxwell stared at me. "Are you always like this?"

"Did you expect anything different?"

Maxwell stepped back, his gaze fixed on me as his hands moved to the buttons of his white shirt. One by one, he undid them with deliberate slowness, never breaking eye contact. The intensity in his dark eyes made my breath catch as each movement revealed more of his chest—a gradual unveiling that felt almost ceremonial.

His fingers worked methodically down the row of buttons, the fabric parting to reveal the strong column of his throat, then the defined planes of his chest. The shirt fell open completely, exposing the expanse of his torso, lightly covered in hair that I so desperately wanted to touch.

Maxwell shrugged the shirt from his broad shoulders, letting it slide down his arms before dropping it to the floor. His trousers followed, then his underwear, until he stood completely naked before me.

My heart danced with a ferocity that surprised me. Why was I suddenly so nervous? Maxwell was the one who'd never had sex with a man before. So why was I battling against anxious butterflies assaulting my stomach?

But this was Theodore Maxwell.

Maxwell, whose magnificent cock now hung heavy between his thighs.

I swallowed hard, my mouth suddenly dry. Dying sunlight streamed through the curtains, drenching his body in a golden, sun-kissed glow that accentuated every perfect inch of him. Broad shoulders, chest just slightly muscled. Taut stomach, powerful thighs. My eyes traced the dark trail of hair that ran from his navel downward, drawing my attention back to his impressive length.

Then he was moving toward me, climbing onto the bed, one hand reaching to remove his glasses.

"Wait," I said. "Keep them on."

His brow furrowed.

"You..." I started, my chest feeling tight, my lungs not quite getting enough air. "You look more like yourself with them on."

Wordlessly, he blanketed me with his weight while supporting himself on one elbow, and the heat of his body pressed against mine sent a lovely shiver through me.

He thrust against me, rubbing our cocks together—an instantly overwhelming friction that pulled a desperate whimper from my throat. I reached down, eager to take us both in hand—

"Let me," Maxwell murmured into my ear, his breath hot against my skin. He brushed his hand across my chin, then stroked my lips with his thumb. My mouth fell open of its own accord, and he slipped two fingers inside. I sucked eagerly, licking around his digits and mustering as much saliva as I could—easy enough, as the man on top of me already made me drool.

With his massive hand, he wrapped it around both our cocks, the wet slide of his fingers easing the way. The feeling of his enormous dick pressed against mine nearly undid me then and there—the velvet-steel hardness of him scorching against my own.

Then he shifted, and I felt the swollen head of my cock brush against something impossibly soft. Maxwell went rigid above me, his breathing ragged, and I realised what he was doing—positioning himself so the tip of my dick was right at the edge of his foreskin. His hand trembled slightly as he held us together.

"I—" he started, uncertainty flickering across his features. "Is this— I don't know if—"

"God, yes," I gasped. "That feels incredible. But only if you want to."

His breath hitched as he tentatively guided the head of my cock inside, the soft skin stretching to accommodate me. Then I was sliding into that warm, wet sheath, my tip completely enveloped by his flesh. The sensation was unlike anything I'd ever experienced—like being wrapped in the most perfect silky heat.

"Fuck," I panted, my hips jerking involuntarily as he began to stroke us together with growing confidence. The wet, obscene sounds of our skin sliding against each other filled the room.

"You feel beyond amazing," he whispered.

I could only whimper and thrust as he worked us both.

His mouth found mine in a kiss that started gentle but quickly deepened, his tongue exploring me with tender thoroughness. His tongue mapped the geography of my mouth, mirroring the strokes until I was moaning helplessly into his mouth.

"I can't—Maxwell, I'm going to come, I can't—" The words tumbled out in a desperate rush as that familiar tightness coiled low in my belly, building faster than I could control.

"Come for me," he breathed against my ear. "I want to feel you come all over me."

And I did, helplessly, my orgasm hitting like a dam bursting. I came hard, shooting directly into that tight, warm space, filling it with my release whilst he kept stroking us. The mess of it, my cum trapped and coating both our cocks, only seemed to drive him wilder.

"Please," I gasped against his neck, still shaking from the intensity. "Please, I need you inside me. Need your cock in me right now."

Maxwell's breath hitched as he stared down at the mess between us—my cum coating his hand, his cock, streaked across my stomach. Something deliciously hungry flickered across his face as he brought his fingers to his mouth, licking them clean with a deliberate slowness that made my spent dick twitch weakly.

"Fuck," I breathed, watching him taste me for the first time.

He lowered his head without warning, his tongue tracing a path along my softening length, cleaning me with careful attention. It was almost too much on my oversensitive skin, making me gasp and squirm beneath him.

"Do you like it?" I managed to ask, my voice barely a whisper.

Maxwell lifted his head, his eyes dark with want. "I'm going to need a lot more of that," he said, the promise in his voice making heat coil in my belly despite having just come.

He reached for the bottle of flavoured lube, squirting some into one hand. Then he gathered the remaining cum from my stomach, mixing the two on his fingers. His eyes never left mine as he slowly shifted, pushing himself back until he was kneeling between my legs. He grabbed my hips, pulling me onto his lap.

"I've... never even watched gay porn," Maxwell admitted, his voice low and slightly uncertain as he stared down at the slick mixture on his fingers.

I pushed myself up on my elbows, studying his face. "Never been at all tempted?"

He met my eyes, a small smile playing at the corners of his mouth. "My eyes certainly wandered over to that section a few times. But I think I didn't want to make my life any more complicated."

I couldn't help but laugh, gesturing at our naked bodies and the ridiculous situation we'd found ourselves in. "What we have right here is pretty darn complicated."

"Well, maybe I like complicated things more than I thought I would," he murmured, his voice dropping to a register that made my stomach flip.

Then there was only our heavy breathing filling the quiet room as his slick fingers traced up and down my crease with maddening slowness, teasing rather than penetrating. I whimpered as his mouth found the tender skin of my inner thigh, pressing soft kisses. The scrape of his stubble created a perfect friction.

"Are you trying to torture me?" I gasped, arching my back.

His eyes locked with mine. "Just being thorough."

When his finger finally breached me, just the tiniest bit, I screamed—a high, unfiltered sound that echoed through the cottage bedroom.

Fuck, I was already being so loud—too loud probably, way too loud. He was going to think I was putting on some ridiculous performance or something, but I couldn't help it, it had felt so good.

Maxwell, finger still barely inside me, used his other hand to trace a path up my leg where his stubble had grazed. "Be as loud as you want. I want to hear you."

As I battled back a strange prickle of wet heat threatening behind my eyelids, Maxwell's finger resumed its careful exploration, easing in so slowly I thought I might combust from frustration. Every millimetre of progress was deliberate, gentle.

"I won't break," I whispered, but Maxwell maintained his maddeningly cautious pace.

Time became elastic as he worked me open with reverent, painstaking care, clearly terrified of hurting me, even a tiny bit. His brow furrowed in concentration, lips slightly parted.

My hand found his elbow, stroking along the firm muscle of his forearm until my fingers covered his.

"Like this," I murmured, wrapping my hand firmly around his and pushing down hard, driving his finger deep inside me in one swift motion.

A gasp tore from my throat as his finger slid all the way in, filling me perfectly. I sighed in satisfaction, my eyes fluttering closed at the delicious fullness.

Maxwell's breath hitched audibly, the sound making my cock twitch against my stomach. I clenched deliberately around him, squeezing his finger, and was rewarded with another breathy choking sound.

Taking control, I moved his hand, fucking myself on his finger while rolling my hips. Fire lit each of my nerve endings as I half thrashed in the sheets, digging my nails into the meat of his thighs to help ground me.

But I needed more.

"Another," I demanded, forgetting to behave.

"What?" Maxwell sounded panicked. "Are you sure?"

I whined, pushing down harder on his hand. "Please." *Please, please, please.*

Maxwell's expression was a mix of concern and desire as he slowly withdrew his finger, adding more lube before carefully pressing two fingers against my entrance. I forced myself to relax, to be patient as he eased them in with that same infuriating caution.

I reached down to guide his hand again, but Maxwell captured my wrist with his free hand, squeezing tightly.

"Let me," he said, voice low and commanding.

His fingers curled inside me, searching, and when they brushed against that spot, I arched off the bed with a strangled cry. Maxwell's eyes widened, watching my reaction with fascination as he repeated the motion, more deliberately this time.

"There?" he asked, pressing firmly.

"Fuck—yes—right there," I gasped, relishing the fullness, the perfect pressure against my prostate. His fingers now stroked inside me with growing confidence, stretching and scissoring.

I couldn't help imagining how his tongue might feel there—hot and wet and—

Suddenly Maxwell's fingers were gone, and I was tumbling through the air. He'd flipped me over, leaving me momentarily disoriented, face pressed into the pillow.

Strong hands grabbed my hips, pulling them up and back toward him. Before I knew what was happening, Maxwell's tongue pressed against my hole, and I forgot how to breathe.

Resplendent.

Divine.

Perfection.

His mouth offered me gorgeous pressure, the wet heat of it pulsing and probing, each sweep of his tongue igniting constellations beneath my skin as he explored me with heady confidence. My cock was stirring back to life, the oversensitive flesh responding to every flick of his tongue with sharp jolts of pleasure that bordered on too much.

Throughout it all, his hands never stopped moving—strong fingers caressing my thighs, kneading the muscle there before sliding up to stroke my lower back, his long arms easily reaching to trace patterns along my spine that made me arch into his touch.

I heard myself making sounds—half words and broken pleas—*please* and *more* and *don't stop* and *fucking hell, Theo,* all tangled together in breathless desperation, my usual sharp tongue reduced to fragments. Possibly, I could come again just from this, if I moved to thrust against the bed, but I wanted Maxwell inside me.

I pushed myself up slightly, glancing back over my shoulder. "Give it to me, *now,*" I gasped out, then remembering my manners, added, "Please."

Maxwell responded with a light smack to my bottom that made me yelp in surprise and delight. I heard the cap of the lube bottle click open, followed by the wet sound of him slicking himself up.

I quickly positioned myself on hands and knees, pushing my ass up invitingly. Blood rushed through my ears as I felt that first press of Maxwell's spectacular cock against me.

Gripping me tightly, he edged in so slowly I wanted to scream with frustration. I wiggled my ass back, trying to take more of him.

His hands clamped down on my hips, holding me firmly in place. "Have you seen the size of my dick?" he growled. "I don't want to split you apart."

I almost joked that I'd had bigger, but actually, I wasn't sure that was true.

"And… I can't bear to feel your pain. You won't be able to hide it from me."

Beneath his commanding grip, I could feel him trembling, his thighs quivering against the backs of mine. With restraint? With… nerves?

"Hey," I said softly. I shuffled forwards, then twisted around, pushing Maxwell sideways until he was flat on his back. "I got this."

He seemed stunned, though he let me position him like a doll, his eyes wide, unblinking. I leaned down and kissed his cheek tenderly, the lovely stubble brushing against my skin.

"You wanted me to be on top anyway," I said with a wink.

Maxwell remained speechless as he stared up at me, watching as I climbed onto his lap, positioning myself above his mighty cock.

His eyes watched me with such intensity that I almost looked away, but something in their depths kept me captivated. With one hand, I reached back to guide him to my entrance, the blunt head pressing against me.

"All good?" I whispered, heart thumping, because for some reason, I still wanted to give him one more chance to back out.

Maxwell nodded, his Adam's apple bobbing as he swallowed hard.

I began to lower myself, the pressure instantly building as his thick head breached me. The initial stretch burned fiercely, drawing a strangled cry from my throat. I paused, panting, adjusting to the intrusion.

"Fuck—you're huge," I breathed, forcing myself to relax around him.

Maxwell's hands found my hips, his grip tender yet firm. "I told you," he muttered.

"It's fucking perfect," I quickly reassured him. "I can't wait for it. Just... can you stroke me? Please?"

His breath hitched as his hand claimed my softening cock, stroking gently. It twitched happily in his hand, already hardening once more. With streams of pleasure coursing through my veins, I closed my eyes and sank down another inch, taking more of him inside. The burning soon morphed into something electric—a delicious fullness that made me tremble. I felt split open in the most perfect way, stretched around him until there was no me and no him. Like every empty space inside me had finally found its missing piece.

My head fell back as I worked myself further down his length, sinking myself onto his thickness with slow, deliberate movements.

"Christ, Rory," Maxwell groaned beneath me.

When I finally bottomed out, I stilled, overwhelmed by the sensation of being so completely filled. Maxwell's eyes found mine in that moment—dark and intense and so fucking tender it knocked the breath from my lungs. I felt like I was falling into those depths, tumbling headfirst into something I desperately wanted to drown in. My hand flew to Maxwell's chest; I could feel each of his heartbeats pulsing inside me.

"You good?" he asked, voice strained.

In answer, I lifted myself slightly before sinking back down. The friction nearly undid me—I couldn't help the loud moan that escaped my lips, echoing throughout the room.

"Fuck yes," I cried, finding a rhythm now, rising and falling on his cock with increasing confidence.

Maxwell's hands gripped my hips tighter, guiding my movements while his hips began to thrust upward to meet me. Each powerful surge drove him further inside—the rhythm we found together meant he kept striking gold, his cock pressing against that spot inside me that made white-hot fractals explode behind my eyelids.

"Right there," I practically screamed, shameless in my pleasure. "Don't stop—fuck—Theo!"

It was so perfect I could have wept. His impressive cock filling me completely, stretching me in the most delicious way. The overwhelming fullness of him inside me, the feel of his body beneath mine, muscles taut as he worked himself to bring us pleasure—all of it combined into something transcendent.

But I wanted even more. More of him.

I wanted my body to carry the memory of him, to feel the ghost of his presence long after we finished. To have this moment etched into my muscles and bones. His cock driving into me, claiming me. I wanted him, and I wanted him hard. I wanted bruises as proof, tangible evidence of this perfect madness.

With a swift, powerful movement, he sat up, shifting his weight and wrapping one arm around my waist while his other hand gripped my hip with bruising intensity. The new position gave him leverage, and he used it mercilessly.

"Like this?" he growled, thrusting up into me with renewed vigor.

The change in angle sent him impossibly deeper, hitting my prostate with unrelenting precision.

I screamed, the sound torn from my throat wild and desperate.

Each drive of his hips sent tremors through my foundations, as if he were reshaping me from the inside out.

Yes. I gasped, clutching at his shoulders, my nails digging crescents into his skin. *Just like that. You're incredible. You're so, so incredible.*

With fingers digging into my hip, Maxwell's rhythm turned punishing, driving into me with a force that bordered on savage yet remained achingly perfect. My body became a vessel for his pleasure and mine, joined in a symphony of sensation that crescendoed with each thrust.

"I'm not coming until you come again," Maxwell hissed. "I want to feel you fall apart again first."

I groaned, the sound desperate and wrecked. "Fuck... I don't know if I—"

"You can," he said with absolute certainty, his hand finding my cock again. "And you will."

This wasn't just sex; this was Maxwell rewriting every definition I'd ever had of pleasure, of connection. And I already knew just once wasn't going to be enough.

"Tell me what you like," I said to him, running a hand over his stubble. "I can't read your mind. It's not fair."

Maxwell rubbed his chin against my hand. "What? This. You. Fucking hell—" His breath came in hot pants against my neck, my name falling from his lips like a prayer, again and again—"Rory, Rory, Rory"—as if he couldn't get enough of the taste of it on his tongue.

Then he nuzzled into my neck for a moment, slowing down slightly, and rasped into my ear, "You feel even better than I imagined, baby."

And suddenly I was freefalling, tumbling through space without gravity, without boundaries. That single word—"baby"—wrapped around me like the warmest blanket on the coldest night, promising shelter and belonging. Of never letting go. It melted through my every thought until I was nothing but raw nerve endings and naked emotion.

I collapsed against him, utterly boneless, overwhelmed in a way I couldn't begin to explain. Maxwell caught me with strong arms, his hands repositioning my pliant body without ever breaking our connection. He continued to thrust upward, using my slack form for his pleasure in a way that somehow felt like worship.

"I'm so close," he growled, one hand snaking between us to grasp my cock. His teeth found my earlobe, sucking the sensitive flesh before whispering against the damp skin, "I think I *like*, like you very much, Rory Thorne."

His words sank into me like stones through still water, creating ripples that spread to every corner of my being. They reached deeper than conscious thought, touching the part of me that was all instinct and wild recognition. The part of me that wanted to bare my throat to him, then claim him back.

Then the world split open.

That now familiar electric current amplified into something that felt like magic, actual fucking magic. It forked through my ribs like captured lightning, radiating outward to every extremity until my fingertips tingled with it. My vision blurred, overtaken by a blue-white flash that seemed to connect our bodies in ways beyond the physical.

That raindrop scent exploded between us, no longer just a subtle note but a torrential downpour filling the room. It was everywhere—in my lungs, on my skin, behind my eyelids—as if the storm that had been building between us had finally broken. The scent mingled with my pleasure, intensifying it, transforming it into something transcendent.

Scorching pleasure fizzed through every pore, consuming everything in its path until I was nothing but flame. "Teddy!" I cried out as I came again, convulsing around him as pulse after pulse of ecstasy tore through me.

Gasping repeatedly, my body jerked with aftershocks—both from my orgasm and the electric phenomenon. Through the haze, I finally caught the look on Maxwell's face—a wonderful softness painting itself across his features. Teddy's features.

"Don't stop," I begged, needing him to keep moving through these overwhelming pulses that seemed to bind us together. "Please don't stop."

He didn't. He held me tight against him, his hips maintaining their rhythm as he chased his own release, fucking me through the zapping aftershocks that made my entire body feel like a live wire. Each thrust seemed to reactivate the current, sending fresh, impossible waves coursing through me.

Hot stickiness glued us together. I pushed just slightly so Maxwell moved back, my eyes fixated on the pearly streaks across his skin. The primal part of my brain went wild as I ran my fingers through the mess, smearing it over his chest in possessive circles.

Mine, now. Mine, mine, mine! My brain screamed with an undertone that bordered on violent, and the primitive part of me wanted to sprout claws and dig into his chest, to mix my essence with his blood.

Instead, I lifted my fingers to Maxwell's lips. He greedily reached for them, his tongue darting out to taste me. He lapped at my fingers, his eyes never leaving mine as he cleaned them with hot, wet sucks.

Then I felt him coming inside me, his face contorting in a blissful silent scream as the first wave hit him. His cock throbbed and surged, each pulse sending fresh heat deep inside me as he shuddered beneath me. The intensity seemed to go on forever, his body trembling with the force of his release as he finally filled me completely. My hands trailed slowly down the side of his sweat-slicked back. I sighed blissfully, collapsing atop him as he softened, gluing myself to his chest, burying my face.

I was too overwhelmed to look him in the eye—that had been so intense, far more than I'd bargained for.

"Fucking hell—" Maxwell cut himself off, breathless. "That goddamn electric shock thing! Are you okay?" His hands kneaded into my thighs as if they might have seized up and needed unknotting.

That's when I felt it—a thread between us. A very real, tangible thing. Just like what I had with Kit, but also... nothing like what I had with Kit.

It stretched from somewhere deep in my chest to his, a silvery-blue connection pulsing with energy that I couldn't see with my eyes but could sense with something far more primal. The bond hummed like a plucked guitar string, vibrating with every beat of his heart.

And with each vibration came raindrops on a hot summer's day—no longer just emanating from him but flowing through the connection between us. It wasn't just a smell anymore; it was the essence of our bond made tangible, as if the universe had distilled our connection. I breathed it in, and it felt like I was breathing him in, like our scents had merged into something brand new.

With Kit, the bond was a comfort, a background presence—like knowing there was always someone in the next room. But this... this was immediate and demanding. It took up space, made itself known. I could feel Maxwell's emotions flowing across it—his confusion, his concern, and beneath it all, a satisfaction so deep it was almost painful to experience.

Fuck, fuck, fuckity, fuck.

What had I done?

I quickly blocked the specifics from my thoughts, but ice-cold anxiety swirled in my gut like a gathering storm.

"Rory? What's wrong?" Maxwell asked, trying to pry me from his chest.

I tried not to groan. It was so unfair that I never had any idea which of my thoughts he'd read.

"Nothing's wrong," I reassured him, forcing brightness into my voice. I reached for that silvery-blue thread between us, instinctively drawing on its warmth to steady my racing heart. The raindrop scent intensified as I did, wrapping around us like a cocoon, and I felt my panic ebbing as calm flowed into me. "In fact, everything is great." I leaned down and pressed our lips together in a long, languid kiss. "That was so amazing. Because you're amazing."

Theo smiled and relaxed—even if he didn't believe me, he wasn't going to push it, because apparently he had the patience of a saint. Who knew? Certainly not me.

We lay together, heat gradually ebbing from our skin like the last embers of a dying fire. I rested my head against Theo's chest, listening to the steady rhythm of his heartbeat. It was strangely hypnotic, the sound of life pulsing beneath my ear. My fingertip wandered through the hair scattered across his chest, charting territories I wanted to memorise.

Theo's hand drifted across my skin in whisper-light touches, fingers ghosting over my shoulder where Callum had bitten me. Though the wound had fully healed when I shifted earlier, he treated the spot with such tenderness that warmth bloomed inside me.

"I couldn't keep away from you earlier," I found myself saying. "Out in the Highlands, when I was a wolf. It was like you were the full moon, pulling me towards my true self."

Maxwell made a strange sound in his throat, heartbeat quickening beneath my ear. For a while, he said nothing.

Then, "Rory... I—"

Squeak!

The sound cut through the moment, followed by a ball of matted grey fur flying directly at Maxwell's head. Sharp claws dug into his scalp as Freddy launched his surprise attack.

Maxwell screeched, his hands flailing wildly. "What the—ARGH!"

I lunged forward, scooping Freddy up before he could take proper offence and sink his yellowed teeth into Maxwell's flesh.

"Fucking hell!" Maxwell muttered, rubbing his scalp where tiny pinpricks of blood were probably forming. I knew this from experience. "That little zombie bastard has it in for me!"

Freddy squirmed in my hands, his tiny body vibrating with unusual intensity. His eerie yellow eyes darted around the room, and he kept making these frantic chittering sounds I'd never heard before.

"Something's wrong," I said, frowning as I studied my friend. "He's never like this."

Maxwell didn't look impressed. "What's wrong is that he hates me and has terrible timing." He glared at Freddy with such resentment that I almost laughed.

I couldn't really blame him for being annoyed. Couldn't Freddy have given us five more minutes of cuddling? Maxwell had been just about to say something...

"No," I insisted, stroking Freddy's ear to calm him. "Look at him—this isn't normal. Something's spooked him."

That's when I heard it—footsteps outside the cottage. Not the casual steps of someone taking a stroll, but cautious, deliberate movements. My wolf senses, heightened with the full moon just two nights away, picked up the sound crystal clear.

I slipped out of bed, placing Freddy on the dresser where he continued his agitated movements, claws clicking against the wood.

"What is it?" Maxwell whispered, staying put, his eyes still fixed mistrustfully on Freddy.

I crept to the window, pulling the curtain back just a crack. It was probably Callum out there trying to spy, the creep, waiting for another chance to assert his dominance or report back to my mother.

The Highland night stretched before me, a canvas of deep blues and blacks. Moonlight silvered the edge of the pines that bordered the cottage property, turning the distant loch into a mirror of liquid mercury. Everything was completely still, the Scottish wilderness holding its breath in that peculiar way it does after sunset.

Except...

There. By the edge of the treeline. A shadow that didn't belong.

My fingers tightened on the curtain as the shadow moved, revealing itself to be a human figure. Not the bulky silhouette of Callum or any of the pack members I'd grown up with. This figure was leaner, standing with a familiar cultivated poise—shoulders back, chin lifted just so, the kind of posture that made me automatically straighten my own.

My heart stuttered, then stopped altogether.

The figure stepped into a patch of moonlight, and I could see him clearly now—the dark hair I'd run my fingers through countless times, the sharp jawline I'd traced with my lips, the lanky frame I'd held against mine on cold London nights.

Dev.

He stood there, staring directly at the cottage. And then, as if sensing my presence, he lifted his gaze.

Our eyes met through the glass, across the darkness.

And he smiled.

Not the warm, crooked smile I remembered. This was something else entirely—cold, wrong, hungry.

The world tilted sideways. My knees buckled. Behind me, I heard Maxwell say my name, but it sounded like it was coming from underwater.

Then Dev raised one hand and beckoned me outside.

17

Theodore

"**R**ory!"

The name tore from my throat, but he didn't even flinch. Just stood there frozen at the window like he'd seen a ghost.

"Rory!" I tried again, louder this time.

Nothing. Not even a twitch.

When he failed to respond for the third time, I leapt out of bed, ignoring Freddy's indignant hiss as I charged towards him. My foot caught on something—our discarded clothes—and I stumbled, nearly crashing into the wall.

"What's wrong?" I demanded.

Fear clawed at my ribs. He looked completely vacant, like someone had switched off the lights behind his eyes. I wrapped my arm around his naked torso, pulling him against me.

Our skin touched, and his fear slammed into me like a tidal wave, so intense and absolute that my knees nearly buckled. It wasn't just empathy or concern; I was experiencing his terror firsthand, as if it had bypassed my mind entirely and lodged directly in my soul. My heart rate shot up to match his, my breath catching in my lungs. For a long, disorienting moment, I couldn't distinguish his panic from my own.

Images flashed through my mind that weren't mine—blurred impressions of trees, movement—coming too fast to grasp. Then a scent—like the first rainfall after drought, when parched concrete exhales its relief—unusually strong, almost suffocating.

I pulled back slightly, staring at my arm across his chest in confusion. In my years as a telepath, I'd never experienced anything like this—this wasn't reading thoughts or emotion—this was something deeper, some-thing else. Like our nervous systems had somehow merged.

"Rory, talk to me. What the fuck is going on?"

He lifted one trembling finger, pointing out the window into the darkness beyond.

I followed his gaze, pressing my face close to the glass. The Highland night stared back—pine trees swaying gently in the breeze, shadows that could have been anything or nothing at all.

"What? There's nothing there."

"Fuck! He's gone!" Rory's voice cracked like a whip.

"What? Who?"

Rory's eyes were wide and wild, pupils dilated with shock or terror or both.

"Dev."

I dropped my grip on him, shuffling away, just slightly. An odd sensa-tion rushed through me—that stomach-dropping feeling of freefalling, the world tilting sideways beneath my feet. "What do you mean?" I asked quietly.

"Dev! I saw Dev out there. And he saw me!"

I stared at Rory, trying to process what he was saying. Was Rory... okay? Too tired from the day's events? Had he hated what we'd just done so much that he'd manifested his ex--boyfriend to come save him?

"It was probably one of your family, Rory."

"No, it was him. He smiled at me. Then he motioned for me to come outside!"

"Are you sure?" I reached out to touch his arm.

The instant my fingers made contact with his skin, another wave crashed over me—this time a volatile fusion of anger and hurt so potent it knocked the breath from my lungs. It was as if Rory's pain had been injected directly into my bloodstream, flooding every nerve ending with his anguish. My vision blurred at the edges, overwhelmed by emotions that weren't mine but felt utterly real.

"Yes!" Rory snapped.

Then his thoughts barrelled into my mind, so clear they might as well have been spoken aloud:

...of course he doesn't believe me...

I jerked my hand back as if I'd been burned. What the fuck was happening to me? In all my years of telepathy, I'd never experienced anything remotely like this. His emotions, his very essence, seemed to be bleeding into me without any barriers.

My mind scrambled for rational explanations. Maybe exhaustion was making me more susceptible to stray thoughts. Maybe spending so much time with Rory had somehow made me more attuned to his particular mental frequency. Maybe—

...why did I even expect him to?...

The thought sliced through me like a blade. I couldn't even attempt to block it—it would have been like trying to stop a tsunami with my bare hands.

I stumbled backwards until my spine hit the wall. The look Rory gave me in return was a knife to my gut. This really was the worst possible timing. Why couldn't Dev have waited until morning to decide to be alive?

"Okay," I said, attempting to inject genuine conviction into my voice. "I believe you, of course."

But even as the words left my mouth, I knew it was too late. The damage was done, written clearly across Rory's face in the disappointed set of his shoulders, the way his eyes had shuttered against me.

...yeah, right...sure you do...

"Did you see which way he went?"

"No, he disappeared when I blinked."

I bit back my question about why the fuck he didn't knock on the door, if he had indeed seen Rory. "Okay..."

I stood there, chest heaving, trying to make sense of what had just happened. Was I reacting like this because I'd been so certain Dev was dead? In my line of work, missing persons cases rarely ended with happy reunions. The statistics were grim after forty-eight hours. I'd prepared myself for identifying a body up here.

Or... was I having this reaction because the idea of the ex that Rory adored being alive meant—

No. I couldn't think about that right now.

I forced myself to focus as Rory yanked his shirt over his head with jerky, frantic movements. The determined set of his jaw told me everything I needed to know—he was about to charge out into the Highland night like a knight in shining armour.

"Rory, wait—"

But he was already pulling on his jeans, hopping on one foot as he struggled with the fabric. Christ, he was actually going to do it. Going to sprint out there in pursuit of what might have been a shadow, a trick of moonlight, or another member of his family who wanted to hurt him.

I grabbed my own clothes from the floor, cursing under my breath.

"Didn't you say your family has CCTV all over their property?" I managed, fumbling with my belt buckle as I tried to catch up with his frenzied dressing.

Rory stopped mid-motion, one arm through his jacket sleeve.

"Yes!" His face lit up with sudden brightness. He slipped his phone from his pocket, fingers flying across the screen. "I'll ring Felix."

I breathed a small sigh of relief. At least this bought us some time, some actual evidence before Rory went tearing off into the darkness.

Felix's phone rang once, then twice. Disappointment threaded through me when I realised he might very well be in mid-air currently—who knew what time their flight had ended up being?

"Felix!" Rory's voice carried a note of desperate relief.

"Rory? What's—"

"We need you to check the CCTV cameras around my family's estate. Now. It's urgent."

A pause crackled through the speaker. "Right, well... we're still at the airport. Four-hour delay, and I've had to check in all my equipment."

"Well, do you think you could do something on your phone?"

Another pause, longer this time. I could practically hear Felix's nervous fidgeting through the connection.

"Umm... not really..."

Rory's face crumpled with frustration. I caught his eye and gave him a warning look.

When Rory spoke again, his voice had taken on an artificially bright tone that almost made me laugh, despite the situation. "Well, thank you anyway, Felix. Have a nice flight."

"Um... okay?" Felix's confusion bled through the phone. "I'll go through any cameras I can get access to as soon as I reach the hotel tomorrow."

Another syrupy thank you, then Rory hung up.

"Great work," I said. "Real growth, here. But next time, try meaning it as well."

A sock hit me square in the face.

"Right, let's go, then," Rory announced, already moving towards the bedroom door. "If you're coming with me."

The challenge in his voice was unmistakable—he expected me to find an excuse, to talk him out of this, to abandon him when it mattered most.

"You know I'm coming with you." I wrestled with my shirt. "But we need to ring Seb first."

"No time for that!"

Before I could reply, Rory was already thundering down the cottage stairs, his footsteps echoing through the narrow stairwell like gunshots. I followed, fumbling for my phone as I took the steps two at a time.

I jammed Seb's name, holding the phone to my ear with my shoulder as I laced up my hiking boots.

No answer.

"Well, we tried!" Rory said.

I grumbled under my breath. "Bloody nocturnal vampire should be answering his phone, for fuck's sake."

The thought of ringing Kit flickered through my mind, but I didn't have the strength for another argument. Besides, Rory already had the front door open, letting in a rush of air that carried the scent of pine and damp earth.

A soft patter of tiny paws on wood announced Freddy's arrival. The ferret scampered across the floor, launching himself onto Rory's shoulder.

Rory turned his head, pressing a gentle kiss to Freddy's matted grey nose. "Dev loved Freddy. Maybe he can help us."

Of course he bloody did. The thought stabbed through me with unexpected venom. Perfect Dev, who is amazing and awesome and does modelling on the side and loves zombie ferrets that bite you. *Perfect in every way... aside from trampling all over Rory's heart.*

I grabbed my rucksack from the side table, slinging it over my shoulder as we stepped out into the night. Moonlight illuminated the path ahead—at least it was a mostly cloudless night, silver light casting everything in sharp relief.

We reached the end of the cottage path, where the manicured garden gave way to wild Highland terrain. Rory lifted his face to the breeze, nostrils flaring as he sampled the air.

"I need to shift to track him properly," he said, already reaching for the hem of his shirt. "Is that okay?"

"Of course."

His clothes hit the ground with lightning speed—the man could undress faster than anyone I'd ever met. While I stuffed them into my bag, he glanced around, apparently searching for somewhere private to complete his transformation.

"You can just shift here," I said. "I've seen you shift now, anyway."

Rory's face twisted. Clearly he still didn't want me to see him all inside out.

"I'll close my eyes," I promised, letting my eyelids fall shut.

"Hold Freddy for a second."

Something cold and wriggling was thrust against my chest. *Great.*

The air grew hushed, broken only by soft grunts of effort. Then pain exploded through my body—muscles screaming as if they were being torn apart and rebuilt, bones feeling like they were snapping and re-forming. I gasped, dropping Freddy as I pressed my hands to my ribs, my spine, anywhere the agony seemed most intense.

Christ, is this what Rory goes through every time?

But more importantly, what the fuck is happening here?

The pain faded as suddenly as it had arrived. I inhaled sharply, opening my eyes.

Wolf-Rory gazed up at me with those same blue-green eyes, now gloriously larger in his lupine face. For a moment, I couldn't tear my eyes off his coat—it was such a rich tapestry of golds—from pale champagne along his belly to deeper amber across his shoulders and back.

Two silver hoops still glinted in his left ear. I reached down instinctively, stroking the soft fur of his muzzle.

"That felt painful."

Rory simply yelped, already wiggling out of my grip and bounding towards a nearby rock. Freddy launched himself onto Rory's head, clinging to the thick fur with tiny claws.

Rory's nose dropped to the ground, working methodically across the terrain. His movements were fluid, purposeful—following some invisible trail that only he could detect. We moved deeper into the thicket, Rory weaving between trees. Finally, he stopped at the huge stone wall, his attention focused on a gap near the base—a hole just large enough for a person to crawl through.

"This must be where Priya and Felix snuck through," I said, eyeing it. Would I be able to fit?

There was only one way to find out.

I threw my rucksack to the ground to toss through, then fell to my knees before Rory could dash through the gap and leave me behind.

I squeezed through the gap in the stone wall, my jacket catching on jagged edges as I scraped my way to the other side.

Freddy scampered through, his tiny paws pattering against the ground, followed immediately by Rory. Then they were off again, Rory's nose pressed to the earth.

He moved so bloody fast I had to break into a light jog just to keep pace with him, my breathing already becoming laboured in the Highland air.

"Christ, Rory, I'm going to have to put a collar on you at this rate," I muttered under my breath.

A sound that could only be described as a wolf's laugh burst from Rory's throat—a huffing, almost wheezing noise that was utterly ridiculous and entirely endearing. Contentment poured out of him like warm honey, and he veered towards me, nuzzling against my legs with his massive head.

For one mad moment, I had a vision of myself walking him through Hyde Park on a lead, tourists stopping to photograph the "unusually large dog."

The moment of levity shattered as Rory's behaviour shifted dramatically. His entire body went rigid—then he started dashing ahead in short bursts, then stopping abruptly to look back at me with urgent eyes.

"What is it?"

He took off again, and this time I didn't bother trying to walk. I broke into a proper run, keeping pace alongside him as we moved through the heather and gorse.

We emerged into a wide, open patch of Highland moorland, the landscape spreading before us under the moonlight. That's when I saw it—a dark shape on the ground about fifty metres ahead. A body, face up.

Rory zoomed off like a rocket.

"Rory!" I shouted, but there was no stopping him.

I sprinted after him, my lungs burning as I closed the distance. As I got closer, details became clearer—tall frame, brown skin, a face that could have graced magazine covers with its sharp cheekbones and perfect symmetry. Yes, this was definitely Dev.

I felt rather than saw Rory beginning to shift back, and squeezed my eyes shut as that same excruciating pain tore through my body again. I kept my eyes clamped closed until the agony faded, leaving only the sound of ragged breathing.

When I opened them, Rory crouched naked beside Dev's still form, Freddy on his shoulder, his hands hovering uncertainly over his ex-boyfriend's chest. Part of me hung back, watching this reunion with a churning mixture of relief and something darker. What if this turned into some Sleeping Beauty situation? What if Dev woke up, saw Rory, and pulled him into a passionate kiss whilst I stood there like a spare part?

For fuck's sake, Theodore, I chastised myself. *There's an unconscious man on the ground.*

I moved forward, dropping to my knees beside Dev to check for signs of life and put him in the recovery position. The professional thing to do.

Pressing two fingers against Dev's neck, I searched for a pulse. There—faint but steady. His breathing was shallow but regular. What was he doing out here? How long had he been unconscious?

"Dev?" Rory's voice cracked with emotion. "Dev, can you hear me?"

Without warning, Dev's eyes snapped open—not the gentle awakening of someone returning to consciousness, but the violent alertness of a predator. His hand shot out with inhuman speed, fingers wrapping around Rory's throat as he launched himself upright and hauled Rory off the ground entirely, Rory's feet kicking uselessly in the air as his hands scrabbled desperately at the iron grip.

What the actual—

Freddy launched himself from Rory's shoulder with a furious chittering battle cry, tiny claws extended as he went for Dev's eyes in a kamikaze dive. Dev's free hand shot out, catching the ferret by his tail mid-flight and flinging him through the air like a discarded toy. Freddy's pained squeak echoed across the moorland as he disappeared into the darkness.

"Dev," Rory managed to choke out, around a strangled wheeze.

Molten fury boiled within me.

We might have found Devraj Bassi alive, but he wasn't going to remain alive for very long at this rate.

"Get your hands off him!" I roared, reaching to fist his grey jumper. "Now!"

Dev turned towards me with cold, empty eyes that held no recognition, no humanity. His free hand slammed into my chest with the force of a sledgehammer, ribs creaking under the impact as I was lifted clean off my feet.

The world became a sickening carousel of sky and earth as I flew backwards through the air: sky and earth trading places, stars scattering like broken glass. Time stretched like toffee—the moon spinning overhead, the distant lights of the village wheeling past my vision, the ground rushing up to meet me with malicious intent.

I crashed down hard, shoulder blades slamming into the unforgiving moorland with a bone-jarring impact that drove the air from my lungs. My skull connected with something sharp and jagged—a half-buried stone. Pain exploded through my head like a firework, white-hot and blinding, as warmth began trickling down my neck in sticky rivulets.

Through the haze of concussion and rage, I sensed rather than saw Rory's transformation beginning—the agony of his shift tearing through my own nervous system like shared lightning as fury poured off him in waves so intense they made my teeth ache. I tried to push myself upright, but my arms wouldn't cooperate properly—everything felt disconnected, like my brain was sending signals through treacle.

Through the ringing in my ears and the pounding in my skull, sounds filtered through the haze. Then, a low, rumbling snarl that raised every hair on my body.

Please, please don't let him get himself killed.

A sudden thud echoed across the moorland—bodies colliding with brutal force. Then another. The wet slap of flesh meeting flesh, accompanied by grunts of effort and the dull crack of bone against bone.

I blinked hard, trying to clear my vision enough to see what was happening. Shadows moved in the moonlight, a violent dance of tooth and claw that my concussed brain couldn't quite process.

A sharp yelp of pain cut through the night—unmistakably Rory. The sound stole what little breath I had, more agonising than my own injuries. I tried again to force myself upright, but the world tilted sickeningly, bile rising in my throat.

Get up, you useless bastard. Get up and help him.

More sounds now—the wet, tearing noise of claws ripping through fabric and flesh. A horrible whining whimper. My own helplessness pressed down on me like a weight, every instinct screaming at me to move, to act, to do something other than lie here bleeding into the heather whilst Rory fought for his life.

The violence reached a crescendo—a final, bone-deep growl that spoke of triumph or defeat, I couldn't tell which.

Footsteps followed—the heavy thud of human feet pounding against the earth. Running. The sound grew fainter and fainter until it disappeared entirely into the night, leaving only the whisper of wind through the gorse and my own ragged breathing.

Rory?

I tried to call his name, but only managed a hoarse croak that barely carried beyond my own lips.

When my vision finally cleared enough to focus properly, Dev was gone, swallowed by the darkness as if he'd never been there at all. Rory knelt beside me in human form, naked and shaking, blood coating his lips and chin in a crimson smear that looked black in the moonlight.

"Shouldn't you... be chasing after him?" I managed to say. "We'll lose him again."

...God, what little he thinks of me...as if I'd just leave him here like this... Oh.

"Hey," I managed, reaching up to cup his face. "Come here, baby."

Weaving my fingers into the softness of his tangled hair, I pulled Rory down and pressed my lips to his, the contact igniting sparks despite my battered state. The kiss tasted of copper and salt, of violence and fear, but beneath those harsh notes lay something elemental—something that somehow reminded me of rain striking hot earth, lightning splitting open the sky. Our breaths mingled as my fingers curled into his hair, anchoring myself to him while the world continued to spin.

Something about his nearness steadied me, as though he'd become my centre of gravity. Through the kiss, I felt the trembling in his body begin to subside, felt his racing pulse gradually slow to match my own. In this moment of chaos, with blood on his lips and terror still fresh in our veins, we found an impossible pocket of stillness—the eye of our personal storm.

Rory pulled away, scanning the darkness around us with sharp, alert eyes.

"Where did he go?" I asked.

The moorland stretched endlessly in all directions, offering countless hiding places amongst the gorse and stone outcroppings.

"Could be anywhere by now."

"Do you think he'll come back?"

"I don't know. That wasn't... that wasn't Dev. Not really. Something's wrong with him. Really wrong." Rory's fingers ghosted over the wet patch on my scalp. "But you need proper medical attention. That's a lot of blood."

I shook my head. No time for that. "Head wounds always bleed more than they should." I tried to sit up, but my muscles betrayed me and I collapsed back onto the damp heather with a groan.

Anxiety spiralled through me—but not my own. This was Rory's panic, sharp and acidic, flooding my system like poison. The sensation was so invasive that it made my stomach lurch.

"Rory, I need to tell you something. Something is happening to me. To us. Something weird." I took a large, unsteady breath. "It's like suddenly I'm feeling your emotions as if they're my own. And earlier—Christ, I *felt* your shift. The actual physical pain of it. And... I hate to tell you this, but your thoughts are even louder now. Crystal clear. Especially if we're touching."

....no, no, no, no...

A look of pure horror crossed Rory's face. He looked away, his anxiety spiking so dramatically that I gasped.

"I can feel that," I said, my voice strained. "What's going on?"

"You're going to be really upset with me."

...he's going to hate me...

The anxiety vanished, replaced by something far worse—pure, crystalline terror that made my ribs feel like they were crushing inwards.

"Tell me," I managed. "Whatever it is, just tell me, and then I can help deal with it."

Rory's hands twisted in his lap. "I didn't know at first, honestly. I mean, I didn't know what the zapping thing was. You know, that electric *thing* that kept happening between us? But then I realised..." He trailed off, staring fixedly at a patch of gorse. "Listen, you have to believe me, it's not my fault. I didn't choose this, and I don't even know much about it, but—"

"Rory."

He took a shuddering breath. "I think I've... accidentally bonded you to me. A bit like with me and Kit, but different." He rubbed a hand over his face. "This one is more, um... romantically charged? Like... a mate."

The word hung in the air between us, and for a moment, I forgot how to breathe.

"But I promise I'll figure out how to stop it. Break it. You won't have to live with it forever." His words tumbled out in a rush. "And when we get back to London, I'll keep away from you so you don't have to deal with it in the meantime—"

"Keep away from me?" It was as if someone had punched me in the gut. A streak of wild panic tore through my chest—definitely my own this time, not his. "Why would you do that?"

"So you don't need to deal with these weird side effects," Rory whispered. "So you don't need to feel all of my turbulent emotions—god help me, there's a lot of those. So you don't need to see me until it's all fixed." His voice faltered. "See the person whose stupid wolf decided it wanted to mate with you just because you told me you *liked*, liked me. But don't worry. I promise I'll stay far away."

I could feel the hot sting of tears threatening to spill over—not my own, but his, flooding through our connection with devastating clarity.

I promise I'll stay far away.

Every syllable was wrong, utterly wrong, and made something violently possessive rear up inside me, an intense feeling like no other.

Without thinking, I reached out and grabbed his arm, yanking hard enough that he tumbled forward with a startled yelp. He landed sprawled across my chest, his naked skin warm against my shirt, and I immediately threaded my fingers through his dishevelled hair.

"You absolute bloody idiot," I said, my voice hoarse. "Do you actually think I want you to stay away from me?"

His eyes went wide, confusion replacing the misery that had been radiating from him moments before.

"Listen to me very carefully," I continued, my fingers still stroking through his hair. "Of course, if you want to, we can figure out a way to break it. But I don't care about the side effects. I don't care about not being able to block your thoughts. And as for your turbulent emotions..." I cupped his face with my free hand. "I've been dealing with those since the day I met you, weird wolf bond or no weird wolf bond."

His breath hitched.

"The only thing that would upset me," I said, feeling the truth of it settle deep in my bones, "is if you disappeared. If you decided that because your wolf chose me or whatever, somehow that made it less real or less wanted."

"But you didn't choose—"

"Didn't I?" I interrupted. "Every choice I've made in the past week has been about getting closer to you. Coming to Scotland. Talking with you. Finally understanding you. Being with you while you shifted. Meeting your family. Sharing a bed. Telling you I like you. Having sex with you." My thumb traced across his cheekbone. "Maybe my conscious mind didn't know what it was choosing, but some part of me did."

Tears spilled over then, tracking down his face to drip onto my shirt.

"Oh my god, I can't believe I'm crying right now." He threw his face into me, mumbling, "I'm so mortified."

...Jesus fucking Christ, Rory, stop that. He didn't sign up to be bonded for life to a hot mess...

"You really thought I was going to be pissed at you?" I asked, genuinely baffled.

Rory's face emerged from my chest. "Well, yeah. I mean, this is literally your personal nightmare, isn't it? Being permanently stuck with me?"

His palm pressed against my ribs. I could feel the way he'd convinced himself that being bonded to him was a burden, a prison sentence for whoever got caught in his orbit.

Was I freaked out about being permanently tethered to Rory Thorne? Absolutely. The idea of never again having any semblance of barrier between our minds, of being tied to someone so impulsive and chaotic, of having my carefully controlled life turned upside down by supernatural forces beyond my control—yes, it fucking terrified me. But Rory didn't need to know that right now.

Instead, I found myself grinning despite the pounding in my skull. "Plus," I added. "Now I'll always know when you're about to do something spectacularly stupid, which should make my job considerably easier."

"Oi, I'm not that predictable." A watery laugh escaped him, and the crushing weight of his self-loathing eased just slightly.

"You literally just ran across the moors after your missing ex-boyfriend creepily beckoned you outside in the middle of the night without giving your safety a second thought."

"Fair point."

The moment of levity faded as reality crashed back over us. Dev's empty eyes, the inhuman strength, the way he'd vanished into the darkness.

"Right, then," I said, my voice turning grim. "What the fuck are we going to do about Dev?"

18

Rory

"**D**id you bite him?"

"Of course I bit him, he hurt you!" Plus, Dev was trying to kill me, but that line sounded good.

My muscles ached from shifting so rapidly into a wolf and then back again, fibres protesting the violent transformation. The pain threaded through my limbs like barbed wire, but it was nothing compared to the chaos in my head. The world felt tilted, spinning on an axis that had shifted somewhere between Dev's hollow smile and Maxwell's unbelievable acceptance of our bond.

In the space of five minutes, my missing ex-boyfriend had almost murdered me, and then I'd confessed to my archnemesis that I'd tethered us together for life.

And he hadn't been repulsed.

And he'd even called me *baby* again.

Dev. Newfound supervillain powers. Almost killed us. Focus, Rory, focus!

"If you seriously injured him, he couldn't have gone far."

"Nah, he bricked it out of here like it was just a scratch. He wasn't *Dev*, Maxwell."

"I could see that. What are you thinking? Necromancy?" he suggested, though I could tell he wasn't convinced.

As if summoned by the word, Freddy scampered onto my lap. I scooped him up, looking for signs of damage to my undead friend. If he died again, there was no Issac to resurrect him this time.

"No... it didn't feel like that. Nothing like the handful of dead-walkers Killigrew Street has come across either."

"Okay... has he... had a psychotic break? Plus taken up martial arts and strength training?" Maxwell shuffled into a more upright sitting position, wincing as he moved. The bleeding from his wound had more or less stopped, though it still looked sore.

"Did you manage to read his thoughts at all?"

He shook his head. "I barely had the chance to try. It was all too chaotic. But should we keep moving? Follow Dev's scent?"

"No. This is too weird. We need time to think." I reached out, fingers ghosting over the tender spot on his scalp. "Plus, you're hurt."

Maxwell's eyes fluttered closed at my touch, and our bond hummed between us, a silver current alive with shared sensation—his pain becoming mine. *If only I could take it away from him.*

A snap of a twig echoed through the darkness.

We both froze.

"Fuck, is that him?"

Terror shot through me like ice water flooding my veins, each drop crystallising into sharp fragments that pierced every nerve ending. The world narrowed to a pinprick of focus—Dev's approaching figure—whilst everything else blurred into insignificance.

I'd barely survived our last encounter. Now we were both in-jured—Maxwell bleeding from his head wound, and I felt like I'd been trampled by a herd of particularly vindictive Highland cattle.

Should I shift again? My muscles screamed in protest at the mere thought. Another rapid transformation might tear something vital, leave me writhing on the ground whilst Dev finished what he'd started.

"Rory!" Dev's voice rang out. "It's really you!"

What the actual fuck?

Somehow, Maxwell hauled himself to his feet, though he swayed like a drunk sailor. He stepped in front of me, arms spread wide in a protective stance that made something warm unfurl within me.

"Stay back!" Maxwell roared, his voice carrying every bit of authority. "I don't want to hurt you, but I will if I have to."

But Dev kept approaching, completely ignoring the warning. His face lit up with what appeared to be genuine delight. "Why are you naked?" he asked, tilting his head with curious confusion. "Have you just shifted?"

What the bloody hell was happening?

I stared at Dev, my brain struggling to process what I was seeing. Did he genuinely not remember what had just happened?

The man before me looked nothing like the Dev I knew. Gone were the designer clothes that had always shown off his model physique—now he wore a plain grey hoodie that swamped his frame, paired with ordinary black slacks. Stubble covered his brown skin in unkempt patches, his dark hair hung limp and greasy, and purple shadows bruised the skin beneath his eyes.

Even his posture was different. Dev had always moved with the confidence of someone who knew he was gorgeous, carrying himself with unconscious grace that commanded attention. But this version seemed uncertain, shoulders hunched inward as if trying to make himself smaller. His left sleeve hung in tatters where my teeth had found their mark, dark stains blooming across the fabric. The man who'd once lectured me about "serious journalism" whilst checking his reflection in shop windows now stood before me looking lost, diminished, and distinctly *injured*.

"Rory?" Dev's voice carried none of the menace from before. He cradled his left arm against his chest, and I caught a glimpse of angry red beneath the torn cotton. "Are you alright? You look terrified."

Because you just tried to murder us!

But the confusion in his eyes seemed real, and the way his forehead crinkled with worry looked exactly like the Dev I'd fallen in love with. He stepped closer, one hand reaching out towards me. "I'm so glad to see—"

"I said, *stay back!*" Maxwell barked.

"It's okay," I told him, stepping out from behind his protective bulk. This Dev seemed... different.

Before I could process what was happening, Dev had moved, throwing his arms around me in an enthusiastic bear hug, squeezing me so tightly I couldn't breathe.

"I can't believe you're here!" Dev sounded like he might burst into tears.

I stood frozen, completely gobsmacked. Wordless, for once.

Click.

Dev was suddenly wrenched backwards, away from me. Maxwell had managed to snap handcuffs around his wrists from behind.

"What the— What the hell? Get off me, man!" Dev thrashed against the restraints, fury replacing joy. He twisted out of Maxwell's grip, gaze locking onto his face, recognition dawning. "Wait... you're the one who arrested us that night! Even though you work with Killigrew Street!"

Tension radiated from Maxwell.

"That was the worst night of my life," Dev spat. "Rory had nightmares for months after that! *Months!*"

I felt Maxwell flinch through our bond, a tsunami of guilt and regret flooding our connection.

"Stop it," I snapped at Dev, before he could elaborate any further and tell Maxwell that being locked in that cell triggered all sorts of memories of being locked up by my father. "That whole thing *was* sort of our own fault, Dev. Anyway, we don't have time for that right now."

"Get these handcuffs off me!"

"You just attacked us!" I gestured wildly. "Look at Maxwell's head. You threw him to the ground! You almost strangled me to death, Dev!"

I touched my neck, where I was convinced there must be a bruise. Dev's eyes followed my hands, his eyes widening.

"Dev, just what is going on here?" Maxwell demanded. "Where have you been? We're up here looking for you."

Dev glanced nervously over his shoulder, scanning the darkness. "They might be watching. We need to go somewhere safe."

"You are safe," I assured him, reaching out to touch his arm. He jumped like he'd been electrocuted. "We'll keep you safe. We'll take you back to our cottage."

"Your... cottage?"

"On my family's land."

Dev looked skeptical.

"It's our best option right now," I insisted.

"Fine, but get these handcuffs off me," Dev said, rattling the metal against his wrists.

"Okay," I said at the exact same moment Maxwell snarled, "Absolutely not."

We turned to face each other, matching scowls etched across our faces.

"Rory—"

"Maxwell—"

I could sense Maxwell's frustration crackling, but underneath it lay something deeper—a bone-deep terror at the thought of Dev hurting me again. The intensity of his protective instincts almost stole my breath away.

And it definitely stole my heart.

"I'm not letting him hurt you again," Maxwell said firmly, his voice carrying the weight of absolute conviction. "You can hate me for it all you want. I don't care."

Though, of course, he did care. He cared very much. I desperately wanted to press a soft kiss to his cheek, to reassure him that it was going to be okay.

Dev shifted impatiently behind us, the handcuffs jangling. "Listen, I don't know what happened before, but now, I just want to get somewhere safe."

I looked between Dev, the ex-boyfriend who I'd spent weeks crying over after he broke my heart, and Maxwell, the man I'd accidentally bonded myself to for life. The man I couldn't bear to see hurt again.

"The handcuffs stay on until you prove you're not a demon wearing Dev's skin," I declared, crossing my arms. "Final offer, I'm afraid."

19

Theodore

Devraj Bassi was alive.

Devraj Bassi was alive, and in our cottage.

More specifically, on our sofa. Asleep, on our sofa.

He'd collapsed the moment we crossed the cottage threshold. His legs simply gave out, seemingly now exhausted. We'd half carried, half dragged him to the sofa, his handcuffed wrists making the manoeuvre awkward.

Rory had tucked a tartan blanket around Dev's shoulders. His breathing had already deepened into sleep before Rory even stepped back.

"We should take shifts watching him," I suggested, though every muscle in my body ached for the warm press of sheets and Rory's skin against mine.

"You sleep first."

"No, you go. I'm not tired yet."

Rory gave me a long, lingering look, and I caught an intense flash of his disappointment—sharp and immediate. The feeling echoed my own sense of being cheated out of having the night to ourselves, to once again tangle our limbs together while we slept. Alongside that came something entirely new: a strange, almost magnetic pull that made the idea of being separated from him—even by a single floor—feel fundamentally wrong. When Rory dragged his feet up the stairs like a petulant child, I had to actively resist the urge to follow him.

Hours passed. Dev snored softly, occasionally muttering incomprehensible words. My eyelids grew heavy despite the uncomfortable wooden chair I'd positioned myself in.

Every few minutes, I found myself unconsciously reaching out through our connection, checking on Rory upstairs. The first time it happened, I jerked back in surprise—I hadn't meant to do it, the action as automatic as breathing. But there he was: a warm, sleepy contentment threading through my consciousness, his dreams apparently peaceful for once.

I was both fascinated and terrified by the strength of this wolf bond—I still couldn't quite bring myself to call it a *mate* bond. Christ, what would it be like when we returned to London? Surely I wouldn't feel this constant awareness of him from across the city? Or, would the distance create some kind of persistent ache, like a phantom limb I couldn't ignore?

And what about Rory? Would he come to resent this? He'd seemed relieved by my reaction earlier, but that was in the heat of the moment. Once we were back in familiar territory, once the novelty wore off and the reality of being permanently tethered to me set in...

When I could no longer trust myself to stay alert, I slipped upstairs and gently roused Rory.

"Your turn," I whispered against his temple.

I set my phone alarm for five hours—not allowing myself any more than that. Yes, because I was desperate to hear what Dev had to say about his disappearance firsthand. But also because the thought of Dev and Rory alone together downstairs while I slept...

When the alarm blared, I wasted no time getting dressed, then padded downstairs in bare feet. I found Rory, dressed in an oversized T-shirt with bare legs, sitting cross-legged on the wooden floor beside the sofa.

He stared intently at Dev's face and when I touched his shoulder, he jumped as though I'd electrocuted him.

"You okay?"

Rory's face broke into a small, sleepy smile that quickly fell. "Look. I think he's waking up."

Dev stirred with a soft moan, his eyelids fluttering open. "Can I please have these handcuffs removed now? Why am I a prisoner? I'm a bloody victim!"

Rory's gaze flicked to mine.

"We'll let you have one hand free," I said. "The other stays cuffed to the banister."

Dev moaned dramatically. "And how about some water? You know, a basic human right?"

Rory practically leapt to his feet, disappearing into the kitchen while I repositioned Dev at the base of the stairs. The metal clicked against the wooden banister as I secured his left wrist. I caught sight of the angry bite mark on his forearm—a perfect crescent of teeth marks.

"So," Rory said the moment he returned, glass in hand, practically vibrating with excitement. "Tell us what happened. Where have you been? But start from the beginning. And tell us everything."

Relief flooded through me—not my own, but Rory's. Pure, overwhelming relief that Dev was alive and coherent, mixed with bright joy.

Dev took a ridiculously long drink of water, his eyes fixed on Rory over the rim of the glass. Specifically on Rory's neck, where the faintest necklace of purple bruises marred his lovely skin.

Fury flared within me, not easily tamped down when the man who put those marks on Rory sat within reach of me.

"Did I really try to strangle you?" Dev whispered. "And you... bit me?"

Rory nodded. "You did. And I did."

Dev's eyes suddenly slid to me. "Maxwell, right? I'm surprised to see you here. I thought you hated Rory. You're a telepath? Are you... reading my thoughts?"

"Not currently, but I certainly will be," I said pleasantly, dripping steel into my voice. "So don't hold anything back from us."

"I just told you, I'm a *victim*," Dev snapped, wrenching his arm away from the banister. I suspected if he wished to, he could snap the wood and free himself. Especially after the strength he demonstrated yesterday.

"We found your phone," said Rory. "In the middle of nowhere. Not close to where you were yesterday."

"I dropped it when they grabbed me."

"Who? Who grabbed you?"

Dev sighed, his free hand rubbing his temple. "My memories... they're like sifting through mud. Everything feels like a dream. Especially being here with you now."

"So you came up here, to the Highlands, of your own free will?" I asked. "We weren't sure if Meridian snatched you in London, and brought you, or what. We've been through the messages on your phone. We know you were talking to a shifter called Carrie MacGregor, from Glasgow."

The name made Dev inhale sharply. "Carrie! They... they have her too. I think. I... remember her face, shaking me awake at one point. And then..." He pressed against his head. "At least, I think I saw her..."

"When we rang her alpha, he said she disappeared around the same time as you," Rory said quietly.

"I wasn't with Carrie when I got snatched. But a couple of hours before, she'd rung me from Glasgow, saying that she thought she was being watched. She sounded spooked. I was looking up buses on my phone, to head back there to be with her."

"So 'they' grabbed you while you were out in the Highlands?" I pressed.

"Carrie managed to obtain information about where they might be keeping the missing shifters. There was this map of an old building complex. Listed online as the Highland Heritage Foundation. So I set out to go look at it in person, for us."

Rory frowned. "We saw that map. Your phone was found nowhere near that."

Dev snapped, "Well I didn't get very far, did I? I got a bus up here from Glasgow. I decided to drop into Glenmoriston to poke around a bit, see if I happened to bump into any shifters."

Rory's eyes blazed with anger. "So you couldn't be bothered to text me to update Killigrew Street with all this new information you kept to yourself, but thought snooping around my old pack was a good idea?"

Dev hung his head. "I fucked up, Ror. I'm so sorry. I promise I was so close to ringing Killigrew Street. I just wanted proper, concrete evidence, you know? They all know me as the guy you got arrested with. I wanted to bring you something solid. Plus, I only have your number. I wasn't sure you'd pick up. Wasn't sure how you'd feel about Carrie being determined your family is involved somehow. Even though you hate them."

I eyed Rory, thinking this half-arsed list of excuses wouldn't be enough to cool him.

But... I was wrong.

The forgiveness washing through Rory was instant and complete, tinged with an old, familiar warmth. "It's okay," he said softly.

I wanted to snap at Rory that it wasn't really "*okay*"—that this woman Carrie was still kidnapped, along with god knew how many others, all because Dev decided he could do it all alone.

Dev looked up and caught Rory's gaze, holding it with a fierce intensity that had my teeth grinding together, irritation flaring hot and immediate. That kilowatt smile spread across Dev's face—the kind that suggested the rest of the world had ceased to exist. I could see exactly what had made Rory fall for him: the way Dev made it seem like Rory was the only person worth looking at in any room.

I felt Rory's heart skip—a flutter of old affection, muscle memory responding to a smile he'd once woken up to every morning.

Two hearts remembering their old song,
while I sit watching from the shadows,
learning the bitter taste of wanting
what was never mine to claim.

"I really am sorry. So sorry," Dev said, never breaking eye contact.

"Anyway," I ground out, before they decided to hug or something. "Back to your story. Talk us through the moment 'they grabbed you.'"

From my rucksack by the door, I retrieved a notepad, then dragged a chair from the table to sit on.

"So, I was walking along, trying to get a signal on my phone to look at getting a bus back to Glasgow because of Carrie being spooked, when I heard something—someone, I guess—behind me. I considered shifting, but decided to keep moving, quickly."

I let my mental barriers drop slightly, brushing against the surface of Dev's thoughts. Images flashed through his mind—a narrow dirt path winding through dense pine trees, the metallic taste of fear on his tongue, the weight of his mobile in his hand as he frantically searched for signal bars.

No deception there. Just the raw memory of panic.

"Go on," I encouraged, scribbling notes.

"I got properly lost. My phone died, and though I brought a portable charger, the wire wasn't working. Night started falling, whoever was following me was getting closer. I could hear them—boots on gravel, twigs snapping. I should have shifted. But I was scared they'd pop out any second, attack me mid-shift."

Dev's hand moved to press against his forehead. "Someone covered my face. There was this chemical smell, sharp and sweet. I tried to shift then, but couldn't."

His thoughts painted the scene vividly—hands gripping his arms, the suffocating press of fabric against his nose and mouth, his wolf straining against some invisible barrier. Again, no fabrication. Just terror, confusion, and the helpless rage of a predator suddenly rendered powerless.

"I think there were at least two of them? Or... maybe even like, four." Dev's gaze flicked from my notepad to me. "Obviously, I could have taken them otherwise."

"Obviously," I agreed dryly.

Dev's fingers pressed against his temple as though trying to massage the memories loose. "I woke up in darkness. Concrete walls, I think. There was this bright, artificial light overhead—one of those harsh fluorescent things that makes everything look sickly. No windows."

His thoughts remained murky, fragmented like pieces of a broken mirror.

"Everything felt hazy, dreamlike. I kept drifting in and out of consciousness." Dev's voice grew quieter. "I remember needles in my arm. Voices discussing 'dosages' and 'compatibility scores.' At one point it seemed like two people were arguing, but I couldn't quite follow what they were saying."

Static filled the spaces where his memories should have been—not the natural blur of trauma, but something artificial, deliberate.

"But, I do have this flash of memory," Dev continued. "Carrie shaking me awake, whispering my name urgently. 'Dev, Dev, you need to wake up. Quickly, Dev.' But then... I think she was dragged away. I heard screaming. I tried to call out, but my voice wouldn't work. Later, I was in a small cell, I think. Not like with metal bars, just a tiny room with a cot and sink. Plain white walls and a security door. I don't even remember attempting to open it."

Dev paused, his hand unconsciously moving to cover his eyes again.

"One time, I swear there was this man looking at me through the cell window. Only saw him once, but the memory stuck because of how unsettling it was. He had this cruel smile and a scar through his eyebrow. He just stood there, staring at me. I didn't know what he wanted. But the way he looked at me..."

Rory gasped. "A scar? Through his left eyebrow?"

...Callum...

The name blazed through Rory's thoughts like a flare.

"I think I know who that was," Rory said, voice tight. "Member of my old pack. He got that scar from scrapping with a neighbouring pack as a teen."

"So he didn't come into the room? Just watched you?"

"Yeah. I think I woke up a couple more times after that. I remember my body being exhausted, like I'd just run a marathon. I had bruises all over my body."

Dev rolled back the sleeve of his grey hoodie, revealing a constellation of bruises that mottled his forearm in shades of purple and yellow.

"Those aren't your clothes, right?" Rory asked.

Dev scoffed, a bitter smile twisting his lips. "Definitely not. I was in my favourite jacket when they grabbed me."

"Oh, the one with the shimmering graffiti phoenix on the back?"

"Yes!" Dev's face lit up, and for a moment the two of them shared a look—the kind of intimate recognition that comes from knowing someone's wardrobe better than your own shopping list.

I coughed pointedly, wiggling my pen between my fingers. "So what happened last night?"

"Well, I don't remember attacking you. Honest." Dev's gaze flicked between Rory and me. "My most recent clear memory is waking up outdoors, alone, completely disoriented. No idea how I got out or how much time had passed. I was wandering through the Highlands until I heard voices—you two. I could smell you, Rory, and I couldn't believe it was you." Dev's voice grew softer, tinged with something approaching wonder. "Finding you felt like a miracle. Though I still felt weird. Like I was watching myself from outside my body."

"I still can't quite believe we found you," said Rory, as he stared at Dev like he was a rare treasure. "I thought you might be..."

"What about Sakshi?" Dev asked suddenly. "My alpha—does she know what's happened to me?"

"I've been keeping her informed," Rory replied. "She's worried sick, obviously. But your pack couldn't venture into Thorne territory themselves—not when my family are famously hostile to outsiders."

Relief flickered across Dev's face. "Good. She'd have my head if I disappeared without a word and didn't tell her where I'd gone. She'll be so grateful for you coming up here."

"Just in case this wasn't obvious," I said, "it was Rory who insisted something was wrong. The moment he realised you'd gone silent on social media, he was adamant you were missing. Then, when Felix found your phone, he demanded we needed to come up here as soon as possible."

Dev blinked, and for a moment his eyes glistened as if he was fighting unshed tears. The expression was almost cartoonish in its earnestness—like something from a sickeningly soppy romantic film before the two characters kiss and declare their undying love to one another.

"Really, Rory?" he said, his voice basically a squeak. "I... don't know what to say. Thank you so much."

It was so tempting to read Rory's thoughts, but I barely needed to—joy radiated from him in warm waves, like sunlight breaking through storm clouds, rich and golden and utterly genuine.

"Of course," Rory said softly. "I wasn't about to let you get kidnapped. Especially not when we started all this together."

Dev's free hand reached toward Rory, fingers stretching as far as the handcuff would allow. Another stupid stab of jealousy punched me in the gut. It was the way they looked at each other—like they shared some secret language the rest of the world couldn't understand, Dev commanding Rory's complete attention.

"Dev, we interviewed Ezra Houston, to see if he had information on your whereabouts. Unfortunately, as you'll see when you get your phone back, he was sent a picture of you meeting those two men—Bradley and Brody—by a friend he had following you. He's sent you a rather angry message about it. You might want to contact him sooner rather than later."

Dev didn't look concerned, or upset. Instead, he rolled his eyes. "God, he does have a flair for drama. I'll ring him."

"Is it safe for Dev to be here?" I asked Rory. "At this cottage?"

My question had absolutely nothing to do with wanting Dev gone as soon as possible. Obviously.

Rory chewed his lower lip. "There's a chance my family don't know he's here. He didn't come to the gate first, like Priya and Felix did. Depends how closely they're watching the cameras scattered around their land. Though there's always a chance they might smell his scent..."

"Well, I suggest Dev returns to London, immediately," I said. "Killigrew Street could organise medical tests to see what they can find—check if there's any trace of drugs still in his system. Blood work, brain scans. Everything they can."

"What? No way." Dev rattled his handcuff against the banister for emphasis, the metal clanking against wood. "I'm not leaving yet. Plus, I feel fine now."

"Well," I said through gritted teeth, fighting to keep my voice level. "We should see what Sebastián has to say about all this."

...Sebastián Salazar has no control over me, and neither do you, dude...

I sighed, dragging my hand through my hair. The conversation felt like it was spiralling in circles, and my head still throbbed from where Dev tried to kill me last night.

"Do you have any idea what they're actually doing with the shifters?" I asked him. "Humans researching, maybe? Keeping you all drugged so you couldn't shift and hurt them?"

Dev's face went blank. "I honestly don't know. That's why the three of us need to go find that building. The one listed as Highland Heritage Foundation. There's a good chance I was kept there. It's our best lead."

"Absolutely not," I snapped. "We're waiting for Felix to send over everything he can about the building first. Plus, the three of us can't go charging in there without backup—they could be armed."

Dev's face shifted, something haunted flickering across his features. He pressed his free hand against his stomach, as though fighting nausea.

"Once," he said quietly, "I woke up and could smell death. Proper death. Not just... not just animal blood or anything. Human death. It was everywhere." His voice dropped to barely above a whisper. "Maybe I don't want to go back there."

Well, why don't you just bloody well head back to London, then?

The thought blazed through my mind before I could stop it, accompanied by a surge of frustration that had nothing to do with the case and everything to do with the way Rory kept looking at Dev like he'd hung the moon.

"Maybe we should all head back," I said aloud, though even as the words left my mouth, I knew what Rory's response would be. "Now we've located Dev—"

"No!" Rory's voice cracked like a whip. "It's the Spring Equinox tomorrow." He turned to Dev. "My pack are hosting a gathering. Fuck knows what its true purpose is."

Dev nodded vigorously, his earlier hesitation apparently forgotten. "Rory's right. We still need to rescue Carrie, and all the others. If we leave now, who knows what will happen to them?"

The handcuff clinked as Dev leaned forward with renewed intensity. "I know I'm scared. But those people—whatever they're doing—they can't be allowed to continue."

I stared at both of them, wondering how I'd managed to find myself surrounded by people who seemed constitutionally incapable of taking the sensible option.

"Right," Dev said, stretching out. "Before we plan our next move, could I possibly have some food, if you'd be so kind as to feed your prisoner? And maybe a quick shower? I feel absolutely disgusting."

I stared at the metal cuff securing him to the banister. The reality was starting to sink in—I couldn't keep him chained there indefinitely. Rory wasn't going to allow it.

"One of you could stand guard outside the bathroom," Dev suggested with a wry grin aimed at Rory. "Maybe arm yourself with a kitchen knife in case I turn into a demon again."

"That won't be necessary," I said quickly.

"God, everything aches. And it feels like there's a clump of mud or something stuck to my scalp." His fingers moved to the fleshy bit at the base of his skull pressing experimentally.

He winced sharply, jerking his hand away.

"What is it?" Rory was already moving, crossing the space between them in three quick strides.

I watched as Rory's hands moved gently through Dev's hair, parting the dark strands with careful fingers. Would Rory mention our bond to him at any point? The thought twisted in my stomach. Probably he was waiting until they were alone. Or perhaps he wouldn't. Perhaps he'd be too embarrassed—or perhaps he wouldn't want Dev knowing if there was a chance he wanted to get back together. They'd spent almost a year together, whereas we'd only had this very strange week. There was no comparison.

Well, if that's what Rory wants, oh well. Probably for the best.

Who was I kidding? I wasn't sure if it was this wolf bond thing amplifying my own organic thoughts or not, but possessive fury bubbled up inside me at the thought of them together.

Christ, what was wrong with me? I'd never been one for obsessing over other people like this. And I was in the middle of a case, for crying out loud.

"Maxwell," Rory's concerned voice cut through my thoughts. "Come see this."

"The mud?"

"This isn't mud."

I closed the space between us, peering over Rory's shoulder. Just above his neck, a tiny portion of Dev's hair had been shaved away—replaced with a neat line of surgical stitches, no bigger than a five-pence piece.

"Dev, there's stitches here," Rory told him. "It looks like you might have had surgery."

"It's a small area," I said. "It's hard to say for sure what they would even be doing. But..." I gestured at the deliberate line of sutures. "This does suggest they opened him up."

Rory and I looked at each other. And I knew without telepathy that we were thinking the same thought.

Someone had inserted something in Dev's brain.

20

Rory

"They must know by now that Devraj somehow escaped," Seb said.

"Unless it's a trap." Kit's voice crackled through my phone's speaker. "And they've released him deliberately to lure Terrier to them."

I'd given Seb and Kit the full rundown while Maxwell took guard duty downstairs.

"Teddy was reading Dev's thoughts. He's being honest."

"That doesn't mean it isn't a trap, Terrier! He just might not know it!"

Seb's voice cut through my brother's agitation. "I'm also concerned that he might have a tracker implanted on—or *in*—him. I suggest you burn the clothes."

"That's not going to help if they've implanted a tracker into his skull," snapped Kit. "We've been staring at the picture. If they were just draining cerebrospinal fluid, you'd expect a simple puncture wound, maybe one stitch at most. But that..." He trailed off. "The three of you could be in grave danger. You all need to come home, *now*."

"Is that an order from Noctule?" I asked flatly.

Silence stretched across the line.

Eventually Seb spoke. "I'll always prioritise the safety of my team, but if Terrier and Teddy are happy to continue, I agree with their assessment that it could be helpful to remain a little longer."

Kit's sigh was audible. I could picture him scowling in his chair, frustrated but unwilling to challenge Seb directly. "It's worrying Dev doesn't actually remember escaping. He only regained control of his consciousness after he'd 'escaped' and attacked you."

"Yes, I know. It's all very *worrying*. That's why we need answers."

"Magpie is searching for information about that cluster of buildings as we speak. You can expect an update from him shortly."

"So what are we thinking about this 'pack gathering' tomorrow?" asked Seb. "Has the whole event been orchestrated to gather intelligence on shifters in the area? Or possibly, are they planning on snatching up over a hundred wolves?!"

Kit inhaled sharply. "Surely not."

"Who knows?" I said. "That's why we can't just walk away right now."

"If Callum specifically wanted you there tomorrow, that isn't good."

"I'll be careful," I promised, and Kit laughed like I'd told the most hilarious joke.

"I need to get back to Teddy, but um, are you free for another few minutes Kit?"

I hoped my meaning was clear—I wanted him to take his phone, and leave Seb's office.

There was some sort of muttered conversation between the pair of them, then Kit said, "Uh... sure."

Scuffling sounds, a door closing.

"What is it?" Kit said, voice dripping with curiosity. We weren't the sort of siblings to have secret, clandestine chats.

I took a breath. "Can a mate bond screw with someone's mind? Like, force the other person to feel attracted to them?"

"What? A mate bond? Rory, mate bonds don't work like—" There was a long pause. "Wait, do you think you have a mate bond with *Dev?* And that sent him crazy?"

"This is nothing to do with Dev."

"What?"

"Just answer the question!"

Kit's voice turned sharp, bitter. "I one hundred percent know it certainly doesn't work like that."

Something in his tone made my breath catch. "What? What do you mean? How do you know?"

"Why the hell are you talking about mate bonds right now?"

Silence stretched as I searched for the words to tell him that my wolf had decided my archnemesis was the perfect choice for a life partner.

Then suddenly—

"Fuck. Do I owe Peacock twenty quid?"

"Umm..." I grimaced. "Maybe?"

"You've got to be shitting me. Seriously?! *Teddy*? And you? You and Teddy? How...? *What*?! Christ, is there something in the water up there?!"

"But listen. Do you know how to break a mate bond? This whole thing was an accident, and I'm worried Teddy will hate me for it."

"I don't know anything about that." His voice went quiet, sad even. "Sometimes I wish there was a way to turn it off."

"Huh?" Why was he again talking as if he had firsthand experience? "Ages ago you told me that relationship you had with that other soldier... You said you hadn't had a mate bond!"

"That's true. I don't mean with them."

My brain struggled to process what he was saying. "Well, who do you mean, then?!"

"Do you want me to come up there?" Kit asked suddenly. "Because I will."

Well that was a subtle change in conversation.

"No," I said firmly, my heart swelling at the conviction in his tone. "I'll see you soon."

Hanging up, I made my way downstairs. Maxwell, now sitting in the armchair with his laptop open, looked up at me, and his face broke into one of those rare, genuine smiles that transformed his entire expression. Something warm and settling flowed into me—like coming home after a long journey.

The realisation slammed into me, stealing my breath. I didn't want to break this bond. Not even a little bit. The thought of severing this connection, of losing this constant awareness of Maxwell's presence and emotions—though it would undoubtedly be challenging—made my stomach lurch with something approaching panic.

What did that make me? Some sort of supernatural stalker who'd trapped an unwilling victim? But Maxwell had said he didn't want me to stay away. He'd chosen to get closer to me, over and over again.

"Everything alright?" Maxwell asked, voice tense.

"Yeah, just... Kit being Kit. Seb says we can keep going for now."

Dev now housed Freddy in his lap, and was gently stroking him. Seemingly Freddy had forgiven him for the whole flinging incident last night. Dev grinned at me. "He bit me twice, then decided we were mates again. Fickle little bastard."

"That's Freddy for you. Zero loyalty, maximum chaos."

Maxwell cleared his throat. "So, Felix just emailed us. Shall I summarise what he's found?"

"Shoot," I said.

"So, Highland Heritage Trust," Maxwell said. "They do have an online presence, though it's pretty minimal. Working email address, basic website—nothing fancy."

I perched on the arm of his chair, close enough to read over his shoulder. Our bond hummed contentedly at our proximity, which was both distracting and oddly comforting.

"Here's the interesting bit," Maxwell continued. "Felix tried to hack into their email system but he's hit a wall. Triple verification security, military-grade encryption. That's not normal for a small heritage organisation." Maxwell scrolled down. "Also, the Highland Heritage Trust doesn't just own that one building. They've got seven other properties scattered across the Highlands."

"*Seven*?!" Seven other properties meant more potential holding sites, more places Dev's captors could have moved other victims. "What was the original purpose of the first building?"

"Used to be a teaching hub for children. Closed down almost a decade ago, after some sort of funding deficiency."

"Doesn't sound like they'd casually have padded cells and operating theatres in a teaching hub."

"Felix managed to pull the original architectural plans," Maxwell said, bringing up a blueprint. "Two-storey building, basic layout. No basement shown on any of the official documentation."

Dev shifted, his expression troubled. "I'm absolutely certain I was kept underground. The way sound carried, the smell of the air, even the temperature."

Maxwell hummed. "It's entirely possible there are underground levels that aren't on the official plans."

"How exactly did Carrie come to know about this building?" I asked Dev.

Dev scratched behind Freddy's ear. "After Ewan went missing, an old friend contacted her. Someone they knew—who insisted on remaining anonymous—worked there briefly. They wouldn't talk to Carrie directly, only gave her friend basic information: that building, and that the Thorne family were involved."

I barked a laugh. "I'm not surprised."

But I *was* surprised. My mother took immense pride in being a shifter. She wouldn't want them cut open, even shifters from other packs.

Then again, how much did I really know her? I'd left shortly after I turned twenty. Maybe desperation had driven them to compromise their principles.

The thought made my stomach churn.

"All we know for sure is that Callum's involved," Maxwell said. "Which doesn't surprise me. The man has 'prick' written all over him."

"So, are we going to check out this building?" I said, at the same time my phone buzzed in my pocket.

Unknown

Is this your number? It's Isla. Let me know if you have any time to hang out or go for a run. Hope you're enjoying the cottage!

"It's my cousin Isla wanting to meet me." I chewed my bottom lip, considering. "Actually, it might be a good idea to bring her in on this. She might be helpful. She's much more in the know about my family than I am, and she keeps reaching out to reconnect."

Maxwell glared at me through his glasses. "Absolutely not."

"Why not?"

"We can't trust that she won't tell Edina everything we've discussed. She's ultimately her alpha, after all."

I shifted on the chair arm, feeling a spike of frustration flow through our bond. "Yeah, but Isla's different. You heard her. She hates the pack almost as much as me. She barely comes back here."

"That doesn't mean she won't feel obligated to report back," Maxwell said, "or feel unable to lie if your mother directly asks her. I'm not a shifter, but my understanding of these things is that pack loyalty runs deep?"

I couldn't help my hackles rising. Maxwell, daring to educate me on shifter politics?

We stared at each other, Maxwell pursing his lips together in a stubborn line. But underneath, I caught flickers of genuine worry—not just about operational security, but about me walking into another potential trap.

The weight of that concern, flowing warm and steady through our connection, deflated my anger.

"Fine," I said, shoving my phone away. "But if we end up needing insider information tomorrow and don't have it, I'm going to be insufferably smug about being right."

Maxwell's mouth twitched. "I can live with insufferable smugness."

Dev's gaze flicked between Maxwell and me, his expression shifting from casual interest to something sharper. His eyes lingered on how close I was sitting to Maxwell, then tracked back to our faces with the sort of look that suggested he was piecing together a puzzle.

"So," he said slowly, drawing out the word. "Are you two... getting along better these days?"

A prickle shot across my neck. I could feel Maxwell tense, probably picking up on my sudden spike of anxiety. The last thing I needed was Dev finding out that I'd accidentally forced this upon poor Maxwell. He'd probably laugh himself sick. *Just don't scare him off by suggesting you move in together,* the Dev in my mind cruelly sneered, even though I knew Dev wasn't actually like that.

"Well," I said, sliding off the chair arm and putting some distance between Maxwell and myself. "Are we going to this building, then?"

A sharp pang of *something* from Maxwell. *Shit.* Was he hurt? Had I fucked up, once again? He adjusted his glasses, not meeting my eyes.

"We could go find it, spy from a safe distance. Set up cameras. Armed, taking precautions. Look for tyre marks around the area, footprints. They'll definitely have their own cameras, so we'll need to be careful. We could bring hiking gear, pretend to be hikers."

I managed a grin. "I'm sure I could muster up a vaguely hiking-appropriate outfit."

"Dev should stay behind, though," Maxwell said, glancing his way. "He can't risk being seen anywhere near there."

I looked to Dev, who'd gone very still. He didn't jump in with an argument—perhaps he agreed. Perhaps he was having flashbacks of whatever horrible things had happened to him in that place.

The idea of spending time alone with Maxwell in the wilderness sent an entirely inappropriate thrill through me.

"There's a tiny tent in the cupboard," Maxwell continued. "We can bring that for the full hiking effect."

My stomach did a little flip. Did he actually want the two of us to camp out there tonight? Together? In a tent?

"But... who'll stand guard over Dev?" I asked. "We can't leave him like this!"

Dev not so subtly rattled his handcuff, Freddy squeaking as if in agreement. "Maybe Rory should stay here with me, in case his family comes round to evict me," he said quietly. "Maxwell could go set up the camera and snoop about a bit?"

The bond between Maxwell and me surged with intense shared panic at the idea of being separated.

"No," Maxwell all but shouted, making Dev flinch. Then he calmly added, "I promised Kit I wouldn't let him out of my sight."

Dev scowled at him.

"And there's no way I trust Maxwell to investigate without me," I added, though it sounded weak.

We all stared at each other in uncomfortable silence.

"The solution is simple," I said finally. "We need Isla to come here and babysit."

Maxwell scowled at me. "Rory, I said no."

Something hot and spiky flared inside me. "Why don't you trust me on this?" I fought to keep my teeth from grinding together. "I've told you, her and Uncle Alex aren't like the others. And we need more hands on deck here!"

"Rory isn't stupid," Dev snarled, shooting Maxwell a disgusted look. "Why aren't you listening to him? If he thinks it's a good idea, then you need to at least consider it."

Maxwell went completely still, his gaze locked onto Dev's face. The air crackled with tension as they stared at each other—Maxwell's expression carefully blank, Dev's openly challenging. Through our bond, I felt Maxwell's emotions churning: frustration, protectiveness, and conflict. Like he was wrestling with himself.

Dev didn't back down, meeting Maxwell's stare with the sort of stubborn defiance I remembered from our relationship. The same look he'd get when I'd ask him to spend less time working, or when I'd skirt around the topic of where our relationship was heading.

The seconds ticked by. The only movement from Maxwell was the rise and fall of his chest. I could practically see him weighing options, calculating risks.

"Fine," he said eventually, the word sharp as broken glass. "But they're not staying here, where Callum can find them stupidly easily. Is there anywhere in town they can stay?"

"There's a large BnB on the outskirts of town that might work. It has a steady stream of tourists, so they won't stick out."

He sprang to his feet so quickly the movement was almost violent, armchair scraping against the floor. "Call Isla, then."

The words were tossed back over his shoulder as he stalked out of the room, his footsteps heavy on the cottage floorboards. A door slammed—possibly the back door. Had he gone out to smoke? Though I hadn't seen him do that since I threw up from the smell.

Dev raised his eyebrows at me. "So, he's still a dick, then, I take it?"

I opened my mouth to make a joke, then, despite the distance between us, Maxwell's raw worry slammed into me. He wasn't simply being difficult—he was terrified. Of losing control, of making the wrong decision, of something happening to me.

I'd just have to pray I'd made the right call.

21

Theodore

The tent strapped to Rory's back caught another low branch, jerking him backwards with a sharp thwack. He stumbled, swore creatively, and kept walking.

"Are you sure you don't want me to carry the tent?" I asked for the second time.

Rory shot me a look that could have stripped paint. "Just because I'm shorter than you doesn't mean that I'm weaker."

I couldn't help but laugh. "Oh yeah?"

A smirk tugged at the corner of his mouth. "What, you think you can take me?"

Fighting my own grin, I shot him a sensual wink. "In a fight?"

Rory waggled his eyebrows at me in the most ridiculously adorable way that made me have to resist the urge to pin him against the nearest tree and kiss him senseless.

But there was no time for forest make-out sessions. We were on a reconnaissance mission.

Earlier, I'd hovered in the corner of the cottage living room whilst Isla stood in the middle, listening to Rory fill her in. I'd probed gently into her thoughts—which seemed innocent enough. She didn't try to block me, and I caught nothing that suggested she'd go running straight to Edina with tales of underground operations and shifters being tortured.

She'd been extremely confused—then horrified. Disturbed, even. When Callum's name was mentioned, she'd visibly flinched. She promised not to tell anyone anything yet, including her father. It wasn't hard to convince her to babysit Dev for us. Until Freddy bit her. Then she was less keen.

Still, the decision to involve her sat wrong in my gut. Every police instinct I possessed screamed that bringing more pack members into this mess was asking for trouble. But I'd relented, not able to bear the thought of Rory believing I didn't trust his judgement. Not when he'd been so certain involving his cousin was the best idea.

The cousin he hasn't seen in five years. I pushed the thought from my mind. It was done now. Dev had agreed to go with Isla to go hide at the BnB, where Isla would find a radiator to cuff him to.

Our connection hummed with his contentment as we walked. At least one of us felt confident about our choices.

"How much further?" Rory asked, pausing to untangle himself from another aggressive branch.

I checked the GPS on my phone. "About half a mile northeast. Felix's coordinates should put us within sight of the building complex."

He nodded and resumed walking, the tent bouncing against his shoulders with each step. Every so often he'd deliberately rub his arm against mine, reminding me of his behaviour as a wolf. It made me smile each time, and certainly provided a welcome distraction from the thoughts circling my mind like vultures.

Christ, I was glad to be away from Dev.

My teeth ground together as I remembered our earlier conversation. I'd been rearranging my bag when I'd asked if he'd contacted Ezra yet. Purely professional interest, of course. Nothing to do with hoping they might reconcile over the phone and Dev declare that they were back together.

"I will do later. I'm still annoyed at him for jumping to the conclusion that I was cheating on him," Dev had said. Then he'd sighed, running a hand through his hair, damp from the shower. "It's sad this happened, but maybe it was for the best. I couldn't see it lasting between us anyway."

He'd looked me dead in the eye, and I knew whatever he said next, I was supposed to listen closely to.

"Shifters date humans all the time, of course. But when it comes to settling down, finding a life partner? It feels more natural for us to be with our own kind. It's just the way we are."

The pointed nature of that comment had hit me like a slap across the face. I'd stood there speechless, processing the deliberate sting of it, the casual dismissal.

Maybe it was that, or maybe it was the way he'd been dressed in Rory's jumper, the one that matched the colour of his eyes. Regardless, the anger surging up inside made me reckless and I let my curiosity get the better of me to ask, "Why did you break up with Rory?"

Dev's eyes had widened in shock before his expression turned thunderous. "That's absolutely none of your business," he'd seethed.

I'd been so embarrassed by my own behaviour that I hadn't even attempted to read his thoughts.

Rory glanced my way, those sharp blue-green eyes narrowing with concern.

"You alright?" he asked, slowing his pace.

Before he could probe deeper into whatever emotional mess he was picking up from me, he stopped short, sniffing the air.

"Can you smell that?"

I shook my head. "What is it?"

"It smells like..." He trailed off, looking beyond me, then checked our location on his phone. "We're almost there, but let's go that way."

I followed Rory through the dense undergrowth, branches catching at my jacket as we climbed steadily uphill. His pace never faltered, even with that bloody tent strapped to his back. My breathing grew heavier with each step, sweat beading despite the cool Highland air.

The trees began to thin as we reached higher ground, granite outcrops jutting through the soil like broken bones. Finally, we emerged onto a rocky cliff edge that dropped away towards a vast, dark lake below. The water reflected the grey sky like tarnished silver, too still, too quiet. Something about this place felt wrong beyond just the obvious.

"Look over here," I hissed, spotting something that made my stomach clench.

Rory followed my gaze to where the ground ahead had been scarred black—a wide circle of charred earth that spoke of repeated use. Ash and debris was scattered across the rock in grey drifts, and the skeletal remains of multiple bonfires dotted the area.

"I thought I smelt it," Rory said, gesturing at the burnt ground. "The smell of... death."

We moved carefully through the bonfire remnants, me pulling on latex gloves from my jacket pocket. Dread pooling in my gut as ash crunched under my feet—Christ, I tried not to think about what we might be walking through.

"What's that?" Rory asked, crouching near the edge of one of the burn circles.

I followed his gaze but couldn't see anything obvious among the ash and blackened stones. "Where?"

"There—" He pointed to a spot where the wind had carved a shallow depression in the debris.

I knelt beside him, brushing away layers of ash with careful movements. My fingers found something hard beneath the surface—smooth, curved. As more ash fell away, the shape became unmistakable.

A large wolf's canine lay in my palm, discoloured to a sickly grey-brown, its surface cracked and brittle from intense heat. But still unmistakably sharp, unmistakably what it was.

Rory stumbled backwards, putting his head between his knees.

"God, I hate them so much, but this is still... It's still my family doing this shit." His words came out in a rush. "Like, how fucked up is that? I can't escape them, can I? Now I have to live knowing the Thornes are literal mass murderers and I'm one of them and... I just wanted to get away from all their shit, you know?"

Looking down at the dark water below, the pieces clicked into place with sickening clarity. "This would be a great place to burn bodies. Then throw the ash into the lake."

Rory made a horrible noise, and I squeezed his hand, offering what comfort I could. No words seemed adequate for this.

My gaze drifted across the lake toward the far shore, where the skeletal remains of an ancient castle perched on a rocky outcrop. Most of the structure had long since crumbled, leaving only jagged stone teeth against the grey sky. But there—atop what looked like the remnants of a tower—something caught the light.

"Can I have the binoculars?"

I handed them over, watching him focus on the ruins.

"There's something there," he breathed. "On top of the castle ruins."

Taking the binoculars back, I studied the crumbling stones. "A tiny solar panel? Could be something? But we really need to go see those buildings."

We set back off immediately. Half an hour later, we spotted wire fencing through the trees, choked with ivy and brambles. The rusted wire had corroded completely in several places, creating gaps large enough to slip through.

"If they're really running a high-tech underground operation here, you'd think they'd invest in better fencing," Rory mused.

"This is very much off the usual hiking routes, but they'll still get people passing through. Like us."

We scanned for cameras—tree trunks, fence posts, even the canopy above. Nothing visible, but that didn't mean we were in the clear.

Once through the gap, we crouched behind a cluster of gorse bushes and surveyed the complex ahead.

Four buildings sat in a semicircle around a central courtyard. Three were modest concrete blocks with flat roofs. The largest dominated the site—red-brick façade with tall windows, clearly some sort of educational facility originally. One smaller building had partially collapsed, twisted metal beams jutting skyward like broken ribs.

"Whole place looks abandoned," Rory whispered, already shifting forward with that familiar restless energy.

"We can't go any closer," I said.

Yet I watched him creep closer to the buildings, tiny step by tiny step, until he was dangerously exposed.

Enough. I moved swiftly, catching his arm and hauling him back against my chest.

"Don't make me handcuff you again," I growled into his ear.

"You gave your handcuffs to Isla!"

"I always bring spares."

He twisted to face me, eyes sparkling with delight. "Promises, promises."

Christ. Even in the middle of a surveillance operation, he could make my blood run hot.

I pulled out my binoculars and focused on the largest building. An old security camera hung at an awkward angle near the main entrance, no red recording light visible. Beyond the complex, I could trace the ghost of an old track—a subtle depression in the landscape.

We found a single tyre track pressed into soft earth nearby.

"Dirt bike?" Rory questioned.

"If they're moving kidnapped shifters, they'd need something bigger. Possibly, they have another way in?"

"I'm going to shift," Rory announced suddenly, already moving towards the cover of a large tree, shrugging out of his jacket. "See what I can smell or hear."

"What?" I said, following him. "Hold on."

But then, he was already down to his underwear, clothes all over the ground. "Shut your eyes," he instructed, and for a moment I considered a joke about being pretty well acquainted with his cock.

I faced away while he shifted, the agony leaking through the bond now familiar.

A soft bark. I turned to find wolf--Rory, dropping to my knees to give him a quick scratch behind his ear, his fur thick beneath my fingers. Rory's bright green-blue eyes were alert and intelligent as they met mine. He panted, his pink tongue contrasting beautifully with his black lips and nose.

"You still can't go right up to the building," I whispered firmly. "Just sniff around the perimeter, understand?"

Rory's wolf smiled at me—an unsettling expression on a canine face, tongue lolling slightly—and then he was off.

I watched through my binoculars as he began a wide circle around the complex, his movements fluid and purposeful. Golden fur caught occasional glimpses of filtered sunlight as he wove between the scrubby bushes and patches of heather.

The circle grew tighter.

And tighter.

My jaw clenched as I realised what he was doing. The bloody fool was spiralling inward like a hunter closing in on prey, each loop bringing him closer to the buildings.

"Rory," I whisper-shouted, as loud as I dared.

He ignored me completely, continuing his methodical approach.

Another loop. Now he was barely twenty metres from the buildings.

"Rory!" I tried again, louder but still keeping my voice low.

He disappeared behind the partially collapsed structure, golden fur vanishing from sight.

Anxiety twisted through my veins. *Why, Rory, why?!*

The connection between us thrummed with his excitement, his wolf's satisfaction at being useful, at tracking something interesting. But all I could feel was mounting dread.

A side door opened.

Two people emerged from the largest building and my blood turned to pure ice.

A man and woman, both mid-thirties. The man was already rolling a cigarette between his fingers whilst the woman clutched a coffee mug, tilting her face skyward as if she hadn't seen daylight in weeks.

Terror shot through me like a bolt of lightning. Surely Rory had heard them by now, even if his wolf senses hadn't picked up their approach long before I'd spotted them.

But where was he?

I couldn't sense anything from him. Did that mean he was too far away?

My mind raced with horrific possibilities. Images of having to ring Kit, of begging him to come help me save his brother from unknown torture. Of explaining to Seb and Priya how I'd lost Rory on my watch.

The woman said something to her companion that made him laugh—a sound that carried clearly across the open ground. They clearly had no idea that a wolf shifter lurked somewhere nearby.

I found myself holding my breath, straining to catch any hint of movement, any flash of golden fur that would tell me he was alive and safe. The binoculars shook in my grip as adrenaline flooded my system.

Where are you, Rory?

Through our connection, I tried to project every ounce of terror coursing through me—the gut-wrenching, desperate fear that something had happened to him. If he could feel even a fraction of what I was experiencing, hopefully that would help.

The thought of losing him now, even though I'd only just begun to understand what this thing between us could become—it threatened to tear me apart from the inside.

No. I couldn't think it.

All I could do was pray that somehow, wherever he was, Rory would hear me and know that I needed him to come back to me.

22

Rory

S moke. Bitter. Sharp in nose.

Hide behind twisted metal. Crouch low. Breathe shallow.

Two-legs emerge. Female clutches hot-liquid scent. Male rolls tobacco between fingers.

Listen. Important.

"Christ, I'm already knackered," female says. Voice tired. Defeated. "Tomorrow night's going to be a nightmare."

"Tell me about it." Male has plant-smoke. Inhale. Exhale. Poison-sweet drifts on wind. "How many new arrivals are we expecting?"

"Could be as many as ten, I hear. Depends on how the extraction goes."

"Overtime again, then."

"Triple shift, more like. I haven't seen my kids in days."

"But ten? Do we even have space for them?"

"Two kicked the bucket last week. Plus, there's a few empty rooms nobody's set up yet."

Wind shifts.

Death.

The scent hits like claw across muzzle. Old death. Recent death. Fills nose. Fills lungs. Choking on it.

Stolen wolves. Dead wolves. Wrong-wrong-wrong.

Terror floods veins. Need safety. Need—

Raindrops-lemongrass-mine.

Panic burns through chest. Must return. Must run. Now-now-now.

Door slams. Two-legs gone inside. Building swallows them.

Run. Fast-fast-fast through scrub. Paws strike earth. Heart hammers against ribs.

Raindrops-lemongrass-mine waits where left him. Crouched. Tense. Binoculars shake in hands.

Relief floods everything. Safe. Here. Together.

"Rory! I told you not to go close to the buildings!"

Raindrops-lemongrass-mine angry. Don't like. I fix.

Launch myself at him. Full weight. Knock backwards into heather. Pin shoulders. Lick face-neck-everywhere. Salt-sweat-fear taste. *Mine-mine-mine.*

"Rory, what the hell—" Muffled under my tongue.

Lick harder. Joy bubbles up. Found him. Safe now.

Laugh breaks from his throat. Deep sound. Good sound. "Get off me, you mad—"

More licking. Can't stop. Need taste of him. Need proof he's real.

"Change back," he snaps, but voice holds fondness. "Now, Rory."

Should hide to change. But don't want to be away. Shift here. With him.

Burns through bones. Human skin replaces fur.

Naked. Cold air bites. But *his* warmth underneath me, solid and real.

"You absolute lunatic," Maxwell breathed, hands coming up to frame my face. "I thought— When they came out and I couldn't see you—"

"I heard them talking," I said quickly, rolling off him to grab my clothes. "Tomorrow night. They're expecting new arrivals..."

I told him what I'd overheard as I yanked on my jeans, the words tumbling out in a rush. The overtime shifts, the casual way they'd discussed the numbers like livestock deliveries.

"I could smell it so clearly," I said, pulling my shirt over my head. "The smell of death. Recent. All over the place. That's what I was tracking, before they came out. I think they might have had bodies in that building. Before they dragged them to their burn site."

Maxwell pulled the small surveillance cameras from his rucksack. "Let's get these positioned."

Nearly an hour it took us to get the bloody things sorted. Maxwell insisted on testing angles three times, muttering about optimal coverage and battery life whilst I held branches out of the way.

All the while, I couldn't stop thinking about the castle ruins we'd spotted from the burn site—grey stones jutting from the hillside like broken teeth. Something tugged at my chest, urgent and insistent.

"I want to go check out those castle ruins," I said.

Maxwell squinted in that direction, then checked his watch. "That's a bloody long walk, Rory."

"We'll go quickly."

Maxwell was quiet for a moment, considering. "I suppose there isn't much we can do back there anyway," he said eventually. "If you think Isla and Dev will still be okay shacked up together in town."

I snorted. "I wonder how they're getting on. Dev's probably trying to charm his way into getting Isla to uncuff him. Sweet-talking her about his journalistic integrity or some bollocks." I grinned despite everything. "Good luck to him, though—Isla's too smart for that. She'll see right through his pretty-boy routine."

By the time we reached the ruins, it was half past seven. The air carried that crisp bite that promised a cold night ahead, while late spring light mellowed to that particular Highland gold that photographers spent fortunes trying to capture, painting the lake's surface in molten copper.

"Castle" was generous terminology for what we found. One wall remained mostly intact, maybe twelve feet high with a stubby tower structure jutting from its corner like a broken finger. The other three walls had crumbled, leaving gaps where wind and weather had claimed victory over ancient mortar.

We tossed our bags into the centre of the ruin. I tilted my head back, scanning the intact wall.

There—something metallic caught the evening light, nestled between weathered stones near the tower's peak.

"See it? Right where the wall meets the tower."

Maxwell shaded his eyes. "How do we get to it?"

Deep grooves scored the wall at regular intervals—too uniform to be natural weathering. "These look like handholds."

His hands settled on my waist. "Right, up you go, then."

Heat burned through my jeans where his palms pressed. That familiar spark zapped between us, making my breath catch.

"Bit higher," I managed.

His hands slid up, fingers spreading just above my hipbones. I had to bite back a groan as he lifted me.

The climb took barely a minute. Up close, the solar panel was clearly expensive kit—sleek black surface with professional-grade cables snaking down into perfectly drilled holes through ancient stone.

"This isn't heritage preservation," I called down. "This is serious tech, and someone's hidden the wiring."

I scrambled back down, Maxwell's hands steadying me.

We moved around the interior, running hands along every stone surface. Found nothing but centuries of Highland weather damage. I wandered towards the collapsed section where one of the towers had crumbled, leaving a pile of weathered stones and deeper shadows. Something felt... *off.*

"Maxwell," I called, crouching in the shadowed corner. "Look at this."

The grass grew differently here—trampled into a faint path that led right to the base of the rubble pile. And where the path ended, the ground looked... maintained. Not wild like everywhere else.

Maxwell joined me. "Someone's been walking here regularly."

I pressed my nose closer to the earth, breathing in. Underneath the Highland dampness and ancient stone, I caught something else—metal, concrete, and the lingering scent of humans who'd been here recently.

"There's definitely something under here," I said, starting to pull away the loose grass. It came up easily, too easily, revealing a rectangular outline in the soil. "This isn't natural."

We cleared the debris together. Underneath, clean edges emerged—metal seams barely visible, a hatch flush with the ground and perfectly camouflaged by its position in the tower's shadow.

"Modern concrete," Maxwell breathed, running his fingers along the edge. "Hidden where no casual hiker would think to look."

The concealment was clever—tucked into the collapsed tower's base where shadows fell even in daylight, invisible unless you knew exactly where to search.

"There's not any visible panels, card readers, or anything..." Maxwell said. "We're not getting into this anytime soon. Let's look around the outside."

We carefully replaced the soil and grass, making the hatch invisible again. Examining the ground near the castle, it wasn't hard to find tyre tracks carved deep into the earth. Wide, aggressive treads designed for serious off-road work.

"SUV," he said, photographing the impressions. "Heavy one. Look how deep these cuts go."

I traced the tracks across the moorland—rolling hills with scattered trees. Perfect terrain for bringing people here undetected.

"Drive right up, unload your cargo, disappear back into the hills," I said quietly.

Maxwell checked his watch. "Nearly eight o'clock."

I looked back across the lake towards the death site, then at our camping gear still piled in the ruins.

"I suppose we should head back to Dev and Isla," I said, watching Maxwell carefully.

"I suppose," he eventually replied. "Though... it'll be dark soon. Trekking back all that way will be a nightmare. We *could* use that tent. Set up down by the lake and monitor the place overnight, see if anyone shows up."

"I suppose..." My face split into a silly grin, as if Maxwell was suggesting we have a romantic camp out together, rather than gather intelligence about wolf murderers. "I suppose that's a very sensible idea."

Maxwell snorted. "I don't know about sensible. I think you might be rubbing off on me, Terrier."

I nudged his shoulder with mine, enjoying the way his expression shifted between exasperation and something warmer. "I know your game. Ancient castle ruins, Highland lake, just you and me under the stars..."

"And potentially armed murderers."

"Sounds like my ideal evening."

But as I beamed up at him, and his lips twitched into that reluctant smile he tried so hard to hide, there was truth behind my words. Something warm and wonderful settled within me. Out here in the middle of nowhere, with nothing but Highland wilderness and each other, Maxwell felt properly mine.

No pack, no Dev, no distractions.

Just us, a tent, and whatever the night might bring. My stomach gave a pleased little flutter at the thought.

23

Rory

Dinner was a disturbing affair: tinned haggis that Maxwell had discovered lurking in the cottage pantry.

The cold grey mass sat in our camping bowls, looking distinctly unappetising in the torchlight. I prodded it with my plastic spoon, watching it jiggle ominously.

"Well," I said, forcing cheerfulness into my voice. "At least it's authentic Highland fare."

Maxwell raised an eyebrow. "I'm fairly certain Burns never intended haggis to come from a tin."

I managed a decent-sized spoonful. The texture was unfortunate—mushy and oddly metallic, with an aftertaste suggesting it had been in that tin since the last century. But I'd eaten worse during my rough-sleeping days in Glasgow.

"Not too bad, actually," I said, swallowing heroically.

Then I caught sight of Maxwell's face.

His expression was somewhere between disgust and genuine horror, nose wrinkled, mouth twisted into the most spectacular grimace I'd ever witnessed. He made a small, wounded sound.

The laugh burst out of me, sending partially chewed haggis spraying across our makeshift camp. I doubled over, coughing and spluttering, bits of grey mush decorating the Highland heather.

"Oh god," I wheezed. "Your face!"

Maxwell watched my haggis explosion with the weary resignation of a man who'd clearly made poor life choices. "Beautiful."

The food situation improved at dessert—shortbread biscuits. I made sad faces at Maxwell until he gave me two extra from his pile.

We'd camped two hundred metres down the lakeside, tucked behind ancient Scots pines that provided concealment whilst maintaining clear sightlines to the castle ruins. Too cold really, especially without a fire, and I already had my thick winter coat on.

"We should check in on Isla and Dev. Check they got to the BnB okay." I pulled out the satellite transceiver. The display showed nothing.

"Bollocks," I said, shaking the device.

"Equipment's probably temperamental out here." Maxwell shrugged. "We'll try later."

"I expected you to spiral into panic mode if we couldn't confirm Dev was still chained to a radiator."

Maxwell scoffed. "I'm really hoping you're right, and Dev is back to himself now. Else we're fucked."

"If he does demon out, Isla can probably take him. She looks small, but like me, looks can be deceiving."

"It *looked* to me that demon Dev was handing you your ass yesterday."

I laughed. "He feels very, very sorry about that now. He grovelled for thirty minutes earlier."

A sudden tension—a tightness that ran through our bond like a plucked wire—made me flinch.

"What?"

"Nothing."

"Tell me."

Maxwell sighed, his shoulders sagging. For a long moment, he said nothing, just stared out at the lake. The water lapped gently against the shore, creating soft ripples that caught the moonlight.

"About Dev…" he began, then stopped, running a hand through his hair. "Look, the way he was talking with me earlier, when you were upstairs, makes me think he might want to get back with you at some point. And I just wanted to say, if that happens, I'll understand, and it doesn't need to be a big deal. The wolf bond thing might sort itself out."

"What?"

The word came out with a harsh snap, but the bottom had just dropped out of my stomach. I stared at Maxwell's profile in the torchlight, trying to process what he'd just said.

He was... giving me permission? To go back to Dev?

The last bite of shortbread turned to ash in my mouth. Of course. Of course this was what Maxwell wanted. He'd been looking for an escape route from the moment he'd realised what the bond meant, hadn't he? And now Dev had conveniently appeared to provide him with the perfect excuse.

"You want me to get back with Dev," I said, voice flat.

Maxwell's head snapped towards me. "What? No, that's not—"

"Right, and you're just being noble about it." A bitter laugh escaped me. "Making sure I know you won't stand in the way of true love, is that it?"

"Rory—"

"No, I get it." I scrambled to my feet, needing to move, needing space. The bond between us was a live wire now, crackling with hurt and confusion. "This whole mate bond thing is terrifying and impractical, like you said. Dev showing up is perfect timing, really. Gets you off the hook."

Maxwell was staring at me like I'd lost my mind. "That's not what I meant."

"Isn't it?"

"I thought you'd want to get back with Dev! You dropped your entire life to rush up here to save him!"

"I'm just a decent human being! Sometimes!" The words exploded out of me, hands flailing in the air.

"Plus, all I've heard about this whole time is how much you adore him. A week ago you were sitting in front of me at Undertone sobbing into your drink about how much you missed him! And you've been going on and on about how amazing his bloody journalism career is, and his 'modelling on the side,' of course, and how much Freddy loves him—"

Something flickered through our bond. Something green and bitter and entirely unexpected.

I stopped mid-pace, mouth falling open.

"Wait... are you *jealous* of Dev?!"

Maxwell's scowl could have curdled milk. "No."

"You *are* jealous. I can feel it." Pure delight bubbled up within me, bright and effervescent. "Oh my god, I can't believe you're actually jealous. This is brilliant. This is the best thing that's ever happened to me."

Maxwell turned away, jaw working furiously. He started aggressively repacking our dinner supplies, shoving the empty tin into his rucksack with unnecessary force.

"Just because I'm glad to find Dev safe and alive doesn't mean I'd just go back to him like that, after he treated me like shit. Do you really think I have that little self-respect?"

Maxwell's hands stilled on the rucksack straps. Something shifted in his expression. "No. But I think you're a beautifully loyal, kind human being who would give anyone a second chance."

I fell to my knees, nudging against his. "Look, Dev was hot and all, but my tastes have changed."

Maxwell's gaze met mine, searching. "Oh? How so?"

Moonlight caught the tiny amount of silver threading through his hair, and I wanted nothing more than to reach out and trace the lines of his face with my fingertips.

Before I understood what was happening, Maxwell caught my hand, pressing my palm against his cheek. His skin was warm despite the Highland chill, and I relished the light rasp of stubble beneath my fingers.

"Well, for a start, it's nice to spend time with someone who's not obsessed with their reflection. Or stops walking every two seconds to take a photo to post."

Maxwell's mouth quirked upward. "I do take the occasional selfie, you know."

"Liar." I shifted closer, my thumb tracing the line of his cheekbone. "But mainly, my tastes have evolved towards men who actually read books instead of just posing with them. Who make me feel like I'm worth paying attention to, not just some accessory to make them look good. Who actually listen when I'm talking."

Maxwell kept so still, he didn't even blink.

"Who drink their coffee black without any stupid syrup in it, just like me. Who get genuinely excited about proper procedure. Who get this smug, satisfied little smile when they solve something particularly clever."

"I do not have a smug smile!"

"You absolutely do. Don't worry, it's somehow ridiculously attractive. Along with how your glasses fall down your nose when you're frowning too much. And the way you pretend to find my jokes annoying when I can literally feel through the bond now that you think I'm hilarious."

Maxwell's hand came up to cover mine, pressing it more firmly against his face. "Anything else?"

"Oh, loads more. The way you care so much about doing the right thing that it actually causes you physical pain sometimes. How you could use your telepathy for evil, but you try not to invade our minds. Oh, and the fact that you dropped everything to drive to bloody Scotland with me, because I needed you to. Even though you could barely stand me at the time."

I paused, studying his face in the torchlight.

"Even if you are an unsociable, grumpy bastard who has refused to ever hang out with us."

"I haven't refused to ever hang out with Killigrew Street," said Maxwell quietly. "You just barely invite me to anything."

"You don't have to be personally invited, you know," I said, my hand still pressed against his cheek. "You're one of us."

Maxwell's laugh was harsh. "No I'm not. I'm someone Killigrew Street contacts when they need something. A resource."

I inhaled sharply. Was that really how he felt? "Maxwell, we don't see you that way at all! Anyway... it doesn't have to be that way. When we get back to London, we can all go to the pub together. You can come to our monthly quiz night—finally we'll have someone who can cheat properly instead of Priya sneaking off to the bathroom to google the answers."

Maxwell rolled his eyes. "They won't want me there. You're not the only one who gets bothered by my telepathy, you know. They all think about it, every time I'm in the room. I've heard them."

The pain in his voice made my chest ache. I could feel the weight of it—years of isolation, of being treated like some kind of walking invasion of privacy.

"If I'm there, it's just a worse experience for everyone. They can't relax, can't be themselves. They're constantly monitoring their thoughts, trying not to think about whatever they don't want me to know." His voice cracked slightly. "Do you have any idea how exhausting it is? Pretending I haven't heard someone's private thoughts? Acting like I don't know they're uncomfortable?"

I could see it now, the careful distance he maintained from everyone. How he'd perfected that professional mask to keep people at arm's length before they could reject him.

"It's not just Killigrew Street. It's stopped me from bothering with most friendships, in general," he continued, staring out at the dark water. "I block as much as I can, but things slip through. The lies, the fakeness, when they actually can't stand me but are being polite. How do you build genuine relationships when you know exactly what people really think of you?"

Oh, how my heart broke for him. I shifted closer, our knees touching now.

"But you know," I said softly, "you've got ready-made friends right at your fingertips at Killigrew Street. They already know about your telepathy! Surely that makes it easier?"

"Does it?"

"They'll get used to it, after a while. Like I have."

Maxwell did one of his frowns that slipped down his glasses. "What do you mean?"

"It doesn't bother me at all anymore." I shrugged, feeling the truth of it settle between us. "I quite like it. Actually, I *love* the bonus applications."

"Rory..."

"What? The sex thing is brilliant. No guesswork. Maximum fun."

"You're incorrigible."

"And you love it." I grinned at him. "Also, Priya was gutted you didn't show up for the Killigrew Street Christmas party. She'd made you a hat and everything."

The space between us grew charged, heavy with something that strangely made my heart pound.

Maxwell took a deep breath. "I did show."

"What? You didn't."

"I came in through the street entrance. The basement door was unlocked that day, propped open." His voice dropped, and he removed my hand from his face. "And then I heard you. Talking about me. So I turned around and left."

The Christmas party? My stomach plummeted like I'd just stepped off a cliff.

I tried to think back to that night, desperately searching my memory for what I'd said. The party had been brilliant—by the end everyone had been properly pissed, and I'd been blessed with that Christmas cracker joke about vampires, after Priya explicitly told me no vampire jokes in front of Emma. But what had I said about Maxwell?

The sick feeling spread through my chest, cold and creeping.

"What did I say?" The words came out strangled.

Maxwell's expression was carefully neutral, but I could feel the old hurt radiating from him like an infected wound.

"Whatever it was, I'm so sorry, Maxwell. I'm so, so sorry."

He watched me with that same careful mask he always wore around Killigrew Street. Professional. Distant. Safe.

"I can feel how much it hurt you, and I just—" My voice faltered. "I'm disgusted with myself. Properly disgusted."

The shame was overwhelming, hot and suffocating. How many times had I been cruel without even thinking? How many careless comments had I made, never considering what they might do to him?

"I'm sorry for being such an asshole. Not just that night, but for the last eighteen months. All of it. Every snide comment, every time I've been horrible to you, every time I've made you feel unwelcome. Every time I called you Detective Dickface." I swallowed hard. "It's no wonder you hated me, seriously. I get it."

Maxwell was quiet for a long moment, his gaze fixed on the dark water. When he finally spoke, his voice was soft.

"I told you before, I never *hated* you. I just thought you were an immature moron and Seb had hit his head the day he hired you."

I stared at him. "You're a bloody saint, do you know that?"

Maxwell barked a laugh. "I'm not entirely innocent."

"What do you mean? You've literally done nothing wrong."

"What about the whole 'throwing you in a cell during a full moon' thing that you've brought up every time we've met for the last eighteen months?"

My face prickled with heat, shame crawling up my neck. "Yes, well, that was my own fault, though, wasn't it?"

Maxwell sputter-coughed, damn well nearly choking on his own breath. "Excuse me?"

I picked at the heather beside my knee, unable to meet his eyes. The confession felt like pulling glass from a wound.

"It was easier to blame you, so I did. But obviously it only happened because Dev and I jumped the gun and didn't wait for Seb to organise sweeping Meridian properly. We went in half-cocked, got ourselves caught, and then I spent eighteen months making you the villain because it was simpler than admitting I'd fucked up."

Maxwell was staring at me like I'd just told him the moon was made of cheese.

"I didn't want to say no to Dev," I continued, the admission tasting bitter. "He had this brilliant plan, and he was so excited about it, and I just... I couldn't bear the thought of disappointing him. Or having him think I was too much of a coward to go through with it. So I said yes, even though every instinct I had was screaming that it was a terrible idea. That it might even cost me my place at Killigrew Street—my new family."

I finally looked up at Maxwell, whose expression was unreadable.

"But in that moment, I was so desperate for his approval that I went along with it anyway. So then, when it all went tits up, when I found myself locked in a cell during the full moon, it was so much easier to hate you than to admit I'd done it to myself."

"You know, I almost had a heart attack when I saw you there that night. At Meridian."

I blinked at him. "What?"

"It was a horrible coincidence. Or maybe a blessed one, I don't know." He rubbed his face with both hands. "I was investigating a drug ring operating just down the road from Meridian. We were convinced it must be them who'd broken into the research centre. Anyway, when I saw you..." He shook his head. "It spun me for a loop. Then you used my name, like you knew me. And my officer heard you."

"Sorry," I said quickly. "I wasn't thinking."

"My career is all I have, Rory." His voice was quiet, almost defeated. "All I have. I couldn't have taken any risks that jeopardised that."

My stomach twisted in knots. "I should never have asked you to."

"But as soon as they processed you and put you in the holding cell, I was a mess with guilt." Maxwell's hands were clenched in his lap. "Did Kit tell you how many times I tried to call him that night?"

"Thirty-three," I said smoothly. "He brings it up all the time. Obviously, Kit couldn't answer the phone, though, because you know, shifter... full moon..."

"Right, but I wasn't thinking straight, and Seb wasn't answering either. But I *did* do all I could. I made sure that you and Dev were given cells away from everyone else. And then I just sat there on the floor. All night."

"What?"

"I sat there, outside your cell, listening to you all night."

The memories hit me with a slap. The crying. The begging. The moaning in pain as my body tried to shift and couldn't. The desperate, animalistic sounds I'd made for hours on end.

I fought to speak around my tightening throat. "But why did you sit there?"

He looked at me like it was the simplest thing in the world. "In case you needed me."

The old Rory would have said, *I needed to get out of that cell.* But sitting here now, looking at this lovely man who'd spent an entire night on a cold police station floor because he was worried about me, I felt tears prick my eyes. Actual tears.

"And then, morning came, and you were shaking so badly I couldn't take it anymore, and I called the nurse. Kit still hadn't answered, and I was in a state by then."

"I don't remember you there that morning."

Maxwell's tiny smile was heartbreaking. "I thought you wouldn't want to see me."

The world tilted sideways, and I had to grip the heather beneath me to keep from toppling over. A horrible rushing sound buzzed through my ears, like standing too close to a waterfall.

This couldn't be real. This lovely, brilliant man couldn't possibly want someone like me. Someone who'd spent eighteen months being an absolute bastard to him. Someone who apparently made cruel jokes about him at Christmas parties behind his back. Someone so desperate for approval that he'd throw away everything good in his life for a pretty face and a reckless plan.

How could someone so decent, so genuinely wonderful, ever want to be with a horrible, selfish, impulsive prick like me?

Maxwell's sharp intake of breath cut through the rushing in my ears.

Fuck, he'd heard! "*Maxwell—*" I started, then clamped my mouth shut so hard my teeth clicked together. It wasn't his fault he heard it when I was probably practically shouting at him.

The satellite transceiver suddenly erupted with static so violent it made us both jump. The crackling was wrong—not the usual white noise of poor reception, but something alive, like the air itself was sparking. Maxwell frowned and reached for the device, twisting the frequency dial, but instead of clearing, the interference grew worse, a symphony of pops and hisses that seemed to pulse with its own rhythm.

"What the hell—" Maxwell started, but his words died as we both looked up.

The sky was bleeding colour.

The aurora borealis unfurled across the Scottish sky like spilled paint on black canvas. Ribbons of electric green danced overhead, twisting and curling in impossible spirals. The lights pulsed with their own heartbeat, shifting from emerald to jade to the palest mint, all threaded through with veins of violet that flickered like lightning trapped in silk.

"You told me seeing the Northern Lights in May was impossible," Maxwell said in a rush, his voice filled with wonder.

I couldn't tear my eyes away from the spectacle above us. The aurora rippled like water, tendrils of light stretching down to touch the mountains.

"I used to think lots of things were impossible," I whispered.

The lights above us flared brighter, as if the universe itself was listening. Pink blossomed through the green, soft as rose petals, while golden threads wove through the display like embroidery on the night sky.

"Impossible things seem to be our specialty," he said softly. The colours reflected in Maxwell's glasses, turning his dark eyes into prisms.

His hand found mine in the heather, fingers sliding between mine with the same gentle certainty he'd shown all evening. His thumb traced across my knuckles as we watched the sky dance above us.

The aurora pulsed again, a symphony of light that painted the ruins silver-green and made the dark lake below us shimmer like molten metal.

In that moment, surrounded by impossible beauty with this impossible man's hand in mine, I felt something fundamental shift inside me.

Something that felt dangerously like hope.

Glancing sideways, I found Maxwell staring at me instead of the sky. His expression was soft, almost dreamy, completely transfixed.

"Oi," I said, grinning. "You're missing the show."

He blinked, startled. "Sorry."

"It's so not fair that I can't read your thoughts," I teased, bumping his shoulder with mine.

Maxwell glanced away, then back again. "I'm trying, for the millionth time, to decide if your eyes are blue or green. And..." He paused, seeming to wrestle with himself. "Lines of poetry keep popping into my head."

"You've... memorised poetry about eyes?"

"No, I..." He ran his hand through his hair, thoroughly flustered now. "I write poems. Sometimes. Well, usually just snippets of ones, really."

Delight bubbled up inside me like champagne. My serious, ultra-professional detective inspector wrote *poetry*. About my eyes, apparently.

"Do they rhyme?" I asked, grinning like a fool. "Please tell me they rhyme."

Maxwell gave me a withering look. "No. Are you five?"

"Come on, then," I said, squeezing his hand. "Let's hear these lines of poetry about my eyes."

"Absolutely not."

"Please? I promise I won't take the piss."

"That's a lie, and we both know it."

"Maxwell, please. *Please. Pleeeeease.*"

He was quiet for so long I thought he'd refuse. Then, he opened his mouth.

"Like broken bottles in an alley that catch streetlights just so—dangerous and beautiful. Like verse that shifts meaning with each reading—green mischief, blue sincerity." He spoke to our joined hands, as if the words were too intimate for eye contact. "Like storm-green and summer-blue caught in the same breath, brightness and chaos, somehow perfect together. Like looking into deep water where sunlight fractures into a thousand shades of... *maybe.*"

My breath caught. Above us, the Northern Lights pulsed brighter, as if responding to him.

"That's..." I started, then found I had no words. "That's really beautiful, Maxwell."

He was still staring at our hands, but I could sense his pleased hum of satisfaction.

"Really beautiful," I whispered.

I couldn't take it anymore—any distance between us.

Before I could second-guess myself, I threw myself onto Maxwell's lap, one leg on either side of his hips. His soft "Oh" of surprise made my stomach flip, but his hands immediately settled on my waist like they belonged there.

I wrapped both arms around his neck, legs circling his waist, and pulled him closer. Coldness had been creeping into my bones all evening, but Maxwell was pure heat, melting away everything except this moment. The aurora above us painted his gorgeous face in celestial light in a way that made me want to kiss every inch of it.

We couldn't call Dev and Isla until the solar storm was over, and I planned to take full advantage of that.

Hopefully, the bloody solar storm lasted for hours. Days, even. Years.

I ground down into him, feeling him harden beneath me, and pressed my lips to the corner of his mouth. The small sound he made—half gasp, half groan—sent heat shooting through my veins. His lips parted, and I flicked my tongue inside teasingly.

Want swelled within me like a tide fighting against rocks, sudden and desperate for release. I fumbled with his belt buckle, my fingers clumsy with urgency, then dragged down his zip with a metallic rasp that seemed obscenely loud in the quiet night.

Maxwell sighed. "You know, we're supposed to be watching the castle."

"Okay then, Mr Proper Procedure," I said, palming his dick through his underwear and watching his eyes flutter shut. I reached up to gently remove his glasses, placing them on top of his rucksack. "Let's stop."

He caught the back of my neck, bringing his mouth to my ear. "Not a fucking chance," he growled, voice dripping with promise. "We'll just have to multitask."

Well, fuck. With that voice, maybe I'd developed a thing for authority figures after all. If he growled at me again, I'd probably let him bend me over the castle battlements.

"Besides, if anyone spots us, they'll just think we're a couple of hikers who couldn't keep their hands off each other," I said. "Perfect cover, right?"

Maxwell's hands gripped my waist, hauling me backwards into the tent with such sudden force that I nearly toppled over. He fumbled for the torch, hooking it from the mesh ceiling pocket.

We attacked each other's clothes like scavengers through a wreckage—buttons popping, fabric tearing as we peeled away layers until we were down to underwear.

His chest rose and fell in quick, shallow breaths, the expanse of ebony skin complete with thick dark hair that I itched to run my fingers through. That gorgeous V-line carved into his lower abs made my mouth water, pointing like an arrow toward everything I wanted. The corded muscles in Maxwell's arms stood out in sharp relief under the torchlight, and something possessive and primal whispered *mine, mine, mine* in the back of my mind. This beautiful, impossible man was mine. *For tonight, at least,* I forced myself to add, though the cord of energy tethering us together seemed to pluck angrily at that last thought.

Maxwell's large hand circled my hip, thumb pressing into the hollow just above my hipbone, and a full-body shiver racked through me.

"Keep your jumper on at least," he murmured. "It's freezing."

"Hold on." I shifted on top of him, one hand braced against his chest while I rooted through my rucksack with the other. My fingers found soft cotton amongst the chaos of spare socks and energy bars.

I tugged it free.

Maxwell's eyes widened in recognition. "Hey, that's my shirt!"

"You gave it to me," I said innocently, shrugging into the sleeves but leaving every button undone so the navy-blue button down hung open like a frame around my bare chest. The familiar scent of Maxwell's cologne wrapped around me like a second skin.

"To wash!"

I leaned down until my lips brushed the shell of his ear, voice dropping to a whisper. "Well, Officer, I'm afraid I've been very naughty and haven't washed it."

Crack.

His hand met my ass with enough force to make me gasp. "That's Detective Inspector, thank you very much."

Heat spread like wildfire where he'd struck me, sending sparks straight to my cock. Something wolfish unfurled inside me—the overwhelming need to claim, to possess, to mark him as mine. Through our connection, I could feel his desire answering mine, feeding the fire until I could barely think straight.

"And is there a punishment for such insubordination?" I asked breathlessly.

Maxwell traced the outline of my very erect dick. "I think you can find a way to make it up to me."

"Are you going to mock me for packing the lube?" I reached into the rucksack again, producing the small tube with what I hoped was a cocky grin. "Being optimistic?"

"Mock you?" Maxwell's hands slid up my thighs, fingers digging into muscle. "I'm going to bloody kiss you."

His mouth devoured mine. Gone was any gentle exploration—this was hunger made manifest, teeth and tongue and desperate need. He kissed me like I was moonlight and he'd been lost in darkness. Like he could pull the very essence of me into himself through sheer will. His tongue swept against mine in claiming strokes that made my toes curl, and when I tried to pull back for breath, he chased my mouth with his own, refusing to let me escape.

Maxwell fell back against the sleeping bag, pulling me with him until I was sprawled across his chest. His hands found the waistband of my boxers, fingers hooking into the elastic.

"These need to come off," he rasped, "before I tear them apart."

The threat made my blood sing. I scrambled to obey, kicking them away. Maxwell shuffled beneath me, working his briefs down his hips until his cock sprang free—thick and flushed and absolutely magnificent in the torchlight.

It looked so delicious I couldn't help myself. My mouth found the tip instantly, one long teasing suck that had Maxwell crying out the most beautiful broken sound, his hands tangling desperately in my hair, tugging with enough force to make my eyes water. I grinned at him wickedly before wrapping my fingers around his head and giving the gentlest squeeze. The breathless curse that escaped him made me bolder—I flattened my tongue and licked across the sensitive tip, slow and deliberate, just to watch him come apart beneath me.

When he was writhing enough for my liking, thrusting his cock towards me, I worked my mouth up and down his length, tongue tracing every ridge and vein, drenching him in saliva until he was slick and glistening. Precum leaked from his head and I greedily lapped it up. The taste of him flooded my senses—salt and musk and lemongrass and raindrops and *mine*.

Maxwell moaned, deep throaty sounds that vibrated through his chest and straight into my bones. His hips bucked beneath me, seeking more friction, more heat, more of everything I was giving him. But when I wrapped my hand around the base of his cock, stroking in rhythm with my mouth, something shifted in the desperate cadence of his breathing.

He captured my wrist with trembling fingers. He guided my hand lower, down past his ass cheeks to the sensitive skin behind them.

"Can you..." he breathed, voice fracturing on the words. "Touch me?"

The naked need in his voice undid me.

Without breaking eye contact, I sucked on my fingers, coating them thoroughly with saliva until they were soaking wet. When he made a soft, needy sound, I pressed one finger against his entrance, watching his face in the golden torchlight.

Thud, thud, thud.

His heart beat a frantic pulse as his eyes fluttered closed, breath coming in heavy pants as I applied gentle pressure.

"Go on," Maxwell whispered, voice barely audible above our ragged breathing.

I pressed forward, just the very tip of my finger breaching him. Maxwell's mouth fell open with the softest whimper, a sound so beautiful I wanted to bottle it up forever. The blissed-out expression that crossed his features was poetry written in flesh and torchlight—lips parted, brow slightly furrowed in concentration, every line of tension melting from his face.

"*Oh,*" he said, bearing down against my finger, trying to take more. His hips shuffled down the sleeping bag, chasing the pressure.

"Easy," I murmured, though my own voice was shaking. "Let me..."

I reached for my winter coat, bunching it up and sliding it beneath Maxwell's lower back to lift his hips. The position opened him up beautifully, and I had to bite back a groan at the sight.

Claim, claim, claim.

Grabbing the lube, I squeezed what was probably a ridiculous amount onto my fingers. The cold gel made Maxwell shiver as I spread it around his entrance, working it in slowly with gentle circles.

When I properly pushed my finger inside, Maxwell's back arched off the makeshift pillow, a broken moan spilling from his lips. I worked him carefully, pulling out almost completely before sliding back in, letting him adjust to the sensation.

Without breaking that careful pace, I lowered my mouth back to his cock, sealing my lips around the head and drawing gently. The dual assault made Maxwell surge up into my mouth, profanity spilling from his lips like a prayer.

The echo of his pleasure crashed through our connection, doubling my own arousal until I could barely think straight. Everything he felt rippled back to me—the stretch, the fullness, the maddening friction of my tongue.

"Give me another," he panted.

I added a second finger alongside the first, working him open with patient strokes whilst my tongue traced patterns around his tip. When I found that spot inside him, Maxwell cried out so loudly I worried someone might hear us across the lake. His whole body went rigid, thighs quaking as they bracketed my head. Through the invisible thread, I felt his body's response like it was my own—the gorgeous tension building in his muscles, the way his nerve endings sang every time I crooked my fingers just right.

"So good," he gasped, then suddenly his hand was capturing mine, stilling my movements. "So bloody good, but... Rory, I need—"

His eyes flew open, wild and desperate in the torchlight, to find mine.

"Fuck me," he said, voice cracking on the words. "Oh, please, fuck me, Rory."

24

Theodore

"**M**axwell..." Rory's eyes, saucer-wide, stared deeply into mine.

I wasn't quite sure where my sudden desperation to have him fuck me had come from.

Maybe it was the miracle of the Northern Lights dancing above us.

Maybe it was my shirt hanging off his slight frame, the way it transformed him into something stolen and precious. Something *mine.*

Okay, it was definitely the shirt.

I met Rory's defiant stare with an equally determined one of my own. The challenge in those blue-green eyes only made me want him more.

He gently removed his fingers from me and I mourned the loss of them, my body clenching around nothing.

...Fucking hell, I want to fuck him so bad, bury myself inside him and claim him inside and out...

"I know you want to," I growled at him.

Rory scowled at me, screwing up his entire face in a way that was so comical, I leaned forward to kiss the tip of his nose. The expression melted away under my lips.

I took his cock in my hand, stroking it slowly. "Listen, I'm sorry to tell you this. This dick of yours is lovely, but really not that big."

"Umm, excuse me? It's perfectly average for my height! I've measured it before! Twice!"

I continued stroking him, watching his eyes roll to the back of his head. "Sorry. I mean, I'm sure I can handle this monster dick of yours. And before you bring it up again, I'm not asking you to fuck me as proof that I'm definitely bisexual. I'm asking because I'm desperate to feel you inside me. And no, I one thousand, one million percent won't regret it. And this has nothing to do with my jealousy of Dev—of whom I'm not actually jealous, for the record."

Rory's lips twitched. "Honestly, mate, you didn't need to make a whole speech about it, you know. I'm absolutely desperate to fuck you." He shrugged one shoulder. "Plus, I'm sort of still feeling you from last night, so this works."

The admission sent pure fire spiralling through me. Plus a ridiculous urge to change my mind, to make him *feel me* even more.

I gripped his cock harder, making him gasp. "My turn to feel you, then, you—"

"Wait," Rory said suddenly, his hands stilling on my hips. His eyes held mine in a way that made my pulse skip. "I need to scent mark you first."

"You need to what?" Confusion briefly cut through the haze of desire.

Rory's lips curved into that wicked smile—one that surely meant he was about to do something that would utterly unravel me. "Wolf thing," he said.

Before I could demand an explanation, his hands were guiding me back down onto the sleeping bag, positioning me exactly where he wanted me, and my mouth fell dry.

"Rory—"

"Shh." His thumb brushed across my lower lip, silencing my protest. "I need you to smell like me."

He lowered himself over me, and suddenly the tent felt smaller, the air thicker. His breath ghosted across the column of my throat as he found the hollow where my pulse hammered against my skin.

The first touch of his tongue was electric—a slow, deliberate sweep along the side of my neck that made my back arch involuntarily off the ground. He moved with purpose, mapping every pulse point with methodical precision. Behind my ear, where his teeth grazed just enough to make me gasp. The sharp edge of my collarbone, where he lingered with open-mouthed attention that bordered on worship.

Mine, his thoughts whispered into my consciousness, primal and possessive. *Mine, mine, mine.*

When his mouth found the sensitive hollow of my throat, I lost all semblance of control. He worked the skin there with devastating patience—licking, sucking, claiming—until I was certain he'd branded something permanent into my very DNA.

"There," he murmured against my skin, his voice brimming with pride. "Now everyone will know you belong to me. And when my scent starts to fade, I'll mark you all over again. And again."

The declaration should have terrified me. Instead, it sent molten heat straight to my core, and I pulled him up to crash our lips together, desperate to claim his mouth as thoroughly as he'd claimed my neck.

Rory broke the kiss with a satisfied hum, his hands moving with purpose, gripping my thigh and lifting one of my legs, positioning me exactly where he wanted me "And now I'll taste my prize properly," he murmured against my skin, his breath hot on my thigh.

His mouth found the sensitive skin of my inner thigh, then the sharp edge of his teeth scraped against me before his tongue soothed the spot. A completely undignified yelp escaped my throat as he moved higher, his teeth finding the curve of my ass cheek.

None of my previous partners had ever done that before, but then again, none of them had been wolves...

"Christ, Rory—"

His teeth sank deeper, not quite breaking skin but hard enough to leave marks, hard enough to make me forget my own name. The bite was possessive and the low growl that rumbled from his chest vibrated straight through me. When he finally released his hold, I could feel the ghost of each tooth, marking me in ways that had nothing to do with bruises.

His tongue found my crease.

Every coherent thought fled my mind. It was intoxicating, intimate beyond anything I'd ever experienced. He lavished attention on me with the patience of worship, his tongue painting slow, deliberate strokes that had me trembling. The molten heat of his mouth turned me liquid, my hands clawing at the sleeping bag as if it could anchor me to sanity.

This wasn't just physical preparation—it was devotion, reverence, something that sent me spinning, dizzy with joy. The way he touched me, like I was something sacred he'd been waiting his whole life to claim.

"Rory," I manage to choke out, wanting to offer him *something*.

He hummed against my thigh, then his finger replaced his tongue. He worked slowly into me, an agonisingly gentle intrusion that had me pushing back against him despite myself.

"You're so tight," he whispered, pressing deeper. "So perfect."

I could feel him watching my face, cataloguing every expression as he worked me open. The intimacy of it, the way he seemed to know exactly what I needed before I did, left me breathless.

"I'm ready," I pleaded. "Give it to me."

...don't bloody tempt me...

"Shh," Rory said, taking another bite out of my thigh, his teeth finding fresh skin to mark. "I'm working."

The sting of his bite mixed with the thrill of him adding another finger, stretching me wider. My body protested the intrusion even as it craved more. My hands found his hair without thought, fingers tangling in the blond strands and pulling until they were thoroughly mussed.

"Fuck, you're so responsive," he murmured against my skin, his voice thick with approval.

His fingers worked me open with maddening patience, each movement deliberate and knowing. When he finally withdrew them, I felt hollow, aching for him to fill me again.

Rory kissed his way up my leg, his mouth hot against my thigh, then my hip. Each press of his lips built anticipation until I could barely breathe.

"Turn around for me, gorgeous," he said, his voice low and commanding. "On your hands and knees."

My hands trembled slightly as I braced myself against the sleeping bag, and I fought to keep anxiety from bleeding through our bond. The last thing I wanted was for Rory to sense any hint of nerves and stop.

His hands found my back, stroking long, soothing lines from my shoulders to the curve of my ass. "So bloody gorgeous," he whispered, his palms warm against my skin.

His fingers traced the curve of my spine, then spread across my ribs, mapping me with the dedication of a cartographer. When his hands moved to my thighs, I couldn't suppress the shiver that ran through me.

The head of his cock nudged against me, and I tensed—couldn't help it—my breath stuttering as my body fought between want and instinct.

"Easy," Rory whispered, one hand settling on my hip whilst he used the other to guide himself. "I've got you."

The first push stole the breath from my lungs. My body seized, rejecting the intrusion even as I desperately wanted it. The stretch was intense, nothing like his fingers had been.

"Can't—" The word escaped before I could stop it, panic creeping up my throat.

Rory immediately stilled, his cock barely inside me. His grip on my hips gentled, becoming a soothing caress.

"I know," he said, oh-so soothingly. "I know it feels impossible right now. Like you can't take any more. But you can."

"I want it," I told him. "Please don't stop."

He pushed in the tiniest bit more, and a whimper slipped out of me.

"Shh, Teddy. You're doing so good for me. Bear down for me. That's it."

The burn was excruciating, like being split open from the inside. My body fought him, clenching instinctively against the intrusion. But through our bond, I could feel Rory's pleasure—the devastating sensation of my tightness around him, the way I gripped him like a vice. His euphoria flooded through me, drowning out my discomfort until I couldn't tell where my pain ended and his bliss began.

Rory tightened his grasp on my hips, pushing deeper. "Fuck, fuck, *fuck,* you're so tight. I'm almost there. You feel so, *so* good. There!"

We cried out together as he pushed inside, finally all the way in. It was utterly overwhelming—too much and not enough all at once. My ass burned, stretched beyond what seemed possible, but the satisfaction of being so completely filled was indescribable.

...fuck, he's perfect. So bloody perfect. Can't believe he's letting me have him...

Rory's thoughts crashed through my mind, pure, undiluted. So many emotions—his wonder at being inside me, his disbelief that I wanted this, wanted *him.*

He breathed hard above me, his hands caressing my back and hips before one finger traced the stretched rim where we were joined. "Feel that? Feel me inside you?"

I could only moan and nod. It still hurt, but the fullness, the way Rory filled every empty space inside me—it was everything I'd never known I needed.

Bit by bit, I relaxed, letting the silk of the sleeping bag caress my skin, letting Rory comfort me with touches and kisses to my spine. Every point where our skin connected burned. I ached for even more contact, craved the weight of him against me.

"Does it feel good?" Rory asked.

I groaned. "So good."

"Shall I fuck you now?"

"Hmm? You're already fucking me."

Without warning, he pulled out almost completely. The sudden emptiness was devastating—my body clenched desperately, trying to hold on to him. Then he slid back in, inch by torturous inch, so slowly I could feel every ridge, every vein of his cock as it filled me again.

Oh.

The groan that tore from my throat was animalistic, primal. Nothing had prepared me for this—the deliberate slide of him into me, the way my body welcomed him back like coming home. Each millimetre was agony and ecstasy braided together until I couldn't distinguish between them.

Rory's hands gripped my thighs, pulling them back towards him until we were flush, his chest pressed against my back. The angle drove him deeper, hitting my prostate so deliciously stars exploded behind my eyelids, brighter than the Northern Lights.

My hand lurched towards my cock, desperate for friction, for release from the building pressure.

Rory's palm cracked against my hand.

"Don't you dare," he commanded, his voice carrying an authority that made me tingly. "That's mine. I'm going to be the one to make you come."

His hand replaced mine, wrapping around my cock with possessive certainty. The contrast was maddening—his slow, deliberate thrusts paired with the quick, sure strokes of his fist. He fucked me like he was memorising every angle, every response, whilst his hand worked me with the confidence of ownership. Each snap of his hips had his cock dragging against that sweet spot inside me whilst his fingers traced patterns of fire along my length. The rhythm was hypnotic—in, stroke, out, squeeze—building something vast and terrible and beautiful inside me.

"Feel that?" he whispered against my ear, teeth grazing my lobe. "Feel how you're mine?"

I could only whimper in response, lost in the symphony of sensation he was conducting. His cock filled me completely whilst his hand claimed me utterly, each movement a declaration that I belonged to him now.

And I wouldn't have it any other way.

There were no other words—I was drowning in him, in us, in the way he played my body like an instrument he'd been born to master.

My arms gave out entirely, and I collapsed face first into the sleeping bag. The silky soft fabric cushioned my cheek, cool against my burning skin whilst Rory continued his relentless rhythm above me.

And then Rory was stretched out over me, his chest pressing against my back—a comforting, intensely satisfying weight. His heart pounded so hard I could feel it, each beat hammering through me like a second pulse. His hands gripped my arms, holding me steady. Soft lips found the space between my shoulder blades as he pressed tender kisses there whilst he moved.

...Never felt anything like this. Never want it to end. Want to stay buried inside him forever...

Rory's thoughts crashed through me, intense, desperate, and I moaned into the fabric beneath me. His lips found my shoulder blade, pressing a tender kiss there before his teeth scraped across. He moved to the back of my neck, sucking a mark into the tender flesh just below my hairline. Lightning shot through me—the wet heat of his mouth, the gentle scrape of teeth, the way his tongue soothed each fresh mark he left on my skin.

His hips ground against me in slow, devastating circles, each movement sending shockwaves through my already overwrought system. I wasn't going to last much longer.

"I want to see you," I gasped, turning my head to catch his eye. "Need to see you."

Those blue-green eyes I'd become obsessed with met mine, pupils blown wide with desire. Without hesitation, Rory pulled out—the sudden emptiness making me whimper—and turned me over. He lifted my left leg, settling it on his shoulder. The new position opened me up, leaving me utterly exposed beneath his hungry gaze.

Rory's slide back in was so easy, we both groaned. This angle was deeper, more intense, but most importantly, it allowed me to watch his beautiful face as he filled me.

"Teddy," he breathed, beginning to rock against me with slow, measured thrusts. "I... I feel so close to you right now."

Before I could attempt to reply, his thumb found the spot on my throat where he'd marked me, rubbing over the tender skin as he leaned down, capturing my lips in a kiss that was bottomless, endless. Everything. I surrendered completely, swallowing down his whimpers and needy moans as his tongue explored my mouth with the same thoroughness he'd shown the rest of my body.

"Rory," I rasped against his lips.

...baby...baby...baby...

The word echoed through his thoughts like a desperate chant. He wanted me to say it again, wanted to be called baby. Wanted it badly.

"My precious baby," I whispered, stroking every inch of him I could reach—the trembling muscles of his shoulders, the flutter of pulse beneath his neck, the fevered heat of his chest under my shirt.

The smile he gave me was beyond blinding, beyond beautiful.

"Feel how perfectly we fit together," he said, voice thick with desperation, like he was begging me to agree that we belonged, that this could work, that we could be something real.

My heart seized.

"Perfectly, baby," I whispered against his lips, my hands cupping his face. "We fit together perfectly." I pulled him closer, needing every inch of contact. "You feel so good inside me. I want to keep you here forever."

The word slipped out before I could stop it—*forever*—and my breath caught at the weight behind it.

But Rory's eyes blazed brighter, and suddenly his hips snapped forward with renewed urgency. The gentle rhythm shattered into something fierce, claiming. Each thrust drove deeper, harder, until I was gasping beneath him.

"I'm so glad I get to fuck you raw," he growled against my throat, his hand wrapping around my cock possessively. "Fill you up with me."

His fist moved in perfect counterpoint to his thrusts, stroking me with the same desperate intensity that drove his hips. It was all too much—being filled and claimed, his hand quickly working me towards the edge.

Something new began flowing through our bond—not just his desire or mine, but something richer, more profound. It poured from him into me like liquid gold, warm and precious and transformative. Tender yet fierce, desperate yet patient.

This felt like making love.

The realisation hit me like a revelation, causing my heart to thump even faster.

"Rory—" His name broke from my lips as my body went rigid beneath him, every muscle seizing as pleasure crashed through me. I came with a strangled cry, spilling across my stomach whilst he continued to move inside me, drawing out every last tremor of release.

He followed moments later, his face contorting in blissful surrender as he buried himself deep. I felt him pulse inside me, gorgeously hot, marking me from within. A primal groan tore from somewhere deep in his chest before he caught my mouth in a long kiss.

Then Rory's tongue found the mess on my stomach, long warm strokes that had me shivering beneath him until I was drenched in his saliva instead. Once I was thoroughly cleaned, he made a little satisfied hum, cocking his head to one side. He collapsed on top of me, and for a moment we lay there panting, hearts hammering against each other through sweat-slicked skin.

...forever...maybe he really means it...

The thought drifted through me like smoke, carrying with it all of Rory's hope and uncertainty.

It was so powerful that my mouth immediately snapped open to reply, to comfort, to reassure.

Though something froze my tongue—the rational part of my mind, beginning to catalogue all the reasons this was madness. We'd known each other properly for days, not months. This mate bond business was supernatural craziness I still didn't fully understand.

But beneath all that sensible protest, something deeper stirred. Something that had been growing since the moment Rory first challenged me, first made me laugh despite myself, first showed me glimpses of the fierce loyalty hidden beneath his chaotic exterior.

Forever: a word that should terrify,

instead it settles like destiny—
inevitable as sunrise,
warm as his eyes meeting mine.

Rory deserved honesty. He deserved someone who wouldn't flinch away from this wonderful thing that was building between us. He also deserved better than empty promises made in the aftermath of earth-shattering sex.

I slipped my hand under the shirt to trace patterns on his shoulder, buying myself time whilst my thoughts churned.

"Forever with you would be…" I whispered against his temple, feeling him tense slightly in anticipation. His breathing fell shallow, waiting. I felt his hope and fear warring with each other, both emotions so acute they made my heart squeeze.

I took a deep, long breath.

"Forever with you would be the greatest adventure I never knew I was looking for."

Rory's eyes widened, those impossible blue-green depths suddenly bright as sea glass caught in sunlight. For a heartbeat, I could have sworn I saw actual stars dancing in them.

Joy crashed through our connection like a tidal wave, so pure and vast it knocked the breath from my lungs. The emotion was effervescent, bubbling up from somewhere deep in Rory's chest and flooding into me with such force I felt weightless. Untethered. As if I might simply drift away on the current of his happiness, floating up through the tent roof to join the aurora still painting the sky above us.

But beneath that brilliant surge of elation, something else flickered—a sharp spike of terror. Brief but unmistakable, lightning illuminating storm clouds for just an instant.

Perhaps that's what prompted the familiar curve of Rory's lips, that signature smirk sliding into place. The one that usually preceded him saying something utterly outrageous or taking the piss.

"Christ, Teddy," he drawled. "That might be the cheesiest thing you've ever said to me. And you once compared my eyes to tempestuous seas and beautiful skies or whatever."

His fingers traced idle patterns on my chest, but I could feel the slight tremor in them. "What's next? How about a sonnet about how my ass is like two perfect moons rising over the Scottish moors?"

I shook with laughter. This was, of course, pure Rory, deflecting sincerity with humour when the feelings became too intense, too real. Too frightening.

It would take months, maybe years of moments like this—actions over words, consistency over grand gestures—to properly earn his trust. But that was okay. I was up for the challenge.

I caught his wandering hand, pressing a kiss to his knuckles. "Actually," I said, matching his teasing tone whilst holding his gaze. "I was thinking more along the lines of comparing your habit of making jokes when you're terrified to a hedgehog rolling into a ball."

His mock scowl was immediate and fierce. "I'm not terrified."

"Yes you are," I whispered, leaning closer until our noses nearly touched. "But that's okay. I'm terrified too."

Rory's surprise rippled outward, followed by something softer. Relief, perhaps, that he wasn't alone in this staggering thing growing between us.

"Come here," I murmured, pulling him down until he was cradled against my chest, his head tucked beneath my chin. As he melted into me, his mouth found that tender spot on my throat once more—a quick, possessive press of lips and the gentle pull of his mouth that made me exhale sharply. Claiming me one last time before surrendering to the quiet.

The sharp edges of Rory's fear smoothed away as contentment began flowing—warm honey spilling into me, golden and sweet. His breathing deepened, syncing with mine as I stroked through his hair, those ridiculously messy blond strands still soft despite how much I'd touched them.

I sighed, reality creeping back in around the edges of our perfect bubble. "We missed the end of the lights. Oops. But anyway, the solar storm is surely over now. We should try Isla and Dev on the sat phone."

Rory grumbled something unintelligible against my chest but eventually reached for the satellite phone. The silence went heavy as he dialled Isla's number first.

It rang. And rang. And rang. No answer.

He tried Dev next, fingers moving more urgently now across the keypad. Again, the endless ringing echoed through the tent.

No answer.

We looked at each other. The torchlight flickered.

And I couldn't help the sinking feeling in the pit of my stomach. The Northern Lights had finished their dance... but something else entirely had begun.

25

Theodore

We made the decision that it wasn't practical to march all the way through the night in rough terrain. I wasn't particularly convinced the torch battery would hold up.

In order to sleep easy, we told ourselves that it was very possible the pair of them were both asleep, phones on silent. Though Isla had specifically said hers wouldn't be.

The temperature continued to plummet throughout the night. We zipped together two sleeping bags, then huddled together, Rory's body heat the only thing keeping hypothermia at bay. His teeth chattered against my shoulder, tiny percussion beats that eventually settled into rhythm with my own shivers. I almost asked him to shift—surely a wolf would generate more warmth—but wasn't entirely confident cuddling a fanged, clawed creature was safe. Particularly when nightmares might strike.

Instead, I wrapped my arms tighter around him, pulling him against my chest until there wasn't a millimetre of space between us.

My alarm shrieked at five in the morning, cutting through the grey light of dawn.

"Rory." I shook his shoulder. "Time to go."

He was awake instantly, no grogginess, just sharp focus as he took in my expression. We were up and packed within minutes—Rory's tent skills were even faster than mine.

"Shall we check the BnB first?" I said, somehow already knowing his response.

"The cottage," he said grimly. It was sensible—we had no evidence they ever left.

Tension radiated from him as we rushed back, both of us moving at a near-jog despite the constant inclines. I rang Isla's number every few minutes. Nothing. Rory tried Dev, then Alex. It was a challenge to convince Rory not to shift to run ahead of me.

Hours later, we were at Primrose Cottage, sweaty and panting.

As we twisted the door handle, I found myself pausing. How was it possible that I just *knew* something was waiting for us on the other side of that door? Some terrible certainty settling in my bones like winter frost.

The door swung open.

Rory inhaled sharply—catching what I couldn't yet see. Horror shot through our bond, visceral and immediate, before my eyes could process the scene.

Blood everywhere.

Splattered across the cream walls in arterial sprays. Pooled on the hardwood floor in dark, congealing puddles. Smeared across the staircase where someone had been dragged.

No sign of Isla or Dev.

My first instinct was to throw my arm up, barring Rory from the doorway. "Don't step in the blood. You'll contaminate—"

He pushed my arm aside, walking straight into the cottage, spinning in dizzy circles as he took in the carnage.

The metallic tang coated the back of my throat, sweet and nauseating. "Rory—" I started, but my next words didn't come. Anxiety and fear assaulted my system—my own terror amplified tenfold by what Rory was feeling through our bond.

"Oh my god... Isla..." Rory said, both hands clutching his head. "What have I done?"

...stupid, stupid, stupid!...

I stared at the amount of blood coating every surface. That girl was surely dead. I thought of her bright smile, those freckles scattered across pale skin. Her father would be devastated.

Rory suddenly froze, nostrils flaring as he sniffed the air. "Wait... it's... it's not Isla's blood. None of it. Well, maybe some. But most of it... It's Dev's!"

"Are you sure?"

His breathing became rapid and shallow, chest rising and falling like he couldn't get enough air. "I'm sure," he said. "I'm sure, I'm sure." His hands started trembling, then his whole body followed suit. The colour drained from his face until he looked ghostly pale. I stepped towards him, but he backed away, shaking his head violently.

"Don't—I can't—"

"Rory, listen to me—"

"I did this." His voice cracked. "I came to save him and now I've killed him. This is my fault. I brought him here, I should have listened to you, I should have taken him back to London but I didn't. I shouldn't have gotten Isla involved, but I did. And now he's dead and Isla's possibly dead too and it's all my fault, all of it—"

The words tumbled out faster and faster, his breathing becoming more erratic with each syllable.

I could feel it building through our bond—the panic rising like a tide, threatening to drown him. His pulse hammered against my consciousness, erratic and desperate.

"Let's sit down," I suggested, reaching for him.

He dodged away from my touch, eyes wild. "Sit down?!" He stared at me like I'd suggested we throw a party. "Sit down? How is that going to help?"

His breathing came in sharp, shallow gasps now. He spun away from me, stumbling towards the wall, his palm slapping against the cream paint—directly into a spray of blood. When he pulled his hand back, crimson streaked across his fingers.

"Fuck!" He began pacing frantically, leaving bloody handprints on his jeans as he wiped his palms. "I'm such an idiot. Always such a fucking *idiot*! But I've really fucked it this time." He held up his stained fingers. "Literally with blood on my hands."

Panic burst through our connection, so intense I had to grip the doorframe to steady myself. This wasn't just fear—this was pure self-destruction, every insecurity he'd ever harboured breaking free at once.

Alarm bells rang in my head, my mind begging me to do something, but it was hard to focus with Rory's emotions flooding my system, dragging me under.

"I was mad to think we could ever be together," he said suddenly, the words tumbling out like he couldn't stop them. "You and me. I was stupid to ever believe that."

Something vital shifted inside me, like a gear slipping out of place. *No.* I wanted to scream at him to take back the words, that he didn't mean them.

"And please don't worry, I'll fix it—the mate bond—because you deserve someone amazing like you and I'm too useless, too stupid, too incompetent. And I'm going to quit Killigrew Street when I get back because—"

"Rory, what—"

"You were right, Maxwell. What you said about Seb. He *did* hit his head the day he hired me. I know it was a favour to Kit. I bet Kit had to beg him, and then beg him not to kick me out so many times." His voice climbed higher with each word, hands shaking violently. "And now I've gotten people killed because I'm so fucking useless at everything."

Irritation flared through me—not at him, but at myself. I'd known leaving Dev here was dangerous. I'd voiced my concerns, but then let Dev's snide comments about not trusting Rory get under my skin. Now we had what appeared to be a homicide scene and Rory was spiralling into a complete breakdown.

I moved towards him, holding out my hands as if he were a scared animal. But he moved backwards, scrambling away from me.

A tiny voice in my head noted that I should really be more concerned with the probable murder than with Rory saying we couldn't be together, but that voice was promptly drowned out by the overwhelming need to stop his panic.

"And you told me! You said we shouldn't do it," Rory shouted at me, eyes wild. "You were right! Aren't you going to say, 'I told you so?'"

"Of course not!" The words burst out of me like I'd been sucker-punched. "This isn't your fault. We both—"

"Stay here," he said suddenly, already moving towards the door, that manic energy propelling him forward. "Please."

My saliva turned sharp and metallic, like I'd been sucking on batteries. "What? Where are you going?"

Don't leave me.

I lunged forward, fingers grasping for his arm, but they closed around thin air. He was too quick, already at the threshold.

"Rory, wait—"

He had the door open now, already shrugging off his hoodie with jerky, desperate movements. Christ, he was going to shift. Shift, and leave me.

"Stay here," he repeated, and there was something almost pleading in his voice that carved itself directly into my skin, hollowing me from the inside out. "And I'm sorry, Maxwell. So sorry. This is all entirely on me, not you."

Stop him! Follow him! my brain screamed, but my legs wouldn't move. The overwhelming tide of Rory's emotions through our bond was crushing—panic and guilt and self-loathing so intense it felt like drowning. My chest constricted, my own breath coming in short gasps as his terror and confusion flooded my system.

The door slammed shut with a bang that echoed through the blood-splattered cottage.

I staggered backwards, one hand pressed against my temple where a sudden, vicious headache had bloomed. The emotional onslaught was too much, too raw, like someone had torn open every nerve ending in my body and poured acid over them.

Through the window, I caught a glimpse of golden fur disappearing into the treeline.

Though as the distance between us increased, it wasn't just his emotions that faded—it felt like someone was slowly dimming the lights in a room I'd only just learned to see in.

Panic receded just enough for me to draw a proper breath, though my hands were still shaking. I stared at the closed door, at Rory's abandoned hoodie crumpled on the blood-stained floor, and felt utterly helpless.

Utterly alone.

We'd been joined at the hip for days on end, and now his absence was like a missing tooth.

My hands shook as I pulled out my phone, caught between relief that I could finally call for help and absolute dread at having to explain what had happened. How would I find the words to tell Kit?

The phone vibrated in my fingers before I could dial. Kit's name flashed on the screen.

My breath caught. Did he already know? Could he sense Rory's distress through their bond, even from hundreds of miles away?

"Hello?" My voice came out shaky, barely recognisable.

"Teddy? You alright? Terrier didn't pick up."

I've lost him, Kit. I've lost your brother.

One deep breath. "I was just about to call you. Something... something's happened."

I filled Kit in as best I could—the blood-soaked cottage, Dev and Isla missing, Rory's complete breakdown. Kit's sharp intakes of breath punctuated my recounting, followed by stretches of silence that made my stomach churn. Each pause felt like an accusation, like he was calculating exactly how badly I'd failed to protect Rory.

"We'll be on the next flight," Kit said finally, before murmuring to someone else. Frantic keyboard typing echoed through the line—Felix, no doubt. "But listen, I rang Terrier to tell him something. Something important. When he was talking about Dev's skull, how it looked like it had been cut open... it picked at something in me buried deep. I didn't say anything much at the time. But then all night I couldn't stop thinking about it. You know that I was in the military, right? Not the actual military, but a black ops unit?"

"Right. Terrier's told me a little."

"A lot of it... especially the beginning... it's all a blur. But last night, in bed, I found myself touching my head. Right where you described."

My pulse quickened. "And?"

"And it's so faint it's no wonder I've never noticed before, but I have the tiniest bump of scar tissue. Noctule even shaved my hair to see it."

"Christ. What does this mean?"

"It means this is the same people I worked for," Kit said, disgust colouring his voice. "Though *worked for* is the wrong term. It was more like they owned me. They called us GREY. Greywatch Reconnaissance and Elimination Unit. I won't go into specifics of what they had us do, but let's say I'm not surprised they've had to resort to these... methods to get more men. All of my unit managed to escape. The ones... the ones that lived." Kit paused. "But what you probably don't know is how I got involved in GREY in the first place."

"Rory was actually talking about it the other day... about how Alex's deceased wife was a bit of a black sheep and set it all up for you."

"Yes. Moira Thorne."

There was a tiny silence. Then it clicked.

"Do you think... do you think *Isla* is working with them? GREY? Meridian?"

I wanted to deny it—that sweet, innocent-seeming young woman. But the memory of her thoughts from earlier now felt different. Too clean. Too surface-level. And those emotions—confused, then horrified, disturbed—had they been too strong? Too perfectly timed?

She'd earned a sliver of trust when she hadn't blocked me from reading her mind, like the rest of her pack. But had I been reading what she wanted me to read? Had someone coached her on presenting specific thoughts to telepaths?

You idiot. I was clearly too used to locking up thugs who looked the part. I'd accidentally profiled Isla as innocent based on her looks and charm and her seemingly innocent thoughts. Rookie mistake.

"It has to be a possibility."

Dizziness swept through me. "I think Terrier might have run off to find her. Find... them? Though he's convinced himself Dev is dead." I surveyed the bloody cottage again. "I'm not sure what he thinks happened here. I'm still not sure myself."

"When did he leave?"

"Ten seconds before your call." I tensed, waiting for Kit to ask why I'd let him leave, why I didn't do everything possible to keep him with me. "Shall I go after him?"

"No. You'll never find him."

Yet something lodged deep within me disagreed. Not Rory's emotions—those had faded as the distance between us grew—but something else. A pull, magnetic and insistent, like a compass needle swinging towards true north. I could *sense* him out there, not his thoughts or feelings, but his presence itself. A warm pulse beneath my ribs that whispered *this way, this way.*

"I might be able—"

"No. It's too dangerous. Fuck knows what's going on here."

"The gathering is tonight. Will you be here by then?"

Murmuring in the background, then Kit's voice again. "Magpie has managed to hack into the airline's booking systems and registered us for the next flight, even though it's full. We should be there late afternoon."

"Thank god," I said, the relief almost making my knees buckle.

Seb's voice interjected, "You must stay exactly where you are until we get there. Barricade the door. That's an order."

"I will," I automatically agreed. But there was no way I could ignore this feeling inside me, urging me to *find him, find him, find him.* The pull in my chest strengthened, as if responding to my resolve.

Fear filled the quiet between us.

"He'll be okay, Teddy," said Kit. "You'll see. He's a tough one, our Terrier."

The gentle reassurance hit harder than any threat would have. Kit was comforting me rather than threatening to kill me for losing his brother. It was almost worse—this quiet faith that it wasn't my fault.

The line went dead.

I stared at my rucksack, dumped on the floor beside the door. My thighs ached from yesterday's march through the Highlands and this morning's frantic rush back. Every muscle in my body screamed for rest, for food, for a hot shower that would wash away the metallic tang of blood that seemed to coat everything.

But something clawed at my insides insistently, stronger now, as if Rory's wolf was calling to me. Something that transcended logic and Seb's very sensible orders to stay put.

I looked around the blood-splattered cottage one more time—at the crimson across walls, the dark pools on the floor, the smears where bodies had been dragged. Evidence that should be photographed, catalogued, preserved.

But instead, I climbed the staircase. *Better bring the gun.* The thought settled in my stomach like lead. But best to be prepared.

I unlocked the cool metal box, sliding the heavy weight of the Glock into my palm.

Closing my eyes, I remembered Rory from last night. The way those green lights had danced across his face, how still and peaceful he'd looked in that moment. How those eyes that I'd spent hours trying to decipher had stared at me with utter adoration.

The compass needle swung again, more urgent this time.

Find him.

I stood up, went downstairs, and shouldered my rucksack.

26

Rory

Paws strike earth. Hard. Fast. Rhythm pounds through bones.

Raindrops-lemongrass-mine fades behind. Distance hurts. Sharp ache in chest where warmth lives. Sad eyes watching me leave. Pain-scent rolling off him like smoke.

Can't think about that. Can't.

Run.

Heather scratches legs. Rocks cut pads. Don't care. Body knows where to go even when mind fractures. Nose down. Breathe deep.

Blood-scent. Sharp copper threading through pine-earth-water smells. Fresh blood. Day-old blood. Same source. Same wolf.

Dev-friend-pack-save.

Trail weaves through bracken. Stronger now. Fear-sweat mingles with blood. Different wolf. Female. Young.

Isla-cousin-trust.

Something else underneath. Chemical-sharp. Wrong-smell. Burning nose-holes. Makes hackles rise.

Trees thin. Buildings ahead. Stone-concrete-metal stench. Human-place where death-smell clings thick as fog yesterday. Body remembers. Wants to turn. Run away.

But blood-trail leads forward.

Sound cuts through wind-whisper. Engine-growl. Wheels on dirt-stone. Getting closer.

Crouch low. Belly to ground. Peer through gorse bushes.

Buggy rolls slow between trees. Same one from arriving-time. Luggage-carrier. But no bags now.

Isla-cousin drives. Knuckles tight on steering. Fear-scent thick around her.

Blankets pile in back. Breathing underneath. Shallow-weak breathing only wolf-ears catch.

Dev.

Rage builds. Hot-red-sharp. How dare she. *Pack-cousin-blood* taking *him*.

Spring from bushes. Land hard in buggy's path. Snarl rips from throat. Lips curl back. Show teeth. All of them.

Buggy jerks to stop.

Isla-cousin stares. No surprise-scent. Only resignation.

She knew. She heard me coming.

Heat floods limbs. Bones crack-pop-stretch. Skin burns as it changes. Pain shoots through skull as face reshapes. Always hurts more when angry.

Human thoughts rush back like dam bursting.

"Isla, what the fuck?!"

I was naked, standing in front of the buggy with fury that made my hands shake. She sat there, walkie-talkie held to her mouth. "Code red confirmed. Begin evacuation protocol, over."

She dropped it into her lap.

"Where are you taking him?" I tried to sound demanding, but my voice came out hoarse.

She glanced back at the blankets where Dev's barely breathing form lay hidden. When she looked at me again, her green eyes held something that might have been regret.

"Somewhere safe."

"Safe?" I laughed, the sound bitter as burnt coffee. "Safe for who? What happened at the cottage? All that blood?"

"That wasnae supposed to happen."

Cold air bit at my exposed skin as I stood there naked, goosebumps prickling up my arms. "Get out of the buggy!"

She shook her head, red hair catching sunlight filtering through the canopy.

"Get out, or I'll bloody drag you out," I threatened, taking a step closer.

She looked conflicted for a moment, jaw working as she weighed her options. Then she turned off the engine and climbed out, movements careful and deliberate.

"They're coming to meet me," she said.

I stared at her. "You mean Callum is?"

She nodded slowly. "And three other men."

"Why are you working with Callum?" The words tasted bitter on my tongue. "Is he forcing you to do this? Threatening you?"

She laughed, but it was hollow, bitter as burnt heather. "You've got it the wrong way around, cousin. I brought Callum into this mess."

I just stared at her, mouth slightly open. The forest sounds—wind through leaves, distant bird calls—seemed muffled, like my ears were stuffed with cotton wool.

She sighed, shoulders sagging under some invisible weight. "You know I grew up believing my mother was murdered by our own pack."

I shrugged. "That was never confirmed. Just rumours floating about." Pack gossip claimed my father might have been involved, as she and Dad had clashed constantly before her death.

"Well, a couple of years ago, she got back in contact."

"Got back in... contact?" My voice pitched higher. "Your mum is still alive?! Moira never died?"

Isla glanced behind her towards Dev's motionless form, then into the distance. "I won't go into the specifics, but she faked her own death. I spent years grieving her loss... it completely fucked me up." Anger sharpened her accent, made the words snap like breaking twigs. "I was only thirteen... I mean, you remember. You were still here then. Anyway, she just merrily popped back up like nothing had happened."

"Are you trying to tell me your mum is involved in all this?" My brain felt like it was going to explode.

A twisted smile curved her lips. "You could say that. She's rather high up in GREY, actually."

I blinked a few times. "Grey?"

"You know, G-R-E-Y, the unit Kit was part of. Mum was the one who organised for him to go, remember?"

"GREY? This... is all GREY? You're GREY?"

Isla snorted. "I'm only a very tiny part of it."

My head spun. The forest around us seemed to tilt sideways. "But... but... you're meant to be studying medicine in Edinburgh. Why the fuck are you doing this, Isla? And *Callum?* You brought *Callum* in on it? I thought you thought he was a creep who was obsessed with you!"

Her face twisted with distaste. "He is a creep who's obsessed with me! But I haven't really been around the pack for years. I distanced myself when my mum came back. So I needed a solid link back in, and Edina trusts him."

"So my mum has nothing to do with this?"

When Isla shook her head, I breathed out a sigh of relief. Small mercies, I supposed. My mother might be a terrible parent and an awful person, but at least she wasn't a kidnapping, murderous psychopath.

"So you got him to get her to organise this multi-pack gathering tonight? So you could identify and capture prime candidates for whatever the fuck you're doing? Were you just going to, what, walk up and grab them?"

"No, obviously there's more to the plan than that," she snapped. "But nobody from our pack will be taken," she added. "Part of the deal I've made is that our pack will be protected."

"Right. Great. Shame that warranty clearly didn't cover ex-pack members' ex-boyfriends."

Isla flinched. "I am sorry about Dev."

"Did you always know I was up here looking for him?"

"I guessed," she admitted. "I saw pictures of you together when I did my social media crawl a couple of weeks ago. I couldn't believe it. Such bad luck."

"This isn't bad luck, Isla!" I gestured wildly at Dev's motionless form. "Is Dev even okay?"

She sighed, running a hand across her face. "I tried at the cottage to bring Dev back under GREY control, but it didn't work. His system has properly rejected the chip."

"The *chip*?! Is that what you've put inside his skull?" I laughed, a horrible manic sound. "You're putting chips inside wolves' skulls to create controllable weapons for GREY."

"Yes. And Dev's chip malfunctioned," she said, almost monotonously. Like she'd resigned herself to her fate of telling me everything.

"How did he even escape?" I demanded.

Isla glanced away. "It was a series of fuck-ups, honestly. Something went wrong with the sedation schedule. Two of the guards went up for a smoke break and decided to prop open the security door. They noticed a couple of hours later, but by that point he was miles away."

"And what if he hadn't escaped? What happens when the chip malfunctions? Because we found your burn site yesterday. There was a shit tonne of ashes there."

Guilt flashed across her features. "That was all meant to have stopped by now. The compatibility tests are *supposed* to be one hundred percent accurate. That's what Meridian promised. But they're liars. That's one of the reasons Mum—"

"Stop. I don't care about that right now. Why is Dev's blood all over the cottage?"

"When Dev understood what I was trying to do to him, we both shifted and fought." She pulled down her T-shirt—underneath, a horrible gash stretched across her collarbone, still slowly closing. "It was a pretty even fight, except that I'd tranqed him five seconds before I shifted. But he didn't drop straight down. And I had to defend myself."

From the buggy, crackling erupted from Isla's walkie-talkie. Callum's voice, asking, "*Do you copy?*"

"They're close," she said quietly, eyes scanning the treeline. "Rory, you need to run."

"What? You'd really just let me walk away from this?"

Her eyes softened, and for a moment she looked like the girl I remembered from childhood—the one who used to sneak extra pudding to me when the adults weren't looking.

"We're similar, you and me," she said. "Both hate the pack. Both rejected their precious traditions." A sad smile tugged at her lips. "I've always admired your choice to leave. Thought of you fondly over the years, actually. You had the balls to do what I never could. Never could officially, anyway."

"Listen," I said, stepping towards her. "I know people who can help you. Protect you. You don't have to keep doing this. You can come back to London with me."

"I can't!"

"Why not?!

"Because I'm in way too fucking deep now!" The words burst out of her, crazed and desperate, eyes glistening with unshed tears. "You think I wanted this? You think I chose any of *this?*"

The wind shifted, carrying scents with it. Callum's familiar musk, sharp with barely controlled aggression. And underneath it, three distinct human signatures—metallic fear, stale cigarettes, and sweat.

"Just give me Dev and I'll go," I said, taking a step towards the buggy. "That's the deal."

She shook her head frantically. "I can't. Rory, you don't understand what they're all like." Her voice faltered, and she paused to inhale a gulp of air. "Mum's made it very clear what happens to people who disappoint her."

As I stared at her, I finally understood. "She's got a hold on you."

"Yes. Yes, she's got a hold on me. On everything," Isla whispered. "My life, my future, my choices. All of it. If I leave, she might hurt Dad. He's innocent in all this. He doesn't even know she's still alive."

"Listen, Isla, I promise I *can* help you," I said urgently. "I can't tell you anything more here, but you need to trust—"

"No." She shook her head again, more violently this time. "You don't understand. She's not just some criminal. She's military. *Government*. She has resources you can't imagine."

The walkie-talkie crackled again. Then I could hear them crystal clear—the deliberate snap of branches, boots on ground. Not trying to be quiet anymore. They wanted us to know they were coming.

"We're out of time," Isla said, panic creeping into her voice. "Just go, Rory. This is your last chance! They'll have tranq guns."

My body betrayed me with tremors I couldn't control. I so desperately wanted to make a run for it. But I couldn't leave Dev. *Wouldn't.*

Then I felt it—warmth flooding through me, followed by a scent that made my heart race. Maxwell, approaching through the trees behind me. I could smell him, smell myself on him—my scent still clinging to his skin from last night.

No, no, no. How did he find me so quickly?

"MAXWELL, STAY BACK!" I shouted over my shoulder.

The sound of crashing footsteps erupted from another direction. Callum burst into the clearing with three other men, each wearing utility belts. Each armed.

"Callum!" I snarled, because I couldn't just stand there and say nothing to the bastard who'd helped torture Dev.

He only smirked, that familiar sneer making me itch to punch him. "I was hoping for a reason to end you. Looks like you've just given me one."

"Hold on, Callum," Isla said, her voice wobbling.

Her eyes widened, looking behind me with something that might have been horror or relief—I couldn't tell which.

I didn't need to turn around to know that Maxwell had ignored my instruction. The bond sparked with fierce pleasure at being reunited even as terror flooded my system like ice water.

He slid into place beside me, raising an arm protectively in front of my chest. His body radiated tension, coiled and ready to spring.

"Oh, look, it's Detective Inspector Maxwell," Callum acknowledged with mock politeness, his brown eyes glittering with malice. "How convenient. Two birds, one stone."

The three men with him shifted their stances, hands moving to their utility belts.

"Callum, please," Isla tried again, taking a step towards him. "We can work this out without—"

"Without what?" Callum cut her off, never taking his eyes off me. "Without giving this little traitor exactly what he deserves? He turned his back on the pack. He doesn't deserve our help."

Maxwell's arm pressed more firmly against my chest, his heart pounding rabbit-fast.

"The only traitor here is you," I spat back, anger overriding common sense. "Working with outsiders—with *humans*—to betray your own kind."

Callum's face darkened. His hand moved to his belt, fingers wrapping around something black and angular. "Should have stayed in London, Rory."

He raised his hand to reveal a bulky pistol-shaped device—a dart gun. I caught the faint chemical smell of sedatives on the air.

Maxwell tensed beside me, muscles bunching, preparing to move even through our shared terror.

Callum looked at the three men flanking him and jerked his chin towards us.

"Take care of them."

27

Theodore

The tranq gun swung towards my chest, Callum's finger tightening on the trigger.

"DOWN!"

Rory slammed into me with the force of a freight train, sending us both crashing to the forest floor. We rolled through bracken and dead leaves, my shoulder striking something sharp—a root, a rock. The world spun in a kaleidoscope of brown and green.

Then the agony hit.

It wasn't just pain—it was invasion. Ten times worse than before, Rory forcing himself to shift ten times too quickly. His bones became mine, fracturing and reshaping with sickening wet cracks that I felt in my own marrow. It felt so real, every snapping tendon and stretching sinew. The transformation was happening inside me and to me, my mind unable to distinguish between his body and mine. Muscles I'd never had tore themselves apart and rebuilt, alien and wrong.

I screamed.

The sound that ripped from my throat was barely human, scraping my vocal cords bloody. For a long moment, nothing existed except the white-hot torture, then—

Whizz.

A dart sailed past my ear, so close I felt the displacement of air. Pure instinct kicked in, muscle memory overriding the chaos in my head. Assess. Move. Survive. My father's voice echoed through the years: *"We never freeze, son. The moment you freeze, you're dead."* My body rolled before my mind caught up, every movement precise despite the lingering echo of transformation tearing through my nerves. Despite my exhaustion from sprinting here like my life depended on it.

My Glock was in my hand before conscious thought caught up. Training overrode everything else—stance, grip, sight alignment.

Where Callum had stood, a massive black wolf now circled a smaller golden one. Rory. Christ, his wolf was so much smaller than I even understood—absolutely dwarfed by Callum's bulk. The bigger wolf feinted left, then lunged, jaws snapping at Rory's throat.

I turned my attention to the three men. "Drop your weapons!"

They froze. The blond one's tranq gun clattered to the ground, hands shooting up. But the dark-haired man beside him didn't flinch, raising his weapon towards me.

I put a bullet through his arm.

Blood sprayed across the clearing in a crimson arc. His scream echoed off the trees as he dropped, clutching the ruined limb.

"Maxwell!" Isla shouted, though she made no move to help her associate.

Callum's massive form struck Rory square in the chest. He flew backwards, hitting the ground hard near the third man. Steel flashed as he drew a knife from his belt.

"Drop all your weapons, *now*!" The words ripped from my throat. I'd never shot to kill anyone before. Dad had. He'd told me about it, voice heavy with something I hadn't understood as a child. Now I did. The weight of crossing that line settled over me, suffocating, but Rory's stream of pain through our bond burned it away. This wasn't about my conscience—this was about survival. "Last warning, or I shoot!"

Ooof. It crashed into me again—sharp, breathless agony that made my own ribs ache in sympathy. Through the bond, I felt his desperation, his fear not for himself but for me. The golden wolf struggled to rise, one leg trembling beneath him, and Callum prowled closer with predatory patience. Every second I spent dealing with these bastards was another second Rory spent vulnerable, outmatched, bleeding.

The cold mathematics of survival crystallised in my mind: three armed men between me and helping him. Three obstacles that needed removing. Now.

The blond man's arm drew back, knife glinting.

I didn't hesitate.

My finger squeezed the trigger. The first shot punched through his chest, the impact spinning him sideways. Blood misted the air. The second man was raising his weapon when my bullet found him, dropping him in a graceless heap. Two lives ended in the space of a heartbeat, and some distant part of me—the part that wasn't drowning in Rory's pain—catalogued exactly what I'd become.

Isla's gasping filled the sudden silence. I turned to find the third man gone, vanished into the trees.

No time to think about what I'd just done. Callum was moving again. Compartmentalise. Focus. Survive.

The wolves crashed together again, a writhing mass of fur and fangs. I circled them, Glock raised, searching for a clear shot. Every angle showed Rory too close—one wrong bullet and I'd kill the person I was trying to save.

Callum seemed to understand. The black wolf deliberately positioned himself so Rory's smaller form blocked my line of fire, tactical intelligence gleaming in those predator's eyes. When Rory tried to dart left, creating distance, Callum herded him back, using his bulk to maintain the shield.

My finger hovered over the trigger. If Rory wasn't so close, I could use a silver bullet, take Callum down possibly just from a grazing wound. But their tumbling and tussling made it impossible.

Despite the noises from the fight, I still heard Isla's breathing, coming in sharp, panicked gasps. In my peripheral vision, I caught her backing towards the trees.

"Stay where you are!" I barked, not taking my eyes off the wolves.

"He's going to kill him!" she screamed, voice cracking. "Callum's going to—"

A strangled sob tore from her throat, forcing me to look at her. She stood frozen, auburn hair wild around her pale face, freckles stark against skin gone white as bone. Tremors spread through her entire body like she was coming apart at the seams.

Then she bolted.

"Isla!" But she was already crashing through the undergrowth, panic-driven and unstoppable. *Brilliant.*

Rory broke free of Callum, beautiful golden fur streaked with horrible crimson, and lunged for the black wolf's throat. He twisted away, but the movement opened up his left flank.

Now.

I squeezed the trigger.

The bullet punched through fur and flesh with a wet *thunk*. Callum's roar shattered the morning air, pure rage. Blood welled from the groove carved across his ribs—a surface wound only.

Those yellow eyes fixed on me with murderous intent. Muscles bunched beneath his coat as he gathered himself to spring. Ice flooded my veins, and through our connection I felt Rory's matching panic crash into mine—pure, animal terror that this was how we'd both die.

Rory's teeth found Callum's back leg, clamping down with desperate ferocity. The bigger wolf stumbled but didn't fall, powerful hindquarters still coiled for the leap that would put me on my back with fangs at my throat.

I emptied my clip into his chest.

Bang. Bang. Bang.

Three shots, centre mass. Callum's body jerked with each impact, dark fur blooming red. Time crystallised, each second stretching impossibly long, Callum hanging suspended for an impossible moment, yellow eyes wide with shock. Then he crashed to the ground.

Callum's massive body hit the earth with a wet thud, but he wasn't finished. His paws scrabbled against the forest floor, claws gouging furrows in the damp soil as he thrashed about like some dying behemoth.

Dark blood pooled beneath him, spreading across fallen leaves in an ever-widening stain.

Just fucking die.

The thought sliced through my mind with vicious clarity. I'd already killed two men, so what more was a third, especially this vile man. All I wanted was for this nightmare to end. For Callum to stop moving, stop breathing, stop being a threat to the golden wolf now collapsed ten feet away.

Rory lay on his side, flanks heaving with each heavy breath. Exhaustion radiated from every line of his body.

Blood frothed at Callum's muzzle, pink foam bubbling with each desperate wheeze. The metallic stench filled the clearing, mixing copper with the loamy scent of disturbed earth. His movements grew sluggish, those massive paws that had been clawing for purchase now twitching weakly. Each laboured breath came weaker than the last until finally, mercifully, the light faded from his yellow gaze.

His eyes fell shut.

I rushed to Rory, knees hitting the ground hard enough to jar my bones. His golden head lifted just enough to rest in my lap, and a soft whine escaped his throat.

"Don't shift back," I whispered, hands finding the soft fur behind his ears. "Not yet. Let yourself heal first."

My fingers moved carefully over his body, cataloguing damage. A deep gash across his left shoulder wept crimson. Puncture wounds dotted his neck where Callum's teeth had found purchase, though none looked dangerously deep.

Images flooded my consciousness—myself as Rory had seen me, gun raised, face set in grim determination. Then terror that had consumed him when Callum lunged transformed into something else entirely: fierce, overwhelming relief that I was alive.

Then new images crashed through: Dev, unconscious under those blankets in the buggy.

"I'll check on him," I murmured, stroking Rory's fur. "But stay here."

I approached the buggy cautiously, lifting the edge of the tarp. Dev lay naked beneath, chest rising and falling steadily. Human form, breathing normally. But Christ—his skin was a patchwork of healing wounds. Angry red welts crisscrossed his torso, some still weeping, others sealed with the pale pink of recent scar tissue. I gave his shoulder a light slap.

A soft moan escaped his lips.

"He's okay," I called back to Rory, returning immediately to his side.

Time crawled past. Rory's whines grew more insistent, restless energy building despite his injuries. Through our connection, I caught flashes of his desires—the burning need to shift back, the desperate urge to chase after Isla. He tried to rise twice, but I pressed gentle hands to his shoulders.

"Not yet. Give it time."

I tried Seb and then Kit on the sat phone. Neither call connected. Were they airborne already?

I kept my Glock ready, scanning the treeline for any sign of movement. But the forest remained silent around us, empty of everything except the sound of Rory's breathing and the distant call of birds.

Rory began to wriggle against my hands. A low whine escaped his throat, and I felt his determination crystallising—he was going to shift back whether I liked it or not.

"Don't," I warned, pressing my palms more firmly against his shoulders. "Not yet."

But he ignored me completely, of course. His body began to change beneath my touch, and I braced myself for the agony.

This time was different. Instead of the violent, bone-snapping transformation from before, Rory moved deliberately slowly. The shift rippled through him like waves, each change measured and controlled. His bones lengthened gradually, joints popping with soft clicks rather than sickening cracks. Golden fur receded in patches, revealing human skin beneath.

The pain that flooded through our bond was manageable—a deep ache rather than white-hot torture. I found myself mesmerised, watching the impossible process unfold in exquisite detail. Muscles reforming themselves, rippling his skin. Muzzle shortening as his skull reshaped itself. His injuries seemed to rapidly close in front of my eyes.

Wonder filled me, pure awe at witnessing something so fundamentally magical. Rory caught between worlds, neither fully human nor wolf but something beautiful and impossible.

"Hi," he eventually panted, human head on my lap, blond hair tousled, blue-green eyes bright.

"Hi," I replied, stroking his hair, fingers combing through the disheveled strands.

"You found me."

I shrugged. "That was your doing. Don't bond us together if you don't want me to be able to track you down."

A soft laugh bubbled up from Rory's chest, the sound rippling through the air like music. Something warm and bright unfurled within me at that laugh—pure joy washing away the lingering adrenaline and horror of what I'd just done.

He shifted, pushing himself up, then climbing onto me so he was sitting sideways across my lap, one arm draped around my shoulders. This close, I could see the flecks of gold in his eyes, the way his pupils were still slightly dilated from the transformation.

I leaned in, drawn by an irresistible pull, and pressed my lips to his.

The kiss began soft, tentative—barely a whisper of contact. Rory's lips were warm beneath mine, slightly chapped. I felt his breath hitch, then his mouth opened slightly, inviting me deeper. My tongue traced the seam of his lips, tasting him slowly. His hand found the back of my neck, holding me close but not demanding more. We moved together with deliberate slowness, each press of lips measured and precious.

Time suspended itself around us. The forest fell away, the bodies, the blood, everything except the gentle exploration of his mouth against mine. His emotions flooded through me, to the point I could taste his exhaustion, his relief, the lingering tang of fear transmuted into something infinitely sweeter. When we finally broke apart, I rested my forehead against his, breathing in the scent of pine needles caught in his hair.

"We're alive," Rory whispered, wonder threading through his voice.

...he's okay...he's okay...it's okay...

"We're alive," I confirmed, thumb brushing across his cheekbone. "I'm okay."

Rory caught me up on everything Isla had said. GREY. Her mother, mysteriously not dead. How he'd begged her to let him help her. After she'd been responsible for so much harm, I wasn't sure I would have extended her the same courtesy.

Then, before I knew what was happening, Rory was scrambling to his feet, naked and bloodied but determined. He swayed slightly, one hand pressed against his ribs where Callum's claws had raked deep furrows. Dark bruises were already blooming across his torso.

"We need to sort this out," I said, gesturing to the surrounding carnage. "It's broad daylight. A hiker could wander off route."

Rory nodded grimly. "The buggy?"

Ever so carefully, we moved Dev to the front passenger seat of the buggy, then completed the grim task of loading the three corpses into the back. Isla's bag was tucked away in there—just toiletries and spare clothes, a thin black jumper and orange corduroy trousers.

"You look ridiculous," I told Rory as he pulled them on, though to be fair the orange quite suited him, somehow. He stole shoes from one of the corpses, though they looked far too big.

"I can hear something," Rory said. "The faintest ringing sound, coming from over near the buildings. An alarm. I guess to evacuate—I heard Isla order it through the walkie-talkie."

"We can head there..."

Rory shook his head. "Don't you think they'll have it all locked down? Besides, we said last time there was no evidence they brought the wolves in that way. It's not accessible by vehicle anymore."

His face crumpled. The light died from his eyes so suddenly it was like watching someone blow out a candle. My chest tightened—not physical pain, but something far worse flooding through our bond. Self-loathing crashed into me with the force of a lorry, bitter and sharp.

Rory sank to the ground beside the buggy, back sliding down the metal frame until he sat with his knees drawn up, head dropping forward.

"Fuck!" The word exploded from him. I caught fragments of his spiralling thoughts:

...useless, always messing up, failed them...should have done more...

The intensity of his self-hatred made my stomach clench.

"Rory." I sank down beside him, damp earth soaking through my trousers. Taking his hand felt natural now, our fingers threading together automatically. "We came to Scotland to find Dev. You found him. You did it."

"But we haven't saved everyone else." His voice came out muffled against his knees. "Carrie, all those missing shifters—"

"This is bigger than we thought. That's not our fault. We've done what we can."

"No." He lifted his head, those blue-green eyes blazing with desperate determination. "We have to do *something*. What if they decide to mass exterminate them all? Get rid of the evidence?"

"The wolves are too valuable for that," I said, though doubt gnawed at me. How could I be certain of anything in this nightmare?

Rory's jaw worked silently for a moment. Then, "Maybe they're taking them to the castle ruins. To get out that way."

"What, underground?"

"Yes."

A laugh escaped before I could stop it. Brief, incredulous. Rory's frown deepened.

"Sorry. What we found there could indeed be connected to GREY. But the chances of there being a direct tunnel from here to there is slim to none. It's what, six, seven miles? It would be a truly impressive feat for anyone to secretly dig that. Impossible, even."

"You're right," he muttered, shoulders sagging further. "It was stupid."

As I studied Rory's dejected profile—the way his shoulders curved inward, protecting himself from another blow—something fierce and protective surged through me. He'd spent most of his life being dismissed and underestimated. Being told his ideas weren't good enough. I wouldn't be another voice adding to that chorus.

"No, it wasn't stupid." I climbed to my feet, extending my hand. "Stand up."

"What?"

"We need to get to that castle."

Confusion clouded his features. "You just said it was impossible."

"And what did we agree about impossible things?"

Understanding dawned across his face like sunrise. That brilliant smile appeared, making my heart skip.

"Though, it doesn't feel right leaving Dev—"

Rory's head snapped up, cutting me off mid-sentence. His entire body went rigid, every muscle coiled like a spring ready to release.

"Someone's coming," he whispered.

I strained to listen but heard nothing beyond the usual forest sounds—wind through pine branches, distant birdsong. But Rory's senses were picking up something mine couldn't. His nostrils flared slightly, testing the air.

"How many?" I kept my voice low, hand instinctively moving towards the gun in my coat pocket.

"Just one wolf." His brow furrowed in concentration. "I think it's..."

A large grey wolf burst through the treeline, powerful legs eating up the distance between us in seconds. The creature was massive—easily Kit's size, with a thick coat that caught the morning light.

"Alex," Rory finished, his voice carrying a mixture of relief and apprehension.

The wolf stopped short, amber eyes taking in the scene before him. First Rory and me, then the buggy with its grim cargo barely concealed beneath the tarp, then back to us again. His intelligent gaze lingered on the bloodstains decorating the forest floor.

"Can you shift back?" Rory asked.

I looked away as bones began to crack and reshape. When the shifting stopped, I glanced back to find a naked Alexander Thorne standing where the wolf had been.

His short grey hair was mussed, but his blue eyes were sharp and alert as they swept over the scene before him. At first, his weathered face lit up with genuine relief at seeing Rory. But then Alexander's expression grew stern as he took in our dishevelled appearance, the bodies we'd clearly been attempting to move.

"What on earth is going on here?" he said, his accent thickening with authority. "And why are you in my daughter's clothing?"

28

Rory

"I promise you, we'll go over everything again later. But right now, I really need you to take Dev back with you."

Uncle Alex's face had cycled through disbelief, horror, and grim acceptance as we'd explained everything. The surgical scars on Dev's scalp, the blood-soaked cottage, Isla's betrayal, Callum's involvement—each revelation had caused visible flinches. When I'd told him about Moira being still alive, he'd turned away from us, needing several minutes to compose himself.

It turned out Isla had rung him around the same time as she'd run off from us. She'd been crying so hard she'd made no sense, then she'd either disconnected the call or lost signal.

"Should've known something was off when I caught Callum's stench mixed with hers," Alex had said, voice bitter. "That lad's been trouble since he could walk."

I opened my mouth to remind him that Isla was the one who brought Callum into the whole operation, then snapped it shut. It was going to take Alex a long time to process this. If he needed to focus on hating Callum rather than his dead wife coming back to life, then I'd let him.

"So, Alex, is it okay if—"

"Where are we?"

We spun around. Dev had pushed himself upright, blinking slowly at our startled faces.

"Dev!" I lurched forward, but Maxwell caught my arm. "You're okay!"

"Bloody hell," Dev groaned, pressing a palm to his forehead. "Feel like death warmed over. Who's this bloke, then?"

"Isla's father," I said.

Dev's eyes widened, pupils still slightly dilated from whatever they'd pumped into him. "She stabbed me with a tranquiliser!"

"She did."

He rubbed at his neck, wincing. "Memories get proper hazy after that. Everything went sideways."

Maxwell stepped forward, his voice carefully neutral. "Alex, I know this is a lot to ask. I know you're probably desperate to find Isla. But can you take Dev back and check him over? I give you my word, if we find Isla, we won't harm her."

Alex looked conflicted, grey beard twitching as he worked his jaw. "I'm sorry, but—"

"If you go back with Dev," I interrupted, "you can sound the alarm to Edina, and bring out everyone. A proper search party."

Alex released a deep sigh that seemed to deflate his entire frame. "Can you walk, lad? Or shift even? It'd be quicker to run over the hills rather than take the buggy. Also, I don't want to bump into any humans like this."

Dev tested his balance, swaying slightly before steadying himself against the buggy's frame. "Think I can manage."

Five minutes later, after hiding the buggy full of bodies deep in a thicket of bushes, we parted ways—Alex supporting Dev as they headed toward the treeline, whilst Maxwell and I turned back toward the castle ruins.

I couldn't help but feel slightly sick at sending Dev off with Alex, the father of the woman who'd helped kidnap him, stuck a chip in his brain, and most recently, almost ripped him to shreds.

I'd have to buy him a drink when we got home. If he wanted to be friends again.

We made good pace, considering my battered condition. Maxwell glanced at me every few minutes, raising his eyebrow every time I fibbed that I was fine. The oversized boots I'd nicked from one of Callum's men kept slipping, making me stumble over rocks and bracken. Finally, I had enough, kicking them off to walk barefoot.

When the castle ruins came into view, I didn't know whether to laugh or cry. A horrible sensation came over me—that this was a colossal waste of time, when we could have been tracking down Isla. That Maxwell knew this was a stupid idea, and was being too nice to me.

Every step towards the ruins felt like walking through sludge. My legs grew heavier with each stride, as though invisible weights had attached themselves to my ankles. Maxwell eyed me, the amount of concern radiating from him making everything worse.

I almost felt irrationally angry at him for a second—for humouring me, for allowing us to exhaust ourselves walking here when we could be doing something useful. Something that actually mattered.

Two hundred metres from the ruins.

One hundred.

Fifty.

A faint hum tickled my ears. I grabbed Maxwell's arm. "Stop."

"What?"

The sound grew louder. Mechanical. Purposeful.

"A vehicle is coming."

Maxwell frowned, tilting his head. "I don't hear—"

An engine roared in the distance, getting closer and closer. Maxwell's eyes widened as the sound reached him too.

Then I saw it—one massive bike tearing across the moorland, two riders hunched together, wearing chunky helmets. The driver handled the rocky ground like he'd been born on a motorbike, while his passenger looked oddly elegant even whilst gripping on for dear life.

"No!" Maxwell exclaimed. "It can't be!"

But it was.

I could feel it—feel my brother through our bond. My legs began to shake, and I stumbled as I started running towards them.

The vehicle slid to a rapid stop, sending up a spray of dirt and bracken.

Kit threw his helmet off, hair sticking up at odd angles.

"Rory!" He ran towards me and we crashed into each other in an extremely rare hug. "You're alright!" he repeated, voice muffled against my shoulder. "I was so bloody scared. I should have come with you from the start. I—"

"Stop, it's fine. It was all fine. Until it wasn't. But Maxwell saved me. I mean, *I* saved Maxwell, to be fair."

"Oi!" Maxwell called from behind.

"How did you find us?"

Kit squeezed tighter, then released me. "I'll always find you, Rory," he said, ruffling my hair in a way that should have annoyed me but only filled me with love.

He'd come. He'd really come for me.

Seb caught up, somehow managing to look immaculate despite having just been on a motorbike—burgundy tailored trousers un-creased, his fancy long black coat with brass buttons pristine.

Maxwell stared. "But... but... how the fuck did you two get here from London so fast?"

Seb looked amused. "We took the private jet in the end. Drove Kit's motorcycle to the airfield, breaking all the speed limits."

"Hey! You tell me I'm not allowed to speed!" I tried to joke.

Maxwell's mouth dropped open like a fish. "You... you have a private jet?"

"I have access to one." Seb's mouth quirked. "We've landed at a tiny private airfield. It's completely empty at the minute. I'm trusting Felix to take care of everything. The pilot and crew are there waiting."

"So... what are we doing?" Kit asked, arms crossed as he surveyed the castle ruins.

I allowed Maxwell to fill them in, keeping a close eye on my broth-er throughout, waiting for his reaction to hearing about GREY. Though his heart rate rocketed, he schooled his expression almost perfectly. I wished he'd shared more about what he'd been through during his time with them, so I could help him. Perhaps now, he'd be forced to.

When we got to the part where Maxwell relayed that I wanted to come here in case the wolves happened to casually pop out of the castle, I cringed.

"Right," said Kit, frowning, looking between Maxwell and me. "And how far away did you say the other place was?"

"Umm... not that far," I said weakly, as Maxwell said, "Almost eight miles."

I could tell Kit was trying not to laugh.

"There's a secret tunnel network all over London!" I protested. "We use it every day!"

"Yes, built during World War Two under a city already connected by an underground train network," said Seb dryly.

"Let's go see this entrance, then," said Kit.

We trudged across to the west wall where Maxwell and I had found the hatch yesterday. I brushed away the layer of dirt and grass clumps, showing them the concrete rectangle with its clean edges, stark against the ancient stone foundations.

"Well, this is all very fascinating," Seb began, "but how are we supposed to—"

"Shut up," Kit interrupted sharply, holding up one hand.

We all froze.

Kit dropped to the ground, pressing his ear against the hatch. "There's people arguing underneath here!"

"What?" I scrambled down beside him, flattening my ear to the cold surface.

Muffled voices drifted up through the concrete—indistinct but definitely human.

"We can't just stay here all day and night!" someone complained.

"Where is Megan?" another voice demanded.

"We're not being paid enough for this!"

I lifted my head, staring at Maxwell in amazement. "There really are people down there." My throat tightened. "There's people, Maxwell!"

"Can you hear me?" boomed Kit in the loudest voice I'd ever heard.

The voices arguing below fell silent instantly.

"You have sixty seconds to open this hatch before we blow it open for you."

"Thanks for consulting me on that plan," Seb deadpanned.

Kit grinned sheepishly. "Sorry, boss."

I pressed my ear back against the concrete, straining to catch every word. More arguing erupted below—panicked this time, voices overlapping in frantic whispers.

"—told you we should have just stayed put—"

"—can't leave the cargo without authorisation—"

"—who the hell are they?"

My stomach lurched. Cargo. They were talking about people like bloody cargo.

"Ten!" Kit bellowed, making me jump. "Nine! Eight!"

Scuffling sounds echoed from beneath us, followed by electronic beeping. Maxwell grabbed my arm, pulling me back from the hatch as mechanical whirring filled the air.

"Seven! Six!"

The concrete hatch opened with a sharp hiss, revealing a ladder descending into darkness. Stale air wafted up, tinged with antiseptic.

"Out you come," ordered Seb in that voice nobody ever dared disobey. "Now."

The first figure that emerged was a burly man in tactical gear who burst through the hatch with a taser raised, scanning for targets.

Kit moved like lightning, tackling him before he could fire. They hit the ground hard, the taser skittering across the grass.

Two more armed figures scrambled up—a tall woman and another bloke with a sidearm. Maxwell's gun was already trained on them whilst Seb simply stepped forward, and something about his presence made them freeze mid-draw.

"Weapons down," Maxwell barked. "Now."

The remaining figures climbed out sheepishly after that—a young bloke in expensive trainers, a middle-aged woman clutching a tablet, others in smart office attire. One wore a white lab coat over a pink shirt. Seven in total, all looking significantly less confident now that their armed colleagues were face down in the dirt.

Maxwell kept his gun raised, expression hard.

Seb surveyed the group with cold efficiency. "Is this everyone?"

The group exchanged nervous glances. Eventually, the woman in the white coat cleared her throat. "Two more are still with the cargo."

"Cargo?" Seb's voice dropped to something dangerous.

"The um..." She swallowed hard. "The patients."

Seb nodded at Kit, who climbed down the ladder without hesitation. A minute later, footsteps echoed up from below, and two more figures joined our ragged lineup.

"There's about thirty to forty wolves down there. One of them fits Carrie's description. All unconscious and restrained on metal trolleys," Kit spat. "Like meat."

"You're all being transported for questioning," Seb stated calmly. "We'll use that airfield's outbuilding," he murmured to Kit.

"*What*?" the youngest man squeaked. "Questioned? On whose authority?"

Seb only smiled. Was I imagining the hint of fangs?

"You can call me Black," he told him. "But do try not to talk to me unless it's truly necessary."

29

Rory

"The gathering is cancelled," my mother said without preamble. "I've sent word to all the packs."

I stood in the doorway of her office, still catching my breath from the trek back to the manor. The familiar smell of old leather and punishment hit me—nothing had changed in here since I was twelve.

"Good," I managed. "Because—"

"Yes, I know." She gestured for me to sit in the chair opposite her massive oak desk. "Alexander told me everything."

Seb and Kit had been clear: Maxwell and I needed to get back to the manor, find Dev, and bring him to the airfield so they could fly him home. Simple enough, except an hour into our journey back, Tariq had materialised out of thin air—stark naked and looking properly frazzled. Alex had indeed sounded the alarm.

And my mother wanted to talk to me.

When we reached pack lands, I'd had to beg Maxwell to go find out where Dev was, to let me deal with Mum by myself. He'd looked like he wanted to argue, but something in my face must have convinced him.

"Is it true about Callum?" she asked, voice tight.

"Yes."

I'd never seen her this rattled. Edina Thorne was always composed, always in control. Now she looked genuinely stricken, her face pale beneath her usual stern expression.

"Alex knows where to find his body," I said quietly.

She turned away to face the window, shoulders visibly shaking. I wondered if she'd have this reaction if she found out I'd died. Kit, maybe. Me? Not so sure.

"So Kit is here?" she asked when she'd turned around again.

"Not here," I said flatly. "He's waiting underground for nightfall, then they're marching them all to the airfield for interrogation. All the people involved in the operation, I mean. Tomorrow, we'll fly all the wolves back to London, then help them get home."

There wasn't a chance in hell that I was flying in that jet. Besides, Maxwell would need company in his mum's car. Before that, though, I had the strangest full moon of my life ahead of me. The late afternoon sun was already casting longer shadows, and I could feel the faintest tug itching at my skin—the moon's pull beginning its ancient dance. I couldn't wait. Kit and me, properly together under the moon for the first time in ages. If the other wolves were up and moving by then, there'd be loads of us running together across the Highlands.

The woman in the lab coat—who seemed to be vaguely in charge—had reassured us that all of the chips were presently deactivated, and the "subjects" could only be controlled using software located back at the site, which was on full lockdown. When Seb had calmly stated he'd put a bullet through her skull the second one of them acted off, she flinched, but didn't change her story.

Tonight, the rescued shifters would be traumatised, confused, probably terrified. But maybe being in their wolf forms would help. Maybe the simple act of running free under moonlight would start to heal whatever had been done to them.

"I see. Very good."

A long pause. I fidgeted with the sleeve of Isla's jumper. "What will happen if you find Isla?"

"*When* we find Isla," she corrected, steel creeping back into her voice, "we'll deal with her."

What that meant, I didn't want to know.

"Killigrew Street will need to talk to her," I said. "We don't yet know the true scope of GREY's operation, but Kit says cutting off this arm won't stop them. There could be wolves all over the world being cut open and tortured and controlled this very second."

My mother pursed her lips. "We will cooperate," she said stiffly. "I hope you know me well enough to know I'd never want harm to come to anyone in that way. What those people have done... I'd tear them apart myself, if I could."

"Did you have any idea Moira was still alive?" I couldn't help but ask. She blinked. "Of course I didn't."

I met her eyes. "I believed the rumours that Dad killed her."

After a long pause, she said quietly, "So did I."

For a moment, something passed between us—an understanding, maybe. Of a sort. I found myself studying her face, really looking at her, but not through the haze of old anger or fear.

She wasn't a monster. The realisation hit me like a punch to the gut—not the relief I'd expected, but something messier, more complicated. All these years, I'd needed her to be irredeemably evil. It was cleaner that way, easier to carry my anger like armour. But sitting here, watching her hands shake as she processed what Callum had done...

She was a terrible mother, yes. Someone who'd failed me in every way that mattered, absolutely. But not the snarling beast of my nightmares. Just a woman who'd made awful choices that had damaged me just as deeply, regardless of her motivations. And somehow, that felt worse. Because now I had to live with the complexity of it all—the knowledge that someone could have "loved" me in their own twisted way and still destroyed me completely.

Before anything else could be said, I stood up.

"Will you come back again?" she said, voice strained.

I tried to shrug casually. "Who knows? Out of all of you, I only really liked Isla, and she turned out to be a murderous psychopath." I walked to the door, resting my hand on the handle. "One final thing. How did you know Maxwell was a telepath?"

The way she smiled told me everything. "You know this pack will always do everything it can to protect itself. And you're not the only one with friends in high places."

I left the office without looking back.

Maxwell was waiting in the lobby. "Dev's back at Primrose Cottage. Alex has already left, joining the search for Isla."

I groaned. "More walking. My legs are going to fall off after this holiday."

Maxwell's mouth quirked upwards. "Holiday?"

I waved my arm. "You know, mission. Case. Whatever. I'm tired."

He caught my hand, squeezing tight as we walked down the stairs towards the cottage. "You did it, Rory," he said softly. "You saved all those wolves."

My cheeks warmed. "Kit and Seb did most of the—"

"No." His grip on my hand tightened. "You did that. And…" He paused, looking like the words were physically painful to get out. "I can't believe I'm saying this—and you better not do it to me ever again—but I'm glad you ran off when you did."

I blinked at him. "What?"

"If you'd listened to me, and if we'd played it safe and waited for backup… Isla would have gotten away. We'd have lost Dev again. All those wolves would still be trapped, or worse."

The validation hit me harder than I'd expected. Maxwell—Detective Inspector Theodore Maxwell, who lived and breathed procedure and protocol—was telling me that my chaotic, impulsive, completely ridiculous way of handling things had actually been *right*.

I had to swallow hard around the sudden tightness in my throat. "Can I have this praise in writing? I want to give it to Seb. He might finally buy me a new car as a reward."

He laughed. "But I'd miss your old car so much."

When the cottage came into sight, it was tempting to break into a run. I was suddenly desperate to get back to London. To Killigrew Street Hotel. To real life. To Priya.

"Hopefully Dev has rounded up Freddy for me," I said.

"I'm sure the pair of them are cuddling as we speak," Maxwell said, followed by a resigned huff.

I sniggered. "Listen, all you need to do to make Freddy like you is feed him. It's really that simple."

"I don't negotiate with terrorists."

"Let's pack at the speed of light," I said. "Good thing my suitcase is still by the door, right?"

Instead of glaring at me, or laughing, Maxwell suddenly grabbed my arm. A particular thread of anxiety seeped into me from him. "Wait a second."

I stilled.

He cleared his throat, looking anywhere but at me. "When we get back to London... I was just thinking... Perhaps we could... That is, if you wanted to..."

"What? Spit it out."

His jaw worked silently for a moment. "Would you like to go for dinner? With me. Properly."

I tilted my head. "We've eaten together loads of times."

"No, I mean—" He ran an exasperated hand through his coils. "A date, Rory. I'm asking you on a date."

"Oh." I blinked innocently. "Like a work thing?"

His eyes narrowed. "You're taking the piss."

"Am I? I mean, we do work together, technically. Very professional dinner conversation about case files—"

"Rory."

"—and evidence logs, maybe discuss some witness statements over pudding—"

"You absolute menace." But he was smiling now. Smiling with *teeth*. "I'm trying to ask if you'd like to go somewhere nice where I can wine and dine you properly without the threat of supernatural kidnapping or your zombie ferret stealing my chips. Or maybe even street food from Borough Market, and a walk along the river?"

I grinned. "Hmm, well I suppose I'll have to check my diary—"

"For goodness sake, Rory," he snapped, exasperated. "Do you want to date me or not?"

I burst into laughter, doubling over. The poor man looked like he was about to combust. Then, pressing my hand to his cheek, I went onto tiptoes to kiss the end of his nose. "Of course I want to date you. Did you forget about the whole mate bond thing? You know, literally tethered to you for all of eternity? I kind of thought dates would be a given. I'm sort of offended we're even having this conversation."

"Well, you said you *accidentally* bonded us. So I wasn't sure—"

I cut him off with another kiss, to his mouth this time. "Trust me, the accidental bit was just the timing. I mean, my wolf basically took one look at you and went 'that one, definitely that one, yes please with a cherry on top.' But like I said, if this is too much for you—if *I'm* too much for you—we can try and—"

Now it was Maxwell's turn to stop me, smashing his lips into mine. Then he kissed me, soft and sweet under the Highland sky. Our bond sang between us, a perfect harmony that made my wolf purr. I pressed closer, practically trying to climb inside his jacket, while Maxwell's grip tightened as if he could absorb me into himself, keep me safe in the circle of his arms. Like he never wanted to let me go, like he wanted to keep me safe and close forever. He still smelled like me—my scent clinging to his skin beneath the crisp Highland air and his own familiar warmth. *Mine.*

We finally broke apart, breathless and grinning like idiots.

"You're not too much. You're exactly enough. And anyone who has ever suggested otherwise never knew what they had."

Well, shit. This is it then. I'm properly gone for him, aren't I? Like, completely and utterly fucked. Head over heels. This is either the best or worst thing that's ever happened to me.

Maxwell blinked rapidly, his warm brown eyes widening. He smiled impossibly wider, then said, soft as starlight: "I think I'm falling in love with you too."

A grey blur streaked through the air towards me. I had approximately half a second to register Freddy's glowing yellow eyes and bared fangs before he collided with my face.

"Ow! Freddy, get off—" I stumbled backwards, trying to peel him off where he'd latched onto my cheek. His tiny claws dug into my skin as he chittered excitedly, tail thrashing against my neck.

Maxwell stepped back, hands raised in surrender. "Don't look at me. I'm not touching that thing."

"He missed me," I said through gritted teeth, finally managing to extract Freddy's teeth from my earlobe. I held him at arm's length, where he continued to wriggle and snap at the air. "Didn't you, you pesky little—"

Freddy made a sound somewhere between a purr and a growl, then promptly bit my thumb.

"Charming," Maxwell observed dryly. "Absolutely delightful."

I cradled Freddy against my chest, where he immediately settled with a satisfied sigh. "You know we're a package deal, right? Me and this mangy ball of undead fury. You'll have to learn to love him."

Maxwell's expression shifted to one of pure horror. "That's impossible."

I grinned, scratching behind Freddy's tattered ears. "What did we say about impossible things?"

Maxwell stared at us both—me with my post-kiss hair and dopey smile, Freddy with his patchy fur and glowing eyes—and let out a long, defeated sigh.

"I'm doomed, aren't I?"

"Completely and utterly," I confirmed cheerfully.

As if on cue, Freddy twisted in my arms and hissed at Maxwell.

Maxwell rubbed his temples. "This is going to be a very long courtship."

30

Epilogue

Rory

3 months later

The afternoon light slanted through the grimy windows of The George, casting everything in that particular golden haze that made even London's tattiest pubs look almost romantic. Almost. The place buzzed with post-work chatter, suits loosening ties and office workers celebrating the end of another Thursday. Kit and I had nabbed a corner table, two pints of bitter sitting between us, both half empty.

I wrapped my fingers around the cool glass, watching the condensation bead on the surface. "Do you have a date for your operation yet?"

Kit shook his head, jabbing at the spot just above his neck. "Little metal bastard has been inside me so damn long, Seb wants Dr Hartwell to run more tests before they attempt removal. Something about mapping neural pathways and ensuring they don't cause more damage taking it out than leaving it in."

The last three months had been a whirlwind of loose ends and careful cleanup. We'd extracted as much information as possible from the people we'd found at the castle. Sadly, none of them were very high up in GREY—mainly lackeys, apart from that one woman. Dr Sarah Chen, according to her university records. Masters in bioengineering, PhD in neural implant technology. Seb had *almost* had to resort to more persuasive methods to get her talking, but she'd eventually cracked, passing on everything she knew about GREY's structure and operations.

The real work had come after. We'd housed the rescued wolves at Killigrew Street Hotel for weeks, nursing them back to full health and sanity. Seb had enlisted Dr Hartwell to remove the chips from each of their cerebellums—delicate operations that had to be undertaken at a private hospital. It was no small feat to keep them off any official records. Though Dr Hartwell made it clear there was a small chance of death from the operation, every single wolf went through with it.

Then we'd sent them home to various cities across the UK. Carrie and her cousin had stayed the longest, meeting up with Dev on several occasions before finally taking a train back to Glasgow. She'd made it abundantly clear that she did *not* enjoy the private jet experience, luxurious as it had been. Something about "rich people nonsense" and "perfectly good trains that don't leave the bloody ground."

My pack had never found Isla. Or, if they had, they hadn't contacted us. I preferred to pretend it was the former of the two options. The alternative—that they'd found her and dealt with her according to their own justice—made my stomach turn, even knowing what she'd done.

Following up on leads was our current top priority. Seb had spent more time than ever on the phone to White, their weekly calls stretching into hours as they tried to track GREY's other operations. Seb had also been pestering her about how my mother had somehow obtained information about Theo's identity and ability. Unsurprisingly, she hadn't been terribly forthcoming.

Now, only Kit's chip remained. A chip that had been inside him for years.

"Well, if it's going to be dangerous, then maybe you'd better—"

"I want the bloody thing gone, Rory! Every day I can feel it in there. Like a splinter under my skin, except it's in my *head*."

I leaned forward, lowering my voice. The couple at the next table were deep in their own drama, but still. "And you really don't remember them putting it in? Nothing? Not at all?"

Kit's eyes went distant, unfocused. He lifted his pint but didn't drink, just held it like an anchor. "There's so much of that time I've forgotten.

Used to think it was PTSD, you know? Combat stress, losing mates, all the usual military bollocks." He paused, finally taking a sip. "But now... now I wonder if some of it was whatever they've put in me."

The thought made my stomach clench—someone scrambling around inside my brother's brain like he was a bloody computer.

"I just can't believe it's been there, all this time. I keep having thoughts about how I might have been acting like a human camera all this time. Like, recording everything I see and sending it to them. Felix has told me it's unlikely, but..."

"But we'd have said that about someone creating an army of wolf robots a couple of months ago," I finished.

Clink. Kit set his pint down harder than necessary. "I understand why they're resorting to controlling wolves. Because the things they had us do..." His voice trailed off, eyes fixed on something I couldn't see.

"Kit?"

"All in the name of 'national interests' apparently. But with GREY completely off any record, there wasn't ever any level of accountability. Who even knows what we were actually doing?" The bitterness in his voice cut through the pub's warmth. "God... the things I did." He covered his face with his hand.

"You know, you've barely ever told me anything about that time," I said softly.

"Yeah, well." He exhaled heavily, shoulders sagging. "It's no secret that I hate talking about hard stuff. I like to keep it all buried in locked boxes in my brain. And when a box opens, even a little, everything rushes out Pandora style, and it's all too much and I just want to lock everything up again."

I nodded slowly. "I get that. I really do. Though... not today, obviously, because the others are coming, but one day soon, I'd really love to sit down and talk with you. About some of the stuff that happened back when we were growing up, that I still think about. I want to talk about it all without you shutting me down straight away."

Kit looked away, his jaw working.

"Even if you mainly just listen," I continued in a rush. "That will be enough. Honest. But, Kit, it's really important to me. You're the only one I want to talk to about it. The only one who will truly understand." Teddy had been nothing short of extraordinary when the nightmares dragged me under—those steady hands and quiet reassurances in the dark hours before dawn. But there were things only my brother could help me make sense of, memories that needed someone who'd been there to witness them.

Kit's chest rose and fell heavily. When he spoke again, his voice came out strained. "I think one of the reasons I hate you talking about that time is because it reminds me of how guilty I feel about it all. You know... because I let Dad manipulate me into being bloody despicable to you." He took a deep, unsteady breath, as if the words were costing him. "I remember how he used to get me to completely ignore you when you were 'acting up.' To pretend you weren't in the room, that I couldn't hear your voice. You used to get so upset. Scream at me until you were red in the face. But I still did it."

My throat tightened. I remembered those days all too well: Kit staring right through me as if I didn't exist, me howling, stamping my feet with rage. Only resisting the urge to punch him because I didn't feel confident he wouldn't strangle me if I did.

"You kept trying to break through to me for so long," Kit continued. "You clearly held some hope that the brother you loved was still in there. But then you just... gave up. And when I left, I knew what I was leaving you with. Knew what would happen. But I still did it. I just... left you there, with them."

Kit's chest began shaking, and I reached across the table, covering his hand with mine.

"But then you came for me," I said. "The second you found out I was living in Glasgow. You came. You rescued me, and brought me back here. You moved me into your flat, got me a job... gave me a new family. A home, here. A real home, like I never knew existed. I'll never stop being grateful to you, every day of my life."

Kit shook his head slightly, as if it didn't excuse anything. "Course I did. You're my brother. My pack. I love you more than anything."

"I love you too. That's why I want to talk about it all, sometimes. You might be able to lock it all away in boxes in your head, but it isn't like that for me. It buzzes around in my mind all the time."

"Okay," said Kit. "Of course you can talk to me, Rory. Anytime."

"And while I'm making demands…" I took a breath, remembering Teddy's gentle nudging from the other day. "When we're at Killigrew Street, in meetings, I want you to stop talking down to me in front of everyone. It makes me feel like you're telling me off. Like a child. Seb is my boss, not you."

Kit blinked, his grip tightening on his pint. A deep frown split his forehead. "I… didn't quite realise I was doing that. I'm sorry."

"I feel like you feel responsible for my actions, because you got me the job there. And that's something I always think about too. But you jump in to criticise me at every tiny thing, and it really gets me down."

Kit's face crumpled slightly. He swallowed hard, Adam's apple bobbing. "Okay. I hear you. I'll really try to work on that."

"Thank you."

Kit cleared his throat, straightening in his seat. He checked his watch with sharp, jerky movements. "They're all bloody late. And… do you know if Felix is coming?"

"Maybe?" I said, shrugging. "Priya will know. If she ever bothers to arrive."

I looked towards the entrance. Teddy should have been here by now. He'd been off work today—he needed to take his mother to an appointment—and we'd parted ways this morning with him promising to meet us at half-past six. It was nearly seven.

A familiar panic started crawling up my spine. What if he didn't come? What if—

No. Stop it. Teddy had been coming to these pub sessions for weeks now, ever since we'd got back from Scotland. The team had welcomed him with open arms. He and Priya even had inside jokes now. About rubber ducks, for some reason. Felix had warmed to him quickly as well, though that might have been because Teddy actually listened when Felix explained his latest tech projects instead of glazing over like the rest of us.

I loved watching Teddy fit into our chaotic little family. The way he'd started smuggling proper crisps in under his jacket, instead of the shit ones the pub served. How he'd learned everyone's drinks and didn't mind queuing for rounds, unlike the rest of us. The way his eyes still lit up every time they called him Theo, not Maxwell.

I grinned at Kit, swirling the dregs of my pint. "So, how much money do I have to pay you for you to tell me who you're in love with?"

Kit coughed, spluttering his drink everywhere. Beer sprayed across the sticky table, droplets hitting my sleeve.

"*Excuse me*?!"

"Oh, come on, you didn't expect me not to ask, did you?" I leaned back, crossing my arms.

Kit's face went bright red, matching the tips of his ears. "It's been three months," he muttered, frantically dabbing at the spilled beer with a napkin. "I thought I'd gotten away with it. Oh look, here they come!"

I turned, expecting him to be taking the piss as a diversion tactic, but there they were—Seb, Flynn, and Priya.

Seb came through the door with his umbrella half up, earning curious looks in the bright afternoon sunlight.

As they reached our table, Priya grinned broadly as she slid into the seat beside me and knocked our knees together.

"Horrible weather, isn't it?" Seb said, settling his umbrella against the table leg.

Priya laughed, then eyed my drained glass before glancing towards the very busy bar. "Where's your boyfriend? I need him to buy me a drink."

I glared at her. "He's not your bar bitch. He's mine."

Flynn said, "You know Theo only volunteers to get your drinks so much because that way he can order you singles, right?"

"Pfft. He would never betray me like that."

I watched as Flynn shuffled even closer to Seb, winding a stray curl around his finger before pressing a kiss to his cheek. I smiled. These two used to make me sick to my core with jealousy. Instead, an intense pang of missing Teddy shot through me—something that happened every time we were apart for too long. Like someone had reached into my chest and squeezed, stealing my breath.

I unlocked my phone to check for messages. My background was my favourite ever picture of Teddy—one of Freddy sitting on his head whilst Teddy scowled at the camera, arms folded. I opened up the contact labelled "Teddy Bear." He'd groaned when I'd shown him the name, but I knew he secretly loved it. Probably.

In his phone, I was listed as "Thorne in my Side." I'd changed it twice to "Thorne in my Ass," but Teddy didn't seem to find that as funny as me.

Then I felt it—a distant tug, faint but definitely there. He was close.

A smile crept onto my lips, that familiar warmth spreading through me.

"Move onto that stool so Teddy can sit next to me," I ordered Priya.

"Are you fucking joking? No way."

She crossed her arms, settling deeper into the booth like she was planning to take root there.

A minute or so later, Teddy strolled through the door, eyes scanning the busy pub. When he locked eyes with me, a jolt shot through my entire body, kick-starting my pulse. *Thump, thump, thump.* The sound of his heartbeat echoed in my ears.

"You're late!" I told him when he reached us. "And now you have to sit on a stool. Priya won't move."

Teddy rolled his eyes but didn't sit down. Something odd threaded through him into me. Almost like... nervousness?

"Sorry. I had to go grab something on the way here. Can you come outside with me for a second?"

I stared at him, confused. Priya looked between us, eyebrows raised.

"Umm... okay?" I said, pushing at Priya so she'd let me out of the booth.

"Oi, watch it!" she snapped.

The short journey to the pub garden felt like walking through treacle. Teddy's anxiety bled into me through our bond, creating a horrible feedback loop—his nerves making me nervous, which made him more nervous, which made my own heart pound so badly I could barely breathe properly.

By the time we stepped into the small courtyard behind The George, my hands were shaking.

Fuck, he's breaking up with me. He's bored of me. He can't take it anymore. He's going to do it right here. And I've missed all the signs again, just like with Dev.

I closed my eyes, trying to steady my breathing. Maybe if I concentrated on the good bits, I could store them up before he took them all away.

Three months of Teddy bringing me coffee in bed every morning I stayed over, even though he thought I drank too much caffeine. The way he'd started buying the expensive beans from Fat Cat's to try and replicate the experience from home.

Three months of him sneakily feeding Freddy crackers when he thought I wasn't looking, to try and bribe him into liking him. Three months of Freddy biting his hand in return.

Three months of the most mind-blowing sex I'd had ever, including the way he'd let me scent mark him whenever I felt anxious, marking every inch of his skin until he smelled like mine for days.

Three months of him learning how to cook all my favourite meals instead of living off restaurant food. Teddy standing in his tiny kitchen, swearing at a recipe book whilst smoke billowed from the oven, refusing my help because he was "perfectly capable of following basic instructions."

Movie nights where he'd pretend to hate my film choices but somehow always ended up completely absorbed, shouting at the screen. The time he'd cried at the end of *How to Train your Dragon* and tried to blame it on hay fever.

Him learning to read my moods through the bond, knowing exactly when I needed space, and when I needed him to hold me until the restless energy settled. Never making me feel broken or too much.

The way he'd started leaving his poetry books around his flat, acting casual when I picked them up. Pretending he didn't notice when I dog-eared my favourite pages. That time he'd randomly caught my waist in the corridor, whispering in my ear, "*I have loved none but you,*" and I pretended I knew what it was from.

Three months of him defending me in meetings at Killigrew Street, backing me up even when I'd been slightly impulsive or reckless. Making me feel like I had someone properly in my corner for the first time in years.

All those nights talking until dawn, sharing pieces of ourselves we'd never given anyone else. The careful way he'd told me about his father, how he hoped he was making him proud. How he'd held my hand when I'd finally managed to explain about the worst bits of growing up with mine.

My chest felt hollow, like someone had scooped out everything good and left me empty. Hot tears prickled my eyelids—

"Rory, Christ, open your eyes. I'm not breaking up with you!" Teddy practically shouted. I opened my eyes to see deep concern etched across his face.

"Then what's going on?!"

Teddy's hand disappeared into his jacket pocket, fingers fumbling with something.

"I was going to do this later, but then I couldn't wait."

He pulled out a tiny box. Rectangular. Thin.

My brain short-circuited.

Oh. My. God.

A tiny, ridiculous part of me went absolutely mental. Because I *had* overheard Teddy's Ma at Sunday lunch last week, insisting she was going to give Teddy his father's wedding ring. "It's been sitting in my jewellery box for almost two decades, Theodore," she'd said, whilst I was in the other room. "Your father would have wanted you to have it. Would have wanted you to *use* it."

But this box was rectangular. And thin. Not ring-shaped at all.

Also, that would be completely bonkers, wouldn't it? Teddy proposing after three months? That was mental. Completely mad.

But what if—

"It's not a ring," Teddy said through barely concealed laughter. "And please, if I ever propose to you outside a dingy pub, say no."

My hands still trembled as I took the box. The velvet was soft under my fingertips, worn smooth. I flicked the lid open.

A silver key gleamed against black silk lining. A house key. A key for a house.

I blinked at it, my brain struggling to catch up.

"I want you to move in with me."

The words knocked me sideways. I stared at the key, then up at Teddy's face, then back at the key. The metal caught the late afternoon sun, throwing tiny sparkles of light across my palm.

Move in. With Teddy. To his gorgeously tidy, spacious flat with its dozen houseplants that were somehow all alive and flourishing. His spotlessly clean kitchen with the spice rack organised A to Z. His bookshelves arranged by genre and author. His bathroom where the towels were always folded properly and the toilet roll never ran out.

"But it's only been three months," I said, the words tumbling out before I could stop them.

Teddy's face flickered—was that disappointment? My chest tightened in response.

Three months. I remembered being so desperate to move in with Dev, forcing myself to wait until nine months to ask so it seemed more acceptable. More normal.

"I know," Teddy said, tucking a strand of hair behind my ear. "But it physically hurts me to be away from you, baby."

The air punched from my chest. Everything went wobbly—my knees, my vision, the entire bloody world. Dizzy with joy didn't even begin to cover it. I felt like I might float away if Teddy wasn't standing right there, anchoring me to the ground.

"I was trying not to stay over too much in case I was annoying you," I managed to get out, thinking about all those nights back in my own bed. Lying there feeling sad and incomplete, staring at the ceiling for hours, struggling to fall asleep without Teddy's steady breathing beside me.

Teddy tutted, shaking his head. "If you wanted to, you could have stayed over every single night. But anyway, let's do it. Move in properly. From tonight."

"Really?"

"Really." Teddy's hand came up, fingertips brushing along my jaw like he was memorising the shape of it. Then his fingers found the hoops in my ear, turning them slowly, absently, like he needed something to fidget with. "As long as Freddy continues to live at Killigrew Street. I don't want to have to install a lock on my fridge."

I pouted at him. "I can't control where Freddy goes. If he happens to follow me home one time..."

"Rory."

"Huh?"

"So is this a yes?"

"Is that even a question? Of course I want to live with you." The grin that split my face felt like it might crack my skull in half. "But just so you know, I don't believe in individual toothbrushes."

"What?"

"Like, having your own toothbrush and stuff."

Teddy groaned, tipping his head back towards the sky. "Why do I love you?"

Those words. I'd never get bored of hearing them, how they made all the colours of the world brighter, sharper, more vivid.

"It's truly a mystery," I said, but even as the joke left my mouth, a tiny sharp fragment of panic sliced through me. What if Teddy hated living with me? What if it ruined what we had, which was pretty damn wonderful. Pretty damn perfect.

"Stop that," Teddy said firmly, cupping my face in his hands.

He kissed me then, soft and sure, before pulling me against his chest. His arms wrapped around me, rocking us gently whilst I pressed my ear to his heartbeat. Raindrops on summer pavement enveloped us, woven into the very fabric of our bond. The steady rhythm of his heart calmed the frantic buzzing in my head, chasing away the worry like sunlight burning off morning fog.

"I'll move all my stuff tomorrow," I said, still grinning like a complete idiot. The key felt warm in my palm, like it was already part of me.

"Half your clothes are at mine already," Teddy pointed out, smirking.

"Um... I hate to tell you this, but that is not *half* of my clothes. Maybe, like, five percent?"

Teddy's eyes widened, genuine alarm flickering across his face. "Five percent?"

"Maybe seven? At a push?"

He groaned, though he was fighting a smile. "What have I gotten myself into?"

"But anyway, Kit is going to be so happy I'm out of his flat!" I joked, though I wasn't completely convinced. Kit had gotten used to having me around, hadn't he? Though it wasn't like I was moving to Mars—I could still pop round to annoy him whenever I wanted. Which would be often. Daily, probably.

"Yeah, well, he'll want someone else in there with him at some point," Teddy said.

Before I could ask what he meant by that, Felix appeared at the end of the path. He raised his hand in an awkward wave.

"Kit is inside wondering where you are," Teddy said as he reached us.

"Umm, okay..." Felix said, giving him a strange look.

When he was through the door, Teddy laughed—a proper belly laugh that made his shoulders shake. I felt like I was missing something important, some sort of joke perhaps, but then Teddy pressed a kiss to the top of my head and suddenly I couldn't remember what I'd been wondering about.

His lips lingered against my hair, warm and soft, and our bond pulsed gently, contentment flowing through it like honey.

"Come on, then," he murmured against my scalp. "Let's go tell everyone the news. Though I suspect Priya already knows—she read my leaves yesterday."

"Huh. That explains her cryptic text to me last night."

Before I could respond, Priya appeared in the doorway, her face unusually serious.

I said, "So this is what you meant when you said—"

"Yes, yes, it's all very sickeningly romantic and I'm very happy for you," Priya cut me off, waving her hand dismissively. "But come back inside. Something's happened."

The happy bubble around Teddy and me popped instantly, my stomach dropping like a stone. Teddy's hand found mine, fingers intertwining as we exchanged a look that said everything—*here we go again.*

"What kind of something?" Teddy asked, slipping straight back into detective mode, shoulders squared.

We followed Priya back through the pub, weaving between tables packed with after-work drinkers. The cheerful chatter and clinking glasses felt suddenly muffled, like we were moving through water.

Kit looked up as we approached, his face pale. Seb sat ramrod straight, mobile pressed to his ear, speaking in rapid Spanish as Flynn studied him, expression grave. Felix was hunched over his laptop that looked extremely out of place in the pub, fingers flying across the keys with even more urgency than usual.

I threw myself onto the stool. "What's going on?" I asked, though part of me didn't want to know. I just wanted to live with my boyfriend and argue about toothbrushes and whether it was appropriate to throw Freddy an unbirthday party in our flat. I wanted ordinary problems.

Seb ended his call and placed his phone face down on the table with deliberate precision. When he looked up, his dark eyes held that particular weight that meant our world was about to shift again.

"Felix received an encrypted message a few minutes ago," Seb declared. "From someone claiming to know the location of surviving GREY facilities."

My blood turned to ice water. "And?"

"The message included coordinates," Felix said without looking up from his screen. "And a list of names. Shifters who are supposedly under GREY control."

"And?" I repeated. Teddy, standing behind me, squeezed my shoulder.

Seb looked at me.

He looked at Kit.

"Your father's name is on it."

The End

<h1 style="text-align:center">Thank you</h1>

Thank you so much for reading Moonlit Nights & Northern Lights! The Killigrew Street Case Files series has been the most fun to write ever, and I'm thrilled so many readers are finding them. If you enjoyed this book, it would be incredibly helpful to leave a quick rating!

Don't miss Killigrew Street's bonus material!

Newsletter subscribers have access to bonus scenes and episodes, including **Return of the Vampire Hunter** (a spicy epilogue featuring Seb and Flynn from Bite Marks & Broken Hearts), and **A Very Killigrew Street Christmas**, a festive special which takes place between books one and two. It contains chapters from Rory, Maxwell, Felix and Kit!

The Killigrew Street Case Files

Thank you for reading!

Don't miss the other books in the Killigrew Street Case Files series! Scan the QR code on the next page to view online.

Acknowledgements

Firstly, thank you so much to Bree for the sensitivity read!

A masssssssssssive thank you to my gorgeous team of beta readers (Bee, Arlene, Evie, Sam, Emily, Anastasia, Jordan, Angela, Helen, Lupita). This book is so much stronger thanks to your input! I'm so happy you guys loved Rory & Maxwell. I'm the luckiest author ever to have such a fabulous team of beta readers, who also champion my books. I'm forever grateful to each of you!

To SJ, my amazing proofreader – thank you for making each of my books shine like the sun. Sorry if there are ten mistakes in this unedited acknowledgements section making your eye twitch!

Finally, to WH - Thank you for graciously accepting my offer to write a book together. Do you fancy something dark and angsty? Let me know your thoughts.

T J Rose is steadily turning her wild imagination into alternate universes, one happily-ever-after at a time.

By day, she weaves action-packed queer romances packed with vivid worlds and characters who dance between sugar, spice, and pure chaos. By night, she's either plotting doomsday scenarios or binging horror movies—sometimes simultaneously.

When not writing or daydreaming, you'll find her wandering through the British wilderness, coffee in hand, sunlight optional but strongly preferred.

Follow her on social media & sign up to her newsletter to stay up to date! For links to my other books, newsletter, shop and social media accounts, scan the QR code: